LUMINATE

TURNING DARKNESS TO LIGHT

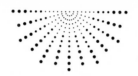

ROBERT FREDERICK

PATRICIA ANDERSON

BANYAN · TREE · PRESS

Luminate, Turning Darkness to Light by Robert Frederick & Patricia Anderson

ISBN 978-1-948261-49-4

Library of Congress Control Number 2021922547

Cover design: Diane Woods

Visit the *Luminate* website: www.luminusuniverse.com

Published 2021 by Banyan Tree Press,
an imprint of Hugo House Publishers, Ltd.
Denver Colorado, Austin Texas.

❋ Created with Vellum

PRAISE FOR LUMINATE

If you love a panorama of wonderful characters in a story with interesting twists and turns. And with a sci-fi plot on planet Earth from beings that travel space and time to protect and defend their friends in trouble. You will fall in love with Luminate, the book and want more. You are in luck since the authors have made it into a series: Turning Darkness to Light and this is the first book that will keep you up at night with a smile and begging for more!
—Lynda Cain Hubbard, Author of *Journey to Nepal*

I thought this was a great story line. A great version of the timeless good vs evil theme. I love when good sets such a great example and then triumphs!

It was action packed and kept me interested and engaged throughout.

I would highly recommend this to any sci fi buff or to anyone who just likes a good uplifting story line filled with plenty of action.

The book left me imagining the possible futures and so wanting for more. I definitely look forward to a future series. Please bring it on!
—Jim DeGrosa

Luminate is an exciting and adventurous tale of the fight between good and evil. It's a captivating plot with Pleiadian star beings who rescue planet Earth from evil doer's with many twists and turns along the way. It's a book well worth reading.

—S.H.

There has always been at the right time in my life an individual who has inspired me, and the person who helped launch a writing career was my friend, Jeanne Powers. Thank you.

EARTH

LOS ANGELES 2060

"TODAY WAS WEIRD."

"Yeah, it was. What's up with the losers anyway? It's like they're zombies or something."

Damien and Juan Carlos meet on the corner, ready to head home. The sun is setting behind the warehouses and junkyards. The fading light casts elongated shadows from the debris littering the gutters. The boys are twelve years old, dressed in baggy T-shirts and jeans, but their eyes are old. They've been drug runners for the gang since they were six, and they just got moved up to collections.

"Yeah, zombies. It was all Day of the Living Dead out there." Damien gives a quick look around, eyes darting into the lengthening shadows. "Let's get off the street." His face is sharp and pale. His long, black hair keeps falling into his eyes.

"Yeah," Juan Carlos agrees. His face is rounder than Damien's, with skin the color of caramel. His dark brown hair is chopped short. He grins at Damien's joke.

"Even Ralphie was out of it. He didn't give me any trouble today," says Damien.

"And it wasn't because Gordo threatened him." Juan Carlos punches Damien in the arm, smiling.

"No." Damien punches him back, pretend frowning.

"Right." Juan Carlos takes off with Damien right behind him. They're laughing and pushing each other when they reach the open garage door of the gang's warehouse. Two men standing guard outside watch them as they pass. Inside, three cars to the left are in various stages of disassembly. No one is working on them. There are four men lounging at the far end of the garage where there's a couple of couches and several chairs in front of a big screen TV.

El Jefe is sitting on one of the couches, watching the TV. He's not a big man but he exudes menace. On the screen, some lady is talking with a real serious look on her face. There's a bunch of bodies lying in a yard pictured behind her.

"Keep it down, *güeyes.*" Rico, El Jefe's second in command, growls at them. His eyes are on the screen too.

Damien and Juan Carlos nod, giving each other one last push, heading for the man sitting at a table behind the TV. They pull out the money belts they wear against their bodies and empty them on the table. They wait while Cambista counts each bunch of bills.

"Okay, you guys are good," he says. He hands four small twists of paper to Damien and watches the boys walk away. Two skinny kids, already claiming a place in the criminal world. He bundles the money and puts it in the safe against the wall.

The boys go stand behind the couch to see what's on TV. The lady is talking about a bunch of people killing themselves.

"What the hell," says Juan Carlos. Damien jabs an elbow in his ribs. El Jefe gives them a look and turns the sound up.

"Scientists have now stated that the earlier projection that Halley's Comet will collide with Earth is confirmed. Collision is imminent. The solution of mass suicide offered by the Eternal Rest Centers has started all over the world. Reports are coming in from Europe, China, Africa, South America, Asia. It looks like many people will escape the horror this way."

"Yeah," says El Jefe. "That's what fucked up our business. It was good until the Eternal Rest Centers started passing out those damn blue pills like candy." He's sneering, ""Take our free happy candy and feel better about your shitty lives.' We should have gotten in on that hustle somehow."

"Looks like it's too late for that," Damien whispers to Juan Carlos, with a glance at El Jefe. They move away from the couch. The sound of the woman's voice follows them.

"The World State Organization keeps sending out the message that all will be well. The Eternal Rest Centers will take away all your fear. Just go to your nearest center for help." The woman looks into the camera. *"I know that's what I'll be doing soon."*

Juan Carlos puts his head close to Damien's, also speaking in a whisper. "We might need to find another job."

"Yeah, but not today," says Damien. "Come on, brother. Let's take the stuff to the parents."

Damien's parents had been drug addicts for as long as he could remember. They pretty much sold him to the gang in exchange for their daily fixes. They'd been using less since the blue happy pills became plentiful, but they still liked the rush of the real thing.

In truth, Juan Carlos wasn't Damien's real brother. He'd wandered into the warehouse one day—a little kid with an attitude. He couldn't or wouldn't say who or where his parents were. Some of the guys tried to knock him around, but he was tough. He took it when he couldn't get away. Juan Carlos never complained to El Jefe, but he got back at the bullies. He'd put salt in their drinks or tie their shoelaces together when they slept. He was sneaky about it. No one saw him do it, except Damien. Damien watched him. The day Juan Carlos saw him watching, he paused and grinned at Damien. Damien paused, grinned back and helped him with his prank. They were brothers from that moment on.

When they arrive at the apartment, the door is locked. Standing in the dirty hallway, a baby crying and the smell of garlic cooking assails them as Damien fishes out his key and opens the door. It's eerily silent inside. Damien and Juan Carlos look at each other. The dusty curtains are drawn. Dirty dishes litter the coffee table in front of the couch.

"Ma?" Damien calls out. No answer. They move through the

cluttered living room. The kitchen is empty. They share another look and head for the only bedroom.

Damien's parents are lying side by side on the bed—dead. Damien stops in the doorway. Juan Carlos moves past him into the room. There's a bottle on the dresser with a bit of pink liquid in the bottom. Cups have dropped from the lifeless hands of the man and woman. Juan Carlos touches the man's hand. It's cool.

"They've been gone a while," he says.

Damien is stiff in the doorway. Juan Carlos looks back at him, "You okay, man?"

Damien shakes his head. He's remembering. Once his mother gave him a cupcake with a candle for his birthday. But more often she slapped him down or locked him in a closet as punishment for something. His father was almost never around and when he was, it was in a drunken rage. The rest of the time he was just a lump of flesh on the couch or bed.

Damien walks to the dresser and picks up the piece of paper next to the bottle. "Listen to this. 'You do not have to suffer the horrible death coming to our planet. Share this drink with your loved ones and you will all drift away peacefully. No sorrow, no pain, just sweet oblivion.'" He looks at Juan Carlos, "Figures they'd go for this." He swipes at wetness on his cheek. "Are you buying this crap?"

"No way. No way," Juan Carlos is shaking his head. He moves to stand by Damien. "I can survive anything. We can survive anything."

"Damn straight," says Damien, turning to clasp Juan Carlos's hand. He looks at his parents one last time, ignoring the dampness still in his eyes. "Let's get out of here."

They leave the apartment, heading back to the warehouse. They know everything has changed.

IN A HOSPITAL not far from the warehouse, a baby girl is born. Her parents, Sven and Rachel Salverson, name her Bridgetta. Rachel opted for natural childbirth to prove how tough she could be. She tried to cave when her contractions came hard and fast, but the doctor told her it was too late. Sven was disappointed with a girl child. If the baby had been a boy, he would have taught him to be the right kind of man. A girl, however… Too much trouble. He had his hands full with Rachel. He didn't need another female. He didn't protest when Rachel insisted that the baby be handed over to a wet nurse and a nanny. Since they're important members of the World State Organization in the western United States, they can't be bothered with a child, especially now that all the WSO's plans are coming to fruition. The World State Organization and its leader, Rhotah Mhene, are the salvation of planet Earth. He will bring order out of the Halley's comet chaos, and the mass suicides taking place right now. Of course, Rachel and Sven will not be taking part in the chemical solution currently underway.

LOS ANGELES 2065

Bridgetta sits outside her parent's office, clutching the doll Nanny Susan gave her. Curly blonde hair frames her cherub face. Her bright blue eyes are somber. She's listening to Mother and Father talking. She doesn't understand all the words, but she knows the tone. Somebody is in trouble.

"We managed to reduce the population significantly with the suicides. The Russian plague got rid of a bunch more. But now we can't bring the *Luminaries* to heel!" Rachel almost spits the name. "They think they're *special* somehow because of their *gifts* and their contributions to the *aesthetics* of *society*. Their only contributions are the mistaken ideas of *freedom* and *self-determination* and *self-expression*. Pah!" Now she does spit. She's a thin, sharp featured woman. Her hair is scraped back into a tight bun, making her appearance even more severe. She paces with hectic energy.

"You know the High Commander has the State Enforcers on it," says Sven. "They were pretty efficient handling the religious nuts who tried to hide in neighborhoods outside the fortress cities." He is shorter than his wife, overweight and balding with sallow skin. He has a nervous habit pushing his glasses up.

5

"Right. I'll give you that. Still, the exalted STEN seem to be taking their sweet time taking care of the *Luminary problem*," Rachel sneers. "Give the job to me—I'd have it done by now."

"It's a good thing only I can hear you. Anyone else and you'd be in a detention center yourself, with those Luminaries."

"I know, honey. I just get so frustrated. It seems like things move at a snail's pace."

"Yes, well, I have some good news. I just heard High Commander Rhotah Mhene is coming to do an inspection of the LA STEN training facility. And we've been invited to attend."

"Oh my God! This is such an honor! We deserve it! I'm getting champagne." Rachel is ecstatic.

Bridgetta hears the click of heels on the floor and she scoots as far as she can into the corner by the door. Her mother doesn't see her as she sweeps out into the hall. As soon as she's out of sight, Bridgetta hurries back to the nursery, hugging her doll. She turns the new word over in her mind: *Luminaries*.

HIGH COMMANDER RHOTAH MHENE strides into the reception, taking in the fancy buffet and the room full of people. He's a tall man, but emaciated. His commanding presence obscures his physical appearance. He's greeted with salutes and respect from the military men and limp handshakes and sighs from the sycophants. He receives their attention, ignoring them all except the Los Angeles commander of the STEN training facility, Colonel Richards, and Colonel Abernathy, the commander of STEN forces in the western U.S., standing together across the room. He walks up to them, returning their salutes. He shakes hands with the STEN commander, and Colonel Richards. Noticing Sven and Rachel Salverson standing behind the Colonels, he nods to them. Those two are still important to the WSO.

"Commander, good to see you again, sir." Colonel Richards looks at the man shaking his hand. Rhotah Mhene has pale blue, piercing eyes, no gray in his black hair although his face is sickly pale and furrowed with heavy lines. He stands with military bearing, but he moves like a dancer. Richards is glad the man can't read his thoughts. He'd disappear faster than you could say Luminary.

"Good to be back," says Rhotah Mhene. "I hear you have some promising recruits you want me to see."

"I do, sir. We'll get started right away."

The three men move to the door. Their aides follow, then the two civilians authorized to go with them—the Salversons.

They travel in two limousines to the training facility housed in what used to be the SoFi Stadium complex. Rhotah Mhene is shown the classrooms, barracks, mess hall and recreation room. The tour ends on the training field where groups of young men and women are practicing various forms of hand-to-hand and weapons combat. They walk to the end of the field where two young men are sparring. They're fine specimens with sleek muscles and quick moves.

"Santos, Johnson, front and center," barks Colonel Richards.

The two men release each other and run to stand at attention in front of the Colonel, snapping salutes. The Colonel returns a salute. The men stand straight, sweat dripping down their bodies and off their faces. Standing to the side, Rachel Salverson enjoys the view. The brass looks at them for several seconds, then Colonel Richards says, "At ease." The men assume the position and relax slightly.

"Commander, Privates Damien Johnson and Juan Carlos Santos. They've been doing very well in all areas of our training program."

Rhotah Mhene steps forward. "How long have you boys been here?"

Damien and Juan Carlos share a quick glance, and Damien speaks, "Three years, sir."

"Why are you still here?"

Another quick glance and Juan Carlos answers. "Sir, we were in a gang before the comet madness. We've been family for each other since we were five. We worked body disposal for a while after the suicides. But when we were given a chance to join STEN... He

7

flicks his eyes to Damien again and flashes a quick grin. "STEN is better than anything we had before."

"It's the best thing we've ever had, Sir," says Damien.

Rhotah Mhene nods and turns away. Colonel Richards says, "Back to work. Dismissed." Damien and Juan Carlos run back to the practice area and square off again. They're grinning.

Colonel Richards and Rhotah Mhene have their heads together as the group walks away.

"Those young men are acing all the training we put them through. Damien is officer material. And Juan Carlos is the sneakiest bastard I've ever run across. We're lucky to have them with us," says Colonel Richards.

"Keep me informed of their progress," says Rhotah Mhene.

"Yes sir."

Rachel has lingered behind to watch the young men grappling with each other. Delicious! She turns away and hurries to catch up.

The group is back at headquarters in the office of Colonel Abernathy. He tells them, "We have planned a raid to pick up a commune of Luminaries. It was reported last week and we've confirmed its existence and location. Commander, would you like to go on the raid with my men?"

"Absolutely. It will be a privilege to see our State Enforcers in action. STEN will always get the job done." Rhotah Mhene looks at Sven and Rachel. "You will come too."

Rachel pales but says nothing.

Sven says, "Of course, Commander."

Transportation for the Commander and his guests is a Humvee. Rachel can't climb in because of her tight skirt. In the end, Rhotah Mhene lifts her easily, placing her feet on the back seat floorboard. Already inside, Sven grabs her arm to hold her steady. Rhotah Mhene gets in the front passenger seat and Colonel Abernathy climbs in the driver's seat, shaking his head. No one speaks. Rachel looks at the back of Rhotah Mhene's head as they drive away. She can still feel his hands on her waist and she shudders.

The raid goes off without a hitch. Seven Luminaries are dragged from an old house near the Silver Lake reservoir—four men and three women, all middle-aged or older. One of the men tries to resist. A STEN soldier strikes him once with his billy club and the man goes down, head bleeding. The others try to help him but are pulled away. Rachel struggles to maintain a blank expression by gripping Sven's hand. He knows she's not upset by the blood, she wants to see more.

The rest of the raid is uneventful. As they drive back to Abernathy's office, Rachel asks, "What happens to those Luminaries once they arrive at the detention center?" Her eyes are shining.

"Didn't you have something to do with designing the detention centers?" asks Rhotah Mhene.

"I did, sir. But I never got to see them being used. I'm just curious."

Rhotah Mhene turns in his seat to look at her. "Of course. All Luminaries are taken to the psychiatric ward. There, they are sedated, put in a bed and given a drip IV that puts them into deep sleep. They are reduced to a vegetative state and kept that way until they die."

"Ohhh." Rachel looks ecstatic.

"What happens to their work, their paintings, sculpture, music, if any is left?" asks Sven.

"Confiscated by the WSO," says Abernathy. Rhotah Mhene looks back again, a smug smile on his face.

Back at Colonel Abernathy's office, Rhotah Mhene's aide approaches Sven and Rachel as they get ready to leave. "The High Commander wants a word with you. Now."

They look at each other, fear in their eyes. They follow the aide into the office set aside for the High Commander's visits. Rhotah Mhene sits behind a large, black desk. There are no chairs in front of it so the Salversons stand in front of the Commander. The aide stands beside the desk.

"You two have proven your worth to the World State Organization. Because of this, I have a new project for you." He nods to his aide who hands a folder to Sven.

Sven opens it. Rachel leans in to look at its contents. They read for several minutes. Rhotah Mhene leans back, resting his fingers on the desk and half smiling.

Sven looks up first, his eyes round. Rachel has a big smile on her face when she looks up.

"This project will need all your attention and resources," says Rhotah Mhene.

"Yes, sir. Of course. No problem," says Sven. Rachel nods, her head bobbing.

"Good. Dismissed."

Sven and Rachel leave the Commander's office. Rachel throws her arms around Sven. "Can you believe it!" she gushes.

Sven hugs her back. "This is a lot of work," he says.

"I know, but we can do it."

"I know we can." They walk arm in arm out of the building.

They reach their car when Sven stops. "Wait. I just had a thought. What about Bridgetta?"

"What about her?" Rachel opens the car door.

"We can't do this project worrying about a kid."

"True." She gets in the car.

"So, what about her?"

Rachel sits back, thinking. "I know! She goes to that dojo for martial arts class a couple of times a week. They can take her in full time. She can live there. We'll pay that place what we pay for nannies. Problem solved."

"What if they don't take boarders?"

"We are on special project for the High Commander of the WSO. They'll take a boarder or they'll suffer the consequences." Rachel's face is hard.

"And again, I'm glad you're on my side." Sven grins at his wife.

Two days later Bridgetta is dropped off on the front steps of the dojo with a small suitcase and her doll. She stands there, looking into the face of the Sensei. She is nervous. She's only seen Sensei from a distance. He looks at her with no expression for a long time. She stands still and looks back. She can see he's a good man, his face is a smiling face. He bows to her. She bows back. He turns and goes into the building. He holds the door open for her and she follows him.

LOS ANGELES 2073

A loud crash and the sound of boots hitting the floor awakens thirteen-year-old Bridgetta. She lies on her sleeping mat and listens. She hears men shouting and cries from Sensei's wife. At first she thinks it may be one of the gangs who roam the neighborhood. Sensei and his wife have talked about the rise of violence everywhere. She creeps to the end of the hall and peeks around the corner into the central room. Sensei is being dragged away by two men in uniforms. Another is holding his wife. Three others stand around. Another man, the one in charge, says "Search the building. Make sure there are no Luminaries hiding anywhere. We know the old man is a sympathizer." He's tall, dark-haired with intense, dark eyes. He'd be handsome if he wasn't evil.

One of the soldiers says, "Yes, Lieutenant Johnson." The soldiers split up and one comes in her direction. She hustles back down the hall to the hidey hole in the closet. She's just pulling the false panel closed behind her when the closet door is yanked open. The soldiers pull all the supplies off the shelves. She can hear them breaking things and laughing.

She waits until it's been quiet for a long time before she ventures out. She does a quick survey of the first floor for damage—it looks like the mess in her closet is the worst. The dojo is empty. The Sensei and his wife are gone. He had always been realistic with Bridgetta about what might happen. The hidey hole was his way of protecting her. He'd also taught her everything he could about the martial arts he'd spent a lifetime learning.

Grief rises up, threatening to choke her. She struggles for control. She goes to the center of the sparing mat and begins T'ai Chi Ch'uan, twenty-four form. The routine centers her and she's ready to move on. She knows she'll have to be very smart and very careful from now on. She kneels before Sensei's shrine and says a prayer to Lao Tzu. She knows it will do Sensei no good, those labeled Luminary disappear forever, but it makes her feel better. She goes to clean up the mess.

On his way back to headquarters, Lt. Damien Johnson reflects on the raid. His squad did well. Not too much property damage, they maintained discipline. Too bad there were only two people in the dojo—just the old man and his wife.

His phone buzzes. A message from Juan Carlos asking if they're still on for dinner. Damien texts him back: *Yes, Lt. Santos. Still on. CU in 30.* He can't wait to hear JC's latest escapades. Spies have all the fun.

STUDIO CITY 2078

Bridgetta walks out into the late afternoon sunshine. She has an iced coffee and nothing to do until dinner. She finds a quiet spot under a tree and sits with her back against the trunk. An impish breeze brushes her sweaty skin.

The image of Sensei sitting cross-legged and teaching rises up in front of her. She hears his quiet voice telling her: *To the mind that is still, the whole universe surrenders.* Sometimes she misses the Master so much... But his words still help her navigate her life. A lot has happened in the five years since Sensei was taken away. WSO runs the world now, from their fortress cities. The people who live there are doped up zombies. Anyone who joins the State Enforcers has a ready-made outlet for their racism, bigotry and religion-motivated rage. They're the WSO's iron fist. She shakes her head at the thought.

She looks out at the grounds around her tree. Sparrows and finches flit, butterflies dance and the breeze carries the scents of summer. She's finally found her place.

Diego comes across the lawn toward her. He raises his hand and waves. She waves back. He's a handsome man, the ideal Latino with smoldering good looks. She thinks of him like a big brother. He and his Uncle Francisco run the survival community centered in this compound. Diego is a medic and Francisco is some sort of ex-Army something. She hasn't been here long but they made a place for her. Of course, her martial arts skills helped. The people in this survival community struggled, but they worked together and built something that supports them and keeps them safe from the marauding gangs.

Now the camp is all excited because of some communication from Australia. It looks like the WSO might have rebellion brewing. She is all for that. It's definitely time for the people left to fight for freedom.

LUMINUS AND LUMINA, SISTER PLANETS, PLEIADES CONSTELLATION

NEWLY PROMOTED Section In-Charge Robey rubs his gritty eyes. What was he thinking? He should have waited to celebrate his birth day. First day of responsibility and he's not a hundred percent. *I'll just close my eyes for a minute. Nothing's happened on these displays for a while. The alarm will sound anyway.* His body relaxes into his chair as he drifts into sleep.

Robey's section in the Luminus Defense Department is tasked with scanning the remote areas of the galaxy for any incursions by the Soulests. Recently, several planets in Earth's sector were destroyed and the circumstances point to Soulest activity.

Robey's dream warps with the sound invading it. He snaps awake, realizing he's hearing an alarm. No, not an alarm. A signal. A communication signal from Earth's sector. Oh crap!

DAY X, SERENITY RANCH, LUMINUS

Angelica gazes out the cottage's back window. A long expanse of shining green grass flows in the afternoon wind. She breathes in the scents of azaleas and herbs. Her world is at peace now, but she feels a storm coming. It's a familiar feeling.

She sees a man in the distance, standing outside his workshop. Stephen is athletic, with handsome, rugged features. He's the man who captured her mind and heart.

Luminus is beautiful and peaceful and exactly perfect. She feels Stephen note her thought and add his agreement. They share a rush of affinity for each other and their home.

Stephen's thought is: *We're lucky to have had this time here, to work with our animals and plants, after many years of war.* His thought of war is colored with sadness which Angelica acknowledges. He goes back into his shop.

Angelica and Stephen were instrumental in saving their planet and sector in the final battle that vanquished the Luminaries' only enemy, the evil Soulests. It was their last active duty following years of service to their planets and people.

They are Soldiers of Light.

Angelica fingers the turquoise blue amulet hanging around her neck. It warms a little. She needs to speak to Stephen face to face.

She walks down the hill toward his workshop. Sunlight glints off her long, strawberry blonde hair. She's caught it up in a ponytail, but wisps float around her face. Her eyes are a mixture of blue and hazel, changing color with her mood. When she reaches the shop entrance, she stands, watching Stephen work. His hair and shirt are damp with sweat and his back and shoulder muscles tense as he works to turn a bolt. She draws a slow breath.

He looks over his shoulder at her and winks.

She smiles. "I do need to talk to you about something."

Stephen sits on a bench facing the meadow. Angelica sits beside him.

She says, "I mentioned that I had the pleasure of seeing Luerin Macobi. He said he still trains new Soldiers of Light in the Way of the Light healing, although he claims he leaves the combat training to younger masters. I suspect he cheats on that statement. I'm sure he works at maintaining his agility and quickness. But he is showing his age. Of course, his wit is as sharp as ever."

Stephen nods.

Angelica looks into the distance. "You know Luerin was very

fond of my mother Elizabeth, many years ago, although they each ended up marrying someone else." Stephen takes Angelica's hand. She squeezes his in return, giving him a small smile. "He mentioned something unusual to me. I didn't say anything because it had no relevance at the time."

"But now you think it does," Stephen says.

"Just now, standing in the kitchen, I got a feeling…"

"A feeling?"

"Yes."

"Tell me."

"Luerin said he was summoned to a meeting with Lars Drail. The Defense Minister wanted to talk to him about some unusual activity reported by the Luminus Defense Department. The Minister wanted his opinion as to whether it needed immediate investigation. I'll not forget the serious look on his face.

"Stephen, apparently there was a faint signal detected, on the amulet wavelength. When it was analyzed, our great AI super computer, the GA (which is much easier to say than its original name, Galactic Authority), gave it an eighty-percent probability of being a distress signal. Drail wanted Luerin's thoughts." As she spoke, Angelica touched her amulet.

Stephen reached for his as well. "The amulet wavelength channel hasn't been used for many years. What did Luerin think? Did he say?"

Angelica shook her head. "You know how he is—always making the student think, making it your choice, even when you're not a student anymore. But he didn't fool me. He thinks it needs investigating."

Stephen and Angelica look out at their ranch.

"So, we'll be taking a trip," says Stephen.

"Yes."

"Alright."

As Angelica and Stephen walk toward the cottage, *pings* indicate incoming messages on their wrist units. The message summons them to the Palace for a meeting with the Minister of Defense in two hours.

"Looks like we're going to get our orders. I'm taking a quick shower," Stephen says.

"Okay. I'll be at the pasture when you're ready."

Stephen nods.

Angelica silently calls to Wind Dancer. The unicorn comes galloping around the stables, almost flying across the ground. She halts inches from Angelica and lowers her head into Angelica's outstretched hand. Angelica leans against her neck. She whispers to her friend in a combination of speech and thought. "I'm sorry we won't be racing this year like we planned." *I'm going to help some friends who've been missing for a long time.* "I know you're disappointed." Wind Dancer nudges her and Angelica gets the idea of Stephen holding her close. *Yes, I know he will. And I'll protect him.* "Wind, I think this will be important in more ways than one. I'll take your strength with me."

Stephen is ready. Angelica touches foreheads with Wind Dancer then goes to him, grasping his hand as they walk to the hovercraft.

DAY X, DEFENSE HEADQUARTERS

As Angelica and Stephen approach the Palace, Angelica remembers the first time she entered it. She was very young, but she was filled with a sense of belonging and purpose and honor. It was at that moment she knew she was a Soldier of Light. She turns to Stephen.

"Do you remember your first visit to the Palace?"

"Yes. I already knew I was a Soldier of Light, but my first visit elevated my purpose."

"Exactly." Angelica and Stephen look at each other in perfect agreement.

The Palace itself is a lush building with many windows, entrances, and gardens. The Ministry of Defense is in a three-story annex, built as a square with a center courtyard and garden. All spaces either look out on or into green vistas. The two Soldiers are escorted to a ground floor conference room overlooking a fountain.

Lars Drail, the Minister of Defense, enters the room with his

Deputy Minister, Lucia Uwani. An aide follows them and stands at attention by the door.

"Thank you for responding to my summons." Drail sits at the head of the table, gesturing for the others to sit. "Would you care for any refreshment?"

Stephen responds, "No, thank you sir."

Drail waves a hand at the aide who slips out of the room. "As you have learned from Macobi, we've received messages. It's been determined they are from Sector Eight, Section Fifty-one, the planet known as Earth. A mission was sent there some time ago."

"Yes, sir." Angelica speaks this time.

"Although the signal was faint, GA has determined it is from two of the group sent on that mission. Records show sporadic reports, then no further contact from them. This is not necessarily unusual, and it's policy to allow circumstances to unfold in cases where there has been no general hostility to our purpose of uplifting civilizations. Up to this point, it was just a pending mission."

Angelica and Stephen nod in understanding.

Drail pauses, looking at them. "The reasons you are here are twofold. First, the message indicates a very real threat to our Luminaries on Earth. Second, two of the people sent on that mission are your mother, Angelica and your father, Stephen." He leans back, interlacing his fingers. "In fact, their mission was to discover if certain sacred artifacts had been secreted on Earth." His gaze pierces each of them. "This information is classified, not to be spoken of outside this room." Angelica and Stephen nod again. Drail continues. "Toward the end of the last conflict with the Soulests, they overran an installation where these artifacts were housed. After the battle, we discovered the artifacts were missing. Of course, we began searching for them right away. It was determined that Earth was a possible hiding place. Mission orders were issued to have Earth scanned for the artifacts and your parents volunteered. This was twenty-five years ago, Earth time. Because of the distress signal, your expertise, and your personal connection, the Defense Ministry is activating both of you for a mission to Earth."

Angelica and Stephen lean forward as one. "We're ready."

Drail leans back as Deputy Minister Uwani speaks. "The signal we received came via the amulet wavelength. As you know, this is one of the failsafe features of the amulet. Unfortunately, amulet transmissions take much longer to travel. It may have taken as many as twenty Earth years to reach us. GA has labeled it a distress signal."

"We have no patrols in the immediate area, but we asked GA to investigate remotely. She determined that the Soulests have infiltrated Earth."

"This means Luminaries on Earth are in great danger," Angelica says.

"Yes," says the Minister, "which is an additional reason your mission has become urgent." He stops, takes a breath. "You are well aware that we Luminaries and Soldiers of Light are a special race of able beings. We represent the elite of many universes.

"Luminaries are creators of new worlds, visionaries, able-minded artists, and bright thinkers in all mediums that comprise the arts and aesthetics. We have helped shape many civilizations and cultures throughout the universe, imbuing them with light force and boundless creation. Our sole purpose is to serve worlds, to create and preserve beauty, aesthetics and new civilizations where all beings can live and create freely.

"The Soulests have a lifeless philosophy that views the universe as soulless—where no individual is truly his own being or soul." Drail passes a hand over his forehead. "I'm sorry. I'm preaching."

"Not at all, sir," Stephen says.

"Agreed," says Angelica. "It is always important to renew our purpose and to recognize our enemy."

"Thank you. We must be vigilant and fight the Soulests when they try to expand their galactic empire. Their conquest of Earth appears to be part of an alarming offensive. Although we've kept them in check for some time, that seems to have changed. We must not lose our advantage. Otherwise, we're at risk on Luminus and Lumina as well." Drail closes his eyes.

Uwani speaks. "For centuries, the Soulests have tried to discover the secrets of the Luminaries' hidden powers, unsuccessfully so far. We have to make sure they never do."

She continues. "GA calculates we have reached a point of no return in our confrontation with the Soulests. The Royal Council is going into action to formulate new strategy and plans. They've begun by declaring an emergency measure: All our Luminaries are to return to Luminus."

Drail speaks. "Since the first message, GA has been working to gather data about Earth. She determined that the population has been severely reduced and that the Soulests are in control through a 'World State Organization.' The infrastructure of the planet is in place but all the energy signatures have been greatly diminished. She continues to monitor the area."

Drail stands. "We'll conclude this meeting now. Please return tomorrow morning at 1000 for a full briefing on your mission." The Defense Minister comes around the table to shake hands with Stephen and Angelica. "I hope your parents are alive and well."

"Thank you, sir," they reply in unison.

Drail steps back beside Uwani. They raise their fists, knuckles forward, toward

Angelica and Stephen, who return the salute.

All four say at once, "Be the light."

DAY XI, MORNING, DEFENSE HEADQUARTERS

Defense Minister Drail greets Angelica and Stephen as they enter the same conference room in the Ministry of Defense. They look around and see Macobi and Uwani already present. The same aide stands beside a sideboard heavy with refreshments. Macobi comes up to them, giving each a quick hug. They look at him in astonishment at this show of affection.

"I'm an old man. I'm allowed to be maudlin," he says gruffly. "Go and get a coffee, the pair of you."

When everyone has coffee, Uwani announces, "Please be seated, we're ready to begin." Angelica, Stephen and Luerin sit on one side of the table and Drail and Uwani take seats on the opposite side.

The conference room door opens again. Drail stands. A young woman in uniform comes through the door followed by the Commander-in-Chief of Luminus, His Excellency Darius Calderone.

Everyone else rises from their seats to stand at attention.

"At ease," says Calderone. "This is my communicator, and daughter, Nicola Calderone. Be seated." He takes the seat at the head of the table and Nicola stands to the left, behind his chair. She holds a large briefcase.

Calderone begins speaking. "There are two critical issues that are now threatening our security, our lives, and the future. We defeated the Soulests in our last battle and assumed they were no longer a threat to us. It now appears they've staged a comeback. The latest intelligence proves the Soulests have made great gains in adding new planets and territories to their empire in Sector Eight. Something changed, and we're just learning of it. They're encroaching again and they're more of a threat than ever." Calderone pauses. "We did not notice until the signal from Earth." He looks at the people around the table. They each nod, acknowledging the lack of vigilance. He continues. "GA's records indicate there are two of our people on that planet plus an uncounted number of Earth Luminaries. The Soulests will spew their evil over our comrades with torture and drugs—as much as they can for as long as possible. Their hatred of us knows no bounds."

He pauses to sip from the glass of water Nicola sets by his hand. "GA has also discovered evidence that some of the confidential texts —texts containing the teachings we use to greatly increase an individual's ability to harness power—were hidden on planet Earth. We have to assume the Soulests have decrypted and studied some of these texts and are using what secrets they've been able to learn to further subjugate the Luminaries and the remaining peoples of Earth." He looks at each person at the table. "They're back. And they're plotting our total destruction." The room is silent.

Calderone continues. "Here's the plan. As Drail told you yesterday, we are initiating a pullback of all Luminaries from Sectors Six, Seven and Eight as soon as possible. They'll return home for an indefinite period of time to further their training and to study our canons and teachings.

"Soldiers of Light Stephen and Angelica will go to planet Earth. Your mission is threefold. You are to rescue the Luminaries in trouble. You will stop the Soulests' reign on this planet. And you must recover the stolen sacred texts that have fallen into the hands of our worst enemy.

"This royal executive order is effective immediately, witnessed by all present."

Calderone stands and the others follow. He says, "Long live Luminus and the Luminaries! Be the Light!"

"Long live Luminus!" they respond. "Be the Light!"

His Excellency nods and leaves the room with his communicator.

The Defense Minister moves to stand at the head of the table. "I've ordered our starship *Lightbearer* and its orbiters to travel to Sector Eight, Section Fifty-one. They're on their way, due to arrive in about thirty days. They'll sweep Earth with our sensors to locate our missing sacred teachings. The captain of *Lightbearer* will be working closely with you. *Lightbearer* will provide assistance in the rescue and rehabilitation of the Luminaries, once you have them secured.

"Your mission begins tomorrow at 1000. Report to the Teleport Station on Lumina. You have twenty-one hours to put your affairs in order. Uwani will brief you on the mission particulars now." Drail clasps Angelica's, then Stephen's hand. "My trusted friends, be strong, be the light." He leaves the room.

Uwani steps forward. "Please sit," she says. "Preparations have been underway for the mission since yesterday's meeting. Stephen, your hovercraft prototype is being requisitioned. You will need a fast form of travel to cover the distances around the planet. You will probably need to build more. My understanding is that the design is much simpler than previous models so you should be able to find what you need on Earth. GA reports that it is rich in many resources."

"I can improvise," says Stephen.

"Excellent. Angelica, we're upgrading your wrist unit with a virtual assistant, Akido, which will interface with GA to give you real time information. GA is already establishing links with select satellites still orbiting Earth so you'll have access to all the data she can gather. You'll also be issued new amulets with enhanced healing power."

"Good," says Angelica. "I'm sure we'll need that to help the Luminaries who've been captured by the Soulests." She and Stephen exchange a look, sharing their resolution to save their parents.

"Finally," Uwani continues, "Angelica, you will head this mission and Stephen will be mission second. Any questions?"

Angelica and Stephen shake their heads no.

"Very good," says Uwani. "Be the light!" She stands and leaves the room.

Angelica, Stephen and Luerin remain at the table. Luerin says, "Before you leave tomorrow, there will be more specific information from GA about the current situation on Earth, so you won't be going in blind. If you need anything, send a message to me through Akido. I'll do what I can." Angelica starts to speak but Luerin raises his hand to silence her. "You and Stephen were—are—two of my best. You never failed in your duty to Luminus, no matter what you were asked to do. I know you will strike a crushing blow to the Soulests on Earth. You make me proud." Stephen and Angelica each grasp Luerin's hands and he bows his head over them.

"Alright," he says, releasing their hands and standing, "time to go to work." He leads the way out of the room. Angelica puts her arm around Stephen's waist and he wraps his around her shoulders and they follow.

DAY XI, EVENING, SERENITY RANCH

Stephen and Angelica sit on the back porch after their evening meal.

Angelica speaks. "Separately, we each chose to be Soldiers of Light. Then we met and discovered the strength that comes from working together toward shared goals. The ranch is an extension of this. But our first duty is our duty as Soldiers of Light."

"When we are called to serve, we go with resolve," Stephen says, "because this is what we know. This is what we've chosen to be responsible for. This is our honor."

"Yes."

They look out over the ranch. Both Lumina and the moon of Luminus are coloring the sky. To the northwest is the purple glow from the mountains. The night is peaceful and fragrant and filled with the sounds of night life. They sit quietly, each with their own thoughts, then stand as one to go inside.

DAY XII

Stephen and Angelica rise early. They carry their backpacks to Stephen's prototype hovercraft parked outside the front door, ready for their trip to the Luminus Transport Center. From there, they and the hovercraft will be loaded on military transport and taken to Lumina, to the Teleport Station. Stephen leaves his wrist unit. He and Angelica don't need mechanical means to communicate.

As he readies the hovercraft for flight, Akido speaks from Angelica's wrist unit. "Updated information for your mission."

"Speak," says Angelica.

"*Lightbearer* has begun its flight to Earth, ETA twenty-seven Earth days. Your mission has been given a name: Operation Blue Whale. GA has gathered more data about the situation on Earth. Eighty-five percent of the current population is either in fortress cities or small, outlaying survival camps. GA has noted some chatter on what's left of the global communication medium, called the internet, indicating there is some resistance to the World State Organization, the government the Soulests are behind. There is some group called STEN that appears to be the enforcement arm of WSO. Okay so far, Boss?"

"Boss?" Angelica asks.

"Yes, Boss," replies Akido. Stephen glances over grinning.

"Yes, okay so far."

"Great! You will be landing on the west coast of one of the large land masses, in the Los Angeles area. There's a fortress and a survival camp in that area. The resistance chatter has two names attached: Francisco and Diego. Look for them. Two other western locations are active. One is near Salt Lake City, about seven hundred miles northeast of Los Angeles. The names there are Garcia and Margo. There are rumors that they come from Earth's gypsy culture. The other is in Denver, east of Salt Lake City. Jeremiah is there."

"This is very helpful, thank you," says Angelica.

"Akido."

"Duly noted by your commander, thank you, Akido," says Angelica.

"Yes sir—ma'am."

"Sir will do."

"Yes, sir."

"Good. Now silent mode unless there are any messages." Angelica exchanges an amused glance with Stephen.

They reach the Transport Center and get themselves and the hovercraft on board the military vehicle for the trip to Lumina. Soon they're up and flying over the pristine Coral Blue Sea. The water glistens in the rays of the morning sunlight. Looking down out the window, Angelica can see humpback whales spouting water and sea mist.

"Do you see them, Stephen? There's at least ten. And there's a school of dolphins following over to the right." Her eyes are shining. "We will accept this sign for our mission's success." Stephen takes her hand.

Leaving Luminus' atmosphere, they look down at their planet as they pull away. They're alone in the cabin. "Beautiful," whispers Angelica. Stephen says nothing, waiting for her to continue. Several moments pass. She stares out the window. Still he waits. When several more minutes go by, he speaks gently, "Say it."

Angelica looks at him with tortured eyes. "It was bad the last time, that last battle." Her eyes unfocus with the memories. Stephen is still. "So much pain. Too much death. Too many lost." Her voice is barely a whisper. "So much horror." She looks up at Stephen. "We have to face that again. Can we?" Another pause. "Can I?"

Now Stephen touches her and she goes into his arms. She holds him as close as he holds her. He says, "Since that time, we've built a sanctuary for ourselves. When we need to, we'll return there to gain strength. We can visit any beautiful time, or any beautiful place, whenever we want—in our minds."

Angelica lays a hand on his cheek. "How is it you always know exactly the right thing to say?"

Stephen smiles. "We have the strength to face this again. We'll find strong comrades to help us. We'll help each other."

Angelica nods. They sit close, holding hands for the rest of the journey.

DAY XII, AFTERNOON

Security is tight at the Teleport Station. Their credentials are verified as they leave the landing pad and again as they enter the station. The station commander comes forward to great them.

"Soldiers. Follow me to the pod bay. Your equipment is being placed in a camouflaged container for teleportation to Earth. Here is a list of what's being sent." He hands a tablet to Angelica. She and Stephen read it together.

"Where will the amulets be?" she asks.

"In the central compartment in the hovercraft. You'll need to key them when you arrive."

"Understood."

"Note the arrival coordinates for the container. We'll send it six hours after you arrive. "

"Excellent."

They have reached the pod bay. The captain in charge stands at attention next to the door. She salutes as they walk up.

"At ease," says the commander. To Stephen and Angelica he says, "This is Captain Shay. She commands the pod bay. She will be responsible for your Luminus bodies while you're on mission."

"Thank you, Captain Shay," says Stephen.

She nods. "Are you ready?"

Stephen looks at Angelica. "Yes."

Captain Shay leads them to two pods, side by side in the back of the bay. Angelica and Stephen touch hands and climb into their pods. The commander and captain stand at the ends of the pods and salute them. As the pods close, the captain says, "Good luck in your mission. Be strong, be the light."

The pods are filling with cryogenic fluid. Angelica and Stephen mind link, holding the image of their destination between them as they race, in essence, toward Earth. They arrive in a blink.

DAY ONE, EARTH, NOVEMBER 2080

ANGELICA ARRIVES

THE NIGHT IS dark but stars fill the sky. A warm wind gathers in the higher tree branches, rustling leaves. The wind is restless, gusting and sighing.

The nearby bushes and plants are ghostly in the dark. A few patches of light in the distance indicate habitation. Far to the west, heat lightning crackles. The wind shifts to blow from that direction.

Earth Time: 0400 Pacific Time (PT). Angelica arrives near a long, dark stretch of road in Griffith Park. Thin moonlight from a gibbous moon shines on the landscape. Below her she sees a parked van. It's white with the words *World State Organization Health Group* emblazoned on the side. It's rocking. She changes her sight to see inside.

A man dressed in white is manhandling a blond-haired woman in simple clothes. Another man watches from the driver's seat. The first man forces sex on the woman. She tries to fight but he overcomes her, beating her into submission. Still she struggles and he ties her, beating her again. She is close to unconsciousness.

The man grunts with his thrusts, punctuating them with vicious punches to her face and body. She is now near death. He finishes, drags her body to the van doors and pushes her out. She slides down, hitting her shoulder and head hard on the road.

The van doors close. It starts up and pulls away from her. It makes a U-turn, coming back to run her over. Angelica creates a presser beam to nudge her out of the van's path at the last minute. It swerves, speeding away. The motionless woman is left crumpled at the side of the road.

Angelica materializes beside the unconscious woman, starting as a faint outline of golden light then forming the shape of a body. Angelica observes the woman. Her dress is ripped and marked with blood stains. She has bruises on her arms, neck, chest and thighs. Her face is bloody. She is not old, maybe thirty. She has a light complexion and even features. Her hair is blonde under the grime. She was beautiful once, but now her body is starved and broken. Angelica understands that she longs for the death that approaches.

The woman's name is Jessica. Angelica reaches out and touches her spirit as Jessica breathes her last human breath. The two spirits begin to enter the white tunnel of space and time.

Angelica acknowledges Jessica, telling her that her life was not in vain. Angelica shows her the plan for Operation Blue Whale. Jessica rejoices. Angelica thanks her for her body. She tells Jessica, "You are no longer the effect of your earthly body. You are free. Look for the light, it's within you, it will guide your journey. Be strong, be the light."

Jessica acknowledges Angelica with great affinity and continues through the tunnel of light. On the other side, she takes one look back before turning into a glow and moving away.

Angelica blankets Jessica's body, taking it over. She explores the damage, using her healing light to fix the most egregious wounds. She knows when she retrieves her amulet from the supply drop, she'll be able to fully repair and upgrade this body.

After a moment, she slowly stands, turning in a circle. She orients to the supply drop point and begins walking down the road.

STEPHEN ARRIVES

Stephen appears on the northwest side of Griffith Park, near a building that was part of Mount Sinai Hollywood Hills Memorial Park. There are no lights visible from his vantage point. He senses Angelica, not far away. He pauses as she guides Jessica, assumes her body and walks away. With Angelica safe, he turns his attention to the chapel that is now a makeshift hospital for the resistance. A doctor and a medic are trying to save the life of a young man with multiple gunshot wounds. The medic, Diego, and the doctor speak quietly to each other as they work to stop the bleeding. Stephen sees the young man's body is failing. The medics have done all they can and turn away.

Stephen talks to the young man telepathically and learns his name is Mark. Mark knows he's about to die. Stephen comforts him, acknowledging his life, his accomplishments, and his efforts with the resistance movement. Mark lets go of the fight to keep his body. His spirit exits and enters the white light tunnel.

Stephen bids him farewell, telling him, "Look for the light all around, but especially within you, it will guide you. Look within you. May the light be with you always."

Stephen moves in and blankets Mark's broken body. He flows his healing light into the areas of injury and they begin to mend. The doctor turns back to pronounce his death. Stephen opens his eyes and lifts a finger off the cot. Diego and the doctor are stunned. Diego can't believe his eyes. The doctor stands back, observing this change.

"Well Diego, we'd better keep an eye on this one for the next twenty-four hours," he advises Diego.

"I thought he was a goner for sure," Diego responds.

"Hmmm." The doctor looks down at Stephen.

Stephen has met one of his resistance contacts. He closes the eyes of his new body, continuing to flow the healing light through it.

ANGELICA ARRIVES at the edge of the Greek Theater parking area as the sun's glow begins in the east. The transporter sled has arrived. She walks to it and uncovers the hovercraft. All is in order. She gets her amulet from the central storage pod and puts it on. She closes her eyes, sending her energy into the amulet to key it. Once the connection is made, she triggers the amulet to send energy pulses through her new earth body, completing its healing. She strips off the bloody dress and pulls on a clean coverall she finds in the hovercraft.

Her thought link with Stephen is wide open. He knows she'll join him soon. She climbs into the hovercraft, aiming it toward Stephen's location. It rises noiselessly into the early morning air. The transport sled disintegrates as she moves away.

Angelica lands behind the building where Stephen rests. No one sees her. She retrieves Stephen's amulet and her wristband and steals inside. It's quiet. She sees Stephen in the corner and makes her way to him. His Earth body is similar to his Luminus body, blonde-haired and strong. She lifts his head and slips the amulet around his neck. He smiles, opening his blue eyes. She sits beside him, clasping his hand. He keys his amulet. She focuses on her amulet, then his, to help him complete the healing of his new body.

"These bodies will do nicely," she says.

"I agree," he says. "They are well suited to the extra energy we can pour into them. Plus, they're not bad looking." He winks at Angelica who grins at him.

Diego appears, staring at Angelica. "Who are you?" he asks.

"I'm his girlfriend," she replies. "I heard he got wounded and I had to get to him. He's going to be okay, right?" She puts a little tremor in her voice.

"Yeah, it's kind of a miracle he pulled through. We thought he was a goner."

"I'm glad you could save him."

"Uh, right. You're welcome."

"Can I take him home now?" Angelica asks.

"No. The doctor wants him to stay til tomorrow for observation."

31

"Okay. I'll stay with him, okay?"

"Sure. You can use that cot over there." Diego points.

"Thank you. What is your name?"

"Diego."

"Ahh. Nice to meet you, Diego." She smiles.

"Yeah."

Diego moves away.

Angelica scoots the extra cot next to Stephen. She lies down, putting her head close to his. "And that's our contact, Diego."

"Yes. But right now, we'll sleep my love." Stephen touches her face. They close their eyes and sleep.

LOS ANGELES SURVIVAL CAMP

Diego sits with Francisco in the common area. "He should have died. His guts were perforated, he was bleeding internally. Suddenly he was okay. Better than okay. Then his girlfriend shows up, like, out of nowhere. It's just weird."

"So, it shouldn't have happened," Francisco states.

"No."

"I guess we'll have to investigate this medical miracle," Francisco smiles.

"I'll arrange it," Diego replies.

DAY TWO

LOS ANGELES SURVIVAL COMMUNITY

In the morning, the doctor checks on Stephen, gazing at him for a long moment before pronouncing him fit. "Someday you'll have to tell me how you did that," he says.

"Someday," says Stephen.

It's noon when Diego walks toward Angelica and Stephen who are sitting up waiting for him.

Angelica says, "We would very much like to meet Francisco. Is that possible?"

Diego's jaw drops but he quickly recovers. "Yeah. He wants to meet you too." He turns to Stephen. "You okay to walk? Doc said you can leave."

Stephen stands. "Yes."

"I brought you some clothes. We had to cut up the stuff you were wearing." He hands pants and a shirt to Stephen.

"Thank you," he says, putting them on.

Diego leads them out of the infirmary and down the hill. They cross over the freeway and LA River and enter the Disney Studio compound. Angelica and Stephen are looking around with interest. They see no one.

Angelica begins thought communication with Stephen as they walk. *From what we've seen so far, things are worse here than our intelligence reported. We're going to have to get moving fast. Our mission orders don't give us much time to do what we need to do. I want to plan a strategy that will coincide with this planet's next solstice. Akido can verify when that is. We'll learn more as we go.*

Stephen acknowledges her with a flow of solidarity and affinity. Angelica smiles.

She is very happy that they're on this mission together. She appreciates the Luminus policy of sending two on missions. Anytime she can get her soul mate on a mission with her, she's a lucky girl!

Stephen acknowledges her again by clasping her hand and they exchange a look. Diego watches this interaction with interest.

Stephen's expression sobers. *This mission does concern me. It has a personal connection to things very dear to us both.*

Yes. Angelica breaks off and looks toward the building Diego is approaching. It's bordered by an odd metal fence—some of the fence posts are topped with three circles, one large with two smaller ones on the top like ears.

Diego leads them inside the building to a common area. A man who resembles Diego sits at a table near the back. As the trio walk toward him, he stands.

"Hello," he says. "I'm Francisco. And you're the miracle man." He extends his hand to Stephen who shakes it. "How did you do it?"

Stephen smiles.

Angelica speaks up. "We've come to help you with the resistance movement. We also know that a number of the brightest and most aesthetic minds have been incarcerated and we want to break them out and help them."

Francisco stares, then takes a step back and indicates the table and chairs with a sweep of his arm. They all sit. He has a very skeptical look on his face. Diego is shaking his head.

"Let us start at a beginning," Angelica says, leaning forward. "I am Angelica, this is Stephen."

"Wait a minute," Diego says. "Your name is Mark."

"Yes," says Stephen, "it was."

"Whaa...?" Diego is dumbfounded.

"It was?" says Francisco. "Wait... Okay..." He's silent, staring at them for two beats. He shakes his head and speaks. "Fine. Continue, I guess."

Angelica goes on. "We've come quite a distance to assist the resistance and to help the Luminaries."

Francisco is still struggling with Mark being Stephen, but here's something he can grasp. "Luminaries?" he asks.

"The artists, the visionaries, the great thinkers whose ideas and creations can change worlds," Angelica replies. "The World State Organization has incarcerated them, hasn't it?"

Francisco looks at Diego. "Yes, they have. There are many instances of people being taken away by STEN. I don't know if they're all what you call Luminaries, but I'm sure some are."

Diego nods.

Angelica says, "Yes. Those are the people we want to help. Now, can you, the resistance, use our help?"

Francisco has recovered his equilibrium. He's thoughtful for a moment. "Diego and I were talking about you earlier. What do you mean, you want to help? And where did you say you're from?"

"We mean, what do you need the most help with?" says Stephen.

BRIDGETTA WATCHES and listens from behind the screen that closes off the kitchen. She's fascinated by the visitors. They remind her of her Sensei. Her attention is fixed on the newcomers as she rubs the small bonsai tattooed on her wrist. *Wow, these people almost glow somehow.* She's sure they'll be able to do what they say they'll do. In that moment she decides she will help them.

"I STILL DON'T GET IT," says Diego. Francisco waits, his eyes sharp on the strangers.

Stephen asks, "What would it take to get the resistance happening worldwide? Do you have communication with other resistance groups? Do you want the incarcerated Luminaries saved?"

Diego glances at Francisco who looks thoughtful now. Francisco says, "A while back, our friend Colin Hainsworth, an Australian, contacted us by means of an 'internet backdoor.' That's what he called it. We got an email one day. Surprised the heck out of us. We'd been keeping in contact by ham radio but now, here was an email. The message started out 'Hey Mates!' He told a story. He said it happened because of Fosters beer. He was at one of the off-the-beaten-path pubs in Northern Australia, having a beer with the locals. There was an old professor type named James Dobbs in the group. He'd had a few and he started talking about a secret U.S. Army project his grandfather worked on many years ago. His granddad got his son, Dobbs' dad, working for the same program. The initial group set up a network only accessible to a select few. It was an internet backdoor. Anyway, this Dobbs guy hacked the back-door and gained access. Somehow Colin persuaded him to give it to the resistance. Then Colin shared it with every other resistance group. We all talk via email now. Colin has passed on every idea the Aussies use to make their communities stronger. And we've shared what works for us. The resistance movement is building."

Francisco pauses. "We call it 'Backdoor Charlie' as a nickname." Another pause. "That changed everything. We have an encrypted way to communicate globally on a network that can't be tapped or broken into."

Diego leans forward. "What we really need is to know what the enemy is doing."

"That would be good," says Francisco. "Many of us had people taken away in the first wave in '70. Since then, the best people, Luminaries, as you call them, are snatched again and again. We know they're held inside the fortresses but we only have sketchy reports as to where. Can you help us with information about what the WSO and STEN are doing?"

"We can," says Stephen. Angelica nods.

"And I will help them." Bridgetta steps out from behind the screen.

Angelica and Stephen look up at her with curiosity.

"Hmm, eavesdropping again." Francisco shakes his head.

Bridgetta looks unapologetic. "It's a good way to learn things."

"This is Bridgetta," Francisco says. "She came to us about two years ago. She's an excellent gardener, she's good with the kids and is good to have with you in a street fight. She's a black belt."

Angelica pulls out a chair for Bridgetta who sits between her and Stephen. They lean in toward her at the same time. "Tell us your story," says Angelica.

Bridgetta begins speaking. "I was born in 2060, when the mass suicides started. My parents told me I was a mistake, and a girl, but they kept me for a while. They're pretty high up in the WSO."

Diego takes a sharp breath. Bridgetta ignores him. Angelica and Stephen have focused their complete attention on her. She continues. "I barely saw them. They hired nannies to take care of me. When I was five, they sent me to my martial arts dojo to live. I was the only one who lived there—Sensei and his wife took me in." She takes a deep breath, looking down at her tattoo. "I never knew any other name for him," she whispers in a choked voice. No one speaks. After a moment, she looks up with determination. "He tended the garden and taught martial arts. And he was my best friend. He was labeled a Luminary and taken away when I was thirteen." Bridgetta pauses again. "After that, I stayed in the dojo and pretended I was much less proficient than I was. I took over the garden, practiced a lot and kept my head down. I left when I was fifteen. No one ever looked for me, that I know of. I haven't had any contact with my parents since the day I went to live at the dojo. I made my way using my martial arts skills. I found my way here."

"We accept your help," Angelica says. She turns to Francisco. "Do you accept ours?"

Francisco looks at her for a long moment. She can see his thoughts moving over his face. Finally, he declares, "We do."

"Good," says Stephen. "The first thing we want to do is examine the interior of the LA fortress to determine where and how the Luminaries are being held. We have access to very good intel including aerial photography and an analysis of patrols in the area."

"Is your source trustworthy?" asks Diego.

"Oh, yes," says Angelica. She holds up her arm. "From this wristband I can access a virtual assistant connected with a very powerful computer. This computer has eyes and ears everywhere."

Stephen continues. "We know the fortress area is patrolled by drones in the air and STEN soldiers on the ground. The surveillance is heavy since LA is a strategic port on the Pacific Ocean and the North American headquarters of the WSO, housed in the LA Convention Center. We think the Luminaries are in an infirmary in the bottom level, in what was an exhibition hall. Buildings and freeways around that section of downtown have been demolished to form a wall around it. The only apparent way in is along a heavily patrolled east/west street."

"Yeah, Figueroa Street," says Francisco. "The regular people inside that area are like zombies. Every kind of drug you can imagine is readily available. The WSO staff and STEN soldiers are everywhere. They live in fancy apartments in the high rises inside the perimeter."

"Can we get in without being seen?" Angelica asks.

"Oh yeah we can," says Diego. "I'm an expert." He grins.

"Why is the WSO targeting these special people?" Bridgetta asks.

"The WSO is a front for a group that condemns any sort of spiritualism and promotes materialism. They're bent on the domination, nullification, and ultimate destruction of all Luminaries. The WSO has been set up to accomplish this on Earth," Angelica says. "We know this group by the name 'Soulests.' In every fortress city, Luminaries are being held under barbaric conditions. They're drugged into deep sleep and feed inadequately so they suffer from malnutrition. It's the worst sort of imprisonment." Angelica

38

becomes agitated as she speaks. Stephen gets up to stand behind her, hands on her shoulders.

Stephen says, "From what we know already, these infirmaries have a secret psychiatric ward that no one knows about. That's where we think the Luminaries are held."

Other members of the survival community have entered the common area and gathered around. Hearing Angelica's speech, they whisper among themselves. Francisco takes note of the reaction of his people. He speaks to them. "You've heard these two strangers. Do you trust them to do what they say they will? Will you join them to increase the resistance and help the ones who've been taken? What do you say?"

Feet shuffle and the people look at each other, then at Angelica and Stephen. After a moment an older man steps forward. "I'm in." Another voice rises, "Me too." More voices chime in. "Count me in." "Me too."

When it's quiet again, Francisco sweeps his gaze over the group. "Anyone opposed?" The silence stretches. He turns to Angelica and Stephen. "Looks like you've joined the resistance."

LATE AFTERNOON

Angelica and Stephen have excused themselves and are walking in the neighborhood.

Angelica says, "Stephen, I can't believe I'm even suggesting it at all, but I have a peculiar feeling, something I haven't felt for a very long time. I can't get it out of my mind. It's a sort of been-here-experienced-this feeling. Our parents could still be here, on Earth. I know they might be lost, or even dead. But they may not be. There's a chance…"

Stephen puts his arm around her. She leans in, resting her head on his shoulder. "If they're alive," he says, "we'll find them."

Angelica looks up at him. "Yes. We will."

They walk a bit more, then she continues. "Now, we have to be practical. One of our immediate targets is to check out the infirmary inside the LA fortress. But we must keep in mind that the creation of a global resistance movement is tantamount to our plans. It will have to be active and thriving to overthrow the World State Organization. The Soulests have had various names over the millennium, but they've all just masked their one purpose—to destroy those who have real power to create. We have our hands full, love. This mission is critical, but in some ways it's beyond the scope of just the two of us."

"Yes, Angelica, but we always find a way to pull off the win and triumph in the end, despite some pretty harrowing scrapes and entanglements. Rest assured, I'm committed to you—and to our mission—as always. We have the same purpose. We'll prevail and achieve our goals for all."

They find a bench in a corner park and sit, watching the sun sink toward the western horizon. Stephen takes Angelica's hand.

"I don't know about you," he says, "but I'm finding the male and female mockups of these Earth bodies a little hard to get used to, especially on a lower gravity planet like this one. They are biomechanical—basically a carbon-oxygen engine. They're sophisticated and efficient biologically, but they do require a good deal of maintenance to operate. I've observed they have to be fed a lot to create energy. It seems that Earth beings don't create their own energy. But they can be attractive when well cared for." He raises an eyebrow and grins.

"Well put, dear. I agree with your observation," Angelica bats her eyelashes and grins back.

Stephen stands, pulling her up for a quick kiss. "Come on. Let's get back, have some food and plan our attack on the LA fortress."

After the evening meal, Angelica and Stephen sit with Francisco and Diego.

"Tomorrow, we'll show you how we do things here," says Francisco. "We've figured out how to stay under STEN's radar. Everything is done on a small scale but in lots of locations so they can never pinpoint anything to attack."

"Plus, they're pretty stupid," adds Diego with a smirk.

"Good," says Angelica. "But we'll want to get into the fortress tomorrow night to check out the facility and to see what we're up against. I figure we're no more than ten or twelve miles from it now, is that right?"

"That's right," says Diego. "It'll take about forty minutes to approach and infiltrate, and we'll do it around three in the morning. The patrols start to get lax about that time."

"Very good," says Stephen. "Angelica, do we have all the equipment we need?"

"Yes. I stored it behind the medical facility on the hill."

"We'll go get that now." Stephen gets up and addresses Francisco. "Where do we sleep?" he asks.

"We've set you up in a place a couple of blocks from here. Diego will show you. If you're going back to the infirmary, be smart about travel. Don't use any light that can be spotted by a patrol. Keep noise down—it carries around the river and the freeway. Diego can go with you…," he pauses.

"That won't be necessary," says Stephen, smiling. "We know how to be stealthy in enemy territory."

"Good," says Francisco. "Let's get you settled." He nods to Diego.

Diego leads Angelica and Stephen to a small house behind a larger one, not far from the Disney complex. The door is not locked. He shows them a small kitchen, living space, bedroom and bathroom. "There's an outhouse out back and a bucket of water for washing in the kitchen. There's a supply of candles on the table. We all eat in the common room. Breakfast is from six till eight in the morning. See you then."

"Thank you, Diego," says Angelica. She shuts the door behind him and turns to Stephen who is setting out a candle.

He says, "Did the hovercraft and supplies come through in good order?"

"Yes," says Angelica, "it was just where we wanted it. I drove the hovercraft over the hill to where I found you. It's hidden behind the building."

"Let's go get it," says Stephen.

NIGHT

They leave the house. It's fully dark, no light coming from anywhere. The moon is a not quite a pale half circle in the sky. They pause to allow their bodies' vision to adjust. They're using the eyes of their bodies but they're also using their soldier-of-light skills. They set off at a brisk pace, retracing their path from the infirmary.

"It's a good thing we can run fast with these bodies," Angelica says. "I believe we could go five to eight miles per hour faster. But we don't want to appear too unnatural right away. We'll just run like top sprinters to be safe."

"I agree," replies Stephen. "We don't want to attract too much attention to ourselves. We're here to blend in, not crash human reality." Stephen grins as he puts on a brief burst of speed that Angelica easily duplicates. They are muffling laughter as they reach the concealed hovercraft.

Stephen checks it out. All is in order. They climb aboard and he sets it to silent mode. They fly back to their quarters, hide the hovercraft and go inside. They find a basket of fruit and another bucket of water waiting for them. Angelica grabs an apple and sits on the couch as Stephen relights the candle. He gets an apple and sits next to her.

"These people are going to make it," she says.

"They are. There's something about them…"

"Exactly. They're resilient and caring and they have good intentions."

Stephen is thoughtful. "At least the ones in the survival camps do. The WSO people will be the opposite."

"I wonder if all of them are, though. I wonder if some are just deluded or didn't realize they could make a different choice."

"Time will tell."

DAY THREE

LOS ANGELES SURVIVAL COMMUNITY

THE NEXT MORNING Angelica and Stephen met Francisco and Diego at breakfast.

"Today we'll show you around, then we'll plan for the mission tonight," Francisco says. He and Diego lead them outside into the neighborhood surrounding the former Disney studio. The area is a strange ghost town with many houses but no people and few animals. They walk and talk.

"We have some information about the LA walled fortress," Angelica says, "but we want to see what the actual scene is. It would be good to find out about the staff in the infirmary, if we can. What are the shifts? Is it covered day and night? How many staff are there? Can we get into the psychiatric section where they're holding the Luminaries?"

"At this point we're interested in surveillance," says Stephen. "We'll also visit other fortress cities. Hopefully they'll follow the pattern of the LA fortress."

Francisco nods. "We've talked to the camps in Salt Lake City and Denver. The WSO does seem to be using a template to build their walled city power bases. The LA fortress has various security towers in key locations around the perimeter with a lighting system much like what you'd see in prison structures. Diego's infiltration route bypasses all the areas covered by these lights."

"That's good," says Angelica. "Our data shows there are a few million inhabitants in the walled cities across North America. We do know these fortress cities were erected quickly by the World State Organization. We don't have details yet about Europe, Great Britain, Australia, Africa, Asia—the rest of the world. Have you received any word from anywhere else besides Australia?"

Francisco shakes his head. "Communication from around the world is sketchy. We've been working on contacting other survival groups using Backdoor Charlie but we've had limited success. They're nervous."

Angelica says, "Remember my virtual assistant? I call him Akido. He's connected to a super computer we call the GA. As a first step, she will tap into communication channels used by the enemy. As a second step, we plan to do some things that will make other survival groups take notice. The resistance has to be world-wide to overthrow the WSO."

"I agree," says Francisco.

"Me too, and can I just say: Wow." Diego grins. "All that would be great. We could be a step—steps—ahead of the bastards!"

"I'll get Akido and GA started on that right away," Angelica says. "Oh, another thing. We'll journey to visit the Utah group in the morning."

"Okay," Francisco says. "Come to the common room anytime for water and snacks. Dinner is between five and seven. Any of our people can answer questions or get you whatever you need. We'll see you at dinner." He waves as he and Diego walk away.

Stephen and Angelica stroll to their house.

Angelica speaks. "I haven't seen these walled cities for some time. I do recall a similar post-apocalyptic world several hundred years ago on a planet in the back side of the Orion constellation. It was being controlled by a lesser skilled race that seized power worldwide. They built colossal fortress cities. They may have had a connection to the Soulests."

"I remember," says Stephen.

They walk on in silence, taking in their surroundings.

When they arrive at the house, Stephen stops at the entrance, tugging at Angelica's hand. She looks at him.

"By the way," Stephen says with a gleam in his eye, "just so you know, I was complimenting you when we were on the park bench before. You look beautiful in that human female body. It has the right height and proportions of a pleasing Earth woman, and it's strong. It's been some time since I've seen you with natural corn-yellow hair. It looks good. You did a good job reconstructing the molecular and DNA patterns of that poor woman's body. She was badly mangled when you found her. Your ability to help spirits repair bodies with your healing power, and skill using the amulet—up close and from a distance—will prove to be immensely valuable on this mission."

"Thank you, Stephen." Angelica grasps his hands and steps back, pulling her gaze up from his feet to his head. "Your Earth body is very pleasing too." She flashes a grin, then sobers. "We've accomplished many successful campaigns. We're a good team. May it continue for as long as the universe exists." Another quick smile. "And we're more than fortunate to be everlasting soul mates!" Their arms go around each other and they stand that way for a moment, holding each other close.

Angelica sighs. "Now, back to our three mission objectives." She breaks away, opening the door. They go in and sit together at the table. She continues, "First is an assessment of how bad the problem is with the Luminaries. According to GA's analysis, it's very serious. Second, how can we help a global resistance movement gain momentum, create a groundswell, ignite against the enemy and overthrow the World State Organization's stranglehold on the peoples of planet Earth? Third, retrieve the sacred scripts. No tall order, right?"

She gets up to pace. "Tonight we'll get a look at the LA fortress, which should give us some idea of the model for the rest of the fortress cities around the world. And since the enemy is basically lazy and not vigilant, the pattern should hold."

Stephen sits at the table, watching Angelica. She stops to stand opposite him. "What is your impression of this LA group?" she asks.

"Francisco and Diego are good leaders. They have a good group. If they're an example of other groups we'll find, then we can succeed. These communities have sprung up out of necessity and kept hidden from the enemy. They need help organizing to work together, but I think they can do it." He pauses. "On a different subject, the people outside must have relatives and other loved ones on the inside of these walled cities. They must have found ways to communicate from the outside to the inside. I'll ask Diego. You should get Akido started on tapping into the enemy's communication network. We have a couple of hours until dinner. We can get some sleep before our fun tonight."

"I like your plan, love. I'm going outside to get started." Angelica blows Stephen a kiss as she walks out the door. Outside she looks around. The afternoon sun shines through a eucalyptus tree and palms wave in the slight breeze. A bird calls and is answered. She stands in the dappled sunlight, savoring its warmth on her skin and the moment of peace.

"Akido," she says.

"Boss," he replies.

"Welcome to Earth. I have a task for you. We need to tap into the communications of the enemy. I want to know what they're doing. As we get the resistance revved up, they will try to stop us. I want to know what they're planning. Tonight, Stephen and I go into the LA fortress for reconnaissance. Keep watch but in silent mode."

"Got it Boss, I'm on it," says Akido.

NIGHT, LA WALLED FORTRESS CITY

"We've come a long way." Damien leans in, lifting his glass for a toast. "To us."

"Yeah, we have." Juan Carlos touches his glass to Damien's. "Both colonels."

46

They drink, silent, eyes unfocused, lost in memories. They share a look, touch glasses again, and drink.

The bar is shadowed, with hooded lamps casting pools of soft light over small tables. Damien and Juan Carlos sit in the corner, their backs against the wall. They can see the entire room and their eyes are alert, despite the alcohol.

"You set up for tomorrow?"

"Yeah."

"Don't mess up. I have to account for you to command."

"When have I ever messed up? Don't answer that." Juan Carlos drinks again. "You never let me forget that time."

"Somebody has to keep you humble."

"You too. You always need a dose of humble."

"Yeah."

They sit in companionable silence, finishing their beer.

Juan Carlos speaks first. "I have to get going. I have an early start." He and Damien stand and exchange a man hug.

"Watch your back."

"And you."

Outside the bar, they walk into the night in opposite directions.

DAY FOUR

PRE DAWN, LA WALLED FORTRESS CITY

STEPHEN, Angelica and Diego are traveling south on a dark road in an electric car. The world is silent around them.

Diego turns to Stephen. "What's your background?" he asks.

"I trained as a design engineer, mainly aircraft. I enlisted and became a pilot. I also trained in martial arts and I have special training in infiltration," Stephen replies. "What's yours?"

"Similar," says Diego. "I was eleven when the suicides started. I was staying with my uncle and my mom wouldn't let me come home. Uncle took me to a ranch in the Ojai area." Diego sighs. "Somehow, we lost her. The ranch was the beginning of our survival community. There's still a good-sized one there. Everyone spends time in both locations. Uncle made sure I learned guerrilla fighting and other survival skills. Education was learning from different members of our community. It was pretty eclectic."

"Your uncle is Francisco," says Angelica.

"Yeah."

"He's not much older than you."

"Ten years." Diego is looking forward. "I wouldn't have made it without him."

It falls quiet in the car.

"I wanted to ask you about the people living inside the fortress," says Stephen. "Are they there voluntarily? Do they communicate with the outside? Do members of your community have people on the inside?"

"In the early years, people gravitated to the fortress because of the promise of safety," says Diego. "It was pretty unsettled. People were scared. It seemed safer with walls around you. A lot of people didn't want to die, but they also wanted to keep their drugs. WSO had been passing out pills like candy and people were hooked. In the cities now, marijuana is grown everywhere so you can just pick it and dry it yourself. At first, WSO encouraged the residents to visit people they had on the outside to convince them to move inside. It worked in many cases.

"After STEN started grabbing folks—Luminaries, as you call them—relations got a little less friendly. Once someone was taken, there was no way to get to see them, no matter how hard you tried. That's when I started sneaking in at night. I wanted to see if I could find where they were, what was happening to them."

"Did you?" asks Stephen.

"Yeah. I found where they were and I managed to sneak in once." Diego's hands clench on the wheel and he takes a deep breath. "I saw, but they almost caught me. Security has been beefed up since then."

"It was bad," says Angelica.

"It was bad."

"When was that? How long ago?" she asks.

"Eleven years."

Angelica and Stephen silently acknowledge Diego. He drives on.

Stephen speaks quietly. "We need to get as close as we can. We're going to rescue whoever is left in that infirmary."

Diego gives him a long look. He says nothing, turning to watch the road.

Inside the city, among the empty skyscrapers, Diego slows the car, moving it behind a building that looms out of the darkness. There's a glow ahead.

"We walk from here. Follow me closely and duck when I do. Keep your heads on a swivel." Angelica and Stephen look confused. "Watch all around you," Diego clarifies. They nod.

Diego slides into the darkness with Angelica and Stephen close behind. They see no one as Diego leads them through alleys and between buildings. The glow gets brighter. They begin hearing the sound of helicopters and patrol dogs.

"Over here," Diego whispers. He leads them into a small space cleared in the debris wall. He crawls through. On the other side, he crouches, gesturing for Angelica and Stephen to join him. "We'll keep to the shadows. We'll go as directly as we can to the infirmary. If we get stopped, let me do the talking. You guys act stoned and horny." Angelica and Stephen nod.

The lights are bright inside the fortress walls. There are intermittent darker areas which Diego uses. They see no guards. As they approach the Convention Center, Diego detours to the back freight area. He stops in a dark shadow near the building.

"The infirmary is on the other side of the freight doors. There's a big space they've divided up. I don't think they've changed anything since I was here last. The people they've taken are in there. They never let them out." He's speaking so quietly Angelica and Stephen have to lean in to hear him.

Stephen moves toward the doors, looking for surveillance cameras. He seems to shrink and disappear as he approaches. He tries the door handles—they're locked.

He opens to Angelica. *We might have to enter from the inside. The doors are locked but this entrance is the perfect way to get the Luminaries out when the time comes.*

Angelica responds. *We'll have to figure out how to infiltrate the building so we can get down to this room. Akido can find out what else this building is used for. If it has any public aspect, we could use that to get in.*

Stephen is moving back to them. Diego pulls them back into the shadows.

"We have to leave now," he says. He moves away, ghosting them to the wall, through it and back to their car. They don't speak until they're on the road heading home.

"Did you get what you needed?" asks Diego.

"Yes," says Angelica. "Thank you for taking us."

"No problem. When we get back, get some sleep. If you leave before I see you in the morning, head northeast for Salt Lake City. When you get close, the camp is actually in Provo, south of Salt Lake City. Look for the temple column with the golden man on top, right up against the mountains. The camp is centered near that structure."

Stephen nods.

The rest of the journey is uneventful.

Back in their quarters, Angelica and Stephen sit in the dark in the backyard. The eastern sky is preparing for sunrise.

"If the other survival communities are like this one, our mission will be successful," Stephen says. "You know, I always feel great when we team together. You leading the mission is always a successful operating basis. You're great with logistics—the best I've ever seen."

"Thank you, dearest. I am assigned as leader but we're a team. I work better when you are by my side." They sit in silence.

Angelica takes a deep breath. "The number of Luminaries that are dying appalls me. How many of them were in that building on the other side of that door? We must see what's going on in these so-called infirmaries as soon as possible. We have to take control and turn things around fast."

Akido's voice issues from Angelica's wristband. "Ready to report."

"Good. Start with the WSO communication set up. Broadcast audio so Stephen can hear," says Angelica.

"The World State Organization uses a proprietary computer network linked to the internet. There are servers in various places around the world. In their offices and common rooms inside the fortress cities, they have computers connected to their network. There are different levels of access. High level communications are encrypted. GA is working on

51

breaking that encryption to give you access. It shouldn't take long."

Akido continues. "Here is a training video accessed from the lowest level. '*Halley's Comet is a recurring event in Earth's skies, becoming visible every 80 to 85 years. It was scheduled to return sometime in 2061. In 2025 a group of scientists studying comets discovered that Halley's had changed its course.*'" Angelica watches the video to its end. She looks up at Stephen.

"This was how they convinced so many people to kill themselves," she whispers. "I think the Soulests have gotten even worse in the time they have been out of our sight. What else, Akido?"

"Right, Boss. Behind the scenes, Soulests recruited every leader already aligned with their philosophy. They infiltrated or took over the power structures in the United States, Russia, and as many oil-rich countries as they could in the Middle East, Africa, and South America. They paid special attention in the United States, targeting North Dakota, Oklahoma, Texas, California, and Washington D.C.

"Currency is now completely electronic, called cryptocurrency, accessed via chips embedded in each person's wrist. The currency allotments come from a WSO welfare system. This is the only currency accepted in the fortress cities. Outside, barter is the method of exchange."

"This data is very interesting, Angelica," Stephen says. "We've seen the same pattern many times. Worlds are ruined again and again by drugs and relentless power grabs. It is ruthless manipulation for evil."

"Yes." says Angelica. "Soulests use the inability of free societies to handle global terrorism and divisions in religious ideology. They spread their message of nullification so they can bring about a world order of radicalism, social and religious contempt, and unrest."

Stephen nods. "But the real reason behind this Soulests' action is their innermost fear. They fight an enemy that is really only within themselves. They have to fight for the extermination of any powerful group and powerful individuals, like those with true personal ability, imagination, and power—the Luminaries."

Angelica nods. "Soulests have enslaved and disposed of their enemies in the cruelest ways as they strive to dominate many worlds. We thought they were vanquished after the last war, but they crept off to this isolated corner of the universe and they've been hard at work, like termites in a beautiful house."

Akido adds, "This location we are in, the United States of America, was once the beacon of hope and freedom for millions of individuals throughout the world. It has been darkened by the Soulests' poison. The top leader, High Commander Rhotah Mhene, is the Soulest in charge here."

Angelica gasps. Stephen grabs her hand, pulling her to his lap, his face grim. She stills with his arms around her, absorbing this news. They sit this way the rest of the night.

MORNING

The sun is peeking over the Verdugo Mountains. The sky is cloudless and a clear, crystalline blue. Birds begin their morning chatter. Angelica has recovered. She and Stephen listen.

"It's moments like these I miss our home," says Angelica.

"Me too."

They watch as the sun completes its journey past the top of the mountain. Each is considering what they left and what they have to do to accomplish their mission.

Akido speaks again. "More information from the WSO database. For more than twenty years, they have been running a basic program to round up anyone who voices opposition, as well as any creative people. The STEN troops have standing orders to detain anyone who's known to speak out, and anyone operating in any form of the arts. Engineers are evaluated as to their usefulness. Most detainees are incarcerated inside the fortress. The ones deemed 'very bad' go to the infirmaries to be given deep sleep 'therapy.' The 'patients' in the infirmary are used as lab animals for psychiatric experimentation. Angelica, Stephen, this is very bad.

"The experiments in the infirmaries have resulted in more and better ways to turn humans into drugged zombies. The free pills in the fortress make the people there very pliable. The Soulests plan to get the entire population left on Earth addicted to their drugs. All Earth's natural resources will be plundered for their consumption." Akido pauses. "In addition, GA says there are hints of some big project in the works but she can't find anything about it on any database. She will continue to search."

"We must get into action!" exclaims Angelica. "First, we leave a note to let Francisco know we'll contact him from Utah using Backdoor Charlie. Stephen, will you prepare the hovercraft for the journey to Utah? Akido, find a route for him. I'll write the note for Francisco and arrange for travel food. I want to leave before anyone comes to see us so we don't have to explain the hovercraft right now. Time for that later."

Angelica goes in the house. She emerges five minutes later with a sack of fruit and a water bottle. Stephen is waiting on the hovercraft.

"Akido downloaded the coordinates. We're ready to go," says Stephen.

"Good." Angelica climbs aboard. "It's a good thing the undercarriage has your camouflage coating. Once we're in the air, no one will be able to see us from the ground."

"And we'll be away from the area fast." Stephen grins as he lifts off and speeds away. Angelica laughs as the air whips across her face and through her hair.

They fly northeast, over a desert crisscrossed with low mountains. The land has a harsh beauty. They see small indications of civilization as they fly across California, then north of Las Vegas. There is more desert and low mountains. As they near the Salt Lake City area, they see the vast Great Salt Lake with its attendant salt flats. Before they reach the lake, they see a smaller body of water with buildings near it, nestled below tall mountains. Stephen points.

"The camp is over there. You can see the golden figure on the spire and some smoke from fires."

Angelica nods. Stephen looks for a place to hide the hovercraft. He flies it into a canyon and sets down in a grove of trees.

"Akido," he asks, "how long to walk to where we'll find Garcia and Margo, our contacts in Utah?"

"Human walking speed, approximately an hour," replies Akido.

"Let's do that," says Angelica. "It will give us a chance to plan."

"Okay."

They set off down the canyon.

As they walk, Akido says, "The idea of a survival community first appeared in Australia. They took the initiative and established the idea of teamwork, with special emphasis on coordinated activity, where each member of the community has a purpose, a skill, and job to do. The resistance movement got its start in these Australian survival communities. The WSO has largely ignored the continent."

"That makes those survival camps perfect to act as the world headquarters for a legitimate planet-wide resistance movement," says Angelica. "Using the Backdoor Charlie communication system will make coordination easy."

"I agree," says Stephen.

Angelica is thoughtful. "Once we've established the state of the survival camps in the United States, we'll want to get to the fringe people. We'll need to reunite them with the rest of humanity and get them involved in the resistance movement. This is the only way things can really change on planet Earth. This is the only way they'll regain any form of freedom. I'm afraid if we don't succeed, the human race will become extinct."

"We have a lot to do, without a doubt," says Stephen. "I am encouraged by our first encounter. Let's see what the next camps bring. Meanwhile, enjoy this beautiful country with me."

They look around as they walk. The air warms as they descend the canyon. There is a small, dry stream bed meandering along the bottom of the canyon. Small animals scurry away from their footsteps. Birds rise in flight. They walk in silence, taking in their surroundings, listening to its sounds.

Soon they hear wood being chopped. Stephen takes out his binovision glasses to look ahead.

MIDDAY, UTAH SURVIVAL COMMUNITY

"The structure with the golden man on a column is not far. The rest of the town is further down the hill. I see activity in that direction."

They reach a young man chopping wood. He looks up with suspicion.

"Hello," says Angelica. "My name is Angelica and this is Stephen. We're looking for Garcia and Margo. Will you give us directions to where we can find them?" She stands with her hands loose at her sides. Stephen is a step behind her, also standing easy.

The young man looks them over, holding his ax with both hands in front of his chest.

"Did you come out of the canyon?" he asks.

"We did," says Angelica.

"You don't look like you've been living rough," he says.

"We get by," says Stephen.

"What you want Garcia for?"

"Francisco in Los Angeles said we should talk with him," says Angelica. "Can you help us?"

The young man stands looking at them a long moment. He lets the ax lower and points down the hill. "They'll be in the training center, in the field. Look for the horses."

"Thank you," says Angelica.

Angelica and Stephen walk down the hill. They see the horses, three have riders who are herding the rest into an enclosed area.

"I imagine two of those riders are Garcia and Margo. They will be good people, compatriots, and strong believers in the resistance movement. Let's see what they've built here," says Angelica. She begins to move with more speed. Stephen strides beside her and lays a hand on her arm.

"Love, remember we have to be certain we move as normal humans. We don't want them to know we're from another planet, at least for now. We should curb nimbleness and quickness to blend better with these Earth folks."

Angelica throws him a look and slows down.

They see the riders stop and look in their direction. They turn their horses, starting toward them at a good pace. As they approach, they become two men and a woman galloping forward. Angelica and Stephen hold their ground. The riders pull their horses to a stop inches away.

"Who are you?" says the older man.

"Garcia, is that you?" replies Angelica. "I'm Angelica, this is Stephen. We've come from Francisco in Los Angeles."

"How did you get here?" asks Garcia.

"We drove. We've been on the road several days. We had to dodge some patrols. We came along the foot of the mountains and hid our car. We've gotten pretty good at avoiding sentries," Stephen says with a smile.

"We'll have to do something about that," growls Garcia, throwing the younger rider a look.

The woman dismounts and walks toward Angelica, holding out her hand. "I'm Margo," she says. "This is my husband Garcia and my son Zack." She shakes hands with Angelica.

"It appears my wife thinks you're okay," says Garcia, looking between the two women. "She's the boss so you'd better come with us."

Margo walks beside Angelica and Stephen, leading her horse. Garcia rides beside her and Zack races ahead.

Garcia is large man—six feet tall and two hundred pounds. Margo is a dark redhead with an hourglass shape. Zack is a more athletic version of Garcia with his mother's hair color.

They thread through a neighborhood. When they reach a larger building, they hand the horses to Zack and go inside to another common room. Garcia heads to a kitchen, calling over his shoulder. "I'm getting a snack. You want something?"

Margo shakes her head. "Let me bring you some refreshments and you can tell us what you're doing here." She follows her husband.

In the kitchen, Garcia turns to her. "You really think those two are legitimate?" he asks.

"I don't know about legitimate, but I think they're okay. There's something about them." She glances through the pass-through window as she gathers peanut butter, jam, and bread. "Look at them." Angelica and Stephen are seated beside each other, legs touching. Zack has come in and sits across from them. They're looking at him with singular attention. "I see a glow around them."

"You and your glow," says Garcia.

"You know I'm rarely wrong."

"I know." Garcia finishes arranging a pitcher of ice water and glasses on a tray. Margo puts the sandwiches on a plate.

They carry food and drink out and set it on the table.

"Now, tell us what you're all about," says Margo.

"We've come to help the resistance. We want to help anyone and everyone who's been incarcerated in the walled fortress cities' infirmaries. You have one here, right?" asks Angelica.

Zack answers. "The Utah WSO Headquarters is in Sandy, near the old soccer stadium. There's a big medical building just south of the stadium. There are reports that they take detainees there. The STEN troops and anyone working for WSO are housed in that area. It's pretty open, easy to patrol. No one in their right mind goes anywhere near it."

"Are there any other survival groups, possible freedom fighters, in this area?" asks Stephen.

Garcia answers. "There's a small survival group in and around Salt Lake City, but they're nomads. Plenty of empty buildings to squat in lets them stay on the move year-round. They never winter in the same place twice. They're not aligned with anyone but themselves." He shakes his head.

"You've had your creative people, your outspoken people, taken away by STEN?" asks Angelica.

"Yes," says Margo. "What do you know about that?"

"We know that it is one of the purposes of the leaders of the WSO. They want to eradicate any person capable of creating beauty and humanity and future. They follow the path trod by past kings and dictators who enslave civilizations to build dynasties. It is an old story." Angelica's voice is grim.

"One of our goals is to rescue the people in the infirmaries," says Stephen.

"Will you rescue all of them, in all the infirmaries worldwide?" asks Margo.

"That's what we want to do," says Stephen.

"Do you have a plan?" says Garcia.

"The beginnings of one," says Angelica. "The first thing we're working on is tapping into the enemy's communications so we know what they are doing and what to expect from them."

"How will you manage that?" asks Zack.

Angelica holds up her wrist unit. "This wristband is a virtual assistant connected to a super computer. The computer is making the arrangements."

"Cool!" exclaims Zack.

"Those of us dedicated to the resistance will be happy with this advantage. I hope it'll help encourage real leaders to come forward to take up the cause for freedom," says Margo.

Stephen reaches for a sandwich and takes a bite. "Mmmm. PB and J."

"Really!" says Angelica and grabs one. "These are good! A taste of home, right Stephen?" He nods, munching with a smile on his face.

"Glad you like them," says Margo. "They're Zack's favorite too." For the next few minutes everyone is eating a sandwich and washing it down with fresh water.

Other people are coming and going in the common area. They look at Angelica and Stephen with curiosity, but no one interrupts them.

"Can we take a look around before it gets too dark?" asks Stephen.

Garcia and Margo lead them out of the building into the community. Zack trails along. They see individuals busy with their daily routines. There's a group in an open area training in martial arts. Angelica and Stephen can see the training includes many styles. They see crops growing in greenhouse gardens fortified using hydroculture and permaculture methods. The plants are flourishing.

Margo shows them outdoor kitchens where groups of women and children are canning fruits and vegetables. Scents of sugar, strawberries, and vinegar waft across the air.

"This whole area was a church training center and university,"

Garcia says. "We've repurposed a lot of the buildings. We have a huge space where we work on building and repairing two-way radios, solar energy set ups, and basic computers. There are guys who know how to fix them and guys learning how. Plus, there's an annex where people are trained to use the equipment."

"Tell them about Joshua," says Zack.

Garcia chuckles. "Old Joshua Henderson runs our weaponry workshop. He's got a lot of experience he doesn't talk about, but he knows everything there is to know about weapons. Zack loves it there."

"Yeah!" says Zack. "Joshua teaches everything—how to find, repair or rebuild rifles, hand guns, anything that shoots a projectile really. He can make any kind of ammo, even gun powder. He makes bows and arrows, knives and swords. He can do all this himself AND he teaches it. He's the best. He says knowledge is worthless unless it's shared."

"He sounds like a very wise man," says Angelica.

"He is," says Zack. "Oh, and he's just added crossbow making and shooting. As soon as we've made enough equipment, it'll be added to the self-defense training program."

The group continues walking in the beautiful neighborhood graced with gardens and trees and mountains in the background. They've arrived at a converted park where the horses are pastured.

Margo looks at Garcia and says "It's getting on time for dinner. Let's take them down to Maggie's."

Garcia nods. "It's a good place to get a meal made by a great cook—who's not Margo, of course. And she's got some basic supplies you can barter for. There's a safe room in the back where we can talk in private."

"It's about a mile to Maggie's, and there's a stable nearby. We'll ride," says Zack. He vaults the fence and gets a horse ready for Angelica and Stephen. "You do ride bareback, right?"

"Yes," replies Angelica. "We ride." She shares a look with Stephen, both thinking of their beautiful horses back home.

"This is my Appaloosa," Zack says. "She's called Majestic. She's a good horse. You both can ride her to Maggie's. Just follow us."

The four riders head to the street, Garcia and Margo leading, followed by Zack beside Angelica and Stephen. Angelica leans back into Stephen, enjoying the feel of riding again.

The shadows lengthen as the sun lowers toward the western mountains. The moon is almost full and hangs in the clear sky.

"Our moon will give you just enough light for a brisk ride," says Margo. "You two are welcome to take horses out later if you want."

"Thank you," says Stephen.

EVENING

Garcia, Margo and Zack arrive first and wait for Angelica and Stephen who are not far behind. The area was once a warehouse district. Most of the buildings are derelict. They've stopped at a makeshift stable set up in a parking lot. The building nearby has a large opening revealing several stalls. They dismount and Zack leads the horses into the building.

When he comes back, they cross the street and enter Maggie's. It's a restaurant with all but one window boarded over. There's a rough, hand-painted sign on the board nearest the entrance. An overhang covers part of the space in front with one table and some chairs under it.

Inside, they're greeted by an old man named Red. His skin looks like dark leather hanging from his bones. He ushers them toward the back, past tables set up on the left and some shelves with items for sale on the right. At the back of the room, Garcia approaches tall shelves pushed against the wall. He rolls them away, revealing a door that opens into a second, smaller room.

"We can have something to eat and talk in private here," he says. He turns to Red and asks for four portions of the special. Red nods and heads for the kitchen.

It's been a long day for the two soldiers of light. They find chairs and sit as Margo lights the lantern on the table. They're the only people in the back room. They're silent as Red brings in plates and places them on the table. He closes the door behind him. They eat the plain but delicious food.

Angelica sets down her fork and sits back. "Will you tell us about yourselves?" she asks, looking at Margo and Garcia. "Stephen and I wonder if you are from a gypsy culture. It's known to be a hearty and sustaining culture, with the ability to muster and wage campaigns. You have demonstrated an ability to survive well as a group, living off the land and fighting adversity the way you have. You are the very soul of a resistance."

Stephen asks, "Where are you from? And where did you grow up?"

"Okay," says Zack. "That's my cue. I'm outta here. I'll go check on the horses." He's out the door in a flash.

Garcia chuckles. "He's heard this story many times." He looks at Stephen. "Well, thanks for asking."

He leans back in his chair. "Our family came from a village called St. Lorenzo. It's tucked away in the mountains of the French Pyrenees, between France and Spain. Margo and I were born there. When we were eighteen, three years before the madness started, the whole clan decided to move to America. We all knew what was coming and our leaders decided it would be better to have a large country to disappear in. We all came here while we still could. Margo and I got married in 2060—right in the midst of the chaos.

"When our clan came to America, we brought our culture. Boys and girls grow up learning life skills from their adult family members. One of the strengths of the gypsy culture is that everyone learns basic survival skills and specializes in a skill needed by the community— building, living off the land, hunting, cooking, and working together. We love music and dance. We mostly marry within our own culture. We have a hearty and beautiful life filled with work and play."

Angelica and Stephen look at one another, smiling.

After that, conversation flows easily. The tone is light, jovial and spirited. Garcia tells how the survival community is increasing in size each year. He credits adding the plan and model for co-ops and survival communities from Australian Colin Hainsworth to the gypsy way of life. Colin's advice has been really helpful.

With enthusiasm, Garcia recounts the story of how they made

contact with Colin. "Out of the blue, we get an email. An email! It started with 'Hey Mates!' and continued with the James Dobbs story."

Stephen smiles, saying, "Francisco told us about that first email and the story that Colin told."

"Right," says Garcia. "That first email was the first of many. He sent messages about survival activities—things like water conversation and hydroculture in backyard gardens. Colin shared organizational ideas and methods. We shared the methods and ideas that made our lives better. That connection changed everything. We had a way to communicate with other survivors who didn't agree with the way things were going. We could talk about resistance without fear of being discovered."

Margo adds, "We had an opportunity to talk with other people going through what we were going through, to discuss our problems and share our solutions. It was and is, wonderful."

The old cuckoo clock on the wall strikes one, then two a.m. They agree it's time to call it a night. Old Red dozes at one of the main room tables. He grumbles as he gets up to lock the door behind them. Standing outside, they're met by the relief of a cool breeze and millions of stars in the Milky Way.

Looking up, Angelica sends a thought to Stephen. *The stars out here are bright and glisten in the night sky. They are a sight to behold. It's so clear here in Utah, the illumination of the stars and constellations is easy to see. And so different from what we're used to.*

Stephen is also looking up. He sends agreement.

"It's a beautiful sky, isn't it?" says Garcia.

Noise from the horses across the way distracts them. They're agitated, reacting to something. All eyes look into the dark searching for what may have spooked them.

Margo and Garcia see a shadowy figure of a man and horse down the road. They're not concerned, there's almost no crime in their community. But Maggie's is a distance from the main settlement.

Garcia lifts his hand to touch the smooth steel handle of the

Bowie knife on his belt. Stephen and Angelica are alert, scanning the scene.

But the shadow disappears in the frosty night air.

"That'll bear some watching," says Garcia.

"Yes," agrees Angelica. "But for now, we need to sleep. May we speak with your key people tomorrow night to brief them on the resistance movement and why we're here? I want to tell them that we're aware of the loved ones being held against their will, incarcerated in the walled fortress cities. And that we plan to rescue them. I think they'll want to hear this."

"Of course," says Garcia. "Tonight, you can stay at our place. It's secure and cozy. You can have the bunk beds in the back bedroom.

"Thank you. We'll take you up on that," says Stephen.

The group makes their way back to Garcia and Margo's house. The horses are unsaddled and let loose in the backyard. Margo shows Stephen and Angelica to the back bedroom. In the bottom bunk, they lie down holding one another, letting their Earth bodies rest. The soldiers of light sleep entwined like they're encased in a cocoon. The space of the room slowly begins to glow with illumination, filled with life energy. They reenergize and their spirits refresh.

DAY FIVE

PRE DAWN, UTAH SURVIVAL COMMUNITY

THREE GUNSHOTS DISTURB the quiet solitude of the night.

Jolted awake, Garcia hustles to the front door. Stephen and Angelica are right behind him, ready for action. Zack enters the room in front of Margo, protecting her.

Garcia holds up his hand as he peers out the door. It's dark and silent outside. They all listen closely. The faint sound of a helicopter seeps into the house. It's so incongruous that Angelica and Stephen look at each other in astonishment.

"Patrol," says Zack.

"Yeah. We don't get them very often. It's always surprising when we hear them," says Garcia.

"What about the gunshots?" says Stephen.

"Probably a hunter, although shots fired within the community are rare. I'll find out what happened in the morning. No need to do anything tonight. Go back to bed everyone." Garcia closes the door.

Angelica and Stephen are grateful to lay their bodies down again. But their minds keep coming back to the mission. Knowing their bodies need sleep, they use soldier-of-light discipline to shut down all thought to let their bodies recharge.

These two have much history together as a soldier-of-light team. They have a relationship based on trust in one another and belief in common ideals. They've saved each other's life on many occasions. They get the job done whatever it takes and wherever it may take them.

MIDDAY

It's midday when they wake. The smell of coffee takes them to the kitchen. Maggie is standing at the stove, Garcia sits at the table, his big hands wrapped around a mug. Maggie gives them each a cup of coffee.

"Cream and sugar on the table," she says. "I've got beans and grits, with homemade salsa and kombucha to get you going."

Stephen and Angelica sit down to eat. They realize their bodies are starved for the energy from food. They look at each other with the same thought. *Sleep and food are essential to keep these bodies sharp and battle ready.*

After lunch, Garcia and Margo leave to take care of their duties. Zack comes in long enough to eat and leaves again. Alone, Stephen and Angelica sit in the backyard, gazing at eastern mountains. The sun is warm. The horses graze at the bottom of the garden.

"Akido. Report," says Angelica.

"Yes Boss," says Akido. "GA has tapped into the WSO networks and will forward all communications regarding the resistance as you work on getting it up and running globally. As soon as I get it, I will give you the data you need from these communications."

Garcia and Margo arrive home, coming into the backyard to pull up chairs opposite Angelica and Stephen.

Garcia reports. "The shots fired were Hank shooting at coyotes going for his chickens. He'll get a better perimeter set up so he doesn't have to wake up everyone."

Stephen and Angelica nod.

Garcia gives them a long look. "I think it's time we had a serious talk," Garcia states. "Who are you two and what exactly you doing here?" He leans forward, looking back and forth at Angelica and Stephen.

"You have probably surmised we are not from around here," Angelica starts.

Garcia growls, Margo pats him on the shoulder. "Remember the glow," she says. Garcia shakes his head but sits back.

Angelica glances at Margo as she continues. "But we heard about the troubles here and we came to help. We have two main objectives: rescue the people held in the special wards of the infirmaries in the fortress cities, and help the resistance become a force that can overthrow the WSO so good people can take over caring for Earth."

Stephen speaks. "With the internet backdoor—do you call it Backdoor Charlie too?" Garcia nods.

"Good. With Backdoor Charlie, all the survival communities who want to be part of the resistance can talk to each other and coordinate raids and attacks on the WSO. It would also be very valuable to know what the WSO is planning. We're working on this."

"We have access to a super computer," says Angelica.

Stephen smiles. "And access is through Angelica's virtual assistant, Akido."

"Say hello Akido," says Angelica.

"Hello, Akido," says Akido.

Margo giggles.

"He often thinks he's funny," says Angelica. "Don't encourage him." She's smiling.

"That's a little hard to swallow," says Garcia, but he's thinking. He says, "Right now we're able to coordinate our efforts and recruit. Knowing what them damn STEN are doing will keep us safer and help morale."

"It will," agrees Margo.

"Okay," says Garcia. "You'll do. But I'll still need to see it to believe it."

"Fair enough," says Stephen.

Angelica leans forward. "You do keep all this top secret and confidential, right? These developments must never be known by the enemy."

"Of course." Garcia looks put out by her question.

Margo glances at her husband and says, "I know that our morale has been greatly improved because of the ideas we exchange. People here especially like the idea that every person, big or small, must have a key role in our community. This has made a real difference for us. Working together as a community is everything."

"It's just a beginning but I think we're finally heading in the right direction," says Garcia.

Margo nods her agreement. "Now we can be part of a resistance movement that means business!"

"This makes me very happy," Angelica says. She smiles and takes Stephen's hand.

"Okay," says Garcia. "Good news all around. I've set up the meeting you wanted, for eight o'clock tonight. I've invited the leaders from the various areas of activity. There's an outbuilding behind the temple we can use for privacy."

"And before then, there's dinner prep and eating," Margo says. "Angelica, come help me with that. The guys can stay here and talk men talk."

Angelica glances sideways at Stephen as she follows Margo.

They spend a pleasant afternoon and evening interacting with members of the Utah survival community. They exchange impressions with each other via thoughts. When dinner is finished and the dishes done, Garcia, Zack, Stephen, Angelica and Margo make their way to the temple outbuilding. They see other figures going the same way.

EVENING

As the confidential town meeting gets underway, there's a feeling in the air that the two visitors have an important message to impart. Only seven key individuals were secretly invited and they all came.

There is the old school master and college professor, Mr. Martin; the former mayor's son, Nick Donaldson and his friend Travis Wilson; the old librarian, Martha Smith; and Maggie Andersen with her husband, David. Old Doc Crawford is a last-minute arrival. He's a mainstay of the Utah camp. He's delivered more babies, fixed more broken bones and stitched up more wounds than anyone can count. He comes in on the meeting already in progress and sits near the back door.

Garcia opens the meeting with Margo standing nearby. Zack is at the door as added security, his six-foot-two-inches acting as an imposing guard.

"Thank you all for coming here tonight," Garcia says. "This is a special briefing. Tonight, you're going to hear from two special guests. Some of you may have seen them around. They'll talk about something that's been considered for some time but hasn't come together completely. I'd like to introduce Angelica and Stephen."

Garcia and Margo step to one side.

Angelica stands up in front of the small group. Stephen stands three paces behind her, eyes on the group. There is no welcome applause. All eyes are on her, a five-foot-six-inch blonde woman, good figure and nice looking, with piercing, but kind hazel eyes. She looks out on the townsfolk who represent the community. She eyes them, commanding the space.

"News came to you, just about one year ago, about the formation of a movement that's shaping up fast. The good news is that this movement will enhance the survival of all communities—here, and eventually the rest of the world.

"I am Angelica, this is Stephen. We may not be from here, but I can tell you that it's time for a special effort. We're here to help get the survival communities going at a fast pace to create this effort—the effort to resist and overthrow the WSO and all it stands for."

There is a sharp intake of breath in the room.

"The main goal for a resistance movement is the restoration of freedom from all oppressors, once and for good." Angelica pauses, surveying the room. "Yes, I'll repeat that. The main goal for a resistance movement is the restoration of freedom from all oppressors once and for good. When that goal is achieved, the work will be to restore a government of the people, here in America and across the planet."

The room is quiet.

Angelica takes in the whole audience, looking into each of their faces intently.

"There has been little hope for many years," she says. "And it's our belief that something can be done about things now. There are folks who believe the same way, who believe we must handle our oppressors now. I think you have the same belief.

"Yet there are those who are stuck in apathy and can't move forward. There are those who have lost people to the STEN raids. The oppressors are taking away your best people. And there are those of you who are scared. We understand. We've lost people too. We can help. Something can be done about all of this." She pauses again.

"Uniting the various survival communities is a key goal. We will all fare better if we are unified this way. The walled fortress cities and their inhabitants are shut off from our outside world. The people there live in a drugged stupor. The World State Organization has good reason for this. They want to control the remaining population of planet Earth, turning them into slaves and pliable zombies with drugs."

Angelica looks at the people in front of her, seeing many emotions moving across their faces.

"This must change," she says in a low voice. "The walled fortress cities must ultimately be taken down, razed to the ground, and the people there taken into your communities and helped to become productive, taught their worth and helped to be free of the yoke of drugs and external control. ALL of the peoples of Earth will be free. Free to live, free to create, free to make life better!"

Angelica's voice rings out and her final words are met with sounds of agreement. She raises her fist and smiles. Now there is conservative applause.

A tall, lanky guy in a blue flannel shirt and tattered overalls gets up and heads to the back door, pulling a pack of tobacco and papers from his pocket. It's Travis Wilson. Garcia and Zack watch him go. Once outside, he rolls a cigarette and lights up, taking a solid puff. Both the smoke and his breath are visible in the heavy, cold night air.

Not more than two minutes later, he hears a voice close by, old Doc Crawford calling him over. Doc has slipped out the door behind the young man. He stands near the corner of the building in the shadows.

Doc whispers, "Don't believe all that you hear in there, Travis, my friend. Those are strong words being uttered by a couple of strangers and they could have some consequences. You catch my drift, Travis?"

Doc throws an arm around the younger man's shoulders. "I think you remember our last conversation, right Travis? What we spoke about? It was over at my house at one of our neighborhood meetings. Remember, it was all about being a good citizen and reporting any and all unusual gossip, occurrences or meetings going on out here in this no man's land. Isn't that right? You know you have a duty to report such happenings and I'm sure you'll follow that advice. You know this is serious stuff. So do the right thing. Report this nonsense about a resistance movement idea. Keep things going along like they always have. It's better not to rock the boat. We all know this. We know the consequences of failing to preserve the status quo.

"Plus, there's always a reward for good information. And we don't want anything to happen to our loved ones, right Travis? Just heard of something the other day over at the Johnson's farmhouse. They experienced some unusual accident or something. Tragic. So keep an eye out for anything unusual around these parts."

Doc Crawford slips away as Travis has his last puff. The cigarette is losing its glow now. It's down to embers and he casts it aside and stamps it out. He goes back inside. Doc's words worm around in his mind.

Doc Crawford is no longer in the back of the room as Travis takes another seat. He listens to the group's discussion about the survival community, the walled cities, a resistance movement, and of all things, regaining our freedom.

He makes a decision. He will report these doings. These guys won't be around much longer. It'll be nice to get the WSO bonus for reporting. He grins.

Angelica is speaking again. "This will be the new role for the survival communities in North America. Survival camps can get their communities thriving in numbers and self-sufficiency. The new projects that are happening in key areas—like permaculture and crops, armaments, water systems, transportation, solar energy, and various others—can be exported to all the survival groups, all over the world.

She pauses again and captures the gaze of every person in the room. "There is something else that will require the vigilance of every member of the resistance. It is probable that the World State Organization has established sleeper cells in every large group of people living outside the walled fortress cities around the world. No doubt, the seeds of these cells were planted by WSO forces sometime after the mass suicides in 2060. They set the stage for a prolonged campaign to eradicate the values that the western world and the American way of life were built on. We see today how they succeeded.

"The major objective of the WSO has always been degradation of individual personal creativity and denial of belief in the spirit. The WSO and its STEN arm believe that man is soulless and nothing more than an animal. But the visionaries, artists, creators—Luminaries—are a major force who can prevent this degradation. They can raise up the spirit of man. WSO knew that Luminaries had to be found and neutralized. They've used STEN for this. The enemy's plan was to encourage the moral degradation of a population by removing the bright lights and enticing everyone else into drugged slavery."

Angelica stops talking and walks back and forth across the front of the room, head down.

She looks up and says, "Help in this fight may come from unexpected places. Conversely, harm may come from somewhere close. Vigilance must be maintained."

Angelica makes eye contact again with each person. Travis is trying not to squirm, looking at her from under his eyebrows. He lowers his eyes as hers reach him. Then he stands and slips back out the door.

Angelica steps back and Garcia steps forward.

"Okay folks, you get the gist of what this lady is saying. We're taking a break here then we'll have some more discussion amongst ourselves. I know Angelica and Stephen will answer any questions you have. Looks like Maggie brought some snacks. Let's tuck in."

As people move to the back of the room, Stephen, Garcia, and Zack huddle to talk about watching Travis. Angelica is with the group getting snacks but she's tuned in to their discussion. She agrees with the importance of keeping a further eye on him.

After the short break Angelica steps to the front of the room. Stephen hangs back by the door, watching the people file back to their previous seats. He sees that Travis and Doc Campbell are missing. He raises a finger to Angelica who gives an imperceptible nod. He exits the room on silent feet. He pulls his binovision from a pocket and switches it to night vision. Making a one-hundred-eighty-degree sweep of the darkened horizon, he spots two shadowy figures standing by a clump of trees at a range of seven hundred yards. He begins running in their direction, turning on the speed, his feet barely touch the ground.

The figures separate, one going back toward the survival camp and the other moving in the opposite direction before stopping to look around. This figure steps out of the shadows for a second and Stephen sees he is a tall, lanky figure—Travis. The man turns back into the darkness and continues to walk to a small cabin nestled under some pines. By Stephen's measure, it's about half a mile from the meeting hall. He sees the suggestion of smoke drifting from the chimney. The man in the cabin is Travis, the other man must be Doc Campbell.

Stephen makes his way back to the outbuilding and enters just as the meeting is finishing. Garcia sees him and comes over.

"I think you have a sleeper cell in your camp," says Stephen in a low voice.

"I think you're right," says Garcia. "Travis?"

"And maybe Doc Campbell," replies Stephen.

Garcia looks shocked. "Surely not!"

"Just keep an eye on them," replies Stephen. Garcia nods.

As they walk back to the house after the meeting, Angelica and Stephen brief Garcia and his family on their plans.

"Tomorrow morning we'll travel to Denver to see the survival community there. We'll share information with you as we get it," Angelica says.

"Okay." Garcia acknowledges. He has his arm around Margo and Zack has jogged ahead. When they reach the house, Angelica and Stephen say good night and go straight to bed. They are asleep in an instant. Margo shoos her husband to bed and after a few minutes in the kitchen, she follows him. She falls asleep to the eerie cry of a coyote.

MIDNIGHT

Doc Crawford and Travis meet in front of Travis's cabin. There's a definite chill in the air. Travis rolls a cigarette and offers it to Doc who waves it off. Travis lights up. "That woman tonight," he says. "The woman from nowhere trying to tell us who we are and what we should do."

Doc Crawford nods. "Yeah. Who is this person and where did she come from is the first question. And where did she come by that message and rhetoric? And that guy with her seemed like some sort of military special forces type."

"Yeah. I think he followed us after we left the meeting." Travis looks out into the night. "Surely this is conspiracy theory stuff and needs to be reported, right? What's your take on her and the guy, Doc?"

"I think they're both highly suspicious. They just came out of nowhere and started mouthing an insurgent message. They need to be reported to STEN right away. In fact, I've already sent a message to my contact. I'm waiting for an answer on how to proceed. Should be very soon." He sits down on the cabin steps. The wood is cold under his butt.

Travis sits next to him. "Beautiful night out here tonight," he says. "Cool crisp air. Almost a full moon."

Doc is quiet for a moment. "You know, they've upped the bonus on reports of any insurgent or resistance stuff—an extra hundred. You make the report, you get the whole thing."

Travis looks at Doc. "Wow, thanks man. I could use that kind of money." Doc nods.

Coyotes are hunting not far away. Their cries echo in the cold air. There must be a pack to the north, hunting feral cats and dogs.

"Doc, who's your contact we're waiting on?"

"It's a new guy, for us. I'm told he's been around a while, knows his stuff. He's started moving between LA, here and Denver. His name is Juan Carlos. I think he's some sort of hot shot in STEN and sleeper cell hierarchy, but there's no way to know for sure. The spy guys don't share much. I got the idea he was in our vicinity, maybe at the WSO headquarters here. He should be here soon."

The coyotes are sharing their kill, talking and yelping their win. Doc Crawford and Travis sit in silence as the night flows by them.

Finally, the sound of a truck engine can be heard in the distance, shifting through gears, coming their way.

Travis breaks the silence. "So, do you think there was anything they spoke about that turned a few heads tonight?"

"Hard to say. Most people don't like change. Especially after the twenty years we've been through."

"But you got to admit it was a gutsy talk about freedom and the time is now stuff. There hasn't been any excitement like this for a while in our community. I'm not sure just what to make of it all, but I agree the big boys should hear about it."

Doc grunts, looking up as an old Ford pickup rolls toward the cabin. "Okay, he's here. Got your pistol in your pocket?" Travis nods. "Good. I've never met this guy, only have a description of what he looks like. Let me do the talking at first. When I signal, you can give him the report."

"Wait. What's the signal?"

"I'll give you a nod."

"Okay."

The old Ford rumbles to a stop in front of the steps. A man who looks to be mid-thirty climbs out with his hands visible. "Doc Crawford?" he says taking a step toward them.

"That's me. You Juan Carlos?"

"That's me." He looks around. "Your call sign?"

"Coyote Bill. Yours?"

"Midnight Creeper." Juan Carlos looks at Travis. His demeanor is friendly but his eyes are sharp.

"This here is Travis," Doc says. "He's just joining. He has something to tell you."

"We'll have to get you a call sign for future use," says Juan Carlos.

"Yessir. Thank you." Travis is nervous.

Juan Carlos leans against the front bumper of his truck and folds his arms. "Tell me what you got."

Travis looks at Doc. Doc nods.

"Well sir, we got this couple who come to our camp, nice looking, youngish. They got real tight, real fast with Garcia and Margo. Well, Garcia called a meeting of the camp leaders. One of them—not Doc—brought me along.

"The woman got up and started talking about freedom and it's about time we did something about our rights and got rid of the WSO. You know, insurgency talk about freedom and resistance." Travis rubs his hands on his pants.

Doc says, "Like I reported, I was there too and heard it. It was a violation of STEN and WSO policy, I can tell you that. That's why we left in the middle of the meeting. I contacted STEN and put in a code three alert."

"And that's why I'm here." Juan Carlos smiles. Travis is pretty sure that smile would fit on a rattlesnake. "What else can you tell me about this man and woman? Ages? What they look like? Any scars or tattoos?"

Doc answers. "The woman seems to be the instigator. She's

76

around thirty-five, shoulder length yellow-blond hair, hazel eyes, about five-six, in good shape. The man is over six foot. He has dirty blond hair that's too long and light-blue eyes. He's about the same age as her, also in good shape. Neither one had any scars or tattoos I could see. The woman called herself Angelica." He looks at Travis. "Did you catch the man's name?"

"Oh, yeah. She said his name is Stephen."

"Doc, I'm going to need pictures of these two. Any way you can provide those?" says Juan Carlos.

"I'll see what I can do."

"The sooner the better." Juan Carlos pushes off his spot on the truck and steps toward Doc, holding his hand out. Doc shakes it. He shakes Travis's hand. "Thank you for this information, gentleman. You'll get payment for this report. And you'll get a bonus when you provide a picture of these troublemakers." He gets back in his truck and drives away.

DAY SIX

MORNING, UTAH SURVIVAL COMMUNITY

ANGELICA AND STEPHEN WAKE at the same time to the glow of the sun on the mountain tops behind the house. A new day is emerging.

They rise, dress and go to the kitchen. They find a sack with a note from Margo wishing them a safe journey. In the sack is a jar of cold coffee, bread, cheese, apples and homemade beef jerky. They look at each other with big smiles. They don't speak as Angelica grabs the bag and they head out the back door.

They move at a brisk pace as the morning air begins to warm and sunlight breaks further through the misty haze of early morning. They munch on apples as they walk. They reach the hovercraft's hiding place, uncover it and climb aboard. Stephen does his preflight check.

"Akido," he says. "Flying time to Denver at one-hundred-thirty miles per hour, please."

"Three hours and fifteen minutes," Akido replies. "As the crow flies."

"Right." Stephen's lips twitch, trying not to smile. "Connect with hovercraft computer and keep me on course. Scan for STEN patrols."

"Yes, Boss."

They fly over the Wasatch Mountains and the valleys and plains tucked between them and the higher Rockies west of Denver.

Angelica speaks softly to Akido as she takes in the beauty below.

"Akido, concurrent task. Run a recon analysis and updates on GPS locations of the STEN helicopters plus flight patterns for a forty-eight-hour period, combing a region of seven-hundred-fifty square miles starting now."

"Right away, Boss." There is a pause, then Akido says, "According to GA analysis, STEN has been flying the same helicopter patrol patterns for some years now, which are from west to east mornings and north to south evenings. The patrol flight patterns are automatic, locked in the system. Patrols don't deviate unless ordered to. I will continue to monitor for forty-eight hours to confirm."

"Good." To Stephen, Angelica comments, "This is good to know. We might need to maneuver around patrols."

"Flying under the radar, right?" quips Akido.

Angelica rolls her eyes. Stephen laughs at her. The hovercraft glides through the bright, crisp air. They fly over patches of snow glinting in the sun. Mt. Evans comes into view and Angelica points at it.

"Let's stop there for a minute," she says.

Stephen drifts the hovercraft to a spot on the mountain top and brings it to a quick stop. Maybe a bit too abrupt as Angelica pokes him in the ribs and shoots him a quick look of dissatisfaction. Stephen grins and shrugs his shoulders. She laughs. They climb out and look around. They're so high their bodies are breathing harder, but the view is stunning. It's a sight to behold—white-covered mountain tops and azure blue skies with pillowy clouds dotting the skyline. Stephen takes out his binovision and they take turns looking at Pikes Peak in the southeast and Denver shimmering in the distance, due east. The space around them is vast and imposing.

They turn to resume their journey then stop, looking deep into each other eyes. For a moment the two soldiers of light see a tense future.

They embrace. An inner light spreads outward and a feeling of warmth fills them. Their spirits rise. They have been partners in battle and in life. They have respect, loyalty and trust for one another as soul mates, and as soldiers of light, protectors of the extraordinary beings they serve.

Sitting in the hovercraft they have a meal of jerky, bread and cheese, washing it down with the cold coffee.

Stephen turns back to the controls. "All clear Akido?" he asks.

"All clear," confirms Akido.

Stephen lifts off and Angelica sits back as if in deep reverie. Stephen knows she's planning the next action steps, setting new strategic plans for approaching Denver's survival camp and walled fortress city.

"Akido," Angelica says, breaking her silence. "Background on the Denver walled fortress and the survival group, please."

Akido replies, "According to GA, the Denver fortress is centered around the Colorado Convention Center in the middle of Denver. Ninety-five percent probability the Luminaries will be kept in a lower-level location like in Los Angeles.

"The main survival group is in Boulder, thirty-seven miles north of the convention center. This community is smaller than the two you have already visited. Many survivors live in the mountains, either in small groups in mining towns or in the mines themselves."

"Thank you, Akido," says Angelica. "We're going to need a closer look at Denver's fortress city so we can plan a way to get in and out, with intel on where the infirmary is and how it's constructed and laid out. Does the Denver facility have the special experimental psychiatric area for Luminaries in the back of the medical ward? Can you get aerial photographs of the Denver walled fortress from GA?"

After a brief pause Akido replies, "Affirmative. Coming in now."

Angelica examines the three-D image projected from her wristband.

"The Convention Center is near a college. The buildings on the north and east, and the freeway to the south have been demolished to form a barrier around the area. It does look similar to the LA fortress. Is that movement from the northwest?"

"GA says it is a sort of gate allowing residents and visitors to come and go during daylight hours. Passage through the gate requires a special pass," replies Akido. "The Convention Center is also a detention center. Residents may not enter that building unless accompanied by a STEN soldier."

Stephen has been flying slowly, skimming along the mountains and dipping into valleys as often as possible.

"Angelica, we're coming up to the outskirts of Boulder," he says. "I'll find a spot to set down where we can hide the hovercraft and you can finish your surveillance."

Angelica nods her agreement.

"Boss, GA just intercepted a STEN dispatch to the Denver commander. Some WSO dignitaries will be visiting in the next two days to inspect the detention facilities, including the new medical/psychiatric ward and its upgraded equipment. They will be carrying blueprints for a next level electroshock Grade IV category machine that can deliver up to a whopping 500 volts of electricity to the skulls of mental health patients."

"Stop," orders Angelica. "Stephen, that amount of voltage can fry a person's brain. Used on an elderly patient, it can kill them instantly. And those that don't die will be human vegetables." She takes a deep breath. "Barbaric!"

"This is all part of the World State Organization's supposed mental health and behavioral modification program, not only for the Luminaries but for the remaining inhabitants of planet Earth," says Stephen. "We will do something about this."

"Akido, can GA get us plans for the new infirmary wards and schematics for the electroshock machine?" asks Angelica.

Akido takes a moment to answer. "No Boss. They exist in hard copy until after the big meeting. Once they've been seen by attendees, they will be copied and distributed in paper form only—nothing electronic."

"Then I'll have to get access to the hard copies."

Stephen looks at her, his face concerned, but he says nothing. He concentrates on locating a landing spot for the hovercraft. He finds one in the foothills just west of the city's Mapleton Hill area. He and Angelica disembark and gather Stephen's binovision and what's left of the food.

"More information," Akido says quietly. "There is a report that the Denver facility has created an additional program. They are forcing sterilization on a select group of women inhabitants. This is another reason the dignitaries are coming to inspect. They want to implement this program in all their cities."

Angelica reaches for Stephen's hand as they walk down the mountain. He can feel her body vibrating with anger.

"I'm sorry, Boss, there's more," says Akido.

"Proceed." Angelica speaks through clenched teeth.

"This sterilization program is linked with sex trafficking by WSO officials and STEN officers."

Angelica is unable to speak.

"Thank you, Akido," says Stephen.

They walk out of the trees into an open space and stop. Stephen steps next to Angelica, lifting his hand to rest on the back of her neck for a few seconds. He skims his hand down her back to her waist, drawing her close. She slips her arm around his waist and steps under his arm. They share their body warmth, standing as close together as they can.

Without uttering a word, the two soldiers of light gain a moment of reprieve from the horror they face, drawing strength from one another, preparing for more of their work.

The moment passes and they continue down into the town of Boulder. The first large building they come to is the Boulder County Justice Center. There are no people around but they feel eyes on them. They stand in the street, waiting. Finally, the building door opens and a man steps out. He's not tall, under six feet. His graying hair sticks out in clumps around his head. His face is tanned and lined so his age is hard to determine, but he has a gray, scraggly beard. He's dressed in a flannel shirt, jeans, and heavy boots. He looks at them, they look back.

"Jeremiah Smith?" Stephen asks, after the pause.

"Stephen?" replies the man.

"Yes, and Angelica."

"Better get inside." Jeremiah turns and goes back through the door. Angelica and Stephen follow him. He leads them to a space within the complex that was once a café. He gestures to a table in the corner. They sit down and an older woman brings them cups of coffee.

"Thanks, Susie," Jeremiah says. He wraps his hands around his cup and takes a sip. "Damn fine cup of coffee." He smiles.

"You heard from Garcia? Or Francisco?" asks Angelica.

"Yup." He takes two more sips of coffee, his light-brown eyes closed in enjoyment. He looks at them and starts talking.

"Our community isn't like the other two you've been to. The people left here in this area are true individualists. A lot were preppers—survivalists. They've always worked at setting up locations in the wilderness and stocking them with everything they'd need to live self-contained for five or more years. After the WSO took over 'officially' they just moved to the places they'd prepared. They don't like to share much."

"Do they ever come to town?" asks Angelica.

"Yeah, they come for supplies and to get any news. They've gotten a bit friendlier as the years go by. Some of the children are older now and not so fixed in their folks' lifestyle. They come around more often."

"What does the WSO and STEN do about them?" asks Angelica.

"They tried to police the area at first but it was like trying to catch a herd of cats. Catch one but fifty get away. Now we just get a few patrols. They've snatched all the best people and taken them to their fortress." Jeremiah looks down, passing his hand over his eyes.

"What happened?" whispers Angelica.

Jeremiah doesn't speak for a long moment. He stares at the table. "They came in the middle of the night. The one in charge was terribly polite with dead eyes. He said, 'she has to come with us.' My wife. He took her arm and led her out the door. I couldn't argue or fight. Ruth was just gone. The kids woke up after. They thought she'd be right back." Another long silence. "That was seven years ago. My daughter Christina was eleven, my son Sebastian was nine. Ten months ago, they decided they'd go find their mother. I couldn't talk them out of it." Pause. "I haven't seen them since."

Angelica exchanges a long look with Stephen. Jeremiah looks up; his eyes shine with tears. He swipes an angry hand across them.

"You two have some sort of grand plan, right?" he says.

"We plan to change things. We plan to rescue anyone who's still alive, incarcerated by WSO and STEN. We plan to help build a worldwide resistance that will overthrow the WSO and its evil and give Earth back to the good people." Angelica's eyes are fierce.

Jeremiah gazes at her, then takes a sip of coffee. "You can do all that?"

Angelica and Stephen speak as one. "Yes."

Jeremiah sighs, giving them a small smile. "Okay then. Specifics. We do have a STEN presence because of the fortress in Denver. But patrols are sporadic. We do have a sleeper cell here. We all know who's talking to the enemy so we're careful around them. And mess with them sometimes, of course. You know, they've been here for some time. Seems the sleeper cell network has always been a tool of the WSO. They must think we're stupid or something." Jeremiah shakes his head and takes another sip of coffee. "There's another community in the mountains, in Vail. It's almost impossible to get to in the winter. Most of the younger folk are up there. The older ones and small children live down here. I go back and forth between the two."

"Will you show us around here?" asks Angelica.

"Sure," says Jeremiah. "We'll head to the communal kitchen for some grub." He gets up and walks toward the door. He waves toward the café kitchen. "See you at dinner, Susie!" Her hand waves back through the kitchen door.

The Boulder survival community is a sprawl. As they walk through the neighborhoods, a few individuals step out of houses to wave at Jeremiah.

They see more elderly and children here than at the other

camps. This location seems to be more concentrated on single dwellings than in Utah and LA. There's more livestock and poultry sharing yard space. Garages have been turned into makeshift barns. Angelica shares these thoughts with Jeremiah as they walk.

"That's what you're supposed to think," he says, winking. "We make it look that way to confuse the enemy."

I like this man, thinks Angelica to Stephen. Stephen agrees. They smile at Jeremiah.

EARLY EVENING, DENVER SURVIVAL COMMUNITY

"Here's the communal kitchen." Jeremiah waves his arm in the direction of a picnic area in a park. Men and women are arriving carrying dishes and placing them on the tables.

"Every dinner is potluck," he explains. "People show up with food, others show up to eat. We bring our own utensils, plates and cups. Don't worry, there's always extras for guests." He smiles. "Dig in."

A little girl brings them each a plate, knife and fork. She takes Angelica's hand and leads her to a table. "I made this," she says, pointing.

Angelica scoops up something orange and wiggly with green bits in it. Stephen does the same. Angelica tastes a bite. "Good!" she says. The girl smiles.

They sample more dishes, eating with people from the community. They get many curious looks but no one questions them. After dinner everything and everyone disappears. Susie comes to sit with them. She's a pretty woman with dark hair pulled into a pony tail.

"Susie is Ruthie's sister and pretty much my right-hand man," Jeremiah says. "We're ready to hear what you have to say."

"The resistance is gaining traction and growing in North America, thanks to the push coming from the Aussies and Colin Hainsworth," Angelica begins.

"This is good news," says Jeremiah. "We've been chatting with Colin for some time. He likes some of our survivalists' preparations and he's shared some good training regimens. I'm thinking you two might be the catalyst needed to get the movement off the ground. Up to now there's just been a lot of talk, at least in our community."

"We have resources that will help the resistance fighters become a unit. We can make planning and execution of skirmishes and battles against the WSO more realistic and doable," says Stephen.

"I hear you have a way to listen in on the bad guys. That right?" says Susie.

"Yes," replies Angelica, "with a little help from our friends."

"Duunnn, ta dum ta dum," sings Akido in a whisper. Angelica taps her wristband to quiet him.

Jeremiah raises an eyebrow but makes no comment. He asks, "And what about rescuing our people in the detention center?"

"Rescuing them is a priority," says Angelica. "What's happening in the detention centers is an outright evil that's out of control. It's a real suppression of life. It is an evil that will not be allowed to continue."

"I forged a pass that I've used to get into the walled fortress many times, looking for my wife and children," Jeremiah says. "The detention section in the convention center is pretty closely guarded."

"Do they lock up the city at night?" Stephen asks.

"Yup," replies Jeremiah. "They have twenty-four-hour guards on the one opening in the wall. They may be lax in the wee hours of the morning. I've never tried to go through then."

"I have to get into the walled fortress to see the lay of the land," says Angelica. "I think going in first thing in the morning will be best."

"I agree," says Stephen. "We'll get started at first light."

"I can't get you a pass that quickly," says Jeremiah.

"Don't worry. I'll get myself in," says Angelica.

Jeremiah looks skeptical, shaking his head.

"Do not worry," says Stephen. "I'm backing her up."

"If you say so," says Jeremiah.

It's late fall in the Rockies. Sunsets happen earlier and there's a nip in the evening air. Night arrives quickly.

An owl hoots in the distance. Jeremiah looks up at the sound.

"We need to get inside," he says, rising.

Susie gets up too. "You two can bunk with us," she says. "We live in a big house not far from here."

"Thank you," says Angelica.

They reach the house in a few minutes. Susie opens the door and gestures them inside.

"Do you need anything?" she asks.

"No," says Angelica after a glance at Stephen. "Will you just show us where we'll sleep?" Jeremiah takes them upstairs and down a hall.

"Through here," he says, showing them a cozy room with two single beds.

"Thank you again," says Angelica. "Good night."

"Sleep tight." Jeremiah smiles as he closes the door.

Stephen sits on one bed and watches Angelica washing her face in the pottery bowl on the makeshift bathroom vanity. She hesitates a moment, studying the lines and contours of a tired Earth woman's face. She thinks about what it would be like to be back on her planet with Stephen, watching the large yellow-orange orb set in the mountains near their ranch. She wonders how her unicorn is and if the golden honey from her hives is being harvested for her friends in the nearby community.

Moving slowly and too worn out to fully undress, she slips off her flannel shirt and sits on the bed next to Stephen. She gives him a quick hug and climbs behind him to lay next to the wall. He crawls in beside her, pulling the blankets over them. She nestles next to her soul mate. They hold each other close and whisper, exchanging sweet affirmations and affection.

Heavy eyes close for sleep.

DAY SEVEN

MORNING

NIGHT SURRENDERS to the first ebb of morning light.

Angelica yawns and stretches. "I hope you slept well, Stephen. It felt good to be snuggled close to you. These Earth bodies are much warmer than I realized. I was toasty all night."

"I know what you mean," says Stephen. "Being next to you through the night gave me a comfortable and new feeling. I've noticed the sensation of feel is magnified in these carbon-oxygen bodies. Their endocrine and reproductive systems are tied to emotions and physical sensations. Interesting." He turns his head and smiles at Angelica.

She reaches up and touches his cheek. "It was comforting sleeping next to you. I liked the feeling. I noticed the sensation of touching skin to skin is greatly magnified in these Earth bodies. No wonder these Earthlings desire sexual sensation. And I can perceive your emotions relayed by these bodies. Also interesting."

Stephen touches her cheek. Their intense affinity flows between them.

They rise, dress and leave the room.

Coming into the kitchen, they see the back door is open.

Jeremiah is just coming across the backyard, dressed in army fatigues and carrying a rifle and bow. He waves good morning to them.

"Hi. I'm just back from some early morning hunting. No luck this time. I must have been thinking too many heavy thoughts or something and scared them off," he says.

"Have you always hunted?" asks Angelica.

"I started when I was a kid. My dad used to take me and my brother hunting. We shot rabbits, squirrels, and anything else we could find. When we were older, we hunted deer and elk. I'm a real believer, as they say, that the early bird gets the worm. Also want to keep a good eye on things." He comes up the back steps into the kitchen.

"Let's have some breakfast before you tackle the walled fortress in Denver. I'll cook. Susie left early to visit some sick folks." Jeremiah gets busy at the stove, making oatmeal and coffee. He is facing the stove when he asks, "Do you think you'd be able take a look for my kids, Christina and Sebastian, while you're looking around inside?"

Angelica and Stephen are seated at the kitchen table. They exchange a look. Angelica says, "Yes, I'll look for them." She takes the coffee Jeremiah hands to her. "I'll need to see pictures of them."

"Here, Stephen, stir this porridge while I get some," says Jeremiah, rushing from the kitchen. He returns clutching a photo and hands it to Angelica. She sees a pretty young woman with long, dark hair and a younger man, skinny and serious looking. She duplicates their features. She hands the photo back to Jeremiah.

"When you find them," he says, "you can let them know I sent you. Here's how. From the time they were very young, Ruthie and I set up a system for communicating in the family. They were taught a hand-signaling technique used by Native Americans. The system communicates basic key words in a finger picture. One or two fingers are combined quickly to form a shape. Here, I'll show you." He teaches them the signs for *father, friend, help,* and *squirrel.* "If you show these to either Christina or Sebastian, they'll know you came from me."

Angelica quickly copies the signals. When she's duplicated them, she asks, "Why *squirrel?*"

"It's a family joke. My wife and I always called them squirrels when we used sign speak," says Jeremiah.

"Okay," says Angelica with a grin. She turns her gaze to the stove. "Stephen, is that breakfast ready?"

Jeremiah takes over and serves them.

After a breakfast of oatmeal, honey and fresh milk, Angelica and Stephen head out toward the hovercraft. Jeremiah asks if they need anything and doesn't question them when they say no. He waves as they walk away.

When they reach the hovercraft, Stephen preps it for the short trip to Denver. He readies his binovision.

"We'll be flanking the Continental Divide most of the way south. It should be another picture-perfect day in the Rockies," says Stephen.

"Today will be sunny and clear with a light wind from the south and visibility of seventy-five miles in all directions," reports Akido.

He adds, "GA now knows this fortress has been a secret training ground for sleeper cell development in the United States going back many years. The training area is on the other side of the fortress from the detention center."

Angelica shoots a direct look and intention towards Stephen and says, "It looks like we have plenty of challenges ahead of us. It's going to be fast and furious. We need to be ready for the challenges, Stephen. They're coming."

Stephen looks resolute. He's flying low and slow. Hovercraft camouflage is engaged which protects them from ground-based detection, but he and Akido are scanning for STEN aerial patrols.

Akido begins speaking to Angelica in a low voice. "GA has history for you. It is a long report, okay to deliver it now?"

Angelica glances at Stephen who nods.

"Proceed," she says.

"You have the information about the electroshock machine to be used by WSO and STEN on the Luminaries and other detainees. This machine was part of mental health therapy for many years before the Soulests arrived on Earth. It was administered by medical professionals called psychiatrists. They believed human behavior was merely stimulus-response. Unhappy people were 'depressed.' Creative and exuberant people were 'manic.' These were terms describing mental illness, which they claimed was caused by a chemical imbalance in the brain. They used mind-altering drugs, electric shock to the brain and surgical techniques to 'heal' any mental illness.

"These psychiatrists were often in collusion with the pharmaceutical companies who manufactured the drugs, and with governments who protected their practices. An elaborate medical and political system was in place to perpetrate this practice. The system was seldom challenged.

"The Soulests slid into this system and took it over. Many psychiatrists and their groups had the same oppressive, cruel beliefs as the Soulests, so they were happy to have them as masters. The GA adds this: 'The Soulests are up to their old tricks, enslaving worlds. This time it is Earth.'"

Silence fills the hovercraft.

"Here's the plan." Angelica's voice is flat and cold. "I will infiltrate behind the scenes in the Denver fortress and see what's happening. I'll get hold of the machine renderings and the infirmary plans that the dignitaries bring. We'll have firsthand knowledge of their plans for the enhanced electroshock machines and for the planned psychiatric ward additions in all the walled fortress cities. It's vital we know what we're dealing with."

"The enemy has been moving fast to obliterate the Luminaries and enslave the rest of Earth's population," says Stephen. He has steel in his eyes. "This will not continue on our watch." He pauses. "It does sound almost impossible, but we've always believed anything is possible."

He's been watching the navigation display, and he spots a parking structure just as Akido alerts, "Patrol!" He dives the hovercraft into the entrance and parks on the other side of a stairwell entrance. They hear the patrol fly over.

Stephen gazes at the daylight framed by the entrance. "This

mission is unique, but it also reminds me of what we had to do in the battle to save the planet Astara in the Andromeda galaxy. You know the one I'm talking about. Remember, Astara was a beautiful place where we almost didn't pull it off. We were behind enemy lines and it wasn't looking good. We were surrounded but you found an ingenuous way to pull it off. It took all we had, but we did it." Stephen smiles at the memory.

"I do remember that." Angelica smiles too. "Here's what we're going to do this time. I'll sneak into the fortress. I'll find Christina and Sebastian and I'll infiltrate the dignitaries' visit and get a copy of the plans. I'll need you to be ready to extract all three of us. I may need a diversion at some point. We'll keep our telepathy open so you'll know what's happening."

"Sounds good," says Stephen.

Angelica climbs out of the hovercraft. She gets a shabby dress and jacket from the storage compartment and changes quickly, handing her Akido wristband to Stephen. She buckles a thin utility belt around her waist, under her dress, checking that the tools and medical items are in easy reach. She rubs dirt on her face and legs. She assumes a downcast, beaten demeanor and turns to leave the garage. At the entrance she looks back at Stephen and winks. He blows her a kiss.

Angelica joins a group moving toward the Denver walled fortress entrance gate. They all carry passes and she makes herself smaller and invisible to the guards. She slips past them while they're busy checking each of the group's passes. There are guards in towers on either side of the gate but they ignore the people coming in, leaving it to the guards on the ground to check everyone. She stays in the shadows as much as possible, walking around the edges of an open, grassy area not far from the detention center. She changes her demeanor, ambling around, copying the walking dead look of the people around her, but taking in every detail.

When she's almost completed a circle of the area, she sees a young woman sitting under a tree. It's Christina! She plops down near her, as if exhausted. Christina gives her a quick glance. Angelica ignores her, but begins signing the four words she knows. She makes it look like she's making nervous motions with her fingers. She sees Christina look over again. She signs *squirrel*. Christina's eyes widen. Angelica scoots over to sit closer to her. She leans in and speaks.

"I've come from your father to find you and your brother," she says.

"I knew you must have," says Christina. "Only he could have taught you the signs. There's a problem, though. My brother was taken into detention two weeks ago."

"That's not good," says Angelica. "What happened?"

"We were here in the yard, trying to figure out a way to get into the detention center to look for our mother again. Some guys near us got into a shoving match and the guards came rushing in. Sebastian realized this was his way in. He pushed into the group being rounded up. They took him into detention. I haven't heard a word from him since then. I'm so worried!" Christina has tears in her eyes.

"Well, this will work out just fine." Angelica leans forward. "I need to get into the detention center too. I'll do that, find Sebastian, and complete the rest of my mission. Then we'll leave and you can reunite with your dad and aunt."

"But what about my mom?"

"That rescue will have to be part of a bigger plan I'm working on. You have to be prepared though; it may not have a happy ending." Angelica's voice is grim.

"I know that," whispers Christina.

Angelica notices two STEN officers looking at them. She groans, grabs her stomach and starts retching. One man turns away in disgust. She feels Stephen's approval, but the other one is leering at Christina. Angelica pretends to faint and Christina leans over her crying, "Oh my poor friend. You must eat. Come on, let me help you. I'll help you find some food." She struggles to lift Angelica off the ground. She looks up at the officer approaching.

"Please sir, will you help me get my friend to the cafeteria? I have to get her to eat." She gives the officer big eyes. He looks her up and down, then at Angelica. He sneers and turns away, catching up with his companion officer.

Christina helps Angelica struggle to her feet, supporting her. They walk in the direction of the detention center. She says, "I was sitting there trying to get up the courage to volunteer for service duty for the big visit tomorrow."

"What are you talking about?" asks Angelica, still leaning heavily on her as they shuffle along.

"A group of officers came around the women's quarters yesterday asking for volunteers to help with tomorrow's visit. Anyone interested was supposed to report to the front of the detention center this afternoon." Christina is biting her thumbnail as she speaks.

"Perfect!" says Angelica. "Let's go!" She straightens, grabbing Christina's hand. They head for the meeting place. They come around the corner of the building and see about twenty women milling in front of the doors.

Signs are posted on the wall around the main detention area entrance, stating, "No Mingling," "No Admittance after 9 PM," "No Public Displays."

Angelica and Christina join the group. A female WSO official comes out and addresses them. "You are being given the great privilege of serving leaders of our World State Organization who will be visiting our city tomorrow. You will stay in special quarters in the Center the rest of today and tonight and will be taught your duties. Those of you who make it will be fitted with special uniforms and rewarded after the visit. Those of you who don't will be expelled from the Center and sent back to your regular place. Follow me." She leads the way into the building.

Once inside, the women are separated. The ones deemed pretty go with a steward to learn waitressing. Angelica and Christina are assigned to a cleaning crew. The crew supervisor directs them to a janitor closet and tells them to start cleaning the front entrance hall and the adjoining hallways. "Everything has to sparkle!" he barks and walks away.

"I guess that's all the training we're going to get," says Christina.

"So it would seem," says Angelica.

As they go into the closet, Angelica thinks to Stephen: *Akido needs to get a floor plan for this building. I need to know where to search for Sebastian and where the dignitaries will be.*

Stephen acknowledges. He relays the request to Akido, who responds, "On it, Boss."

Within minutes, Akido is showing Stephen a three-D image of Sebastian's possible location in the Center. Looking at the image, Stephen thinks to Angelica: *Here is where Sebastian should be.* Angelica acknowledges.

Stephen requests the next image from Akido. He complies and Stephen shows it to Angelica. She thinks: *Got it. Thank you, love!*

As she sweeps, Angelica whispers to Christina, who is dusting. "The plan is to find Sebastian by searching Population Center A, one floor down. I have something important I have to do after the dignitaries arrive tomorrow. When I've finished that, we'll find Sebastian and get out of here. You're with me, right Christina? You can do this."

Christina takes a deep breath. "Yes, I can."

"Good." Angelica grips her hand. "Now let's get to work."

Angelica and Christina work their way slowly around the main level, copying the lethargic pace of the other workers.

"Sebastian will be on the lower level in the larger ballroom area, Population A. That's the incarceration area for the less violent troublemakers. Before we get to him, I have to go to the theater. Let's make our way in that direction," says Angelica in a low voice.

The rest of the day, Angelica and Christina learn their way around the convention center. By late afternoon, preparations for the arrival of the dignitaries are complete. The women recruits are sent to a cafeteria on the street level for a meal, then to barracks on the upper level for the night.

DAY EIGHT

MORNING, DENVER DETENTION CENTER

THE NEXT MORNING they're given a shapeless uniform and sent to the theater. There are tables of food and drink set up in the lobby. Half the women are told to stand at these tables and serve. Angelica is sent downstairs to make sure the lower level is clean. She whispers to Christina as she leaves, "Meet me at the top of those stairs when it's over." Christina nods.

Walking in the lower level, Angelica sees a long corridor with several cameras on the ceiling and a guard at the end nearest her. At the other end is a large sign on a door: NO ADMITTANCE.

This is the infirmary and its psychiatric ward, she realizes, taking in everything in the area. She hears a commotion behind her. She's roughly pushed aside by a soldier leading a group of well-dressed people. She keeps her face averted, making herself smaller, and they ignore her. The guard by the door salutes them. She peers at them as they walk away.

The group is five World State Organization personnel, all talking loudly, being escorted to the theater stage. It's four men in suits and one female executive dressed in a tight-fitting skirt and long-sleeved blouse. She's young and nice looking, close to Angelica's height. Her hair is light brown with highlights and she struts in high heels with confidence and authority. Her body is poised like a tigress looking for her prey.

The men wear the same uniform-type suits with white shirts and ties showing STEN insignia. Each man leans on the woman's every word and movement, hoping to score the prize of some chill time to party with her after work.

She is the assistant of the chief architect who has come to show his new plans for infirmary additions in psychiatric wards. For this conference, she's also been assigned to assist the doctor presenting the Grade IV electroshock machine. She's discussing the live demonstration using one of the new electroshock units that will be set up in the infirmary by the doctor's team. A difficult patient, a dissident, has been chosen. This demo will show the VIPs how well the machine works.

Anger swells in Angelica when she hears this. Her fingers tighten into a fist. A calming wave from Stephen washes over her. *Remember the greater mission, love.* She calms herself, unclenches her fist and drifts after the group.

The men are all vying for the assistant's attention and conversation. Angelica overhears various comments. One of the WSO execs is admiring what the Organization is sending their way now—good-looking females with nice cleavage. The woman throws him a haughty look.

Angelica learns her name is Alliana.

She has an instant bright idea about this female assistant.

The group is coming into the stage area. They pass a dressing room door. Behind them a few paces, Angelica stumbles against the wall, pulling the fire alarm as she slips to the floor. The alarm screams out, throwing everyone into confusion. Angelica jumps up, grabbing Alliana. She pulls her back, shoving her into the dressing room. Alliana's absence is overlooked in the confusion of the moment and the mandatory evacuation that ensues. Angelica quickly applies a two-finger nerve stun to Alliana's neck (similar to the famous Vulcan nerve pinch) and she goes down in a heap.

Angelica drags Alliana's body behind a screen and strips off her clothes. She takes a small, silver syringe from her utility belt and injects Alliana with a sedative that will render her unconscious for up to an hour. She pulls thin zip ties from her belt and secures the assistant. She dresses in Alliana's clothes, making sure her utility belt is hidden at her waist but easily accessible, and exits the dressing room, locking the door behind her. She hangs up a "Closed for Cleaning" sign.

The fire alarm has been turned off and the dignitaries are back in the theater, moving toward the stage.

As she rejoins the group, she takes on Alliana's identity, walking and talking like her. By the time she catches up with the men, she *is* Alliana. She steps up as if nothing happened. Her clothes are a perfect fit except for the tightness of the push-up bra. It isn't exactly what she's used to wearing.

Stephen, I'm in the big meeting now. He acknowledges her with the equivalent of a thumbs up.

The key engineers, executives, and scientists are filing in and sitting in the pit area in front of the stage. A man steps to the edge of the stage and speaks.

"Welcome! I'm Gerald Grimes, the executive director of the Denver Detention facility. We are very happy to host this historic meeting. What we see here will revolutionize our work." He gestures to the two large, standing bulletin boards in the center of the stage with blueprints attached to them.

He continues, "Our main speaker is Dr. Dale Burns, head of the WSO Mental Health Division. He'll explain these renderings." He gestures to the standing boards. "We also have Mr. Steven Stein, WSO Senior Architect. First, Dr. Burns."

A short, dumpy man comes forward. He's wearing a crisp, white lab coat and thick glasses. "We have drawings here of the Grade IV electroshock machine and the proposed infirmary additions for Denver and all the walled fortress cities in North America." He goes back to stand between the bulletin boards and gestures proudly. "You are the first people to see these!" He bobs his head to acknowledge the brief applause. He raises his voice to continue.

"This first drawing shows the juiced-up Grade IV model electroshock machine, just approved by the big boys." He laughs nervously. "This second drawing shows the layout of the installation where the machines will be used. There will be five beds with straps to hold the patients in place while administering the shock treatment. We'll set up at least two installations in each infirmary."

Dr. Burns steps to the edge of the stage again. "We have perfected the use of a muscle relaxant drug that's given to the patient prior to treatment. With it, there's no need for an anesthetic to prevent convulsions when the shock wave hits the frontal lobe." He rubs his hands together with glee.

"A wooden or rubber bit is placed in the patient's mouth so they don't bite off their tongue. The electrical charge surges through their skull, triggering a rebound effect in the body like a tsunami tidal wave. This causes a series of grand mal seizures. This does kill some patients, but most will become quiet and malleable, a bit like wilted lettuce. This machine is truly amazing. Much more efficient than earlier models, it will turn the most difficult, disruptive, hard case individual into a completely tractable doll who won't speak much and will follow any order. And that occurs using lower-level settings. At the higher levels, the patient is placed in a permanent vegetative state. In many cases, death follows in short order. The miscreant is punished, and ceases to be a burden on the state.

"The installation can accommodate five patients every two hours. A fully staffed one could process sixty people a day. They do require some care the first few hours after processing, but after that they just need a chair to sit in." He chuckles. "It's an excellent device to use on enemies of the WSO."

Now the audience breaks into enthusiastic applause. Dr. Burns beams, nodding his thanks.

Gerald Grimes steps forward. "Thank you, Dr. Burns. An inspiring talk. Now we'll hear from Mr. Stein." He gestures toward the second bulletin board. A thin, pale man steps up. He adjusts his tie with nervous fingers. He speaks about changing space configurations and time needed to complete renovations. His talk is weak compared to Dr. Burns. He finishes quickly and receives desultory applause.

Grimes takes over. "Thank you, Mr. Stein. Now we invite you to come forward to look at the renderings more closely. In fifteen minutes, we'll go to the infirmary for a live demonstration of the electroshock machine. After that, there will be a dinner upstairs in the atrium."

The attending engineers, scientists and executives gather around the boards, chattering amongst themselves and clapping their approval like school boys.

A WSO executive, Helmut Laird, lauds the work that's been done. He says, "This is a moment to celebrate, as this project has been in the works for many months. It's great that the machines will soon be installed. They will be a major asset in handling dissent and insurrection—most especially the Luminaries. Those thorns in our side will go poof and be gone from us for good!"

Everyone on stage applauds. Angelica stands to one side, sick. Stephen holds her through their psychic connection. They steel their purpose and intention to end this barbarism.

There's a crash at the back of the theater and four STEN body-guards armed with assault rifles enter through the center doors. They are escorting two unanticipated guests.

There are murmurs on the stage as the people standing there peer into the gloom of the theater to see who's coming in. When the figures walk into the light there are gasps of surprise.

Holy crap. Angelica sees the tall, emaciated and sickly looking man in the middle. Her heart begins racing from a jolt of adrenalin. She can't believe her eyes. She knows Stephen is with her, also registering shock at seeing their enemy walking toward them—the one they thought they defeated long ago.

Holy crap. It is *him.* They share the same thought, along with a rush of emotion and images of the last time they saw this evil being. Angelica is reeling, even though she knew he was the Soulest in charge on Earth. Stephen is trying to anchor her.

The sudden recognition of an enemy makes an impulse to act in rage surge in Angelica. Her immediate urge to wrap her hands around his throat almost propels her forward. She feels out of control. Her mind is a jumble. Her hands and body are rigid and her teeth clenched. She has enough presence of mind to stay in the shadows at the back of the stage.

This new arrival is a Soulest supreme commander, now High Commander of the World State Organization, Rhotah Mhene. He's flanked by Earth human flunkies.

Gerald Grimes grabs a microphone and makes an excited announcement. "Our Fearless Leader! I've just been informed he flew in from his secret compound to our conference via private military jet to enjoy this day, a celebration and victory lap for our glorious WSO. Welcome High Commander!"

The applause is thunderous.

The High Commander stops at the bottom of the steps to the stage, looking up at the collection of people. His face is impassive, showing only his usual haughty composure. He's casting his attention outward, ready to bathe in the expected adulation when—wait.

Something is wrong. His mind starts screaming *Something is wrong!* But what is it? Then he feels it. *A whisper? A presence. No, it couldn't be! No, NO.* But his mind touches an essence, an identity and he knows. *She should be millions of miles away, but she isn't. Somehow she is here. The Soldiers of Light have found us and they have sent Angelica.* He touches her mind with a needle point of his and they both recoil, slapping up blocks. He begins shaking with aftershock, but quickly controls it.

Seconds after stopping at the bottom of the stairs, he's collected himself. He walks onto the stage and stands, looking at the collected World State Organization scientists, engineers and executives. Flutes of champagne are being handed out by waitresses. He appears to bask in their adoration. He begins speaking. "The day of reckoning for any and all despicable lowlifes is soon upon us. It also marks the beginning of the annihilation of the Luminaries. We should give thanks to the science that has brought us to this point. Let us raise a glass and toast the opposition's final days." All on the stage raise their glasses, shouting "Hip hooray!" and drinking deeply.

Angelica is struggling to control her deep rage. Stephen is beside her in thought but he is also struggling. *I cannot believe my eyes. I can take him out right now. I want to kill the evil bastard of all bastards, right now, and end the suffering for the Luminaries and all the others.*

His personal bodyguard and assistant standing close by his side, Rhotah Mhene continues speaking. "I have nothing but contempt for the Luminaries. They are close to their extinction. This gives me great satisfaction and relief. To be able to carry out our mission and not be threatened by their presence will be a new day of great celebration!"

At this point Angelica cannot restrain herself anymore.

Her left-hand fingers draw together to form a clenched fist and her body's adrenaline mobilizes and peaks as she readies for action.

She feels like a caged animal with the cage door sprung, presenting the opportunity to strike its captor.

In a flash, Angelica plans her attack: bodyguards first—one, two, three, four. Then Rhotah Mhene, his assistant, and escape out the back in the confusion. She shifts her weight back and forth, flooding her Earth body with endorphins. She is ready to rush across the stage in full action mode.

She's still connected with Stephen telepathically. He is fighting his own battle with his Earth body. It's ready to defend its mate in her time of need.

Akido recognizes the physical crisis and tries to get Stephen's attention. Stephen is not hearing him. GA transmits a suggestion which Akido instantly implements. Stephen feels a sharp stab in his wrist under Akido's wristband. At the same time, Angelica gets a sharp stab in her waist from the tiny digital camera hidden in her utility belt. The pain brings them to their senses.

Angelica slows her breathing as Stephen does the same.

I can kill him.

He answers. *But what about Christina and Sebastian? What about getting a copy of the plans we need? What about Project Blue Whale?*

I know. I know my duty.

Angelica finds her Earth body is shaking from the surge of adrenaline. She takes a deep breath and forces calm into her thoughts and body. She slips the camera out of her belt. *I'll get photos of the blueprints now.*

The stage is becoming crowded with people who've heard Rhotah Mhene is in the building. He's speaking to the fans milling around him. Angelica uses the confusion to get pictures of the two sets of plans.

As she walks off the stage to make her way back to the dressing room, she wonders. This is a rare appearance by her nemesis. He almost never leaves his hidden compound, wherever he establishes it. He must feel it's very important to travel across the world to expound on the virtues of the World State Organization's mental extermination plan.

Today, our paths have tangled again—he's come to this place at this moment where we both are. Interesting how fates intertwine.

Stephen echoes her thoughts.

Angelica hurries toward the dressing room. Her motion is stopped by one of the male engineers who steps in front of her. It's clear he has his attention on corporeal things. His hands fumble at her jacket. He motions with his head toward the dark area behind the curtains. Angelica tries to sidestep him but he stumbles back into her path. He's tipsy, on his way to drunk, and holding on to her.

"Come on Alliana, come over here. Quit playing hard to get. You know you want me. I want to show you something," he slurs.

He lunges toward her and to his surprise and dismay, he finds himself down on all fours in serious pain, holding a certain part of his anatomy. A swift knee jab communicated Angelica's answer to his suggestion. A couple of the other engineers laugh at his rejection. Angelica puts her nose in the air and stalks off.

She lets herself into the dressing room and sees that Alliana is still out cold, sprawled behind the screen where Angelica left her. She should be coming around soon.

Angelica strips off Alliana's clothes and puts them back on her. It's an awkward task that takes her some time. Once they're both dressed, she props Alliana against the wall and gives her a dose of adrenal stimulant.

Alliana starts awake, looking around in confusion. Angelica is dressed in her cleaner's dress. She leans over Alliana and says in a subservient voice, "Are you okay? You fainted or something. I brought you in this dressing room." She lowers her eyes.

"Get away from me," Alliana snaps. Angelica scurries out of the room. Alliana stands, using the wall for support. She doesn't move for a second. She shakes her head and straightens her jacket.

She goes to the mirror, combs her hair, applies some makeup and straightens the collar of her suit. Feeling better, she turns and walks out the dressing room door as if nothing happened. "Guess I should've eaten breakfast this morning," she mutters to herself.

MIDDAY, WSO, WESTERN HQ, LOS ANGELES

Damien stands at the window in his office, thinking about the report he received. A sleeper cell member in Utah reported disturbing news to Juan Carlos. Newcomers are stirring up unrest in the survival community there. They seem to be well organized and the leader is charismatic. And a woman.

He looks down at the dispatch in his hand. He needs more information. He needs raids in the Utah camp, the Denver camp, and the Los Angeles camp, since it's well known the three locations have close ties. His troops will look for any evidence of insurgency—any gossip about it, any evidence of individuals who may be spreading such ideas. They'll make the camp inhabitants tell them what they know, what they've heard. And they'll use any means to get this information, however unpleasant. This will augment whatever Juan Carlos comes up with using his methods.

His aide comes in and gives a sharp salute. Damien returns it.

"Your order is ready to go out on the STEN communication channel right away, sir," the aide says.

"Mark this order urgent. Inform me once it's sent," says Damien. His aide takes the dispatch, salutes, and leaves. The raids it orders will happen simultaneously tomorrow morning.

Damien turns back to the window, his hands clasped behind his back. He doesn't see the Los Angeles skyline in the window's frame. He's seeing the dirty warehouse he reported to as a boy, when he was a runner for the local drug dealer. That gang was his family. Now he has the WSO and STEN. He and his brother Juan Carlos worked hard, proved their value. They both made colonel. Now he runs the worldwide network of sleeper cells that keep tabs on the sheep. And Juan Carlos provides the kind of intel you can only get when your boots are on the ground. Together they make sure the sheep don't get any ideas about trying to overthrow the wolves.

But this latest report is unsettling. He has a bad feeling about what it means. Something is brewing.

MIDDAY, DENVER DETENTION CENTER

There are still many people trying to get close to the High Commander. Angelica slips through them to the staircase and runs up it. She spots Christina hovering at the top in the theater lobby. She goes to her and takes her elbow, moving her toward the Population Centers. Near the west entrance, she steers Christina into a corner.

"Christina, go out this entrance and make your way to the tree where we met yesterday. Don't let anyone stop you. I'll find Sebastian, get him out and meet you there at dusk. If you need to move around, do that, but don't get detained! Once I have Sebastian and we meet, we can all leave the walled fortress. What was he wearing last time you saw him? I've seen his picture but I'll have to ask people if they've seen him."

"Okay, I can do what you said." Christina thinks a minute. "Last time I saw him, he was wearing a light blue T-shirt and tan khaki pants with lots of pockets. He does have a dark birthmark the size of a quarter on the back of his left calf, shaped a little like a spider."

"Good. Thank you for that. I'll find him and I'll get you both back to your dad. Okay?"

Christina nods. She looks around, squares her shoulders and makes for the door. Angelica watches her for a moment, then heads for the stairs down to Population Center A. There's just one guard at the top of the stairs. He looks disgruntled. Right now, he needs to be someplace else so she can get down the stairs. She throws a strong intentional beam at him, commanding him to take a bathroom break.

The guard walks across the corridor to duck into the men's room. Angelica hustles down the stairs. The guard at the Population Center entrance has stepped away to talk to another guard. She can hear him complaining that they'll never get to see the High Commander. He's left his jacket hanging on a chair. She grabs it and slips through the unlocked doors.

She's in a large space, with many men wandering, sitting, playing cards or talking in low voices. She puts on the jacket and walks slowly into the room, looking around. She projects the idea she is some guard's playmate and she's on her way to meet him. No one looks at her directly.

There are no younger men in this area so she moves on. She holds the image of Sebastian in her mind and *knows* she will find him. This technique has worked for her many times in the past.

Stephen hovers with her in the back of her mind.

The room is half again as large as the size of a gymnasium, with rows of bunk beds placed about eight feet apart. Men sit on the bunks or stand in small groups talking quietly. There is no decoration, no pictures. Angelica can see some belongings stowed under bunks and there are a few paperbacks visible.

Making her way further into the room, she perceives that Sebastian was in a fight with not just one guy but two. He's banged up, and close by.

Angelica steps up to a man cleaning his fingernails with a toothpick. He looks at her with suspicion. She asks, "Have you seen a young man in a light blue shirt and khaki pants? He may have been in a fight recently."

He takes a long look at her, up and down. "No," he answers and starts to turn away. "But if I did know something, what's in it for me?"

"I don't tell my STEN boyfriend how you were ogling me when I was coming to him." The man makes a scoffing sound. Angelica puts her hands on her hips and says, "Or how you tried to grab me in an inappropriate fashion."

Fear crosses the man's face and he leans back, hands raised shoulder height. "Wait, I just remembered. There was a fist fight here about five days ago. The guards broke it up. They took one of the guys away. Another one fighting was smaller and dressed like you said. He got hurt pretty bad. Should've gone to the infirmary but he didn't. I think one of the older guys is taking care of him."

"Where they are now?"

"Most likely in the far-left corner. The guy that's taking care of him hangs out there. He used to be a boxer. Now he's sort of the resident medic."

"Fine," says Angelica, turning away.

"Wait," calls the man. "We good?"

Angelica looks back over her shoulder and gives a brief nod.

Angelica walks fast toward the far corner. *I knew I would find him. I could just see him. Sebastian is right there. Amazing how things work out when you trust what you know.*

Stephen's agreement brushes her mind.

She sees Sebastian in the row of beds closest to the wall. The man near him looks spry—he must be the boxer. He looks forty but Angelica senses he's approaching seventy. His dark skin is wrinkled, his short black curly hair is heavily sprinkled with gray. He's sitting next to Sebastian reading a book. Sebastian is asleep.

Angelica walks up to the boxer and greets him softly. "Hello." The boxer looks up with narrowed eyes. "I'm Angelica. I've come from Sebastian's father Jeremiah, and Christina, his sister."

"So you say." The boxer's face is expressionless.

"I have a message for Sebastian from his father."

"Uh huh."

Sebastian opens his eyes and sits up. The boxer looks at Sebastian. "Here he is." Sebastian sees Angelica's jacket and frowns.

"Sebastian," she says. "I've met your father and your sister." As she speaks, she's making the words with her fingers. Sebastian is looking at her face. Then he notices her hands as she makes the figure for *squirrel*. His eyes get big. He leans forward.

"Ben, she's okay. She has met my dad."

"You're sure?"

"Yeah, I am." He smiles at Angelica.

"Have a seat, Angelica." The boxer gestures to the opposite bunk. She sits, leaning forward.

"How are you, Sebastian?" she asks.

"I'm good, almost completely healed."

"You can travel?"

"Travel?" says the boxer. He looks at Angelica. "And how did you get in here? This section is reserved for males. You're definitely not a male." He looks Angelica up and down. "That's for sure."

Angelica smiles. "I have a few skills," she says.

"Yeah, I bet you do." He looks her over again, and sticks out his hand. "I'm Ben Norton. Sebastian here got beat up pretty bad by a couple of lowlifes. I fixed him up and he's been on the mend. He's coming along now." Angelica shakes his hand.

Ben continues. "The creeps that jumped him were just being bullies, blowing off steam. See, you either blow off some steam in here or you go into big time apathy and take the drugs they pass out daily. The folks who take that route are walking zombies. Some of the aggressive types fake taking the blue pill then flush them down the toilet. It was a couple of those guys Sebastian tangled with. I stepped in and gave those boys a pretty good ass kicking. Even got some applause." He grins. "They'll be thinking twice about fighting where I can see."

Angelica smiles at him. "I want to take Sebastian out of here, back to his people."

"Yeah, he talks about his sister a lot." Ben looks at her closely. "What's your involvement in all this?"

Angelica regards him. She leans toward him, speaking in a quiet voice. "My partner and I are here to help jump start the resistance. We met with Sebastian's father Jeremiah. He was worried about his children. We were coming to the Denver fortress for another reason and he asked us to help his children. So I am."

Sebastian speaks. "You've seen Christina? She's okay?"

"She is." Angelica looks around to confirm they are unobserved. "She's meeting us at dusk and we're leaving the fortress."

"Did I hear you correctly?" Ben asks. "You're from the outside? Holy sh—, crap. Sorry.

I didn't know you could get in here and out. Why do I have the feeling there's way more to this than you're saying?" Ben rubs his chin and stares at Angelica.

"You get that feeling because it's true," says Angelica. "Want to come along with us?"

"Are you serious?"

"Completely. The resistance movement is beefing up. It could use a man like you. You could help train freedom fighters." Angelica gets a twinkle in her eyes. "I hope you say yes because I really don't want to have to fight you. I'm not a boxer, but I am a bad ass in martial arts and it would be a brawl." She winks at Ben.

"I'd rather join forces and be on the same team. Smarter move I think," says Ben. "I'm with you."

"Great," says Sebastian. "Can we get going? I want to find my mother and get out of here."

Angelica takes his hand. "I know that was always your plan. I've talked to Christina about it, and your dad. The fact is, finding and rescuing her is not simple. What happened to her has happened to a lot of people. My partner and I are working on a way to rescue everyone being detained, but it's going to take a little more time."

Sebastian is shaking his head.

"Look at me Sebastian." He raises his eyes to hers. "Your mother would not want you to risk yourself. She wants you alive and whole. She would want you to find people who could help you help her. That's me and my partner Stephen. We need you. Will you join us and help us rescue all the stolen people?"

Sebastian looks at her for a long moment. She holds his gaze. She can see when he makes his decision.

"Okay," he says.

"Good. Let's get out of here." She stands. "Do either of you need to bring anything with you?"

Ben and Sebastian shake their heads no. Ben stuffs his book in his back pocket.

"If anyone stops us, this is our story. I'm taking you to the big meeting in the theater. The guards told me to bring a young man and an old man. You've been taking your pills so you don't care about anything. You'll need to be zombies, okay? I'll get us out of the building. You got it? You can do it?"

They nod.

"Good. Here we go."

CHRISTINA MAKES it out of the building without being stopped. Something is happening in the theater and many people are rushing in that direction. She is ignored. She walks to the tree and sits down. She tries to think positive thoughts but she's worried about her brother. She's gazing at nothing and wringing her hands. The same STEN officer who approached her and Angelica before appears above her.

"Hey beautiful. You look like you could use a little diversion. I'm your man. I'll take your mind off your troubles." He leers at her and grabs his crotch.

"Oh," says Christina. "Oh, oh. My master said I couldn't leave this spot till he came back. He'll beat me if I move. Please." She looks up at the officer, big eyes filled with tears. She lowers her head and looks at him from under her long eyelashes. "Maybe I could sneak out later and meet you. By the gate? After dark?"

"You little hussy. Want a real man, huh? My name is Miguel. Women call me Mig because it rhymes with big." He leers at her. "Okay, at the gate just at dark. Don't be late." Miguel strides off without a backward glance.

Christina sighs in relief. *I'll either be long gone or Angelica will help me deal with that creep.*

IN CHARACTER, Angelica pushes Sebastian and Ben toward the door and they walk through Population Center A. When they meet a guard at the entrance, Angelica puts on a show that gets them past him. They make it out of the Population Center and up the stairs to street level. There are many people milling around, trying to get a glimpse of the High Commander. Angelica knows that by now he'll be at the banquet in the atrium on the other side of the convention center.

She guides Ben and Sebastian through the crowd to the west door. They stop in the shadows nearby.

Angelica whispers to them, "We'll go out one at a time. There are enough people trying to come in, the guards will be busy checking IDs. When they are occupied, slip out. You first, Sebastian."

He nods. They watch the doors. A moment comes and Sebastian slides along the wall to the far-right door then out, unseen. Now it's Ben's turn. He gets out the same way.

Angelica is watching for her chance when there is noise from the area behind her. The two door guards come to attention. She glances back and sees the enemy's entourage coming. The High Commander, his bodyguards, assistant and a crowd of followers is flowing from the atrium toward the door near her. She ducks down an adjacent hallway, out of sight.

She watches from the end of the hall as the group walks past.

Rhotah Mhene is looking around. His gaze sweeps past her hiding place and she feels his mind. He misses a step, stops, and stares down the hall toward her. She feels his mind searching. It's like crackling lightning stabs through the hall toward her. She fortifies her block. He turns away and continues walking. He's out of sight now but she's trembling in the aftermath of the brush with him. Stephen's mind reaches toward her as she fights for control. At last, she's able to move again. She knows Stephen is worried but she doesn't answer his unspoken concern. She concentrates on getting out of the center.

She comes back down the hall toward the doors. Now the space in front of them is almost empty and the guards are alert. Angelica pauses, considering the situation.

In the next moment, the guards perk up, looking at something outside. The guard nearest her closes his door and goes over to join the other guard. They're talking to someone outside. Now they're flirting! They're trying to step out the door at the same time and catch each other in the doorway. Angelica uses this brief confusion to slip through the far-right door. She sees Christina talking to the guards, swaying her hips back and forth. She's still dressed as an event worker.

Angelica takes off the guard's jacket, stuffing it behind a bush. It's late afternoon and the light is soft. She takes a deep breath of clear air. She moves around the side of the building and steps away, circling back around to where Christina is trying to flirt but also stay away from the guard's groping hands.

Angelica walks up, hands on her hips. "What are you doing?! Where have you been?! You are in so much trouble. Come with me right now!" She grabs Christina's arm and tugs her away. Christina cringes and looks subservient.

Angelica looks at the guards. "I'm sorry men, you'll have to catch up with this one later." She doesn't give them time to question her. She jerks Christina's arm. "Come on," she says, marching her off across the street into the trees. When the guards are out of sight, Angelica releases her arm and gives her a hug.

"Thank you!" she says. "That was a perfect diversion!"

"I was waiting where I could see the doors. I saw Sebastian come out and I grabbed him. He told me about Ben, we grabbed him. Then we saw all those people leave. We thought you might need a diversion, so I made one." Christina smiles shyly.

"It was brilliant." Angelica gives her another hug as Ben and Sebastian come up. "Now, let's get out of this fortress."

The sun is disappearing behind the buildings as they make their way across the open space to the walled fortress gate.

"The gate is open for thirty minutes after sundown," says Christina.

"We'll need to get out of these outfits," says Angelica. "Do you know where we can get a change of clothes, Christina?"

"I do," Ben says. "If it's still there—behind that building over there. We had a sort of dump. Mainly trash, but we'd hide usable things too. Let's see if it's there."

He leads the way and finds the dump. He goes to a section near the corner of the building and digs around. He comes up with a couple of ragged pairs of pants and two holey T-shirts. He and Sebastian turn around while Christina and Angelica change.

Angelica has Christina and Sebastian lead the way. She and Norton bring up the rear, checking for any unhealthy interest in their group.

Stephen, on our way to the gate.

Ready.

The guards are alert in their posts. None of the group have a pass that will let them through the gate to the outside. The traffic is sparse. They move to one side and sit down pretending to talk among themselves. One guard glares at them but doesn't leave his post.

The sun is setting.

Christina is biting her thumbnail again and looking around with a worried expression.

"What is it?" asks Angelica.

"While I was waiting under the tree, that officer from before, Miguel, came back and tried to proposition me. I got rid of him but I had to promise to meet him by the gate at dark." She looks at Angelica. "If he shows, I was hoping you could help me with him."

Angelica looks up in the waning light. "I can take him, of course, but it would be better if we're gone before he comes."

Ben takes off his shoe and pulls a paper out from under the insole. "I only have this one forged pass. It's not very good but maybe we can use it?"

Christina sees the soldier Miguel in the distance, coming toward the gate. She gets Angelica's attention and points to him.

Angelica talks fast. "Sebastian, you're trying to get out to take care of your sick mother and you've lost your pass. Argue with the guard. Ben, you are a good neighbor wanting to help—you try to talk them into letting him leave with your pass. Christina, you're really drunk and I'm helping you out. Make lots of noise. Everyone keep moving toward the other side of the gate. When we get close,

I'll take out the guards and we RUN toward the tall, good-looking man with blonde hair. He'll be waiting for us. GO!"

It's almost full dark but the gate is well lit. Sebastian goes first, engaging the guard on the right. Christina is falling down. Angelica is trying to pick her up while keeping an eye on the approaching soldier and the action at the gate.

Ben goes forward, showing the guard on the left his pass, but veers over to where Sebastian is and joins the discussion. They swing around and take steps toward the exit as they wave their hands, petitioning the guards.

Angelica comes up, trying to hold up an agitated Christina who is waving her hands and shouting slurred, unintelligible things.

All four of them push toward the far side of the gate with the guards moving beside them, arguing with them. Miguel has almost reached the inside part of the gate and he's opening his mouth and raising his arm.

Stephen has been keeping pace with Angelica and is in the shadows outside the gate.

Angelica whispers in Christina's ear, "Now." She lets go of Christina who sprints out the gate.

Angelica pivots toward the guards who are facing Ben and Sebastian. They're pulling out their radios to call for backup. Her first kick knocks the radio out of the hand of the closest guard. Ben grabs Sebastian and they take off after Christina. Angelica's second kick snaps the guard's head around and he goes down.

The other guard takes a step toward her as she steps up to him, putting all her weight behind a sharp jab to his throat. He goes down and Angelica races for the shadows beyond the gate.

Miguel runs after them. He's outside the gate now. Angelica puts on a burst of speed and catches up to Stephen. He's pointing Christina, Ben and Sebastian toward the parking garage. Miguel doesn't see Stephen as he reaches for Angelica. She turns, thrusting both hands hard into his chest as Stephen steps behind him, sweeping his legs. Miguel flips onto his back, knocking out all his air. He's down.

Angelica and Stephen catch up with the other three at the

entrance to the parking garage. They duck inside and Stephen points to the hovercraft peeking out behind the stairwell.

He turns to Angelica and pulls her into his arms, holding her for a moment. She holds him back.

They release each other and walk to the others.

"Christiana," he says, touching her shoulder. "And Sebastian." He shakes the young man's hand.

He turns to Ben. "And who is this?"

Ben steps forward, hand extended. "I'm Ben Norton." He and Stephen shake hands.

Angelica says, "He's one of us now, escapee from the Denver detention center and new recruit for the resistance. He's a freedom fighter."

"That's great," Stephen says, looking at Norton.

As he's greeting Ben, Stephen sends a thought to Angelica. *Everyone into the hovercraft to get back to Boulder?*

Why not?

"This way to the taxi home," says Angelica.

"You have wheels?" says Sebastian.

"After a fashion," replies Angelica as they walk up to the hovercraft. "We'll be snug, but the trip isn't long."

"What kind of car is this?" demands Sebastian, walking around it.

"There will be time for inspection when we get back to Boulder," says Stephen. "Everyone in. Akido, all clear?"

"All clear right now, Boss, but patrols are due in five point four minutes," reports Akido. The disembodied voice draws a sharp glance from Sebastian, but he stays silent.

"Thank you."

Christina and Angelica share a seat, Ben and Sebastian wedge into the space behind the seats. Stephen sets the camouflage and takes off. He flies out of the garage, rapidly climbing to cruising altitude in the darkness of night with a full moon rising.

NIGHT, DENVER SURVIVAL COMMUNITY

Stephen points at the firelight coming up below them. "Your dad's signal," he says. He lands the hovercraft in the darkness beyond the fire. Jeremiah and Susie rush forward. Christina is out and hugging Jeremiah in seconds. Sebastian is not far behind. The night is quiet, except for the lonely sound of coyotes calling in the distance. Angelica and Stephen are witnessing a very happy family reunion.

Ben climbs out of the hovercraft, standing to one side with Angelica. Jeremiah sees him over Sebastian's shoulder.

"Who's this?" he asks.

"Oh," says Sebastian. "This is my friend Ben Norton. He basically saved my life."

Jeremiah comes forward to shake Ben's hand. "Thank you. Thank you for taking care of my son."

"No problem. Happy to help."

"Wait," says Jeremiah. "Ben Norton. The boxer. You were a big deal."

Ben shakes his head.

"He's joined the resistance," says Angelica.

"That's right," says Ben. "I had a gym before all the madness. I was training people back then. I can still train people."

"Maybe you can use him here," says Stephen.

"Boy, can we use him! Welcome aboard, Champ!" Jeremiah pumps Ben's hand again. Sebastian is beaming.

Susie moves in to shake Ben's hand too. "I'm Susie. Come on, I'll get you something to eat and show you where you can bunk."

Ben looks around at everyone in the yard. "Thank you." He rubs his hand over his face. "It's really good to be needed again."

AUSTRALIA

Colin Hainsworth is sitting on his veranda, enjoying the beautiful spring afternoon and drinking a Fosters with his lunch. He's not a big man, compact and well-muscled like an MMA fighter. His mouse brown hair is cropped close to his head. His most striking feature is his green eyes. People he's not pleased with have called them piercing.

His house is in Nightcliff, not far from the ocean. It was built in the tropical style, on stilts with louvered windows and ceiling fans. The breeze carries ocean and jungle scents across the veranda and through its rooms.

Life is good right now. He's happy with the survival community in Darwin. They're far from the major population areas in southeast Australia. It takes some dedication to get to this location. The people who've come have been receptive to the idea of having a job that contributes to the welfare of the community—something they can do that helps them and others. He grins, thinking about the fierce bunch of grannies who cook, sew, knit, quilt, teach. Even kids have essential jobs. He is glad he's been able to tell the other camps about some of his community's successful actions.

This leads to thoughts about Backdoor Charlie. That has been the salvation of humanity. If Dobbs hadn't come forward when he did, well, we'd still be trying to coordinate a revolution with ham radios. We could've done it, but having a dedicated, hack-free communication system sure makes things easier. We can plot the overthrow of WSO and its STEN flunkies right under their noses. Colin grins again at the thought.

He picks up the report he brought with him to the veranda. Soon three-hundred-seventy-five elite commandos will finish their training at the secret East Point Military Complex. He liked the poetry of using a location from World War II to train the fighters for the next great war. *If I can swing it, some of these men and women will become trainers in other survival communities. Dreams.*

He sits back, sipping his beer. He hears footsteps on his stairs and a knock at his door.

"Come through," he calls. "I'm on the veranda."

He watches as Kenny, his main communicator, comes onto the porch. Kenny has an odd look on his face.

"What's up, mate?" asks Colin.

"I just got the strangest message." Kenny plunks down on a

chair by the cooler and grabs a Fosters. He takes a long swallow. "You know Frisco from California. He just sent an email saying they've had visitors who are doing and saying some unbelievable things. Supposedly, these blokes have tapped into the WSO/STEN communication network somehow. He says they can give us any information found in any WSO computer system. He says they've been to the Utah camp and they're at the Denver camp right now." He wipes a hand across his face.

Colin looks at him a moment, taking a swig of beer. "Have you heard from Garcia and Jeremiah?"

Kenny nods. "I knew you'd ask about that, so I sent off emails to them."

"And they said…?"

"Yeah, they both got visits. It's a man and a woman, Angelica and Stephen. Garcia says she's a fair dinkum speaker. She talks about the resistance and about saving the stolen people. She calls them Luminaries. Jeremiah said she and her man rescued his young uns from the Denver detention center and walled fortress. He was pretty impressed."

"Where are they from?"

"There's quite a bit of speculation about that. The consensus is 'don't look a gift horse in the mouth.'" Kenny takes another swig.

"They sound like people we want to know, don't they?" says Colin.

"Ya think?" Kenny smirks.

Colin flips him the bird. "So. How do we reach out?"

"Evidently they seem to have some sort of assistant with a funny name: Akido. You just address an email to him, no dot com or anything, and they'll get it."

"Curiouser and curiouser."

"Yeah. Want me to send an email right away?"

"Ya think?"

Kenny flips him off. "Cheers. I'll let you know what happens."

Colin leans back with his beer. *Things may be improving. And if they are, there's a lot of work ahead.*

DAY NINE

MORNING, LOS ANGELES SURVIVAL COMMUNITY

ANGELICA AND STEPHEN. I have to see them again. This is Bridgetta's first thought upon waking. She dreamed about them, Angelica in particular. *I have to connect with her, to join her. She has something. I need it. I want the kind of power I know she has so I can do good things like I know she does.*

She gets up and dresses. She has a full morning of training but after lunch she'll figure out how to connect with Angelica.

She grabs a hasty breakfast, eating an egg sandwich on her way to the training area. She'll be working in the outdoor space doing hand-to-hand training with the teenagers. She's happy with this group. They do the work and they're getting good. She doesn't stop to think that she's just past being a teenager herself.

I hope John Boy is there today. I need a proper workout. Her wish is granted. She spends the morning honing the skills of the young men and women in her class. Today she can give them reasons why they have to train—there's focus to the activity now. She gives them the resistance message again and again as they train.

At the end of the session, she taps John Boy.

"Ready for some sparring?" she asks.

John Boy makes his pecs dance and flexes his biceps. "You bet!"

Bridgetta bats her eyelashes and sweeps his legs, tumbling him to the ground. He growls and leaps up.

They're on. Kicks and parries, jabs and blocks fly.

The class surrounds the pair at a safe distance, cheering. John Boy is starting to breathe harder as Bridgetta dances around him. She's not winded at all.

Then she lands a kick to his chest and he goes down again. He sits on the ground, raising a hand in defeat.

"Thank you, John Boy. That was a good workout." Bridgetta offers him a hand which he clasps, pulling himself upright.

She looks at the class. "Often a larger opponent will tire more quickly. Because they have more mass, they have to use more energy to move it around. Stay beyond their reach as much as possible. Make them work for everything they get and poke them when you can. I heard an old saying when I was young: Float like a butterfly, sting like a bee. It works. You bigger guys, don't let a smaller opponent work you til you're tired. Hang back and wait for your openings—then make them count. You can always reach in, wrap them up and squeeze til they go limp." She laughs and the class joins her.

"Oh, and keep those hips loose and flexible. Keep doing your flexor drills. That's it for today," she says, waving as she walks away.

OVER UTAH

Angelica and Stephen are in the hovercraft on their way from Denver to Los Angeles to brief Francisco and Diego in person. They spent a peaceful night with Jeremiah's family and got a predawn start.

"Navigation shows two and a half hours flying time," says Stephen. He glances at Angelica. "You look a little drained from the events of the last couple days. Things are more serious than we thought, aren't they?"

Angelica looks away, then at the ground. After a moment she looks back at Stephen. "Yes, love, it's far worse than I could have imagined." She sighs, now looking at the land shining in the morning sun. "But, I'm fine, Stephen. I really am." She leans into him. "Let me rest my head on your shoulder for a second. You know you're my most favorite being. You take such good care of me. I'm lucky to have you."

Stephen gives her a kiss. He points the hovercraft southwest and opens the throttle. It leaps forward, quiet as a whisper and quick as a thief in the night.

"Boss. GA intercepted a STEN dispatch from a Colonel Damien Johnson ordering a morning raid on the survival camps in Denver, Utah and Los Angeles. GA alerted Francisco, Garcia and Jeremiah. They had just an hour's notice," says Akido.

"It must have happened right after we left," says Angelica. "Any reports on what happened?"

"Not yet," says Akido.

"Alright," says Stephen. "Ask the GA for information on Colonel Johnson. I'd like to know more about this man."

"On it."

They ride in silence, each taking in the land they're flying over. After a moment, Angelica begins speaking in a quiet voice.

"I keep picking up my mother's presence in my space. That's why I believe she's still alive. It's like she hovers at the edge of my awareness. If I could focus her in, sharpen her signal, I'd know where she is." More silence.

"There wasn't enough time to check when we were at the walled fortress in LA or when I was in the Denver Detention Center. I saw the door to the infirmary and I felt the despair flowing out of it. I couldn't do anything." Angelica leans closer to Stephen. He holds her tight, knowing she's thinking of what she experienced in the detention center. It saddens her heart. The thought of her dear mother possibly being close to death, or having already succumbed, is hard to take.

"The idea that my mother and your father could be in such a place disturbs me. That if they were taken to a place like that, they were, or are, in harm's way." She clings to Stephen, then straightens. He lets her go.

"Coming here has made me begin using one of the skills we

learned as soldier-of-light cadets. It's the ability to use heightened perception to see and understand—*looking* rather than only *thinking* in a logical, purely analytical way. It's liberating."

Stephen nods his understanding.

Angelica gazes into the future and sees the storm clouds massing and the fight that looms to save planet Earth. It's coming.

DENVER, OUTSIDE THE FORTRESS CITY

Rhotah Mhene sits in his private jet on the runway in Denver. The meeting went well yesterday, but he can't get her presence out of his mind. He shakes his head to rearrange his thoughts. *I have come a long way with the WSO and the plan to overtake this sector of the galaxy, starting with planet Earth. The plans are good plans and I'm on schedule...So why am I feeling unfulfilled and restless?* He knows the answer. It's because he was reminded of *her* yesterday. *Not just reminded—she's here. She is on Earth. She and that* man *whose name I won't mention are working to thwart my plans, just like they always have. That must not happen this time! Will not happen!*

He sinks into a deeper reverie, returning to a scene he's tried to forget. *I told her how I felt and she rejected me! For him! I was the rising star but she chose someone else.* The ache is still there, always, after all this time. *I loved her from the very beginning. Ever since I saw her dancing at the Intergalactic Federation contest. She made me feel alive. There was a special excitement and joy in her.* Now the ache of rejection has been poked at, no, electrocuted. *I want to hurt her like she hurt me. I will not be the only one to bleed.*

His flight crew is waiting for orders. They know not to interrupt him when he's sitting, looking into space. They exchange worried glances. This pause is longer than usual.

He looks up and they snap to attention.

"We go to Los Angeles," he says.

The pilot and copilot stride to the cockpit and the stewardess places the Commander's hookah on the table in front of him, a bowl of his personal marijuana/opium blend beside it. Rhotah

Mhene sits back in his chair and smokes, a plan forming in his mind.

He gestures to his aide. "Get me the name of the sleeper cell commander in Los Angeles." The aide salutes smartly.

It's time for the sleeper agents to get to work. This is the exact thing the cells were set up for—to provide information about threats to his plans and to act as saboteurs for him.

With a wicked smile, he nods his head in satisfaction.

MIDMORNING, NEAR LOS ANGELES SURVIVAL COMMUNITY

Angelica and Stephen approach the northern edge of the San Fernando Valley. Stephen and Akido are on alert for STEN patrols as they skim over the mountains north of the valley. The rooftops of the first houses appear and Akido speaks.

"Boss, I have a briefing from GA," says Akido.

"Go."

"First, Colin's people have reached out via email. He definitely wants to meet you."

Angelica smiles at this. "We will definitely make that happen."

"Absolutely," says Stephen, also smiling.

"Should I respond saying that, Boss?" says Akido.

"Make it so," says Angelica.

"Done," says Akido. "Here is the rest of the briefing." He projects a three-D image. "This is the most recent update of an aerial view of the World State Organization's domination of Earth, as seen by satellite. The map is marked with red flags showing the WSO/STEN controlled strongholds in walled fortress cities across the planet. They are clustered in North America, Europe, the British Isles, and parts of Africa and South America. As you can see, there is nothing in most of Asia. The WSO has no interest in that area. They consider that the people there are no threat.

"Mexico has no WSO presence, making it a potential staging ground for delivery of resistance equipment, arms and commando teams into the United States by land via California, Arizona, and Texas.

"Northern Africa is well covered by air patrols, but the heartland is open and untouched. It could provide another area for staging bases and the training of global freedom fighters."

Stephen says, "It sounds like Africa represents a productive area for the new civilization. It could spark from there using the area's wealth of natural resources."

"Yes," says Angelica. "Their people could be a real asset for the resistance. We want to get them involved."

"There is good news about the resistance in other parts of the world," Akido says.

"The survival camp in Japan has started a special forces training camp, like what is being done in Australia. The same thing is happening in Scotland and Ireland."

"This is good," says Angelica. "The resistance is picking up momentum on its own. It will become a wave that becomes a tsunami. It's force will be a rally call to people craving freedom around the world. It's happening now. The battle is beginning."

She sits back. Her face turns thoughtful. "There is still the matter of sleeper cells and how WSO is using them. We'll need to talk to Francisco and Diego about them. Jeremiah mentioned they know who they are in Denver—I wonder if that's true in Los Angeles. And in Utah. We'll have to address this."

Angelica reaches for Stephen's hand. They know their mission will be even more intense in the days to come. She whispers to him, "I want to thank you for your patience, for always being there for me, for watching my back. You mean everything to me."

Stephen squeezes her hand and a moment of closeness wells up. Angelica leans closer to him and breaks the beautiful silence, saying both telepathically and in a whisper, "Thank you, my love."

Stephen answers her with a thought. *You've always been my joy and inspiration, Angelica. There's no one like you in all the universe.*

Akido clears his throat. "Ahem. STEN activity ahead," he warns.

Stephen is already looking for a place to set down. He spots a large area behind a house, with trees and shrubs that can be used to obscure the hovercraft. He lands and he and Angelica jump out, pushing the hovercraft into the bushes under the trees.

"Akido, tap into the STEN communication and put it on speaker," Stephen orders.

Angelica and Stephen climb back into the hovercraft, leaning forward to hear. There is a crackle, then a voice. They listen to individual voices reporting the activities of the raid. There are shouts and some screams. Clipped sentences report the absence of any leaders, just a bunch of old women and small children. A disgusted voice orders all troops to pull out. Angelica draws a deep breath and leans back. "We have to find out how Garcia, Margo, and Jeremiah fared in their raids."

"We'll find Francisco and Diego. Then we'll find out what happened." Stephen starts the hovercraft. He maneuvers it out of the bushes, through the yard into the street. They cruise at a slow pace, watching for people and troops. They see neither.

LOS ANGELES SURVIVAL COMMUNITY

Bridgetta watches the STEN bastards climb back into the two troop carriers. Twenty-five heavily armed soldiers trying to capture the people working to restore freedom. It was very lucky the community had some warning. She was glad they'd practiced how to handle such an emergency. The women and children were brilliant!

She comes out of her hiding place and embraces Nancy.

"You guys were fantastic!" she says.

"We were scared shitless," says Nancy in a shaky voice. "But we knew what to do because of the practice. Thanks for making us do that, Bridgetta."

"Hey, I know how panic can mess you up. You have to have some knowledge about situations so you can control them, even if you're not the one supposed to be in control."

"Yeah, well, anyway, thanks." Nancy gives Bridgetta a quick hug before hurrying away.

Bridgetta heads for the bunker to find Diego. She makes her way to the basement, through the maze and knocks on the door, not waiting for an answer to enter. Diego looks up.

"Everything okay out there?" he asks.

"Yes. In fact, it's great. The ladies were scared but they handled it like champs. Any word from Angelica and Stephen?"

"They're on their way. Should be here within the hour."

"Finally!"

Diego rolls his eyes.

Bridgetta sticks her tongue out at him. She asks, "You okay down here?"

"Yeah, my shift is over soon. I'll see you topside."

When Stephen and Angelica reach the meeting place in the Disney complex, Stephen parks the hovercraft in a secluded spot. They walk into the common area looking for Francisco. They see him sitting at a table talking to Diego and Bridgetta. Bridgetta glances up and squeals.

"You're here!" she cries, rushing forward to give Angelica a hug.

Angelica is surprised at this show of affection.

"Ever since I met you, I've wanted to see you again. You are the coolest person I know. I want to learn everything from you," Bridgetta says, releasing Angelica.

Angelica exchanges a quick look with Stephen, then gives Bridgetta her full attention. "Thank you," she says. Bridgetta beams.

Angelica turns to Francisco. "You just had a STEN raid here," she says. "How did you fare?"

"We had enough advance notice, thanks to Akido, that we were able to put a protocol into effect. Bridgetta's been drilling everyone for the past month. The raid found nothing and no one."

"It was brilliant," says Diego.

"Very good," says Angelica. "Do you have news of the other survival camps? Utah and Denver?"

"I just received an email report from Garcia," says Francisco. "His group has been drilling the same protocol and they used it successfully. He said Jeremiah reported a bit more difficulty. We're waiting for his email report with details. In general, the bad guys had a bit of a bad day today. The only trouble is that they'll probably try to retaliate with something designed to mess us up."

"If they do, when they communicate to each other about it, Akido will alert us before their plans go into motion," says Stephen, "and they will be unsuccessful again."

"That's right!" says Diego.

"It's the reason for the raids that has me concerned," says Francisco. "The timing seems indicative that someone on our inside is reporting on our activities. All since you two arrived. That's pretty quick."

"Yes," says Angelica. "Stephen and I saw evidence of sleeper cell acitivity in Utah, and Jeremiah said they know who the agents are in the Denver area. This means active sleeper cell activity. There are hidden enemy forces at work on the ground in the camps."

Stephen adds, "Maybe you, Garcia, and Jeremiah can dig deeper on this. How many sleeper agents are there in each area? How and who are they reporting to? It won't be easy but we need to find this out. And how to deal with them is another thing."

"Akido, what have you got on the history of sleeper cell use by the WSO?" Angelica asks.

Akido's voice issues from the bracelet band on Angelica's wrist. Bridgetta looks surprised. Francisco lifts an eyebrow. Diego smirks.

Akido says, "According to reports, these sleeper cells have been a real problem in various countries for many years. They have existed and caused havoc since people began creating borders around themselves. One or two individuals posing as trusted townspeople are, in fact, loyal to some other group. In the time prior to their complete takeover, the WSO sleeper cells worked to undermine the prevailing system.

"Vigilantes, extremists, disgruntled youth—such men found the WSO sleeper cell system sensitive to their voice and their causes. They could vent their frustration by working against the status quo.

"The current sleeper cell network is run by a Colonel Damien Johnson. According to his personnel file, he is a rising star in STEN. He is intelligent, resourceful, and very ambitious. He's a STEN man through and through. He will bear watching."

"Your data gathering is impressive as usual, Akido. Thank you," Angelica says.

"We definitely need to find out who's behind the scenes in our camps, spying and reporting to STEN," says Diego.

Angelica says, "The fact STEN staged simultaneous raids in Utah, Los Angeles, and Denver camps concerns me, mostly because of how fast they reacted. I'm sure the sleeper cell 'critters' are to blame. Stephen spotted two at the town meeting in Utah. They could be the source that prompted the raids. He asked Garcia to keep an eye on them. Heightened surveillance should probably be next. We need to find out who they report to and how. We'll have to work together to expose the whole system. This is very important to the further success of the resistance, and to building stronger survival camps."

Stephen says, "We'll work on the Colonel Johnson aspect if you and Garcia and Jeremiah will work on ferreting out the agents in your areas. But I don't think you should expose them. We can use them to pass on disinformation."

"That's a plan," says Francisco. He glances at Diego. "We'll work out the details with Garcia and Jeremiah." Diego nods.

"We must pick up the pace," says Angelica. "Time is of the essence. My biggest fear right now lies with the enemy using all their surveillance tools to pick up the increased resistance activity in the survival camps. We don't know if they know anything about the successful Darwin operation in Australia, or how bustling the survival camps really are in North America. That's information we will be watching for as we scan their communications."

Bridgetta watches this back and forth conversation with great interest.

A young man comes into the hall and heads for the table. He hands Francisco the paper he's holding.

"Email report from Jeremiah about the raid in Denver," Francisco says, reading it aloud.

"'This morning, STEN guards stormed the area around the Boulder courthouse. That area is fairly wide open so access was pretty easy. They established a perimeter and the officer gave orders to about thirty-five STEN troops to assemble every member of the camp they could find. Because of the warning, that was mainly old women and younger children, but they did find three teenage boys. Every other able-bodied person was either absent or well hidden.

"'It was comical watching the hard-core troops trying to wrangle little kids and grandmas. They were rougher with the older boys. The officer tried to question them but they acted stupid. He got frustrated and cuffed one of them. The other two tried to run away and were restrained by the soldiers, none too gently. Since I was the only man around, the officer concentrated on questioning me. He was most interested in finding out about new people, any new links or leaks to outsiders or the outside world, any propaganda, or any small, unannounced meetings or gatherings where counter World State Organization beliefs were expressed. He wanted to know about dissent or insurrection or talk of resistance, etc. I managed to answer all his questions without saying anything.

"'No one was seriously hurt. The one boy will have a black eye. When the officer was done with me, the ladies ripped the soldiers a new one for coming in and scaring the kids. The officer ordered his troops back to the vehicles.

"'There was damage to some of property when the troops got heavy handed in their search, but nothing serious.

"'They were gone within two hours. Our people went back to their usual activities. The men will have questions when they get back, but they'll be able to watch the video. The people in hiding watched the whole exchange via a button cam set up I had on my shirt.

"'I have to say, the timing of this raid is suspicious. Looking forward to everyone's thoughts on the matter.'"

Francisco says, "We'll talk with Garcia and Jeremiah and put together a plan to implement what we've discussed about the sleeper cells."

"You all will need to be hyper vigilant now that we know how close their connection is to STEN," says Stephen. "We'll be helping any way we can."

"There is another factor you should be aware of," says Francisco, "since we're discussing facts of life under the WSO. It's not uncommon for wanderers to drift between the survival camps, even though the camps are often hundreds of miles apart. The actual whereabouts of drifters are not known to people in the camps or the walled fortresses cities. These people prefer to live on their own in remote areas away from civilization.

"They do find ways to communicate with people in the fortress cities. They use barter to trade with the WSO troops and fortress city inhabitants for some of what they need and also for information, which is often pretty accurate. They do the same with the survival communities."

Diego takes up the story. "These wanderers drifted among the camps that grew up outside the fortress cities. Some began to carry messages between people inside and those outside as a side hustle. People separated from their loved ones would always pay somehow for news. Even now, they keep a form of communication going."

Francisco continues. "Diego and I and Garcia and Margo were all part of gypsy bands before we decided to settle and make survival camps."

"Are the outliers good people?" asks Angelica.

"No, most of them are not," replies Diego. "There are many lowlifes and criminals who roam the interior. When we travel, we go in well-armed groups."

"Hmmm," says Stephen. "Recruits for the resistance."

"They'll be a hard sell," says Bridgetta. "I've dealt with some."

"Angelica can be very persuasive," says Stephen. Diego looks skeptical.

"There's news about the resistance around the world," says Angelica. "The effort is gaining traction and there are future locations for development in China and Africa. As you know, Colin in Australia has created a resistance machine. He'll be instrumental in the forward motion of the resistance, as will you all. Stephen and I need to meet with Colin face to face." Angelica looks at Stephen, opening her mind. He sees her plan as she continues speaking. He approves.

"Physically meeting Colin will allow Stephen and me to move all the tactical and strategic plans for the resistance movement to the next level. Since Colin is seventy-nine-hundred miles away from Los Angeles, I plan to meet in the Hawaiian Islands. They're away from usual routes and we can rendezvous in secret to go over plans and to get well coordinated. We want to see what we can do to ramp things up."

"I've heard the Hawaiian Islands are beautiful," says Francisco.

"Aside from that, it's about halfway between the mainland and Darwin. Logistically it works well," says Angelica.

"Yes. Well all right," says Francisco. "I say we finish all this serious talk and planning and take some down time. You'll be heading back to Utah tomorrow, right?"

Angelica nods. "Yes. And we'd like Bridgetta to accompany us. We have a mission in Denver and could use her help."

"Oh yes," says Bridgetta. "YES!"

"Good," says Francisco. "Now, outside for some play, then dinner, then a good night's sleep."

The group ends up in a large grassy area. Bridgetta starts with a martial arts exhibit. Angelica joins in and the two women spar, looking more like dancers than fighters. Stephen joins them. The flow and art of the three bodies moving together, apart, entwining, is hypnotic and beautiful. When they stop and bow in unison, they are acknowledged with thunderous applause from the people gathered to watch them.

Bridgetta is flushed with pleasure. Angelica and Stephen are smiling. They clasp hands and walk away, across the grass and around a building. No one follows them.

"Things are moving quickly. This is good. The faster the resistance gets moving under its own steam, the better," says Angelica. "Akido, what do you know about Hawaii?"

"GA started looking into it as soon as you mentioned it," he replies. "There are few Hawaiians left. There is a survival camp on the north shore of Oahu in a place called Turtle Bay. It used to be a resort, before 2060. There's a partial airstrip about ten miles down the coast, or the Australians might be able to land on the Kamehameha Highway."

"Sounds perfect." Angelica walks on, hand in hand with Stephen.

"Something else," says Akido. "The Hawaiian new year begins with the rising of Makalii, the Pleiades constellation, in mid-November, signaling the beginning of Makahiki. It is a time of peace and plenty and an opportunity to fortify existing relationships and to forge new ones. It corresponds with Luminus's Celebration of Creation and Divine Light."

"December begins in two days. Can we do that? How long will Colin need to put together a trip to Hawaii?" Angelica wonders aloud. Stephen raises her hand to his lips, nibbling her fingers. She lets him, looking into his eyes, then pulls her hand away, laughing. Stephen grabs it again and they walk, shoulders touching.

"I didn't tell you," she says, "when I thought of Hawaii as a meeting place, I asked Akido to find creation or god stories about the islands. He's been whispering them to me."

"Has he," says Stephen.

"Yes. The Hawaiians share many gods and goddesses with other Polynesians. There are stories of humans who go to live in celestial bodies. They remind me of our creation story.

"There is a Hawaiian legend about the goddess of enchantment and golden light guiding ancient mariners to the island of beautiful beginnings, the big island, Hawaii. This goddess was the star constellation Pleiades. It's said that in the full moon phase, the goddess shines her light to show the exact path to take, creating a narrow corridor upon the sea, the same path the ancient seafarers first saw, the same heavenly light glistening upon the waters, beckoning the way. It's a sign of eternal friendship for all mariners on the waves. It must be a sight to behold." Angelica sighs.

"In any case, the Hawaiian Islands are a spiritual place. They are a halfway point between Darwin and Los Angeles, but they're also a place for us to renew our spirits, escaping our bodies for a bit to experience the joyful divine light itself, its energy and endless space all around. What do you think, love?" They pause and Angelica gazes up at her soldier-of-light soul mate, standing close with her hands resting on his chest. She feels the hum under her fingers as he answers.

"Hmm… still the most beautiful eyes I've ever looked into," says Stephen. He reaches up to cover her hands with his.

They stand like this for a long moment, souls reflecting and together as one.

"I like it all," says Stephen, hugging her to him.

The moment ends and they step apart.

"Will the hovercraft have any trouble with a twenty-six-hundred-mile trip across an ocean?" asks Angelica. "We may have to fly low sometimes."

"The old girl shouldn't have any trouble. We'll travel light. Her top speed is about five-hundred mph so the trip will take almost ten hours. We'll fly mostly at night, of course. The views will be spectacular."

"Wow, Stephen. I'll have the pleasure of a midnight serenade of the planets and stars from aboard the hovercraft as we cruise the Pacific, with the heavens above and the glistening ocean below, and you close by my side. What more could a girl want?" She grins at him.

They walk in silence, back to join the others.

As the group heads toward the community area, Angelica and Stephen fall in step with Francisco and Diego. Bridgetta walks ahead.

Angelica begins. "In my thoughts, the resistance has good footing. But it is time for it to start moving at a faster pace. Everything Stephen and I are doing is to help that happen. But we do need to talk with Colin and his people in person. We'll meet them in Hawaii in mid-December. We'll talk of his plans for the resistance and what more we can do. I also want to talk with him about rescuing the Luminaries in the detention centers. I have the beginnings of a plan that I will flesh out while we're there."

Angelica walks several paces. "I have more thoughts. As you know, the World State Organization and STEN are well equipped with soldiers and resources. Would you agree that at this point any resistance movement is undermanned, under trained, and light on resources? Do you agree we must get everyone on board and coordinated for full maximum effort?"

"I agree with both those statements," says Francisco. "I've had many long email exchanges with Colin. You two definitely need to get in the same room together."

"Akido," says Angelica, "send Colin an email requesting a meeting in Hawaii, in Turtle Bay on the North Shore of Oahu on December 5th."

"On it, Boss."

Stephen speaks. "Our ultimate goal for Earth is to bring about the day when all individuals can trust one another. A new civilization can only be founded on this principle."

Angelica continues. "This intention is from the heart. It is the universal message of peace and truth."

Francisco and Diego nod, not speaking. They are touched by Angelica and Stephen's dedication and willingness to see things become better. They're also wondering where these guys come from.

DAY TEN

LOS ANGELES SURVIVAL COMMUNITY

AFTER A GOOD NIGHT'S SLEEP, the five meet for breakfast. Bridgetta has stuffed what she needs in a backpack. After eating some toast and black coffee, Stephen leads the party to the hovercraft. He waits to one side with Angelica while the Earth men walk around it, looking. Francisco comes to stand beside them.

"The three of us are going to have a real heart to heart, very soon," he says.

Angelica and Stephen smile and nod.

"Time to go," she says.

Stephen opens the doors.

Angelica shows Bridgetta how to climb in the back. She and Stephen board and they're off. Stephen takes a different route to Utah this trip. He flies more north at first, then east to travel over north central Nevada.

As they fly over California, they see pockets where homes are hidden under trees near streams. Where roads are passable, there are small communities showing signs of life—vegetable gardens, penned chickens and small livestock. Where there is water, there is life, but the land between is barren and rocky. It has a harsh beauty.

As they fly over the salt flats, they veer toward the Utah survival camp. Stephen says, "Akido, STEN patrols?"

"Started scanning a ways back, Boss," says Akido. "We're in the clear so far. STEN hasn't changed their patrol routes yet. GA will alert me if and when they do."

"Good."

"Angelica Boss, incoming email from Garcia. Here it is."

"Thank you." Angelica reads the email displayed above her wristband. Bridgetta stares, open mouthed.

"Stephen, Garcia has already been talking with Francisco about the sleeper cell situation. He's checking into Doc Campbell and Travis Wilson. Doc has been part of the community for years but Travis is a newcomer. He drifted in a couple of years ago, taking the cabin you saw. Garcia says he got on fine with other folks in the community. Garcia's got a plan to find out what is going on in his group. Margo will be helping him. He says Doc and Travis haven't been seen much in the community in recent days."

"Good. We'll count on them to handle the snakes in their garden," says Stephen. "We'll follow up on their STEN connection."

"Yes, we will," says Angelica.

Bridgetta has been following this conversation with interest. "So Francisco, Garcia, and Jeremiah will take care of the sleeper cells in their communities," Bridgetta says. "How are you going to follow up on the STEN side?"

"I can answer that one," says Akido. "We have not been introduced. I'm Angelica and Stephen's virtual assistant."

"Oh," says Bridgetta. "I'm Bridgetta. Pleased to meet you."

"Thank you. I am pleased to meet you," says Akido. "At this moment I am awaiting a report of a scan being done on all STEN computer files for mention of Colonel Damien Johnson. When I receive the report, I'll relay it. Then the bosses will have enough knowledge to know what to do."

"That is cool!" says Bridgetta.

MIDDAY, UTAH SURVIVAL COMMUNITY

Stephen slides the hovercraft into a secluded spot near the Utah camp. Everyone disembarks and walks toward Garcia and Margo's house. They see Margo coming from the opposite direction as they reach the front porch.

"Friends!" she calls.

"Margo." Angelica steps forward. The women embrace. "Let me introduce Bridgetta," she says.

"Oh yes," says Margo. "I know about this one. Diego is always talking about Bridgetta's escapades. Welcome!" She gives her a hug.

"Garcia is finishing up with some folks. He'll be along directly. Come on in for some tea. Or coffee." Margo heads into the house.

Four people are arranged on his living room furniture when Garcia comes in.

"So, you must be Bridgetta. Welcome to Utah." Garcia shakes her hand. "And you two, what mischief do you have planned now?" he asks Angelica and Stephen.

"We're going back to the walled fortress in Denver. Bridgetta and I will infiltrate the detention center and get a look at the infirmary psychiatric ward where the Luminaries are being held. I need to see how the wards are operated so I can finalize the plan to get the Luminaries out—in Denver, Los Angeles, and Utah," says Angelica.

"I'm going in with you?" asks Bridgetta.

"Yes."

"Holy crap. Okay." Bridgetta looks a bit breathless.

"People need to know the full extent of their torture," says Angelica. "I can tell them, but I'm an outsider. You are not. You'll be the advocate for Earth's Luminaries."

Bridgetta looks a little shell shocked, sitting deep in an easy chair. She blinks, rising slowly. She stands taller and looks at Angelica.

"I am the advocate for our Luminaries," she says.

The room is silent.

"Well, that's settled," says Garcia. "What can we do to help this mission?"

"Will you show Bridgetta around? We'll need a vehicle, food, extra gas and camping gear. Bridgetta, will you collect that and meet back here around dinner?" Angelica issues her orders, then asks, "Akido, driving time from here to Denver?"

"Eight hours forty minutes," Akido answers.

"We'll leave before dawn tomorrow morning. I want to travel an overland route so we can meet any wanderers in the area. It's time for them to be briefed on the resistance and the rescue of the Luminaries," she says. "If their network is as good as Francisco made it sound, the message will travel far and fast."

Zack comes in as Angelica is speaking. He hears her last statements.

"That's a great idea," he says.

"Meanwhile," says Garcia, "take this young lady and show her around. She has a shopping list she'll need help with. She's Bridgetta from LA."

"Wow, good to meet you!" says Zack. "There's a new guy waiting for me outside who can help, Juan Carlos. He arrived yesterday. Let's go."

"Awesome," says Bridgetta, waving to the others as she leaves with Zack.

Angelica turns to Garcia. "Stephen and I will stay here, if that's alright. There are some plans we need to look at. You both have duties—you don't have to stay."

"I'll be back around four to make dinner for everyone," says Margo. "Make yourselves at home. Come on, Garcia. We'll leave these kids alone." She grabs his hand and they go.

Angelica moves to the big kitchen table. "Akido, display the psychiatric ward plans and the electroshock machine plans."

The schematics appear above the table.

"These medical wards and the proposed extensions will beef up the psychiatric wards where secret interrogations, drugging, electroshock treatment and deep sleep coma programs have been going on for years. It's all designed to suppress our artists and visionaries,"

Angelica says. She starts shaking, leaning on the table. Her face goes ashen. She's overcome with rage and grief, gasping for breath. Stephen is at her side in an instant, holding her when she crumbles.

She struggles to catches her breath, clutching Stephen. "This is bad, very bad," she whispers. "It's almost too much to confront and deal with—the extent of the evil of the Soulests and their World State Organization. Once again, those evil beings are responsible for the perpetration of it all. These new plans make it clear that the WSO is dedicated to the extermination of humanity, either with drugs or with death by torture. I'm afraid that if they get this special equipment up and running soon, we'll have lost the game here."

"That will not happen." Stephen speaks with conviction. He grasps Angelica shoulders, turning her to face him. He looks into her eyes. "Will it?"

Angelica looks back at him. He watches as her eyes fill with fire. "No. It. Will. Not." Stephen releases her and they sit, face to face.

"The humans here have been indoctrinated by the Soulests," she says. "They have no idea what they're giving up. They cannot care for their fellow man and still use such vicious, barbaric techniques on their own kind. It's as cruel and inhuman as you can get. If those allied with the Soulests don't realize their crimes, they'll be punished the same as their supposed mentors."

Her face is fierce. Stephen smiles.

Garcia, Margo, Zack, and Bridgetta arrive back at the same time. They have an old pickup truck loaded with extra gas cans and a footlocker that Bridgetta opens to reveal camping gear for three, plus dried fruit, nuts, jerky, bread and water.

The group spends a lively evening eating an excellent meal. They all go to bed early.

DAY ELEVEN

UTAH SURVIVAL COMMUNITY

STEPHEN AND ANGELICA are up before the sun, packing the clothes Margo has loaned them in a knapsack. Stephen takes it to the truck while Angelica goes to wake Bridgetta. The sound of a rooster signals the new day as the light softens behind the mountains. The morning air is crisp with the scents of winter. Within twenty minutes they're in the truck and on the road. Each nurses a cup of coffee handed to them by Margo as they pulled away.

Angelica has picked a back route through Heber City, Roosevelt, and Vernal in Utah to Steamboat Springs, Silverthorne and Denver in Colorado. This way goes through rugged terrain. It will keep them out of the way of STEN patrols and take them into wanderer territory.

Stephen drives. Angelica and Bridgetta act as sentries, scanning for STEN aerial or ground patrols and for hostile wanderers.

Stephen drives with one hand on the wheel, the other pointing to sights beyond the windshield. "Look, you can see for miles. The views are incredible, magnificent along this road. The diverse scenery from desert terrain to mountains looks natural and untouched, like it's been undisturbed for thousands of years. I imagine it's been some time since people have traveled in these parts. North America, the United States is really a beautiful place to behold." He sits back, enjoying the view.

But soon, Stephen is thinking about Bridgetta. He has the word of Francisco and Diego that she is a skilled fighter, but he's only seen her spar once, in play. How will she handle herself in real battle? Accompanying Angelica into the Denver walled fortress will be a test for her.

Angelica feels his concern and looks at his thoughts. *Worry not love. She will step up. I know this.*

Stephen sends her acquiescence, respect, agreement in a single flow. Angelica smiles.

They drive for three hours then stop to stretch and eat. Stephen turns the driving over to Angelica. Bridgetta asks Angelica what she should expect inside the Denver fortress and Angelica gives her a briefing about her first visit.

Bridgetta nods and is silent for a moment.

"I need to tell you something," she says.

Angelica nods and waits.

Bridgetta looks straight ahead. "I have spoken with some wanderers. There's a group that comes to our LA community for food and a shower. One of the girls told me this story. I know it's true because I heard the same story from another girl later."

She pauses. "This girl had been inside the LA fortress for a couple of weeks. She said every person has to take the blue pill every day. If you refuse, you go to detention. If you're pretty, you land in the infirmary. They say it's for a special health screening program by a doctor. She said it's not a health screening, it's prostitution. It's a so-called sex therapy program for lechers—doctors, government officials and STEN officers. They dope up the women with uppers and downers then rape them while they're semi-conscious. This all happens behind closed doors and after hours in the medical and infirmary psychiatric wards. The first girl said she heard a man bragging about how he'd used the *service* in every walled fortress he'd been to." Bridgetta shudders.

"Any girl who tries to fight back is taken to detention in the general population B section. That's where all the really bad men are kept—the ones that are too bad for even the WSO. There are no privileges there at all. No exercising, no talking to friends during breaks. The girls are thrown in there for a night. Some of them don't survive the treatment they get."

Angelica takes Bridgetta's hand. No one speaks for another mile, watching the landscape roll past.

Stephen says grimly, "The WSO has a lot to answer for."

They roll through more miles and the countryside continues to be amazing in all directions. They can see for miles around. It's clear as a bell and there is so much space. They are coming up to the Continental Divide, the majestic Rockies.

"It's really beautiful here," says Bridgetta in a quiet voice.

Each time they approach a town or clusters of buildings, they slow, looking for people but they see no one. Angelica is disappointed.

The roads are clear and the weather is good, but there is a winter snap in the air. Stephen is watching the skies and sees movement. He signals Angelica. Angelica heeds his directive, cuts the speed in half, and heads off the main road. She stops, pulling the pickup into a grove of trees. She turns off the engine and they sit in the cab, listening.

They hear the plane making its way in their direction. It circles past them to the north. There's no change in its sound—the patrol is oblivious to them below. The sound fades, the coast appears clear. They scan the sky, but only more and more clouds dot the beautiful skyline. All they hear are the birds of this region calling out.

The rest of the journey through the mountains is uneventful.

EVENING, DENVER

They cruise into the Denver suburbs. It's twilight but they drive with no lights. Stephen is at the wheel now.

"Akido," says Stephen, "be alert for any STEN patrols. Also, suggestions for a place to park that's walking distance to the walled fortress?"

"Got it Boss. How about the parking lot of the Mile High Stadium?"

"There's cover there?"

"Yes, Boss."

"Good. Show me the way," says Stephen. Akido does.

Once the truck is hidden near a loading dock, the sun is close to the western horizon.

"If we hurry, we can make it to the gate before it's closed for the night," says Angelica. They grab two blankets, a handful of dried fruit and nuts and head for the walled fortress, about two miles away. They slip quietly through the city neighborhoods at a brisk pace. Stephen leads, Angelica and Bridgetta follow. They cover the distance without incident. They stop when the gate is in view.

Stephen watches the road to the gate as Angelica reveals her mission orders to Bridgetta.

"We'll go into the fortress city and find a place to spend the night. In the morning we will refuse to take our meds—the daily blue pill—so we can get sent to the infirmary ward for handling and treatment.

"Since this is the time that the sex crazy doctors pick out and prey on the women who come to the clinic, you and I will be part of the herd. We'll refuse to comply with their so-called treatment plan. They'll try to send us to General Population B as a punishment. My plan is to get into the psychiatric ward before that happens, so I can see what's happening to the Luminaries. I need to get behind the scenes to see exactly what they're doing to them. Once I know, we can finalize our plan to change things for them. We'll find our way out the following day. Stephen will be there to swoop us away. This will be dangerous, Bridgetta."

"I'm ready."

Stephen raises his hand. "I see a larger group heading for the gate. You should walk in with them."

"Yes, good idea." Angelica takes off her wristband and hands it to him. "Bridgetta, you can pretend to be a little stupid and follow my lead, okay. Be prepared to use your feminine wiles."

Bridgetta grins. "No problem. Feminine wiles on tap and ready."

"And whatever happens, stay close to me!"

Bridgetta nods.

Angelica gives Stephen a hard kiss and walks away with Bridgetta on her heels. As they approach the group heading for the gate, Angelica puts a swing in her hips and hooks her arm through Bridgetta's.

She leans in and whispers, "We are a couple of empty-headed girls looking for some fun and maybe a way to get ahead." She giggles and so does Bridgetta.

The guards take one look at them and wave them through without asking for passes. They're in the fortress.

EVENING, LOS ANGELES

Damien looks at his aide. The man is standing stiffly at attention, eyes locked straight ahead. The High Commander has been in town for almost two days and no one at HQ has seen him. Damien knows he'll be getting a visit sometime. He needs to know when.

"Report."

"Sir." The aide only moves his mouth. "High Commander Rhotah Mhene's private jet arrived at the Santa Monica airport day before yesterday, late morning. He went to his retreat house on the ocean and has been there ever since. He's seeing no one. Deliveries have been made—food, his drugs of choice and, on separate occasions, two women, both with similar looks."

"At ease, Sergeant," says Damien. "What else?" His aide relaxes a little. He's learned long ago that his boss always wants particulars, so he made sure to grill his sources for every bit of firsthand knowledge and gossip.

"I'm sorry sir, but that's all I have. No one from his entourage has communicated with HQ at all. No one I could find can even explain this behavior. It seems it's totally uncharacteristic."

"Yes, it is." Damien walks to the window, looking out. His aide recognizes this habit. Whenever his boss is thinking he looks out the window.

The intercom on his desk sounds. "Sir, the High Commander is in the building, heading for your office." Damien looks sharply at his aide.

"Sir. He was still at his retreat an hour ago. I'll set up the conference table." Damien waves his hand and the aide rushes from the room.

Damien paces from the window to the conference table and back. He stops himself from repeating this nervous action. The sound of the door handle turning announces his guest. He assumes the at-ease pose.

Rhotah Mhene sweeps into the room, his assistant and two guards close behind. He wears a short cloak over one shoulder. Damien is surprised at how thin and pale he looks. But he still exudes a palpable force. Damien snaps to attention and salutes, memories of the last time they met on the training field running in his head

"Sir," he says.

"Ahh, young Damien," says Rhotah Mhene, sketching a return salute. "At ease. So. You've lived up to your potential. I've been hearing good things about you." He steps forward and sits in the chair at the head of the conference table. The window is at his back leaving his face in shadow. "Sit, sit. We have much to discuss." Rhotah Mhene indicates the chair to his left.

Damien's sergeant rushes in with a carafe of water and a plate of sweets, placing it near the center of the table. As he leaves, Rhotah Mhene waves his hand at his guards, who follow the sergeant out. His assistant takes a chair to a corner and sits.

Damien seats himself, his face impassive.

Rhotah Mhene leans back and steeples his hands, eyes unfocused. "Tell me about the operation you run."

Damien is thinking hard. "I run the Intelligence Division for the United States. I have an active sleeper cell network in the bigger, organized survival camps. I have agents in the fortress cities keeping track of who comes and goes. I have an efficient disinformation machine. I also have a training center in the Denver fortress." He stops, looking at the Commander.

Rhotah Mhene's eyes are still closed. "Yes, yes. I know all this. I want to know about *you*. And not just what's in your personnel file. Tell me who Damien is. What motivates *him*. Why is he here?"

Damien looks at his commander for a moment. He knows he's looking at the equivalent of his old gang leader. The only difference is that this man sits at the top of a worldwide gang. Damien wants this man's job. He also knows how to stroke the head guy. He knows how to make himself appear competent but unthreatening.

"Sir, I started my STEN training in 2062, when I was fourteen. I knew STEN was for me because of the time I spent in the number one gang in LA. In the gang, I was best at information gathering. I did Level IV basic training in one of the LA groups. You came to our training facility once and I met you. Later I worked in squads rounding up Luminaries who were named insurgents in LA. We got a lot of them, sir.

"After that, I was promoted to lieutenant in 2070 and commanded my own squad. We were efficient. I was good at organizing and keeping track of my men and the survivors who went outside the fortress cities, supposedly beyond our control. I worked with Colonel Santos and we started building a good network of spies. This morphed into sleeper cells in the outlying areas. We are able to monitor the people who think they're out from under our control. It has become an efficient early warning system."

"Yes," says Rhotah Mhene, spearing Damien with his eyes. "That's what has been reported to me." He pours himself some water and takes a sip. "What has your network heard about organized resistance to the WSO?"

Damien leans back in his chair. "We've been monitoring this closely. Five days ago we received a report from one of our most consistent paid informants. He reported an organized meeting in the Utah survival camp. The meeting was run by a couple of newcomers—a man and a woman."

"Who did most of the talking at the meeting?" Rhotah Mhene interrupts, leaning forward.

"Apparently, it was the woman. Our man was disgusted by this."

Rhotah Mhene takes another sip of water. Damien watches him, realizing he's disturbed by this report. It's an unexpected weakness and Damien makes note of it.

He continues. "This is the first time we've gotten a report of a formal gathering talking about resistance. We've been watching LA, Utah and Denver as their communities grow. There have been grumblings, but nothing organized. They don't have any way to communicate with each other so any resistance would be localized and easily quelled."

"You're sure they are not communicating among themselves?"

"No sir, not one-hundred percent. Because of this, Colonel Santos has gone to Utah. He'll get to the bottom of what's going on there."

Rhotah Mhene nods once. "It's also possible there's something happening in Denver. I was there two days ago for an event. There may have been someone there…"

"I haven't received any report about that yet. Can you give me any more information, sir?"

"No."

Damien waits a beat for more. "Yes, sir."

Rhotah Mhene gazes at nothing for a minute. "I want daily reports on what you and Colonel Santos find. I don't care if you just say 'nothing today.' Daily reports, understand?" His voice is loud at the end of this statement.

"Yes, sir, daily reports no matter what. I understand." Damien salutes to punctuate his acknowledgement.

Rhotah Mhene stands. "I'll expect your next report end of day tomorrow. Find out what this woman is doing. Find her. Bring her to me." He strides out of the room, his assistant close behind him.

Damien is standing at the window when his sergeant comes back in. He has a lot to think about.

NIGHT, DENVER

ANGELICA AND BRIDGETTA follow a group of women into a building that was once a hotel. The rooms are full, with several people to a room. Others camp out in the lobby and other common areas. They look around for a place to sleep.

Angelica sees an alcove near the elevators. "Let's try over there," she says to Bridgetta. "That seems to be a spot where more elderly and kids are sleeping. It will be lights out soon and we've got to blend in and get some sleep like everyone else. Just do what the others around us are doing."

Bridgetta nods and lays out the blankets they brought.

Large sounds become less frequent as the building's population calls it a night. The interior is dark but some illumination filters in from the fortress security lights outside.

Angelica and Bridgetta lie quietly, close together for warmth. But Angelica cannot find sleep. Somewhere nearby she hears a mother who is very worried about her child.

She casts her attention out, searching for the troubled person. *There, behind the reception desk. It's a mother with her son. He appears to be sick—not doing well at all. She's worried and in despair. I can feel her heavy stress.*

The anguish of the mother is in her soft voice when she cries, "I know he's going to die. Can someone help us? Please." Bridgetta sleeps but Angelica is caught by the mother's quiet tears as she holds and rocks her child. She hasn't used her turquoise amulet since teleporting to Earth, except to help heal her and Stephen's Earth bodies. Now she takes the crystal from around her neck and presses it between her fingers. It starts to warm and glow. Angelica goes to the woman and sits down beside her.

"You need to get some rest," she says. "I will tend your boy while you sleep. Let me help you." Angelica takes her hand.

The woman doesn't answer for a long moment, staring at Angelica. She makes a decision and nods her head.

Angelica puts the warm amulet in the woman's hand and closes her fingers around it. Its power radiates. She puts two fingers on the woman's forehead while they hold the amulet between their hands. She calms the space around them and the woman relaxes and falls asleep.

Her boy is restless, trying to fight his pain.

Now Angelica takes the amulet and moves closer to the boy, her back to the room. No one can see her hands.

First, she puts the amulet on his chest over his heart to begin the healing process. When he sighs with relief, Angelica touches the amulet again. She places her hand over it and a faint glow begins to emanate from it. She puts her other hand on his head and concentrates on sending the glow through his body. He sighs again. The amulet changes, its glow becomes concentrated, seeking the dark areas in his body. It's changing the spectrum of light and the electromagnetic wavelength of his pain.

Angelica holds her touches and watches the visible light change color from dirty brown to dark blue, to green blue, to light green, to golden, as the crystal's energy penetrates the boy's body. The amulet is working as it's supposed to. He's doing better physically and mentally. His body is relaxed, he looks calmer and has fallen asleep. Angelica removes her hands, puts the amulet back around her neck and moves the boy to his mother's side. They're sleeping now.

Bridgetta, pretending to be asleep with eyes closed to a slit, watches with wonder as Angelica, a soldier of light, first soothes the mother then attends the child. She sees her placing her hands on the boy's chest and head, using the turquoise crystal. She sees the faint glow becoming stronger, changing color until it is golden.

Wow. I've never seen anything like that. It was out of this world in a way I don't understand. Who is she anyway? Angelica possesses some extraordinary power. She stays still when Angelica lies down beside her.

Later, the mother, Nidera, starts awake, reaching to check on her son. She sees the difference in him right away and says aloud, "This is a miracle! Thank the gods! What angel has come to save my son? Where is she?" Her frantic eyes search the room. She sees Angelica and rushes to her.

"Thank you, thank you," she says, kneeling down to clutch Angelica hands. She speaks in a low voice. "When Sabal was four years old, his father was killed by STEN guards, in front of him. The guards thought his father had a weapon. He didn't. He was carrying a large plastic spoon and a bowl, trying to get more food for us. A guard shot him in the chest because he refused to obey. Sabal has been silent and sickly since that moment. He's been getting worse…"

Bridgetta pats her shoulder. Nidera wipes tears from her face, looking at Angelica.

"But you," she says, "you are an angel. You saved my boy. Thank you."

Angelica lays a hand against Nidera's cheek. "You are welcome."

A siren starts in the distance, wailing low and high, louder and louder. Angelica goes to the window to look out. She sees searchlights aimed at the sky and sweeping the ground. There are figures with guns and dogs moving along the streets. She reaches to Stephen.

Do you know what happened?

Some teenagers fooling around tripped something near the gate. They have guards with dogs checking it out. Nothing for us to worry about. Stephen pauses. *Good work with the boy.*

Thank you. Angelica is smiling.

Bridgetta leaves Nidera with her son and comes to stand next to Angelica. She looks at her with increased admiration and respect. She says, "I saw some of what you did, with the crystal thing and how it lit up. There was a light all around that kid's body. Pretty incredible. How does it work?" She reaches to touch the amulet that's back around Angelica's neck. "Could you teach me how to do that? I know a lot of people who could use that kind of magic. Can it help anyone?"

"Yes, it can," says Angelica. "There are two important aspects to healing, Bridgetta. One is to know that almost all illnesses and maladies are caused by spiritual distress. The second is that all problems, when viewed completely, will vanish. When you address the individual or the spirit, you can help them handle the distress or the true source of the problem. The crystal helps handle the light spectrum in and around the body.

"We'll talk more about this as we go. I'll teach you to help others in this unique way. The more you can help and serve others, Bridgetta, the more valuable you are. This is how Stephen and I operate. This is our core belief."

Bridgetta's eyes are shining. She nods.

They go back to their blankets to sleep. The rest of the night passes without incident.

DAY TWELVE, DECEMBER

MORNING, DENVER WALLED FORTRESS CITY

THE SUN IS bright outside when they wake. They hope the routine of the fortress city hasn't been changed because of the incident last night.

Angelica turns to Nidera. "When do they dispense the daily meds? What line do you usually stand in for the blue pill?" she asks.

Bridgetta says, "Yeah, I want my blue pill. How about you Angelica? Aren't we just like everyone else ready to receive our daily pill?"

Nidera responds with a new found enthusiasm, "It starts at nine a.m. til ten a.m., so everyone has a chance to get their pill. Right after breakfast at the cafeteria you just get in line and you get your pill. That's the way they do it here."

"What happens if you miss your turn or are sick and don't go to the cafeteria to eat? Can you go to the medical ward in the detention center to get your pill?" asks Angelica.

"Yes, yes you can," says Nidera. "Folks that miss getting their meds in the morning do just that. There's an incentive if you take your pills. You get privileges like extra food. But you have to wear your 'I got my blue pill today' ribbon."

"Thanks for the information, Nidera," says Bridgetta. "Very helpful, dear. But how do you get into the medical ward? Do you need a pass or something?"

Nadira responds as she keeps a watchful eye on Sabal. "All you need to do, I'm told, especially if you are a woman, is be passive and consent to the whims of the guards and the doctors when they want to examine you. Don't resist letting them feel your private parts if they want to. You have to allow sexual acts with them, if they want it. If you don't, they send you to the Population B center. It's on the bottom floor where they keep the toughest, most degraded individuals. Believe me, you don't want to end up there. My friend Jane did and she said it was a real hell. Another girl I know refused to go along with the doctors. She tried to slap and punch her way out of there but they caught her. I heard she was taken away. All I know is she never came back. You have to do what they want."

"Thank you for your insight," says Angelica.

Angelica and Bridgetta leave the hotel, waving to Nidera and Sabal. They find their way to the blue pill dispensing station and get in line. They move forward at a steady pace. Angelica begins complaining in a loud voice.

"I don't know why we have to do this every morning. Some days I want to stay *awake*, you know, so I can *enjoy* stuff." She leers at the people around her.

"Yeah," says Bridgetta. "I don't want to sleep through all the fun. Girl's gotta have some fun, right?" She wiggles her hips.

Other people in the line are shrinking away from them.

Now they're at the table.

"We've decided we're not taking that pill today," says Angelica. She crosses her arms and pouts.

"Yeah," says Bridgetta and does the same.

The technician seated at the table motions to one of the soldiers standing by.

"Take these ladies to the detention center," he orders.

The soldier grabs them each by an arm and drags them away. He hands them over to the guard at the detention center door.

"Blue pill protestors," he says with a leer.

The detention center guard leads them to a line filing through a wide door at the end of a corridor. This is a part of the center Angelica didn't enter when she was here before. There are fifteen women with them in the line. Six of them are younger and more desirable, like her and Bridgetta. They exchange a glance and duck their heads to hide their smiles.

They have to submit to a body scan machine searching for any weapons. Two soldiers watch each woman's scan with sharp eyes.

On the wall to their left is an obvious propaganda poster—a massive picture of the globe with the caption, "Power to The World State Organization."

As she passes through the scan, Angelica sees an enclosed monitoring station to the right. A large display of monitors and computers is visible inside. The monitors show images of spaces throughout the entire detention center complex. She figures there must be over seventy-five cameras sending images. Several guards are keeping tabs at various consoles.

Angelica links to Stephen. *Here's a computer room I didn't see before. I imagine any lockdown orders, emergency situations, or closures will be handled from this room. Let Akido know.* She receives Stephen's acknowledgment.

They make their way further into the detention center.

She turns to Bridgetta and whispers, "At no time are you to engage with the guards or doctors using force—martial arts—unless a life-threatening circumstance arises. I need your full agreement on this. You'll have plenty of opportunity to use your skill to help the resistance movement. I understand how you might feel about men who cross the line and try to take liberties with your person. I do. But our objective is getting in, finding what I need to know and getting out in one piece."

Bridgetta frowns, but says, "I promise."

"Thank you."

Now they're prepared for whatever happens. Angelica sees

they're heading for the lower floor of the detention center where she saw the entrance to the medical/psychiatric ward. They're taken through another door in that same corridor.

The entire group of women is now in a big room where they're herded together. They're told they will participate in a special study on the best ways to handle depression in the fortress city. They are told to take their blue pill and to undress or they'll be sent to Population B. Most of the women comply, especially the ones who have been through this procedure before. But Bridgetta and Angelica do not, sitting on the floor in protest.

A doctor's assistant picks the more attractive, compliant women and they are escorted to private rooms. The protesting women are hauled up and dragged to a smaller room with one guard.

When she's hauled past the door of a private room, Angelica notices one of the medical doctors already having sex with one of the women. She's bent over the examining table and he stands behind her, his pants around his ankles. He is working closely with his "patient," helping her with her fortress city "depression."

Just past the room, Angelica launches her diversion. She starts screaming at Bridgetta, lunging at her to stage a mock fight. She starts hitting Bridgetta, knocking her to the ground. Bridgetta is surprised but lets Angelica jump on top of her. Several doctors rush in to see a good old girl fight. Bridgetta plays along, trading punches, kicks and hair pulling with Angelica. The guard stands back, letting them go at it. There's nothing like two good-looking women slugging it out. The doctors catcall with amusement. Everyone is entertained for several minutes.

Bridgetta doesn't know that Angelica is going to employ a special choke hold that she learned in her elite combat training. Bridgetta will be unconscious briefly—enough time to be a diversion. She performs the move. Bridgetta slumps to the floor and Angelica sprints away toward the door marked NO ADMITTANCE.

As she runs, Angelica reviews in her mind what needs to happen: *Get into the special ward, see what's going on. How many guards,*

attendants, how deep sleep drug is being employed. How do they keep it oper-
ational?

Two guards stand over Bridgetta's body with one of the doctors. One says, "Wow, those women really went at it. Wonder what got into them. This one is still unconscious and the other one bolted. Haven't seen anything like that for a while." He shakes his head. To the doctor he says, "You might want to chase up the one that ran, Doc. We don't have clearance for that area." The doctor nods, leaving reluctantly.

The guard picks up Bridgetta's limp body and hauls it into a nearby room. He puts her on an examining table. He leaves the lights off and closes the door as he leaves.

Another doctor from the medical ward enters the room a few minutes later. Using a flashlight in the darkness, he tries to wake her up. She's still out and he realizes he's got an opportunity to take liberties with her.

Making the best of this opportunity, he wrestles Bridgetta's jeans down, pulling off one leg. He quickly undoes his belt and pulls his pants down. He begins to mount her, holding her hands down to administer his version of the sex therapy program.

As he fumbles between her legs, Bridgetta starts awake and finds him on top of her. She realizes she's about to be raped. She jerks a hand free and smacks him across the face. Heaving her body, she throws him off. They both tumble to the floor. She's angry. She rolls over on him, pinning him down with the weight of her hips. She begins to whale away on him and in less than a minute, he's out cold.

Meanwhile, Angelica is through the NO ADMITTANCE door and in the room on the other side. The doctor comes in behind her, his hands making the "take it easy" motion in front of his body. He speaks softly, telling her how impressive she was in the fight with Bridgetta and how beautiful she is. She lets him move up close, pushing her against the wall.

He plays with her hair, saying, "Listen, I can make special arrangements to get you a whole lot of privileges. All you have to do is be my research assistant and have sex with me. Just with me, a few times a week, after the staff leaves for the evening."

With a sneer, Angelica says, "What makes you so sure you could handle me? I have quite an appetite for what you desire. Wouldn't want you becoming *my* sex slave now would we, Doctor?" She narrows her eyes at him. "I'll have to think about it."

In an instant, he's all over her, trying to fondle and kiss her. Angelica utters a foreign sounding expression. Angry now, she drops him to the ground with a one-two-three punch and kick combination. She adds a few more kicks to the side of his head and he's out cold, down like a fallen tree. He'll be out for some time.

Bridgetta hears the commotion from the room down the hallway and figures it has to be Angelica. She's pulled her pants back on and slides out of the room. She sees no one. She sprints down the hall to the NO ADMITTANCE door. She slips into the room and sees the body of the doctor on the floor. Angelica steps out from behind the door. She turns and gives Angelica a high five. It's a bit clumsy because Angelica doesn't know the gesture. They giggle.

"Did you have to incapacitate anyone?" asks Angelica.

"Yes, I woke up with a doctor getting ready to rape me. I knocked him out."

Angelica takes a silver locket from her waist belt and opens it. She hands Bridgetta a small white pill. "Go and put this under his tongue. He'll sleep at least an hour. Quickly now, we have a lot to do."

Bridgetta dashes from the room.

Angelica administers a white pill to the doctor she knocked out.

Bridgetta rushes back in. "I did it."

"Very good," says Angelica. "Let's go."

They grab white medical coats from the wall next to the door into the ward and slip them on. Angelica puts a finger to her lips, signaling quiet to Bridgetta, who nods. Through the door, they duck into the special psychiatric ward looking like two hip nurses. They have less than an hour to accomplish what they need to do before the doctors wake up.

Angelica and Bridgetta are in the restricted area that many

inhabitants of the fortress city have no idea exists. There is a distinct medicinal odor in the air and the light in the space is low. Ahead of them is a nurse's station where an older, rotund nurse is seated, pouring over some papers—and a crossword puzzle. She's wearing thick, round glasses. Her thin, grey hair is short, hugging her head. She's not aware of the two as they approach.

Angelica speaks. "Hi, we're here to check out the drug administration system. It needs its six-month inspection and maintenance check. We'll make sure everything is working the way it should."

The nurse looks up, squinting at them. "Never seen the likes of you before. It's always a bunch of guys who make the rounds. They like to hang around and hit on the younger nurses." She pats her hair. "They don't know what they're missing. There's a lot to a mature woman, I can tell you. Those sassy young staff nurses got nothing on me." She glares at Angelica and Bridgetta. "You two look the type. What are you really doing here?"

Angelica raises her voice. "We have orders to inspect the system in the special infirmary ward. Regional wants to makes some changes to it on the orders of the head psychiatrist, who reports directly to Dr. Burns. I need all the numbers: how much drug you have in stock, when was the last shipment, was it delivered by the usual guys and did it come from the usual source. Get this information together while we inspect the equipment in the ward."

The old nurse says, "Wait a minute, sister. You're not going in there til I get authorization. We got protocols." She reaches for her phone.

Angelica nods to Bridgetta who gives her a quick one-two punch and chokes her out. The nurse slumps back in her chair, out like a light. Angelica gives her a white pill to make sure she's out for more than a few minutes.

"Bridgetta, you'll need to get the data I asked her for. Her computer is still open. When you've got it, come in."

Bridgetta nods and steps to the desk. Angelica slips through the second door marked NO ACCESS AREA. On the other side of the door is a semi-dark hospital dormitory. There are a few dim lights

158

overhead. The room is full of small beds that look like pods stacked three high in neat rows.

Angelica does a quick estimate. There are enough beds here for seventy-two people. Every bed has an IV drip coming down from overhead, ready for insertion.

Angelica moves through the space, checking all the beds. She can see that just twenty-five are occupied. The darkened dormitory has little ventilation and the stink of unwashed, unhealthy bodies is extreme. The atmosphere is more like a morgue. Every person she looks at appears to be in a deep coma, and near death. Angelica is stunned into motionlessness. She can't move for an unknown length of time. She comes back when Bridgetta touches her arm.

Bridgetta has a stricken look on her face. "Angelica, this is really creepy. There's an atmosphere of deadness here."

Angelica shudders. She grasps Bridgetta's hand, holding it tight. She doesn't speak at first, then she whispers back, "Yes, this is what we're looking for. Did you find all the information I asked for?"

"Yeah, I got it all."

"Thank you. Seeing this, my deepest concerns and suspicions are confirmed." She takes a deep breath. "The enemy has put these secret psychiatric wards in every fortress city. They're conducting mind control and deep sleep programs." She waves her hand. "This is what it looks like. The enemies of creativity, freedom of expression, personal growth, and true mental health have always used these methods. The men who order this are convinced that power over others is the only goal. We must stop them here, now. We must stop them everywhere else they are, forever." Angelica is trembling, speaking almost to herself. "If they get the new electroshock machines up and running, all these people will be killed. This is very bad. Evil is too small a word for their treachery and their intention to annihilate Luminaries."

Angelica's universe is spinning away. She is enraged and wants to lash out in anger. The anguish and pain are stifling. She utters a curse in a foreign tongue.

Bridgetta looks at her in dismay.

Angelica's eyes are flashing and her fists are clenched. "I will kill all the bastards!" Her rage and hate are directed at Rhotah Mhene and for an instant she sees his surprised face in front of her. She recoils, automatically throwing up blocks. Stephen steps into her mind with comfort. *Take that energy and give it to our mission. We will act quicker and work harder. We will pull this off. We will not fail. We will protect the future not only of the Luminaries but also this planet. And the people of this world will help.* Angelica begins to calm.

Bridgetta senses she needs to help Angelica. She takes her hand again to give her comfort and support. Angelica grasps Bridgetta's hand in dire need of the solidarity and compassion of kindred sisters.

This connection helps Angelica get back to battery. She and Bridgetta approach one of the beds to examine the IV drip mechanism. The IV needle is inserted in the patient's arm with a feeder tube and a switch mechanism for adjusting the flow. Each IV line is connected to a specially constructed delivery system running across the ceiling.

"There must be some sort of pump system outside the room to keep the flow going," says Bridgetta.

"We need to find it," says Angelica.

They run to the back of the room, following the lines and looking for something to tell them where the pumping equipment is located. Bridgetta spots a door and yanks it open. They stand in the doorway of a small room, just wide enough for a man to pass the pump machine inside. There's a tank full of liquid on a shelf above the pump. An arrangement of hoses connects the tank, pump and ceiling delivery system. As they look at it, the pump turns on for a minute, then off.

"They have some sort of timer or pressure sensor to keep the flow going," says Bridgetta. "Look, the extra containers of the drug are stacked beside the pump. There are only two. The records I found show there's a delivery every week."

Angelica steps into the room to read the label on a container. "The drug mix is made by IB Proben. It's a sedative and psychotic drug cocktail used to induce a comatose state that can be maintained indefinitely." *Stephen, give this data to Akido.*

He acknowledges.

They leave the room, closing the door behind them. Angelica walks past the beds, looking at the occupants more closely. She discovers most of the patients are only just alive. She decides to communicate with them on a telepathic level.

"Bridgetta, I'm going to communicate something to these people in a special, nonverbal way they'll understand." Angelica closes her eyes and begins. *Brothers, sisters, true Luminaries. Wake up! Come back to life! You are needed. We miss you. You are appreciated. There's more to accomplish. Don't go! Life is still within you. You are still needed. Rejoice, renew in spirit. Long may you work to create new worlds of wonder. Long may you create tomorrow.*

I will come back for you. Be ready.

She opens her eyes and smiles.

In the bleak room there is a feeling of great relief and a discharge of grief and sorrow.

Bridgetta senses a dark mass dissipating. It's replaced by a warmth, and she sees a faint, golden shimmer of light illuminating the space. Angelica's turquoise amulet is glowing.

Angelica looks around for any amulet glow on or near the bodies in the pods. She sees none. She hurries to the side of the nearest person, taking off her amulet. She lays the turquoise crystal under her hands over his heart. Slowly, his breathing eases. She needs more time but she has to leave.

I think I was able to reach them on a telepathic level. Stephen's mental touch contains approval, joy, resolve. Angelica has tears flowing down her cheeks. Bridgetta touches her arm. "We need to get out of here, and out of the detention center. We have to move like the wind, Angelica."

Angelica nods. She rests a hand on the man's cheek, taking her amulet off his chest and putting it around her neck. She moves quickly down the row and out the door into the nurse's area. Bridgetta is right behind her. The nurse and doctor are still out cold. Somehow, no one is in the "sex therapy" area when they reach it, except the guard Bridgetta took care of. They don't question this luck. Angelica steers them to a loading dock entrance behind the theater. They only have to dodge one pair of guards before making it to the unguarded door. They slip out into the afternoon air and walk at a sedate pace toward the gate.

Angelica to Stephen: *On our way to the gate.*

I'm in the same place as last time.

Angelica acknowledges.

When she and Bridgetta reach the gate, the guards are involved in getting control of several groups trying to enter at the same time. Using this confusion, they walk out unnoticed.

Angelica slides her arm through Bridgetta's. She speaks in a low voice. "Now you have firsthand experience with the enemy and their level of evil. Stephen and I are here because of the atrocities we just witnessed, which we linked with the disappearance of many artists and visionaries around the world—your Luminaries. We discovered it was worse than we imagined, and now you've seen it."

Angelica lowers her voice to a whisper. Bridgetta leans in to hear her. "Stephen and I think his father and my mother are prisoners in a walled fortress city somewhere. My mother is an artist of great renown. Stephen's father is an inventor, working in computers. We're sure they are here. We're looking for them."

Bridgetta says nothing but squeezes Angelica's hand. Angelica returns the gesture. They see Stephen come around a corner, heading toward them. Angelica rushes forward and he folds his arms around her. They stand silent, holding each other for several moments. Bridgetta waits.

"Let's get back to the truck," says Stephen.

The three hurry through the deserted streets. The sun is bright, but the air is chilly. They arrive at the truck. Stephen looks around, alert. Something is off.

Bridgetta opens the door, ready to climb in the truck when ten men materialize in a semicircle around them. They carry various weapons—knives, baseball bats, and a tire chain. Most of them are young and in good shape. They present a formidable front.

The one older man speaks. He's tall and wiry, with a scruffy beard and a tanned face. He holds a sawed-off shotgun. "You need to cooperate. Surrender any weapons or face the consequences. Do it right now and nobody will get hurt."

Stephen steps forward. "We have no weapons," he says, holding his hands up palms out. Angelica and Bridgetta do the same.

"Okay," says the man. "But there's something odd about you folks being out here on your own. Smells peculiar. You all might be spies or informants or something else foul. Who are you and what are you doing with the truck? Functional trucks are a rarity around these parts. Did you steal it?"

"We did not," says Angelica stepping forward. Bridgetta closes the truck door and stands beside it. "My name is Angelica; this is Stephen and Bridgetta. You all clearly have the upper hand. We're not looking for trouble but we'll make a stand if we have to." She pauses, looking thoughtful. "But maybe I have a better idea. Instead of us brawling, why don't we do this: We'll offer our best fighter against yours." She pauses again, looking at each man in the semicircle. "In fact, we'll go one better. We'll offer this woman here to fight your best fighter, right now. If our Bridgetta beats your top man, you let us go. And we drive off with the truck. If she loses, the truck is yours, and we're your prisoners." She smiles. "What do you say?" She looks at the bearded man, waiting.

He looks around at his men, scratches his beard, and grins, showing a couple of missing teeth. He likes the idea. His men grin back at him. This will be good for morale, plus give his gang a bit of amusement. Nothing like watching a woman fight, and getting her sweet ass kicked.

"I agree," he says. He waves his men back, making room for the fight.

Angelica turns to Bridgetta. "Here's your chance to use your martial arts skills to kick some serious ass."

Bridgetta nods, a smile on her face. Angelica smiles back. "Have fun." She thinks to Stephen: *Now we'll see what she's really got.* He sends her a grin.

The man who steps forward is big—over six foot and at least two-fifty. He's in good shape, with the bearing of a soldier. He has a scar along his left cheek and a tattoo on his right arm that says

"Born to Raise Hell." He comes out of the semicircle, light on his feet. Bridgetta moves up to stand opposite him, feet apart, hands loose at her sides.

Stephen and Angelica move nearer the truck, sizing up the band of men. They're ready for their next move.

The two fighters circle each other. The big man makes the first move, darting in with a right jab. Bridgetta dances out of reach. He keeps throwing punches but she evades them. He drops his guard for a second and Bridgetta catches him in the head with a round house kick. He's stunned, and she kicks him again. He goes down on one knee and his gang shouts at him.

Bridgetta steps back. He shakes his head again and lunges forward, catching one of her legs. She goes down, her head thumping on the asphalt. Her opponent pulls her toward him and punches her in the chest. She's stunned now. He releases her leg and starts to stand, one hand and a knee on the ground. In a flash, she scissors her legs around his neck, twisting her body to leverage him to the ground. She lifts her upper body and slides onto his chest, putting one knee on his throat. She leans in, adding her weight on the knee. He tries to move but she's cutting off his air. He scrabbles at her but she's immovable. Finally, he taps her thigh. She releases him, climbing off and stepping back. He stays on the ground, breathing heavily. Bridgetta gives a small bow.

It's all over. The gang is speechless. Their best fighter just *lost*.

Bridgetta turns toward Angelica and Stephen, grinning. Her opponent struggles to his feet, holding his throat. And lunges at Bridgetta. He catches her off guard and knocks her down hard.

Bridgetta rolls away from him, leaping to her feet. He barrels forward, wrapping his arms around her, pinning her arms to her sides and forcing her face into his chest. He squeezes. She brings her knee up sharply into his crotch. He releases her and staggers back, bent over, holding himself. Bridgetta dances back and delivers another kick to his head and he goes down again. This time Bridgetta stays alert, hands up in fists, watching him. He stays down.

The members of his gang are shocked, but they recover quickly and start to close in on Angelica, Bridgetta, and Stephen. Bridgetta steps toward Angelica and Stephen. They all move together, backing up against the truck.

The bearded man stands aside as four of his men come forward holding knives. Angelica glances at Bridgetta. She nods, ready. Angelica and Stephen watch the four men as they come toward them. The men jump. Angelica and Stephen spring into action. They move together in a blur. Three men hit the ground, disarmed and unconscious. Bridgetta handles the fourth. Stephen and Bridgetta stand ready while Angelica gathers all their weapons, tossing them in the back of the truck. She looks at the bearded man.

"Are we finished?" she asks.

He laughs, looking at his men on the ground. "Yeah, I think we are."

"Good. What is your name?"

"I'm Clayton," he says.

"Well Clayton, we don't really want any quarrel with you all. We have some news you might be interested in."

"I'm listening," says Clayton.

"There's a resistance movement that's growing day by day. We're a part of it. We're just coming back from trying to locate some lost relatives and loved ones in this fortress city. Will you tell us about yourself and your people?"

Clayton glances at his men. One of them sits down on the loading dock. Another sits cross-legged, back against the wall. The rest look at each other and do the same. Angelica leans against the truck with Stephen and Bridgetta flanking her. The unconscious men roll over and groan.

Clayton paces as he talks. "We roam around. We have no allegiance to anyone. We live where we please. There's plenty of deserted areas in towns, abandoned farms, parks, mining cabins, barns, and countryside homes to choose from. You name it. If it suits our needs, we use it or inhabit it."

His defeated men start to stir. One tries to sit up, shaking his head. Clayton goes to him grasping his hand to pull him up. The man puts a hand to his head and goes to the loading dock to sit.

"We despise the World State Organization," Clayton continues.

"We do whatever we can to disrupt their activities. We figured you were part of their sleeper cell informant system—we hate those bastards most of all. One of them got one of our guy's parents locked up some years ago. He never saw them again. They're probably dead. We also heard they were experimenting on some of those unfortunate folk with drugs and the like." His face is dark with anger. "That's us in a nutshell. Now, your turn. Spill."

A soft voice comes from Stephen's wrist. "He means tell what you know," says Akido. Clayton snaps a look at Stephen who grins at him.

"You've heard talk about a resistance?" asks Angelica.

Clayton nods. "Truth is," he says, "we're as close to a resistance movement you're going to find around here. There's some people banded together in their survival communities but they're just trying to get along."

"That's true," Angelica says. "The one thing that binds every one of the groups is the loss of loved ones taken into the detention centers. That atrocity is galvanizing. We're here to fan that spark into a flame that will become a wildfire. The WSO cannot be allowed to continue."

"That's a mighty fine speech. What're you doing about it?" Clayton folds his arms across his chest. All his men are awake now.

"Right now, talking to you," says Stephen. "What are you doing about it?"

Angelica lays a hand on Stephen's arm. "Are there more roaming bands like your gang? Does your group have a name?"

Clayton scratches himself. "We go by Clayton's Marauders. There are several other gangs roaming around this territory. Most of them stay out of the cities. You thinking of talking to them too?" Angelica nods. "Well then, there is one group I should warn you about. They're a lot bigger than we are. Last I heard they were close to a hundred strong. They're tough, with a real bad reputation. Their leader was a soldier and he runs his men and women like an army. Our first run in with them, we got stomped. Then the head man told us how it'd be when we met again. We agreed, so things are okay between us. But they do not like strangers."

Clayton pauses, looking off into space. "It could be they're looking for a bigger fight—like taking down STEN and the WSO. Anyway, be careful if you come across those guys."

"They sound like the kind of people we *do* want to run into," says Angelica. "What else can you tell us about them?"

"The leader's name is Big Mike. Like I said, he runs the group like a military organization. His followers call him 'Sir' but it's out of respect. He's older, maybe fifty, but there's no one in his group who'll take him on. Now that you're out here talking about resistance, he'll probably find you."

"Good," says Angelica. "Will you tell me more about how you communicate with people in the walled cities?"

"Sure. It's like this. Right now, we're in the vicinity of the Denver walled fortress. We go in and out and we have contacts inside we talk to. They give us messages for people outside. We go into Utah, all over really, and deliver the messages. Once, years ago, we went as far as California to see if I could find my daughter. I had a daughter. I got a tip on her whereabouts through the grapevine but it proved to be wrong." Clayton stops and swallows. "I'm pretty sure she's dead."

"I'm sorry."

"Yeah. Anyway, our contacts are information brokers on the inside. They're a mix. Some are in it because they're good people, others are in it for what they can get. We do some barter for the bits and pieces we pick up, but mostly we exchange information."

"How does that work? How do you get your information from your contacts on the inside?" asks Angelica.

"It's pretty simple, really. We have forged passes. And, the STEN guards have gotten lax since most of the people in the cities are like zombies. As soon as we come through the gate, we get word out with the children. Did you notice them hanging around just inside the gate?"

Angelica, Stephen and Bridgetta look at each other. Angelica shakes her head no.

"Yeah, I'm not surprised. They're cagey. They're also the best communication system. They see us and run to tell the brokers. We have a meeting place where we can do our business. There's always a list of people to find and contact. And we bring back any news from the last list we got. It's a system."

"Thank you, Clayton, for sharing that. Now, to answer what we are doing. Bridgetta and I were just inside the detention center infirmary, the facility where they're keeping all your kinfolk. I don't know if you noticed but STEN rounded up creative people, free thinkers. The first thing we will do is rescue those people from STEN. Here, in Los Angeles and in Utah."

Clayton snorts. "There's no way you can pull that off," he says. His men nod in agreement.

"We'll see," says Angelica. "We're also spreading the word about resistance. People in survival communities are getting organized."

"We haven't seen any evidence of that."

"Next time you visit Jeremiah's group, or go to Garcia and Margo's place, look," says Angelica. "Now, let's consider that our business is concluded. No hard feelings. I'll keep these three baseball bats, as a precaution. We also want our gas cans back, please. Understand that we will not tolerate you following or trying to make any future trouble for us. Clear?"

Clayton stands still, glaring at Angelica. They wait. Clayton frowns and gives a brisk nod. His men stand and step back. Except one. He is staring at the trio. He turns to Clayton.

"What the hell, Johnny?" says Clayton.

"Boss, I want to join the resistance."

"What are you talking about?"

"You saw the way that girl fought. I want to learn how to do that. And if these guys are connected to a resistance, I want in. I'm going with them, if they'll take me." He walks forward and grabs the two gas cans. Clayton stares at him.

He makes it to the truck and heaves the gas cans into the back. Angelica watches him. Stephen and Bridgetta keep their eyes on the rest of the gang. Johnny stands by the back of the truck. Angelica steps behind Stephen, toward Johnny, stopping three feet away. Everyone freezes for three heartbeats.

"Get in," Angelica says. Bridgetta turns, opens the passenger door and slides in. Stephen leaps into the truck bed and back out on the driver's side. Johnny and Angelica jump into the bed. Stephen has the truck started and moving in an instant.

Clayton takes a step forward and begins running as the truck pulls away. One of his men runs up behind him, handing him his shotgun. At the sight of the gun, Angelica and Johnny duck down. Clayton fires it at the truck, dinging the tailgate and bumper. The truck charges out of range.

Stephen turns a corner, driving fast. He races down city blocks at random. After ten minutes of this, he pulls off into a driveway that curves behind a house and stops, out of sight of the street. He slides out, with Bridgetta behind him. Angelica follows. The three of them face Johnny, sitting in the middle of the truck bed.

Johnny looks at Bridgetta with admiring eyes and with a desire in his heart to be a top-notch martial arts fighter like her. Will she teach him all she knows? She's his sensei now.

"Thank you for letting me come with you," he says. Nobody speaks. "It's okay, right?"

"Tell us why you came," says Stephen.

Johnny bites his lip. "I was born after the comet scare—no one in our family took the suicide solution. My parents had a small homestead in the mountains north of here. One night, soldiers were banging at our door. We'd planned for this, practiced what to do. I hid in the bolt hole under the floor, but they took my parents away. I haven't seen them since." He lowers his head. When he looks up, tears sparkle in his eyes. "Clayton took me in, but they don't do enough! When I saw you guys, I knew. Then she fought and..." He shakes his head. "I totally knew. You are the ones. If I stick with you, I can do something."

Angelica reaches out her hand and touches his face. "Welcome," she says.

Johnny takes a shuddering breath, and smiles.

Stephen reaches over and claps him on the shoulder. "Time to get moving." He climbs back into the cab. Bridgetta gets into the back with Johnny, Angelica takes her place next to Stephen.

The four head back in the direction of Utah.

Angelica scoots next to Stephen, laying her head on his shoulder. She is tired, body and soul. She lets Stephen's presence, the motion of the truck, and the beautiful countryside soothe her. "I planted a tracker on one of the guys we took down, just in case we need to find Clayton and his marauders again."

"Good job, love."

Johnny finds a way to get some sleep in the back of the truck. Bridgetta watches him for a while. She lays down to sleep too.

The old pickup can still muster close to fifty miles an hour with the four of them on board. They drive on as the sun is setting in front of them. The late afternoon light sparkles through the cab creating a beautiful array of dancing colors. The winter sun warms their skin, but as it dips behind the mountains the temperature drops quickly.

Stephen stops to cover the truck's headlights with a rumpled t-shirt he found under the seat. They have to travel at a slower pace in the darkness, but they make steady progress. Everyone listens for any sound of activity outside. Akido delivers occasional reports in a quiet voice. Slowly the brown pickup makes its way to the outskirts of their destination.

Stephen heads to Garcia and Margo's house where they're greeted warmly. Zack has night duty so there's room for them. Margo waves Angelica and Stephen to the room they had before. Bridgetta gets Zack's room and Johnny has a couch in the living room. After a brief snack, they all go to bed.

In their room, Angelica asks, "Akido, has Colin responded to our request for the Hawaiian summit on December 5th?"

"No Boss, not yet."

DAY THIRTEEN

UTAH SURVIVAL COMMUNITY

WHEN THE TRAVELERS get up in the morning, Margo already has breakfast on the stove. A pot of coffee sends out a wonderful aroma.

Angelica and Stephen come in together. Margo hands them each a cup of coffee and they sip with pleasure. Bridgetta comes in and gets the same treatment. Angelica sits at the kitchen table; Stephen sits beside her. Bridgetta sits opposite them.

Garcia comes through the back door, blowing on his hands. "Chilly out there this morning." He takes a steaming cup from Margo and sips. "Oh, that's good coffee." He sips again and sits beside Bridgetta. "That young man you brought came out with me this morning. He was very interested in the workings of the camp. Had a lot of questions about the resistance too."

"Where is he now?" asks Bridgetta.

"He's having breakfast in the communal kitchen," says Garcia. "He had a lot to say about you, missy." He takes another sip. "All about how you kicked the butt of the best fighter in his group—a man. And how you're going to teach him, be his sensei."

Bridgetta is embarrassed. She shakes her head in disbelief and hides behind her cup.

Margo turns from the stove with food: homemade bread, scrambled eggs with cheese, butter and her special kombucha. She takes off her apron and sits with them. Everyone digs in and talk ceases while they eat.

Garcia breaks the silence. "What can you tell us about your trip?"

Angelica takes a breath. "I'll give you the brief version with conclusions, okay?"

Garcia nods. "Works for me."

"We arrived in Denver before nightfall and Bridgetta and I were able to get in the city and spend the night in a sort of hostel. The next morning we got ourselves in the detention center infirmary. From there we broke into the psychiatric medical ward. Bridgetta was a real asset. She was courageous and strong and I would not have succeeded without her." Angelica reaches her hand to Bridgetta who takes it. They hold hands for a moment.

"We got inside the ward itself." Angelica stops again. This time Stephen holds her hand. "The Luminaries in that place are barely alive. They're kept drugged. Many are very close to death." She stops, eyes unfocused. In a whisper, she says, "They have to be our first priority."

Everyone at the table is silent, in solidarity with Angelica and her statement. She looks up, in control again. "I have an idea of how to change out the medication. Stephen and I can administer special light therapy, but they'll need medical care too. They are all in such bad shape. We can and will help them."

"Yes," says Margo.

Bridgetta takes up the report. "After we left the walled city, we ran into a marauder gang run by a scruffy looking guy named Clayton. They jumped us, demanding weapons. They wanted to take the pickup. Angelica proposed a one-on-one fight with their best fighter —against me." Bridgetta blushes.

Stephen says, "And she gave them a lesson. She demonstrated some incredible street fighting and martial art tactics. She beat their champion. She put on such a display that one of their number chose to join us so he could learn from her and help the resistance."

"Johnny," says Garcia.

"Johnny," agrees Bridgetta.

"Clearly you had quite a day," says Margo. "What's next?"

Angelica says, "Stephen and I are finalizing our plan to meet with the Aussies. Colin will know the location but otherwise we'll keep it a secret. No sleeper cell will find out and report it. We think coordinating with Colin and his people will give a boost to the worldwide resistance."

Stephen turns to Garcia. "What do you think is needed to turn the resistance into a driving force to overthrow the WSO?"

"Francisco, Jeremiah, and I have been batting this around for a while—even more since you two showed up. Colin has weighed in too." Garcia leans back in his chair. "Getting Backdoor Charlie was major. The way we see it now, we need to get the individual survivalists, the marauder gangs and all the survival communities activated as resistance fighters. We need more local leaders and we need military organization. A bunch of villagers with pitchforks won't cut it." He takes another gulp of coffee. "The Aussies have been an inspiration and a driving force. We need to improve our strategic and tactical planning and focus on turning all the survival camps into viable military outposts for the eventual fight."

"That sounds like exactly what's needed," says Angelica. "We'll add that to the agenda for our meeting with Colin. I have high hopes for this gathering. The WSO doesn't view Australia as an aggressive nation so it's been largely ignored by STEN. This means things can happen there under their noses."

"No, not aggressive," says Margo with a smile. "Sneaky."

Angelica nods, taking a sip of coffee. Her eyes are unfocused, looking at something besides the room and her company. The others at the table are quiet.

"Stephen and I have seen three survival camps. Each has a different physical setup, but the people have the same survival intention." Angelica pauses. "Earth is a large planet. Humanity is sprinkled across the surface now. If the resistance is going to succeed, there will need to be an organizational model that can be used by every sort of survival group. Do you agree?" She looks at Garcia. He nods. "Margo, may I have a piece of paper and a pencil?"

Margo gets up, goes to a drawer and pulls them out, handing them to Angelica.

"This is what I propose." She begins sketching. "In any group, there is a head, the guy in charge." She draws a circle with a line extending down from the bottom of it. "Next, there are three generals, division heads—some sort of title—who are in charge of the major functions of the group. Right now, those functions may be survival groups, military groups, information dissemination." She's drawn three more circles in a row with lines coming from the top of them, connected to a horizontal line below the top circle's line. "Below each of these three, the pattern repeats—a person in charge with people working below him in that area. Each distinct area has someone in charge with others helping him. Do you see what I mean?"

Margo answers. "Yes. Here in Utah, we have something like this. I see how beneficial it will be to lay out the plan in a chart like this. Plus, it simplifies it for any type of group. Can I work with this?"

"Of course." Angelica smiles, handing her the paper. To the group she says, "What do you think of this idea? It seems to me that right now, the resistance needs to be military. The whole WSO hierarchy has to be demolished. Because of this, I think that Colin might be a good person to fill the top circle. He seems to be the most military minded. What do you think?"

"That makes sense," says Garcia. "If he'll do it."

"It will be our job to convince him," says Stephen.

Margo is looking at Angelica's rough sketch. "The beauty of this is that it makes a place for everyone. Even children can have a spot in this organization. Every person can contribute. I like it!" She looks up grinning. "I'll be working on this."

"Garcia, do you know how many survival groups there are in the U.S.?" asks Bridgetta. "I never heard it talked about in LA."

"Colin reports he's had messages from Columbus in Ohio and Norfolk, Virginia. He said there seems to be something happening in Scotland and Japan," says Garcia.

"Do you think the pockets of resistance can be linked together?" asks Angelica.

"I do," says Garcia. Bridgetta and Margo nod in agreement.

"Good," says Stephen.

"We'll be going over all of this with Colin when we meet," says Angelica. "Should emissaries be sent to the recognized survival communities in the United States?"

Garcia answers. "No, I don't think so, not yet. You talk with Colin, and we'll talk with Francisco and Jeremiah, about the best way to get groups activated. I'll use Backdoor Charlie to contact Columbia and Norfolk and find out what they're doing."

"Now, a new topic," he continues. "Bridgetta, how about you take over martial arts training at our camp, at least until Angelica and Stephen get back from their meeting with Colin. Maybe you can train some other instructors. Maybe apprentice that new kid, Johnny. What do you think?" Bridgetta looks at Angelica, who nods.

"That would be great. I'd love to!" She leans back with a grin.

"Good. That's settled. We'll get you a house you can live in," says Garcia.

"Cool!"

Akido speaks. "STEN has sent out a network-wide alert. They have circulated pictures of two women wanted for questioning about a disturbance at the Denver Detention Center. The pictures are blurry, but do show you, Angelica, and Bridgetta. There are also written descriptions that are accurate."

"Well. We'll have to stay away from STEN troops then," says Angelica.

"No problem," says Bridgetta.

"Now," says Stephen, "Angelica and I are going off by ourselves for a bit. We'll be back for dinner."

"Have fun, kids!" Margo waves to them.

Stephen leads Angelica to the room they share. He pulls her through the door, shutting it behind her. He traps her body between his and the door. He holds her face in his hands, leaning forward to kiss her lips, softly at first, then with more passion. She wraps her arms around him and kisses him back with enthusiasm. He moves his hands down to enfold her body. They move to get closer to each other. Their bodies are braced together against the door. When they

175

separate, both are breathless. "Wow." Stephen leans his forehead against Angelica's. "These bodies have quite the chemical reactions."

Angelica clutches him tightly. "My knees are weak."

"I'll hold you as long as you need."

They stand together. Stephen leans his head against Angelica's. She rests her head against his chest. Their hearts beat together. Each opens their mind to the other sharing a flood of emotions. Angelica looks up at Stephen.

"These bodies…"

"They're a playground, aren't they?"

Angelica giggles. "You said it. A playground." She laughs out loud. Stephen joins her. They separate, but still clasp hands.

"Let's go sit in the garden," she says.

They make their way to the backyard, dragging a couple of chairs near a large lilac bush in the bottom of the garden. There's evidence of the horses but they've been moved. They position their chairs out of sight of the house, close together so they can hold hands.

"This is a beautiful planet. It's peaceful to have a moment to sit in its sun," says Angelica.

"It is," says Stephen, eyes closed, head back to catch the sun on his face.

They're quiet, soaking in the sun, hands entwined.

"Akido, what has GA concluded was the downfall of the humans on this planet?" asks Angelica.

"GA accessed every database available. She started her research when the first Luminary message was received. She has concluded that human downfall began when they started using substances to affect the body and its connection with the mind. They chose to rely on the crutch of drugs instead of their own capability. Life became all about the physical, leaving the spiritual behind."

Angelica has her head back, eyes closed. "Maybe they reach for the physical—either to enhance sensation or dull it—because they can't have mind to mind connection." She squeezes Stephen's hand. He joins their minds and they have a moment of perfect harmony.

Akido speaks softly. "Boss. Just received an email from Colin Hainsworth. Read it aloud?"

"Proceed."

"'Dear Angelica and Stephen. Hawaii sounds like the perfect place to meet. I know Turtle Bay. Will arrive December 5 noonish. I'll be bringing some friends. Can't wait to meet you in person! Love, Colin.'"

"This will be fun." Stephen is grinning. "I'm going to get started on drawing up modified hovercraft plans so it can be manufactured on Earth. I'll ask Garcia for a place I can spread out."

"Good. While you're working on the hovercraft, I'll see how Bridgetta is getting along setting up her martial arts training. I can use a good sparring match. I might be able to teach her something. Or maybe I can learn something. Or find a trainee I can pin quickly." She gives him a sideways glance. "You remember our Academy days. I took on anyone and beat them, except you, of course."

"Of course." Stephen laughs. "I recall those days with fond memories—and bruises. We were the best. Still are. You were awesome in the training ring. That's another thing I like about you."

"Thank you." Angelica bats her eyes.

Stephen stands. "See you later, beautiful." He walks toward the gate.

Angelica sits up. "Stephen." He turns. She blows him a kiss. He grins as he leaves.

Angelica stays in the garden, leaning back with her eyes closed. She's perfectly relaxed, perceiving her surroundings without using her eyes. She lifts out of her Earth body, floating into the air as herself, a being with no corporeal substance. Continuing to rise, she looks out over the landscape. She sees the people below as shining spots—white hot, but also tinged with colors. Still rising, she directs her attention north, to the Utah STEN outpost. It looms dark brown, gray, and black on the horizon. She searches for the Luminaries confined within. They are just a few faint sparks buried below the dark colors. She wills it and is in the space near them. She moves into the middle of the faint dots of light and radiates her own light outward, like a sun. She radiates health and love and strength.

She radiates until the pinpoints brighten, weakly. She promises to return. She lingers, emanating hope and intention. She swells to encompass each dot. She acknowledges their fight, and affirms the choice they have: endure or move on, leaving their corporeal form. It's an instant of communion that briefly holds off the blackness oozing toward them.

"Angelica. Angelica!" Bridgetta shakes her shoulder and she snaps back to her Earth body. She opens her eyes and blinks.

"I'm sorry I woke you. I just wanted to talk to you alone."

"It's okay, I was just thinking. What is it?"

"I'm not sure how to say this." Bridgetta perches on the chair next to Angelica.

"Just speak your mind. You can't say anything that will make me think less of you." Angelica smiles gently.

Bridgetta bits her lip. She's sitting on the edge of the chair, wringing her hands. Angelica is surprised at this show of nerves. "What is making you nervous?" she asks.

"Well, two things." Bridgetta pauses, looking at her feet. "I'm not sure I fit into this new order you and the others are creating. I know I'm good at martial arts. I had an amazing teacher. I know I can train others—I did that in LA. But it was more fun and less serious."

"And smaller?"

"Yes! Smaller. You guys are talking about the entire planet. That's too big for me."

"You grew up in Los Angeles?"

"Yeah."

"Tell me about your life there."

"When I lived with Sensei, it was good. We didn't go out much. He had a garden, we grew a lot of our food. We had to go out for some things. I'd do that but I was afraid. I knew martial arts but I was small. I was always watching for STEN troops." Bridgetta sits back in the chair. "After Sensei was taken, I got very good at becoming invisible when I had to go out for supplies."

"Did you have to avoid many people?"

"No. There were a lot of buildings but almost no people."

"I understand that before 2060, the greater Los Angeles area was home to nineteen million people. Now there are maybe a million people there." Angelica watches Bridgetta. "If you were to look at the stars in the night sky, you see many. What if the next night the sky was almost empty of stars? That's what's happened to the population of Earth since the WSO took over."

Bridgetta looks toward the house. The sun has gone behind it. She doesn't speak for a long moment. "The Earth is large but the number of people is small." She looks at Angelica, who nods. "If I can train ten, twenty, a hundred guys in martial arts, that's a lot compared to the total number of people." Angelica nods again. "And I'd be in that structure you drew for Margo, right?"

"You would."

Bridgetta is quiet. After a moment, she says, "Okay. I can do that." She pauses again. Angelica waits. "But there's something else. There's still the matter of my parents."

"Yes?"

"I mentioned it when we met. They're pretty high up in the WSO. How can I be part of the resistance if I have parents like that?" Her anguish is palpable when she raises her eyes to Angelica's.

"When was the last time you spoke to your parents?" Angelica asks.

"The day after STEN raided our dojo and took away my Sensei. I hadn't spoken to them for years, but I begged them to help him. They refused. It got pretty ugly. I had to back off because they threatened to send me to STEN training. We haven't spoken since. I slipped away and made my own way."

"They haven't tried to contact you at all?"

"No, not that I know of."

"Would you speak to them, connect with them now, if they found you?"

"No."

"Do you feel any connection to them?"

"No. No, I don't." Bridgetta seems surprised at this. "I hadn't thought of it that way. My mother gave birth to me but she and my dad ignored me. I always had nannies. They did send me to the dojo but that was to keep me out of their hair. And that's where they dumped me when they couldn't be bothered with a kid anymore. Being left there was the best thing. I never missed them."

"It sounds like you made a sound decision about your relationship with your parents."

"Yes, I did. I made the decision to jettison them, way back then." Bridgetta sits up straighter. "I have no connection with them." She's relaxed and smiling now. "I *can* do what you need!"

"Good," says Angelica. "How about we go look at the facilities here right now?"

"Yes!" Bridgetta and Angelica stand. Bridgetta throws her arms around Angelica. "Thank you! I know I can help now. This is great!"

"You're welcome," says Angelica.

As they leave the garden, she touches Stephen's mind. *Bridgetta's parents are high level WSO. We may have to deal with that later.*

We will if we need to.

Bridgetta leads the way to the outdoor training area where several men and boys are practicing. Angelica and Bridgetta watch them. Bridgetta keeps her eyes on two teenage boys sparring. She's quiet, then strides over to the mat.

"You guys have some pretty good moves. Can I show you a couple of things?" she asks. The boys look at her, shaking their heads. The older one says, "You're a girl. What can you show us?"

"Come at me."

"What?"

"Come at me. If I can repel an attack, can I show you a couple of things?"

The boys look at each other. The younger one answers, "Sure, if you can." He leaps at her. Bridgetta easily steps aside and flips him on his back. She gives him a small bow.

The older boy comes forward, hand outstretched as if to shake her hand. Bridgetta doesn't move. He takes one more step, she grabs his hand, pulls him forward and flips him over her hip. Both boys are on the floor, looking sheepish.

"Okay," says the older boy. "You can probably teach us a thing or two."

"Cool," says Bridgetta. "I'll be in the gym tomorrow morning. See you then?"

"Yeah," the boys answer. They walk away, whispering and looking back.

"Well done," says Angelica. She and a grinning Bridgetta head for home.

DAY FOURTEEN

MORNING, UTAH SURVIVAL COMMUNITY

IT's NOT much past the crack of dawn and light is just beginning outside. Not even a rooster has announced the new day. Stephen and Angelica are up and in the kitchen. Roosting birds nestle in the bushes outside the window, their soft sounds filtering through the glass. Stephen makes coffee, Angelica has her head in the refrigerator looking for eggs.

Garcia comes into the kitchen through the back door. He goes straight for the coffee, pouring a cup. He leans against the counter, sighs, and takes a sip.

"What's happened?" asks Stephen.

"Travis is dead and Doc Crawford has disappeared."

"Oh," says Angelica. "Did Doc kill Travis?"

"Don't know. Probably," says Garcia.

"Wow. What do you suppose it means, Garcia?" asks Angelica.

"Well, I guess one spy down, but another one on the loose." Garcia rubs his face. "I think it means we're going to have a lot more trouble from STEN because of sleeper cell spies."

"I agree," says Stephen.

"We'll need to be very sure of people we let into resistance activity planning and execution," says Angelica.

"I'm not happy about the need for paranoia," says Garcia.

"Not paranoia, vigilance," says Angelica.

"Okay." Garcia shakes his head. "Enough of that. What are you two up to today?"

"Angelica and I have some plans to go over," says Stephen. "Then we'll be spending time with Bridgetta in her training center."

"Stephen and I will be leaving early this afternoon. We'll check in with Francisco in LA, get a little rest and leave at sunset for our meeting with Colin."

"Sounds good," says Garcia.

Stephen leads Angelica to the space where he spread out his plans for the Earth edition hovercraft. She looks over his drawings with interest.

"I remember when you won first prize for the newest design and technology advancement for your hovercraft prototype," she says. "I was impressed by it, but more impressed by you. I liked how confident and smart you were. And there was that touch of brashness. And I remember how our science professor grabbed the patent on it before you even graduated." Angelica shakes her head.

"My life might have been much different if he hadn't done that." Stephen pauses. "I'm glad he did."

"Me too." Angelica looks back at the plans. "I see you've altered the power source to solar. How long does the battery hold charge before it needs recharging?"

"I did a bit of modification so it will run the craft for twelve hours. And there's a spare for emergencies."

"How long will it take to charge?"

"With my solar technology, charging for a day gives you the twelve-hour running time."

"Clever, as expected." Angelica traces her finger over a part of the drawing. "I like the change in the body shape."

"I've made it in a six-person configuration, but it can be modified for larger numbers. Just add a second or third main battery for power. If there are manufacturing capabilities on Earth, they should have no trouble making this hovercraft. Even a small machine shop could put it together."

"You've done it again, my love." Angelica comes around the table and leans in to give him a kiss. "Now, I'm going to see Bridgetta in her new training center. Want to come?"

"I'm done here, so yes." Stephen gathers his papers, putting them in a satchel. "Let's go."

They leave the house and walk toward the training area. The sun is out and the sky is clear but there's a chill in the air. As they walk, they hear snatches of conversation from both men and animals.

"Yesterday, Bridgetta was questioning her ability to do what we're asking her to do. I spoke with her..."

"And she changed her mind."

"She did. Then she slipped right back into teaching with a couple of young men last night. I'm curious about how she's doing this morning."

"Let's find out." Stephen holds the gym door for her and they enter.

Bridgetta is a picture of confidence as she conducts a training class in front of about thirty interested men and women, young and old. They study her every move as she demonstrates a takedown with Johnny. He stands and she executes a flurry of one-two punches. Johnny staggers to the ground. He shakes his head and jumps up, ready for more.

Angelica watches Bridgetta. Her attention is drawn to a young man standing off to the side. He's watching Bridgetta with a calculating look. In the next instant, the look is gone and his face is blank. She asks Stephen, "Do you know who that is over there?"

Stephen looks. "No." He feels Angelica's mind link.

Something about him. You get it?

Yes, there is something. He doesn't feel quite right. We'll ask Garcia to keep an eye on him.

Bridgetta spots them and speaks to her class. The students pair up for practice and she runs over to Angelica and Stephen. The watchful young man follows her at a slower pace.

"Do you see how many people came today?" She's excited. "Those boys from last night spread the word. And Johnny is like a sponge, soaking up everything."

"You made an impression," says Angelica.

"She sure did," says the young man as he walks up. He extends his hand. "I'm Juan Carlos, a friend of Zack's."

"Are you new here?" Stephen asks in a pleasant tone, shaking his hand.

"Yeah, I arrived just a couple of days ago. I've been wandering," says Juan Carlos.

"How interesting! I'd like to hear about your adventures sometime," says Angelica.

"I'd be happy to tell you," Juan Carlos replies. His smile seems a bit false.

"Juan Carlos is also an instructor. He's going to help with the training. He's excellent with sword work. We're lucky he wandered our way." Bridgetta smiles, looking at Juan Carlos shyly.

"Happy to help," says Juan Carlos. His face is more watchful than warm.

"I'm glad everything is working out," says Angelica. "We'll leave you to it. Until later, Bridgetta. Juan Carlos." She gives Bridgetta a brief hug.

That young man will definitely bear watching.

Agreed.

Stephen and Angelica make their way back to Garcia's house, exchanging greetings with community members as they walk.

JUAN CARLOS WATCHES the couple walk away. He looks back at Bridgetta working with one of her students. He's sure those two, the couple, are the troublemakers. They are the pair Doc Crawford reported at their midnight meeting. He's going to have to find a way to get to the Utah STEN office to send a report to Damien and to get the latest intelligence dispatches.

Soon.

Margo is in the kitchen when Angelica and Stephen arrive. She says, "I made you a lunch to take." She indicates bread, fried chicken and apples in a small basket. There's also a flask of water and a jar of kombucha.

"You are too good to us," says Stephen, giving her a kiss on the cheek.

She blushes. "It's you who are good to us."

Angelica gives her a hug. "Is Garcia around?"

"No, he's gone on a reconnaissance run. Can I help with anything?"

"We wanted to ask him to keep an eye on the new man, Juan Carlos. Not to worry, it's just that Stephen and I get a feeling of *something not quite right* from him. If he is working for the enemy, he'll need to go somewhere to report. It might be better if he doesn't get that chance."

"We can watch him."

"Thank you."

Angelica and Stephen put their lunch in the satchel with the hovercraft plans. They wave good bye to Margo and head for the hovercraft.

UTAH STEN DETENTION CENTER

Doc Crawford sits in the conference room at the top of the Utah detention center. He can see all the way to the Great Salt Lake through the windows that look north and west. He's nervous about this video conference with the head guy. He turns his chair as the screen on the wall comes to life. A STEN soldier appears. He says, "Colonel Johnson will be with you in a moment."

Doc nods. The soldier moves out of view. Doc waits. Minutes pass. He taps his fingers on the table, his face twisted in annoyance. As soon as he sees motion in the other room, he stills his fingers and quiets his face. Colonel Johnson appears. Doc stays seated.

"Damien, how are you?" he asks.

Damien frowns and remains standing. "What have you got to report?"

"I told you about the two strangers talking resistance in a meeting of the camp leaders."

"Old news. What new information do you have?"

"They disappeared, went to Denver."

"I know that too." Damien folds his arms across his chest. "Do you have new information or not?"

"While they were gone, I talked to as many people in the camp as I could. There's something strange about those two—they pretty much appeared from nowhere. And they're getting people into the idea of resistance. They seem to have a way to talk to other resistance-type people in other parts of the world. They may even have a way to spy on you guys."

"Do you know this for sure?"

Doc shifts in his seat. "Nooo. As usual, everything I learned is rumor and gossip. I *was* at that first meeting, but you know that."

"When can I expect some workable intelligence?" Damien's voice drips sarcasm.

"Well, about that." Doc turns away from the screen, shifting his eyes to the windows.

"What have you done?"

Doc is silent for a moment.

"Well?"

Doc turns around to face Damien. "There was a kid, Travis. I was working on recruiting him. I talked to him while that meeting was happening. He looked receptive. He even met the new contact, Juan Carlos." Doc pauses. "So, I'm talking to people, asking questions while I patch up cuts and breaks. It's what I've always done, no problem. Then, a couple of days ago, Travis came barging into my house after dark. Something happened, something changed his mind. He's belligerent, raising his voice, poking me in the chest, calling me a traitor. I tried to quiet him down. He wouldn't shut up. I punched him, bloodied his nose. He went crazy, pulled out a knife and lunged at me. In the struggle, he got stabbed in the neck. Got his jugular and—he died." Doc stands and paces to the window and back. "He made a hell of a mess. I figured my time in the Utah camp was finished so I came here." He looks up at Damien.

Now Damien is pacing. "You're no good to me now. I need people who blend, listen and report. Did you even find out what happened to change this Travis guy's mind?" Doc starts to speak, Damien holds up his hand. "No, you couldn't even do that."

"Sir." Doc is standing now. Damien stops, looking at him. "Sir, I'd like to serve in another location."

"You can't go to LA or Denver. If the camps are talking to each other, you'll be recognized eventually wherever you go."

"Yes, sir, I thought of that. Maybe I could work at the training center in Denver. I did a good job for the WSO and STEN for many years. I could teach the new recruits what I've learned."

"Hmmm. Possible."

"You could arrange transport for me to the Denver walled fortress—"

"I have a different idea. You make your way to Denver however you can. When you get there, report to the center commander."

"But—"

"Did you think there would be no consequence for your action?" Doc stares at Damien. "No."

"Good. Dismissed." The screen goes black. Doc sits back down. After a few minutes, a soldier comes in, holds the door open and gestures to Doc. "This way." Doc gets up and leaves.

In Los Angeles, Damien turns from the screen to look out his window. The sky is dotted with clouds, allowing intermittent sun. It doesn't match his mood. "Damn it, Doc!" he mutters. Doc was a good agent but he's clearly past his prime. "If he makes it to Denver…" Damien shakes his head. "Juan Carlos, I'm counting on you to find out what's happening."

AFTERNOON, LOS ANGELES SURVIVAL COMMUNITY

The trip to Los Angeles is uneventful. The skies are quiet and the air warms as Angelica and Stephen head southwest toward the coast. Stephen is flying low, hugging the terrain. Angelica stills her mind to be in the present. She observes the surroundings, using all her Earth body's senses. She smells dust and feels the breeze on her skin. Stephen is doing the same as he drives. It's peaceful.

When they arrive, they park the hovercraft in the backyard of the house they first stayed in. They walk to the meeting place in the Disney complex. Francisco is sitting outside in the sun.

"Back again," he says.

"Yes, briefly. We leave at dusk for a summit with Colin," says Angelica.

"Garcia just sent out an update on everything you all talked about yesterday and today." Francisco tips up his sunglasses and grins at them. "You don't waste any time, do you?"

"We haven't found time wasting to be advantageous," says Stephen with a serious expression which he holds for two seconds before laughing. Francisco laughs with him.

"Best to move quickly in these sorts of circumstances," says Angelica.

"I hear you," says Francisco. "Do you need anything from me?"

"May we use the house we stayed in before? We need to sleep before we leave," says Angelica.

"Of course," says Francisco. He tips his sunglasses back down and leans back. "See you when you get back."

Angelica and Stephen wave and walk away. After sleeping until the sky is darkening, they rise. Someone has left them sandwiches, oranges, and a bottle of water in the kitchen. They eat the sandwiches with pleasure and pack the oranges to take with them. They make their way to the hovercraft and take off, once again heading southwest.

There's still a glow left by the sun as they fly over the island of Catalina. The ocean ahead of them is blue, darkening to black as night falls. A quarter moon is rising with its thumbnail of light. The smell of the sea seeps into the hovercraft.

Stephen has activated the hovercraft's camouflage, making it invisible to radar. He sets the autopilot and sits back, head against the head rest. Angelica does the same beside him.

"Akido," says Angelica.

"Yes, Boss?"

"Silent mode, until I call you again."

"Yes, Boss.

Angelica and Stephen are at rest. It's another moment of peace. The hovercraft flies on. Sometime later, they see whales and porpoises breaking the water, making it shimmer in the faint moonlight.

"Look Stephen, just like at home." Angelica watches the spectacle with delight as they pass over it. Stephen takes her hand.

"Now that we're on our way, the idea of being on an island during the Celebration of Light is even more appealing," she says.

"I agree. It will be beneficial for us to experience the spiritual aspect of this planet."

They fall silent, watching the sky and sea as they fly. The moon is small, high in the sky. The stars and planets shine like jewels. The constellations are a storybook on night parade. It's quiet, floating in space with the heavens and stars. In the distance they see the lights of a vessel, too far away to identify.

"What do you think?" Angelica asks.

"It could be a STEN patrol. It's traveling north to south. It could be a family living on the sea, following the currents and living on the bounty of the ocean."

Angelica opens her mind link with Stephen and enfolds him, acknowledging his beautiful thought. He responds, duplicating her action. They travel on.

The moon is shining a narrow path down on the water in the same direction they're traveling. *Just like in the Hawaiian legend,* Angelica thinks.

She serves the food Margo sent with them. They eat and drink. They rest and watch the universe. They sleep. As they near the islands they spot another pod of whales.

"Can we hear them?" asks Angelica.

Stephen makes adjustments to the controls and the sound of whale song fills the hovercraft. Their sounds are melodic, sensual. A spiritual harmony flows through the octaves and harmonics. Angelica is enthralled. She flows her joy and happiness to Stephen through their link. The whales are following the same route to the islands, but the hovercraft pulls ahead. Angelica and Stephen listen to the whale conversations as long as they can. As the songs fade, a meteor shower begins streaming overhead.

"The universe loves us tonight." Stephen is grinning.

"If we believed in signs, the events in this journey would certainly portend good things." Angelica is grinning too. They lean back in their seats and enjoy.

A soft beep from the console signals the approach of their destination. They see faint outlines of islands in the moonlight. Stephen makes a course correction to take them to the north shore of Oahu. They see no lights in the dark landscape on any of the islands.

Stephen uses his binovision to spot the Turtle Bay buildings, heading for a spot east of them. He brings the hovercraft in for a landing on the beach of a shallow cove, moving in under the trees and plants for cover. He turns the hovercraft to face the beach and ocean. He and Angelica sit quietly, listening to the waves lapping the shore.

"We've been at this for a long time—rescuing extraordinary beings throughout the universe," says Angelica. "Back home, the Celebration of Light will be starting. And here it's the Makahiki, taking place at the same time. Our ceremonies always started with telling the Myth of Creation."

"Tell it to me now." Stephen reaches for her hand.

Angelica takes a deep breath. The hovercraft doors are open and a tropical breeze plays around them, bringing sounds of night creatures and the rich scent of blossoms and earth. She recites:

In the beginning, before life as we know it, the Gods played.
Their game was good, but they wanted more.
They chose to give life to new forms. The first form was light. The light was warm.
The light flowed, sparked, burned, healed.
The light was gathered into stars and their planets.
The Gods gave lifelight to smaller forms, made in the image of the Gods.
The Gods called them beings and placed them on the planets.

To the Luminaries, they gave two planets.
To the Luminaries, they gave stewardship of the light of the Gods.
To mark this legacy in this time, the heavens explode with starlight and we are
reminded.
Light brings life to all things.
Darkness is the absence of light.
Light can be or not be.
The will of the Gods is the will of Luminaries.
Be the light!

Angelica and Stephen are silent. The eastern horizon is pale gold, ready to receive the sun. In a single motion, they climb out of the hovercraft and walk toward the beach, shoulder to shoulder, minds linked, expanding, expanding to encompass the ocean water, the sand, the rocks, the plants, the sky, the moon, the stars.

Their Earth bodies stand at water's edge. They leave them, and free from earthly bonds, they frolic in the dawn sky, rejoicing in their celebration of light.

DAY FIFTEEN

MORNING, TURTLE BAY, OAHU, HAWAII

THE SUN CRESTS the horizon with brilliance. Two dolphins rise from the water in front of them, calling in their high, clacking voices. Angelica and Stephen come back to their Earth bodies, laughing with joy.

"Thank you, brothers, for reminding us of our duty!" Angelica runs into the ocean, diving under the waves. The dolphins come to her and they swim together. Stephen joins them and the four play in the warm water.

With a final nudge at the humans, the dolphins swim away. Angelica and Stephen walk onto the beach and flop down in the sand. The sun is already warm on their skin and a faint breeze dries them.

After this interlude, they make quick work of setting up a camp. The hovercraft is hidden with undergrowth after they unload their supplies. Angelica discovers a cache left by Margo.

"There's beef jerky, fresh water, and kombucha. Oh, and bread and cheese. A feast! Let's eat then take nap. We want these bodies rested for the rest of the day." Angelica hands a jar of kombucha to Stephen.

"Good idea," he says, drinking with pleasure.

They finish their meal and rest, sleeping for several hours. They wake refreshed and stroll toward the water.

Motion up the beach catches their eyes. People are fishing— several Hawaiians fishing with handmade poles. A basket of fish is behind them on the sand. Angelica and Stephen walk toward them. As they get closer they see it's two older men with a boy. The boy stares. The men dart them quick glances.

Angelica watches them carefully as she and Stephen approach. She knows Stephen is alert. She takes his hand and they slow their pace. She stops, turning toward the water. She steps beside Stephen so she's hidden from the fisherman. She points to the water, whispering to Stephen. "The older men are signaling to someone out of sight in the jungle behind them."

"I saw that too. We'll go toward them without any threat and you can do your 'friendly with the natives' thing."

"Right, my 'friendly with the natives thing.'" She punches him lightly on the arm and laughs. He joins her.

The older fishermen are now watching them openly. Angelica and Stephen raise their hands in greeting as they walk up to them.

"Aloha," says Stephen.

"Aloha," says the oldest man.

"I am Stephen, this is Angelica. Your fishing is good this morning." Stephen indicates the basket.

"Yes, *Ku'ula* has smiled on us today. My name is Haku and this is my son Kapueo and grandson Kaholo." Haku has a quizzical look on his dark, weathered face. His eyes and mouth show heavy laugh lines. "What are you doing here? How did you get here?"

Angelica steps forward. "First, we are very happy to meet you. We came last night from the mainland, in an experimental craft. We're representatives of the resistance movement that is growing all around the world. We're working to help make it a strong, world-wide movement. We came to your beautiful island to meet with people from Australia, who should be arriving soon. We'll be making plans that will result in a new future for Earth and the people left on it."

The three Hawaiians stare at her.

"Are there many people on the islands?" ask Stephen.

Kapueo speaks. He is a younger, less wrinkled version of his father. His arms bulge with muscle. "No, not many." He eyes them with barely veiled suspicion.

"Is there a WSO or STEN presence?" asks Angelica.

Haku spits. "No. At first they came around in planes and a few ships but we made ourselves scarce. They tried to stay but we harassed them—sinking small craft, sabotaging supplies, dumping vehicles into bodies of water. They never caught us. Finally, they left. We get an occasional flyover, that's all."

Angelica smiles, turning to Stephen. "We've picked a very good place for our meeting."

"Yes, we have," he says. He addresses Haku. "Do you and your people live in the resort building?"

"Some do." He pauses, examining Stephen's face before he continues. "Most of us have dwellings in and around the grounds."

"Are there many of you?" asks Angelica.

Haku doesn't answer at once. Kapueo puts his hand on his father's arm and speaks to him in Hawaiian. Haku shakes his head. "My son is not sure we can trust you. He doesn't want me to reveal any more about our village."

Angelica nods. "I understand." She squats down in front of Kaholo. He has the same stocky build as his father. She speaks to the boy. "We arrived before dawn. We flew most of the night with the moon and stars. Where we come from, it's time for the Celebration of Light. This is similar to your Makahiki celebration. That starts soon, yes?" The boy nods. "This morning Stephen and I had our own ceremony. Then we swam with dolphins."

At that moment, two dolphins chatter from the water, diving and leaping in unison. Kaholo is open mouthed. Kapueo shakes his head ruefully.

"Fine," he says, staring at the dolphins. "The gods are speaking." He gives them a hard stare. "To answer your question, we have about eighty-five people living on this end of the island. I have a wife, Lani, and two other children. We live quiet lives, following the old ways."

The boy Kaholo speaks up. "When we saw you walking up the beach, we thought you might be part of the gang."

"The gang?" asks Angelica.

"You may have seen me using a signaling system," says Haku. "We have to be vigilant because of a roaming gang of thugs, mostly teenagers and young men. They live on Maui but they have boats and think of themselves as pirates. They raid the coastal villages periodically, demanding tribute. They steal food and livestock. And they harass the younger women. It's become a threat to our safety. They demand our best catches and rob even the poorest of our community. They're a real problem. They show up almost every month, making their demands. We can't defend against them, mostly because we don't want to harm our youth."

Kapueo continues the story. "Our community has been up in arms about this for some time. But there's not much we can do. We never know exactly when they'll come. They're really just a symptom of a greater disease. These young people are more apathetic than anything else. They reject the old ways and have nothing to replace them." He shakes his head. "They seem lost. They have no sense of being part of a group. The days are gone when they are willing to listen to their elders, taking pride in becoming apprentices and mastering our way of life. The way of the Kahuna is dying." Kapueo sighs. "That's got to change."

"Way of the Kahuna?" says Angelica.

Haku answers. "A kahuna is a life specialist, a professional, a tradesman, one who helps his community and people with his skills. He can be an almost mystical specialist. He or she has a skill like navigation and canoeing, knife making, cooking and herbs, leadership. The kahunas hand their skills down each generation, teaching the children so our families, community, and culture will survive."

"Thank you for telling us this. We may be able to help you," Angelica says. "We mean that sincerely. It sounds like these young men pirates have lost their sense of purpose." Haku and Kapueo nod. "Maybe we can help rekindle their purpose." She pauses. "May we meet with your community leaders?"

"We have a Chief and two Elders," Haku says. "If you can help us with the young pirates, the Chief will want to speak with you. His name is Akela."

"We'll be staying just a few days, then we have to go back to the mainland. May we come to your village tomorrow evening?" asks Angelica.

"I'll arrange it," says Haku. "Be in the courtyard in front of the building as the sun touches the ocean. You can join our Makahiki."

"Thank you."

The sound of a plane sends them into cover under the trees. They peer through the fronds at a low flying plane.

"That's our Australian friends," says Stephen. "Let's go meet them." He grabs Angelica's hand. They turn to the Hawaiians. "Thank you. We'll see you tomorrow night."

AFTERNOON, AUSSIES ARRIVE

Stephen and Angelica run inland, following the motor sounds. They arrive just as an old plane is taxiing off a paved roadway south of the beach and resort buildings. The propellers wind down to a stop. The back end of the plane cracks open, descending to become a ramp. A small vehicle rolls down the ramp with two men inside. A third person, a young woman, follows on a small motorcycle.

The man driving raises his fist shouting, "Angelica and Stephen! G'day, mates!" The vehicles roar across the grass toward them. Angelica and Stephen, both grinning, raise their hands in greeting.

The vehicle skids to a stop, the motorcycle right behind.

The driver leaps out. He's deeply tanned with smile lines etched around his mouth and green eyes. "I'm Colin," he says. "This is my second in command, Liam. And Missy, clearly the prettiest of us three. She's the logistics whiz for our organization." Liam is tall and blond. He's dressed in shorts and a T-shirt, both showing well-muscled limbs. Missy is a stunning redhead with pale skin and a sprinkle of freckles across her nose. Her bright blue eyes sparkle with intelligence.

"We're very happy to meet you!" says Angelica.

"Very happy," says Stephen.

"So, do you have a camp, somewhere we're going to hunker down for our big meeting?" asks Colin.

"Yes, just north, on the beach. Not far," says Stephen.

"Great. Climb aboard, we'll drive up there. This dune buggy loves to roam."

Liam helps Angelica into the back of the dune buggy. Stephen hops up beside her. They're sitting on stowed gear.

In minutes they're at the beach. Stephen speaks over the engine, "Just there, on the right." Colin steers off the beach, stopping near the hidden hovercraft.

"A bit sparse, but no worries. We can handle that," says Colin. "Okay children, let's get set up."

Liam and Missy start taking bundles out of the dune buggy. In minutes there are two small tents under the trees. A camp stove is set up on the sand with a cooler next to it. A pot of water is set on a burner.

"Tea will be ready shortly," says Missy.

Angelica and Stephen stand by, admiring the coordination.

"Once we all have a cuppa and some biscuits, we can get down to business," says Colin.

Liam has cups for everyone and tin of tea. Colin makes tea, tossing a handful of leaves in the pot. After a minute, he pours cups and Missy hands them around. A tin of biscuits is opened. Angelica and Stephen sit cross-legged on the sand with their tea. The Aussies sit, completing a circle around the biscuit tin. Colin snags one and bites it with pleasure. He takes a sip of tea.

"Oh, I needed that." He nibbles and sips. He gestures to Angelica and Stephen. "Tuck in. The biscuits are made by the granny bakers. You'll love them."

Angelica and Stephen each grab a cookie and take a bite.

"Oh, that is good," says Angelica. She takes another bite followed by a sip of tea. Stephen mirrors her actions.

"Good. Now everyone is fortified," says Colin, "we can get started. I'll begin. As you know, we come from Darwin, located in northeastern Australia. Our country has been largely ignored by the WSO. They have one walled fortress in Sydney, which was the largest city. Most of our continent is wild, with population clusters on the coasts. Darwin is a coastal outpost, but it's far from everything else. We've developed a very workable model for a survival community. Lately we've been establishing a resistance organization. We even have a name. We call ourselves the New Civilization Freedom Fighters—NCFF."

Liam interjects, "Yeah, they have WSO and STEN—now we've got a cool acronym."

"That's right. And the letters look good on uniforms," says Colin. The Aussies grin.

"Word has been spreading," says Missy. "We've been getting a steady stream of people who want to be NCFF. The inflow has put some strain on our internal structure but we've adapted."

"Missy is instrumental in this," says Colin. "She's a genius at figuring out how to use people."

"Thanks, Boss." Missy smiles.

"Now, tell us about you," says Colin. He fixes them with a penetrating gaze.

Angelica and Stephen exchange a glance. Their minds link. They sip more tea.

Angelica: *I think we tell them the simple truth. Colin is very perceptive. He'll know if we prevaricate.*

Stephen: *Agreed. And I get to watch you use your gift.*

Angelica: *???*

Stephen: *You can talk to anybody about anything in a way that they understand.*

Angelica: *Thanks, love.*

Angelica says, "We were first alerted to the problem here by a distress call from our people. Earth has experienced the capture and incarceration of her most creative, innovative people. We call these people Luminaries. They called for help and we heard. And we realized you were fighting a powerful enemy—one we've fought before.

We were given a mission: we must rescue the Luminaries and help overthrow the WSO."

Stephen continues. "The first people we met were Francisco and Diego in Los Angeles. We asked them how we could help them. Diego said what they really needed was to know what the enemy was doing. We are able to help with that."

"How?" Liam asks sharply.

"Akido, explain," Angelica says.

"Yes, Boss. Hello, Liam, Colin, Missy. I am Akido, a virtual assistant. I am connected with a super computer we call GA." Akido pauses. The three Aussies have expressions of surprise on their faces, but they don't speak. Akido continues. "This computer can hack any system, and now it is inside the WSO/STEN computer network. I am alerted to any communication related to the resistance. For instance, Angelica, Doc Crawford had a teleconference with Colonel Johnson. The colonel was not happy that he killed Travis and blew his cover."

"Damn!" Liam sits back with a whistle. "That really is handy. Who are Doc Crawford and Travis?"

Angelica answers. "They are suspected members of a STEN sleeper cell in Utah."

"Definitely a subject to cover," says Colin. "And right there you've demonstrated your value. I suspect you have more for us."

"We do," says Stephen.

Missy's jaw cracks with her yawn. "Sorry, mates. I'm going to need some sleep if my brain is going to function at all."

"We all could use some down time," says Colin.

"Understood," says Angelica. "Tonight, we've been invited to visit the Hawaiians living in and around the structure we came past on our way to the beach. They're starting a celebration called Makahiki. They also need some help with the local criminal element. Would you like to come with us?" says Angelica.

"That would be good," says Colin. Liam and Missy nod.

"All right. You all sleep. Stephen and I will take the watches."

The afternoon passes quietly. Stephen and Angelica take turns sleeping while the other watches over the group. It's late afternoon when everyone rises. Liam gets busy making tea.

Sipping hers, Angelica says, "After this snack, we will go visit the Hawaiians."

"Here's some background," says Stephen. "We spoke with a family of fisherman when we first arrived. They told us about two things, a festival they will begin tonight and their trouble with a gang extorting them. If the gang operates true to form, they'll come tonight. Angelica and I have a plan to help the villagers. We may need your help too."

"Of course. It'll be a good chance to see how we work together," says Colin. "Do we need to know details?"

"We don't have specifics, but I think you'll know what to do if the time comes," says Stephen.

"Okay then," says Colin. He shares a glance with Liam and Missy.

"Good," says Angelica. "Let's go."

The five freedom fighters head along the beach to the resort. They arrive at the luau, coming into a clear space where a pig is roasting over a pit of coals. Tables are laden with dishes filled with fruit, fish and other things they can't identify.

Kaholo runs up to them. "You came! Come and meet my mom." He grabs Angelica's hand and tugs her toward a group of women and children. "Mama, this is the lady I told you about."

One of the group turns. She's a round woman, draped in colorful cloth. She has long, black hair caught in a thick braid reaching to her waist. "Kaholo! Let go of that poor girl!"

Angelica smiles and gives Kaholo a quick hug. "I'm very happy to meet you." Looking around she continues, "This looks like quite a party. Thank you for having us."

"My husband and father-in-law tell me you have a blessing from the gods. And that you will help us with the hooligans trying to intimidate us."

"We will. We're happy to." Angelica waves to Stephen and the others. They come over to her. "These are my friends—my partner, Stephen. And Colin, Liam, and Missy."

"Welcome," says Lani.

More islanders come toward them saying aloha. Several men lead Colin and Liam away and give them a beverage. Missy is waved over by a group of women holding babies and small children. Kapueo waves to his wife and she leads Angelica and Stephen to him.

"The Chief wants to meet you right away, before the luau starts. He's this way. Come," he says.

They make their way toward the building. They walk around to a courtyard in the back. The Chief is there, sitting by a fire. He's an imposing figure. He has a lei around his thick neck and a flowered sarong around his hips. His face is lined and weathered like Haku's, but fuller. His chest and arms are slabbed with ropy muscle. His black eyes bore into them. Kapueo introduces him. "This is our leader, Akela. Chief, Angelica and Stephen."

The Chief examines them. They stand quiet under his scrutiny. He says, "I'm happy you've come here. We'll take any help you can give us. I cannot tolerate the pain and trouble my people are receiving from these wicked children. But that's not the only reason you have come to our island, is it?"

"No sir," says Angelica. "We have a mission we'd like to tell you about. We have friends with us from Australia who are part of our mission."

"Good. I feel in my heart we'll all benefit from our meeting. You and your friends are welcome here. You'll tell us about your mission after we eat and celebrate Makahiki."

The Chief walks with them back to the luau. The sun has set and the crescent moon hangs over the ocean. The cooking smells circling the clearing make their mouths water. Kapueo takes them to where his family is sitting. They sit and eat and eat.

A group of women of all ages, dressed in grass skirts, colorful tops and leis move into the center space of the clearing. Several carry a large, gourd-like instrument. Lani leans in. "It's called an *ipo*." Angelica nods. The dance begins—it's mesmerizing. More dances follow, involving both men and women, accompanied by ukulele and guitar. Their movements are graceful and athletic.

After the dances, the whole village walks to the beach, each person carrying a lei. They line up in the shallows, singing. At the end of the song, everyone raises their arms, tossing their leis on the water. The flowers rise and fall with the waves. Angelica reaches for Stephen's hand, linking their fingers. Thin moonlight glistens on the water. Dolphins appear, gliding among the flowers, then rising up under them so they're wearing the leis. Each dolphin flows up on his tail, skittering across the water. They dive as one and disappear below the waves. There is complete silence on the beach.

The Chief begins to sing. Every person joins the song. When it ends, the sound reverberates on the water, sand and trees. When the sound dies, the people drift away in small groups. The freedom fighters are deeply moved by what they witnessed. The Chief walks up to them. "Come. We'll talk."

Back in the luau clearing, they sit next to the fire pit.

The Chief speaks. "There is a legend about how Hawaii was formed and founded. Ancient mariners from the Marquesas Islands sailed their two-hulled vessels upon the oceans for weeks in search of new lands. Guided by the Goddess of Light near the end of their journey, they found refuge in the magical island chain they later named Hawaii.

"Our people have always had a rich heritage. No matter which way the world goes, we continue with our traditions. But some of the young people reject tradition. They resent guidance from their elders. The kahunas teach a Polynesian and Hawaiian code of conduct based on reason and optimum conduct. We are taught it as the Way of the Kahuna and we live our lives by it. A kahuna is a specialist, but Kahuna is also a message passed down through the ages in our Hawaiian culture.

"First, we help one another, our brothers and sisters. We work to be industrious, courageous, and kind. We want life to have value, integrity and honor. We encourage our children to return to these teachings. When each of us has a purpose and skill in life, it helps the community. That's the strength of our people, passed to us by our ancestors."

"You've just expressed the way of life we are working to put together for all the survivors on Earth," says Colin.

"All gods speak the same message to us in the language we understand." The Chief looks to the heavens and back at Colin. "Have you been successful?" he asks.

"We have, in Darwin, where we live. We've been telling other communities about what we've done. Others are working to be successful. Our structure will be the backbone of the resistance movement and the new civilization that follows when we win."

"The resistance movement." The Chief looks thoughtful. "We're been isolated here on the islands," he says. "You're the first friendly visitors we've had in years. Tell me about this resistance movement."

"It is action to resist all the tyranny of the WSO and STEN. There is an active movement beginning to swell," Angelica says. "Colin and his people are in the forefront and Stephen and I have come to help. We have experience with the sort of evil that conceives and runs a group like the WSO and its STEN arm. We also have a mission to save the Luminaries the WSO have incarcerated."

"Luminaries?" asks the Chief.

"Luminaries are the creative force in any civilization. They are teachers, makers, innovators, builders, storytellers, artists. Your Kahunas are Luminaries. The WSO has been systematically hunting, capturing and jailing Luminaries. They are kept drugged and comatose." Angelica pauses. "We plan to do something about that."

Colin speaks. "And we're using these two in our drive to make the resistance movement worldwide." He looks at the Chief. "We want your people to be a part of the resistance effort."

Several pops sound from the direction of the beach.

"Gunshots." Liam jumps up.

"Wait." The Chief stops him with the word. "It's the pirate boys. They've come for their loot."

The pirates flood into the clearing. There are ten young men armed with knives. One has a pistol. The few villagers in the clearing scramble for cover. The Chief steps forward, speaking to the one with the pistol. "Tommy," he says. Tommy holds the pistol with a steady hand. He's wearing jeans and an open shirt. An indistinct tattoo shows on his chest.

"Time for you to pay up, old man," Tommy says. "We'll start with all the food you have laid out here. We'll empty out the storehouse as usual. Shorty, Dutch, you go."

"No." Angelica steps forward. "That won't be happening this time."

"Who's going to stop me? You?" Tommy laughs.

Stephen steps to Angelica's side. "She'll have a little help."

Tommy stares at them. He walks forward, gun held out. He pushes the gun toward Stephen. In a lightning move, Stephen bats it out of his hand. Tommy jumps back, but Stephen grabs him. Tommy tries to twist away, kicking at Stephen's shins. Angelica grabs the gun.

Colin, Liam and Missy move toward the pirate group, cutting between them and the fighters.

Now Tommy holds a knife. He's making sideswiping motions towards Stephen, trying to back him off. Stephen evades his thrusts easily, finding an opening to deliver a sweeping side kick to Tommy's chin. He follows with a sharp blow to his neck. Tommy goes down, hitting the ground like a felled tree.

Silence creates its own presence as the stunned gang members look at the scene before them. This is totally unexpected. They're used to having their way.

Tommy is out cold.

The villagers join Colin, Liam, Missy, and Angelica, setting a perimeter around Tommy's gang.

Stephen checks Tommy's pulse. He pulls off his amulet. He lays it on Tommy's forehead, holding it in place with his palm. The stone begins to shine green, the exudes a golden glow that moves to encircle Tommy's head. Tommy moves, groaning. He's slowly coming around. Stephen removes the amulet, putting it back around his neck. Tommy stays down. He struggles to a sitting position on the sand. He won't look at his gang.

The villagers watch Stephen's actions in perfect silence. They understand he is a kahuna at work.

The gang members huddle in a group, guarded by Kapueo, Haku and other village men. They look like scared children now.

The Chief speaks to Tommy. "You have been a weed in our garden for too long. That stops now. Our village and the rest of the islands are joining the resistance against our common enemy, the WSO and STEN. You can choose to contribute to this effort or you all can sit quietly in a hut until you change your mind. However long that takes."

Tommy looks up at him sullenly. The other young men look at each other. The Chief waits. A boy in the back steps forward. "I'm with you, sir."

"Good. Go with the men over there." The Chief stands in front the rest of the boys, arms folded across his chest. He looks every inch a warrior. They won't look at him and shift nervously.

Another boy says, "I'm with you too." He looks at Tommy. "I told you, man. I told you this had to stop. You know it wasn't right." He glares at the rest of the boys on the sand. "Do the right thing!" Now they're looking sheepish. One by one they come forward, shuffling their feet, keeping their eyes down. "We're with you too."

Now just Tommy is sitting on the sand. Angelica sits down in front of him, matching his body position. She waits until he lifts his head, his expression sullen and antagonistic.

"You're a good leader," says Angelica, "but you're leading in the wrong direction. Your people are not the enemy. The enemy is out there, drugging everyone, stealing all their dreams. That's who needs fighting. That's who needs to be destroyed. Can you lead against that enemy?"

Tommy's eyes narrow but he doesn't speak for a long moment.

"They took my Auntie." It's barely a whisper. "Nobody did anything to help."

Angelica holds his gaze, speaking fiercely. "Now *you* can do something. *You* can do something to help."

He looks at her for a long time. Finally, he says, "Okay."

"Good," says Angelica. She looks at the other pirates. "But you will all have to prove yourselves and make up the damage caused by your reckless and irresponsible actions." The Chief is nodding. She looks at Colin. "Commander, can you use a leadership trainee who needs to make a lot of amends?"

Colin looks down at Tommy. "You'll have to come to our training camp in Australia. You'll have to work your ass off, doing the shit jobs nobody else wants to do. You'll have to learn martial arts and military strategy. When I think you're ready, you'll have to travel to enemy strongholds to perform acts of sabotage. Are you ready for that?"

As Colin is speaking, Tommy's eyes go wide and harden. He answers without hesitation, "Yes, sir." He gets to his feet. "What about my boys?"

The Chief steps forward. "The others will stay here to make up the damage. There are many things they can do to help defend this island. When we're satisfied they've made amends, we'll help them find where they can contribute best. For now, we'll feed them and give them a place to sleep. Tommy will stay with his men tonight."

Angelica looks at Stephen and Colin. "This is good. Chief, may we come talk with you tomorrow afternoon? We'll have specifics about the resistance to share with you. We'll take Tommy with us then."

The Chief nods, shaking each freedom fighter's hand as they leave.

NIGHT

Back at the camp, no one is ready for sleep. They sit, looking out at the midnight sky, covered with a blanket of stars. The breaking surf pulses against the beach. Night sounds and smells fill their senses. Meteors are hundreds of darting light arrows in the sky above them. The group watches the display with wonder.

Soon Missy stifles a yawn, moving quietly to her tent. Colin and Liam follow, going into theirs. Angelica and Stephen lie close on the warm sand, eyes on the velvet sky overhead. They are content in the shared knowledge that their mission is on track and will succeed. The good people of Earth have joined them.

DAY SIXTEEN

MORNING, TURTLE BAY

The sun is rising, the moon is fading, the sky is blue glass, the sea breathes against the beach. Liam is making tea, Missy sets out food.

Angelica gives Stephen a quick kiss, standing to walk to the water. It laps at her toes.

"Akido, report."

"All quiet, Boss. No new STEN activity since we've been in Hawaii. Margo says, quote, 'the new boy Juan Carlos and Bridgetta have been working *very* closely. Garcia and I are watching.' end quote. Nothing new from Francisco or Jeremiah.

"There have been some emails flying in the WSO network about the possibility of resistance. GA has been validating each one and directing them to Backdoor Charlie."

"This is very good. Thank you, Akido."

"You're welcome, Boss."

Angelica walks back to the others. "Word of the resistance is spreading," she says, sinking down to sit in the circle.

"Good news," says Stephen. The others nod.

Liam hands her a cup of tea. Missy hands her a plate of food. Everyone eats in companionable silence.

Colin finishes and sets his plate aside. "Okay, let's get started. Here's what we've got so far. The plan for organizing survival communities is up and working. Our conversation with the Chief last night proves the plan we use is a universal concept.

"Now we need to organize the resistance. I know we need fighters—fighters trained in martial arts, battle tactics and sabotage. We have an excellent training program in Darwin. Later, we'll need divisions of fighting expertise, like commandos, pilots, artillery, foot soldiers, spies. We'll need someone in charge, to coordinate resistance activity worldwide. And maybe an overall plan of what that activity will consist of. Do we blow stuff up? How do we take back the walled fortresses and do we want to? What do we do with WSO STEN people who want to switch sides? Stuff like that." He grins. "How I'm doing?"

"Perfect," says Stephen.

"Great. Your turn."

Stephen looks at Angelica. She says, "We came here with a twofold mission. We will rescue the incarcerated Luminaries. We'll help get the resistance up and running. We found out what Francisco and Diego needed and we're providing that by tapping into STEN's communications. What do you need, Colin?"

"A resistance needs men and women, but it also needs equipment and a means to transport people and things," Colin says. "The WSO and their STEN thugs are pretty much absent from Australia. We're a big island with lots of wild country. We have planes and ground vehicles and travel at will.

"Getting here pointed out our limitations. Our old plane, Mongoose, made the trip because we didn't meet any patrols. If we had, it'd be a different story. We need something reliable to move stuff around that can avoid patrols."

Stephen looks at Angelica, smiling widely. She smiles back.

"What?" says Liam.

"Come with me," says Stephen walking toward some bushes. "We flew here in a special craft. We call it a hovercraft. I designed the first prototype in my school days. It's had modifications over the years and now it's battle ready." He sweeps the branches away to reveal the hovercraft.

"Ohhhh," says Liam.

Colin walks around the vehicle, looking. He comes back to stand next to Stephen. "You have design specifications for this?"

"I do."

"Can it be made bigger?"

"It can."

"Like cargo plane bigger?"

"Yes."

"Oh, boy. This will work." Colin claps Stephen on the back.

"It will require manufacturing capabilities to make the parts that become the hovercraft," says Stephen.

"Funny thing about that," says Colin. "We have a couple of plants we've been tooling up, preparing to manufacture aircraft. We're just at the point of deciding on a design, so this is perfect." He throws his arms around Stephen, lifting him off the ground in a bear hug.

"Ooof. You're welcome." Colin sets him down and goes to examine the hovercraft.

Liam is peering inside it. "Tell me about this beautiful machine," he says.

Stephen goes to stand next to him. "It maneuvers like a helicopter but can attain and maintain a speed of five-hundred mph. There's a camouflage device that makes it invisible from the ground. It can be configured for passengers or cargo or both. It runs on solar batteries."

Liam is grinning ear to ear. Colin is shaking his head. "This is almost too good to be true," he says. "You're sure we can get all the materials we need to build this miracle machine?"

"I'm sure," says Stephen. "On the plans, I've included a list of materials needed for construction. If you have plants ready, you should be able to start building as soon as you gather the materials. Once you work out the processes, you can export them to other plants."

"That'll be good for the future," Colin says. "We'll have to be very certain the enemy doesn't get wind of this until we're ready. We'll need tight security."

"We can handle that," says Missy.

"That brings up the sleeper cell problem," says Liam. Everyone nods.

Colin says, "We've run into a few problems, but there's not much for STEN to find in our area. We've been able to fool them the few times they've come sniffing around. With the resistance going into high gear, there's much more to lose."

"The communities we've visited on the mainland have had the same experience," says Stephen. "They're discussing how to handle it. You'll be getting emails."

"We'll figure it out," says Colin.

"Good," says Angelica. "Back to the hovercraft. Once production gets underway, what do you think about Hawaii as a staging area between Darwin and the mainland?"

"That's a brilliant idea," says Missy. "I've been listening to Colin and Stephen, thinking about how we can make this work. Angelica, you said exactly what I was thinking. We can work on getting hovercraft of different sizes made, then stockpile them here, in Hawaii. Meanwhile we can train pilots in Darwin. Later we can export the pilot training program first to the places where other plants are and then to places where we can put fleets. Oh, this will work!" She claps her hands in delight.

Liam looks thoughtful. "And we could expand our training program into Hawaii. The big island would be great for commando training."

"I asked to speak to the Chief tonight. I'll present this plan for his approval," says Angelica.

"So we have a general outline of the resistance, right? Missy, you got the basics? You can put them all on paper so we can export to the survival communities who want to be resistance centers?" Colin asks.

"Yes, Boss, I got it." Missy smiles.

"Good," says Colin.

Liam rubs his hands together in glee. "Yeah, and I'm all over the training section. And the hovercraft. I can't wait to learn to fly one! Can we each have a personal hovercraft?"

"We'll take care of the resistance, then we'll see," says Colin.

"Fine." Liam tries to pout but can't hold it.

"There's just one more thing," say Angelica, her eyes on Colin.

"What's that?" he asks.

"We have the organization of survival communities, but what about the organization of the resistance? The enemy has someone in charge, I've seen him. Who will be in charge for the resistance?" She pauses, looking at Colin. He looks back at her. "Stephen and I think you are the person for the job, Colin."

Colin rubs his face, taking a deep breath. Liam and Missy say nothing, waiting.

"Thank you for the vote of confidence." He doesn't speak for a minute. Everyone keeps their eyes on him. He takes another deep breath, gazing at the sky. Moving his eyes back to Angelica, he says, "Okay, I accept." He grins.

"Good man," says Stephen.

Liam and Missy shout, "Yeah, Boss!" They're grinning too.

"That's settled. Excellent," says Angelica. "Now, I'm going for a swim." She jumps up, peeling off clothing as she runs for the waves. She dives, surfaces and swims. Within minutes, she's joined by several dolphins. Stephen strips down and runs into the waves. Colin, Liam and Missy are transfixed.

Angelica shouts, "Come in!"

They discard clothing and wade in. The five freedom fighters play with a pod of dolphins for an hour. When they finally say goodbye to their new friends and head for the beach, they see a group of village women standing a few yards up the beach, staring at them. Angelica approaches them. Lani holds a platter of food. She hands it to Angelica without speaking. Angelica takes it and the two women lock eyes for a beat. Lani lowers her head in a small bow which is copied by the other three women. They turn and walk away.

The rest of the crew are out of the water and back in the camp. Angelica brings the food to them.

"This will taste good after our swim," she says.

"I'm getting the tea this time," says Missy. Liam finds plates and utensils. They sit down and tuck in.

Colin finishes and leans back with his tea. "Liam, Missy and I sort of grew up together. When I was twelve, my dad moved us to a place outside Darwin. My mother was a community leader, working with several charities. I was so mad that we moved. I had to leave my whole life. After the mass suicide, when things began to change, my dad and mum had an idea how things would go. My dad sat me down and explained the new facts of life. I was thirteen." He looks into his mug. "I became a man that day."

"I was born in 2058," says Liam. "My dad was a regular guy with regular problems. My ma was the strong one. She was friends with Colin's mom and she followed her to Darwin, bringing me with her. My dad didn't make it."

Missy speaks. "My parents were artists, originally from Darwin. They sold their art all over the world. They lived in town but bought a place way out when they saw what was happening. It was our ranch that became the center of the survival community. Colin and his parents, Liam and his ma, all ended up at our place. I was born in 2061. They still live there. They had to change their names—go underground to escape capture. They still make art but no one ever sees it. They truly are Luminaries."

A breeze blows across the ocean, rustling the foliage above the group. In front of them, birds call over the waves. Others answer from the vegetation behind them.

"What's your story?" Colin asks.

Angelica and Stephen share a look. She begins. "It could have been just yesterday. One meeting, and we knew we'd be together. We click on every level. We decided long ago that we would gain the skills to help any Luminary in need. That's what we're doing, that's what we've always done. Right now, there are Luminaries in the walled fortress cities in dire need of help. We have a short-term plan. The resistance is the long-term plan."

Stephen speaks. "Our parents are Luminaries—her mother is an artist and my father is a programing genius. They were part of an artist's colony. It was in a very remote location, not much contact with the outside world. They were raided by STEN troops. There's nothing left of the colony." He pauses. "We're hoping to find them."

After a moment, Colin says, "I'm sorry. There are too many stories like that."

"Exactly," says Stephen. "That's why Angelica and I are here. To turn around as many of those stories as possible." He clasps Angelica's hand.

Colin nods. Connection, togetherness and a shared sense of purpose flows in and around the group.

"There's one other thing." Angelica speaks in a low voice.

Stephen sees what she will say. *Are you sure, love?*

Angelica: *Aren't you?*

The sum of their experiences with humans on Earth rises between them.

Stephen: *Yes. You're right.*

Angelica fixes her eyes on the Aussies. "We know something else about the enemy. It's not just the WSO and STEN. They are the tools of a much older, more evil enemy, one that Stephen and I have faced before. This battle for Earth is the first in a new war. We intend to make it the last battle and end the war for good."

Colin, Liam and Missy are motionless.

Angelica continues. "I went to the detention center in Denver, into the room where Luminaries are incarcerated. It was the worst thing I've ever seen—another example of the depravity of the enemy." Her eyes turn hard. "Stephen and I *will* rescue Luminaries from the detention centers in Los Angeles, Utah, and Denver. And we want to coordinate Luminary rescues at the same time in every other walled city across the globe. With your approval and help, it will be the first salvo from the resistance."

Colin and his people stare at Angelica and Stephen. They stare back. They can see when each of the Aussies come to a personal decision. Colin says, "That is an excellent idea. As the newly appointed commander of the resistance, I approve your plan, whatever it is."

"Thank you, sir." Angelica smiles, then turns serious. "It will have to happen soon. STEN is planning to start using an advanced electroshock machine on the Luminaries, and anyone they consider subversive or a criminal. The new machine is far worse than its predecessor. It's the worst kind of torture. It fries the brain of the victim, turning him or her into a zombie or killing them outright. We have to get the Luminaries out before the new machines are in use."

"That's horrible!" gasps Missy. Her face hardens with a fierce look. "Whatever you need, you'll have."

"Absolutely," says Liam.

"Thank you," says Angelica. She looks at each of them in turn, emphasizing her gratitude. "Now, let's walk in the jungle. I want to explore this beautiful island before we have to leave."

"Yes! I'm with you," says Missy.

Colin, Liam and Stephen join them. They spend two hours discovering wildlife, exotic plants, flowers, and waterfalls. The landscape is breathtaking. They're reluctant to return to their camp, but it'll soon be time to go back to the village to speak with the Chief.

LATE AFTERNOON

The freedom fighters are back at the luau clearing, meeting with the Chief.

"Your island can play an important role in the resistance," Angelica says. "Our friends here will go back to Australia with plans for a new aircraft. They have manufacturing plants there to build the craft. But we'll need locations to stockpile them once they're finished. We would like Hawaii to be the first one. From here the aircraft can easily be brought to the mainland of North and South America. Plus, the WSO leaves this area alone. Will you agree?"

The group waits. The Chief looks them over, his eyes speculative.

"Yes, I agree," he says. "I spoke with our Elders this morning. I told them about your intention to ask for our help. They know a little of the resistance and they're determined to help. Then the women came and told us about you swimming with the dolphins. That confirmed our choice. You are *ohana* now." He smiles.

As one, the group bows to the Chief.

"Thank you, sir." Angelica and Stephen speak in unison.

"Good. Now we eat." The Chief leads the way into a different part of the resort. Bowls of fresh fruit, platters of grilled fish, and a bowl of *poi* are laid out. Haku and other men join them for a lively meal.

Twilight is creeping in when Tommy arrives, carrying a small satchel. The Chief puts his arm around Tommy's shoulders. "These young men are proving themselves," he says.

"I knew they were basically good men," says Angelica.

"Thank you for a great meal and good company. Thank you for joining the resistance," says Colin. He shakes the Chief's hand. "Now we have to get back to our camp, we have an early start in the morning. Come on, Tommy."

With a wave, the Aussies, Tommy, Angelica and Stephen leave their new Hawaiian friends. Back at the camp, they make it an early night.

DAY SEVENTEEN

EARLY MORNING, TURTLE BAY

IT'S THREE A.M.

Angelica and Stephen wake with their bodies spooned together. His arm holds her close, she grasps his hand. He hugs her, rolling to his back. She hugs him and rolls to her back, keeping their shoulders touching. They look up at the night sky, resplendent with stars. The air is still, just the gentle pulse of waves sounds nearby. Small night sounds come from the jungle behind them. Their minds link and they look into space. Planets are aligning, swirling around stars that are rotating in galaxies. They see their Pleiades constellation—the Seven Sisters.

As spirits, they leap from of their bodies, moving freely up and out into moments of forever. Space is limitless but their love fills it. They look back at Earth, a blue-green planet floating in black space. Shifting viewpoint, they see the black cancer fouling its surface, concentrated in the fortress cities. They also see golden lights, some faint, some glowing and dancing. They envision the golden lights reaching, flowing together, enlarging, encompassing and dissolving the cancer until all of Earth emits a golden glow.

They know life sustains and renews itself in the endless celebration of divine light. They see this happening for the life of Earth. They watch the stars wheeling in the heavens and are filled with the joy of life.

Rustling and a cough from the nearby tents bring them back to their bodies on the beach. Colin and Liam emerge, then Missy. It's not yet dawn. Tommy rolls out of his sleeping bag under a tree.

Missy begins striking one tent, Liam works on the other, Tommy helping him. Colin sets up for tea, Angelica puts together a breakfast. All packed, they sit down to eat.

"All in all, an excellent, productive visit," says Colin.

"Agreed," says Stephen.

"I'm going to look into setting up Fiji as a stockpile spot on our way home," says Colin. "We've spoken with the people there and they're on board with the resistance."

"Excellent idea," says Stephen.

"Yes," says Angelica. "From now on, we need to activate resistance cells wherever we go. The light from these freedom fighters will begin to spread across the whole world until it burns away the WSO cancer."

"Wow," says Missy, "that's a beautiful way to put it."

Angelica ducks her head, looking a little embarrassed. "Thank you."

"We have six large aircraft, like Old Mongoose, that we can get into the air on pretty short notice. A couple are long range so we can fly people and cargo from Darwin to the west coast of North America if necessary," says Colin.

"When our rescue plan is finalized, we'll probably take you up on that," says Angelica. "How many commandos could you send, if we asked?"

"I've got this one," says Liam. "We have two-hundred-fifty elite men in training right now. They're ready to go anytime. And we have a plane that can bring them to you. How soon will you be mounting this rescue?"

"We haven't worked out the details yet. The first step is to decide on the timing of the raid," says Angelica.

Tommy is quiet, watching each speaker as the conversation flows.

"Uh, Boss," says Akido. Tommy is surprised, looking around for the speaker.

Angelica addresses him holding up her arm to show him her wristband. "Tommy, this is Akido, our virtual assistant. Continue Akido."

Tommy nods, looking a bit stunned, but he listens.

Akido continues. "Hi, Tommy. I just got a WSO system-wide announcement. In fifteen days, all WSO and STEN operations will be celebrating Founding Day. There won't even be skeleton crews in the facilities. They plan on just locking everything up for twenty-four hours. Drunkenness and debauchery are encouraged for this day. Could that be our window?"

Angelica and Stephen look at each other, then at Colin, Liam and Missy. Tommy leans forward.

"That sounds like exactly what we need. Can we pull it off in fifteen days?" says Angelica.

"We can provide the commandos, and any other help you need from us," says Colin.

"Deal," says Angelica. "Okay. We'll put this together and send you the details within the next three days."

"The overall plan should stay between the six of us," says Missy, looking sternly at Tommy.

He shakes his head, "Who am I going to tell?"

Missy continues, "If you feel the need to speak about it at all, you only talk to me, Liam or Colin. STEN has their sleeper cell network in place. No hint of this can get to them."

"Yes ma'am."

"Agreed," says Colin. He turns to Angelica. "How will you handle it in the survival communities involved?"

"We'll work with Francisco and Diego, Margo and Garcia, and Jeremiah. We'll brief them. Anyone else necessary to the plan will only know the part they'll play. Two weeks is not a lot of time to plan what we want to do. We should be able to keep it quiet."

"We'll be very careful," says Stephen.

"All right." Colin stands. "We'd better get going. Liam, Missy, Tommy, you take the dune buggy and gear and get it all stowed on Old Mongoose. I'll grab the hovercraft plans and follow you on the bike."

"Sure, Boss." Liam and Missy grin at him, Tommy gives a salute. They climb in, wave, and take off with a roar and a plume of sand. Stephen hands the satchel to Colin who slings it across his body. He turns to face Angelica and Stephen. It's clear he wants to say something.

"I won't beat around the bush," Colin begins. "Speaking for us Aussies, this was nothing short of an extraordinary meeting. We're impressed with you two—you're very special people in an out-of-this-world way." His gaze sharpens. "I know there's much more to you than you've said. I expect to hear your full story sooner rather than later."

Angelica steps closer to Stephen and clasps his hand. They reach out to Colin with their free hands. He steps closer, takes their hands. They stand in a small circle of three. Colin begins to feel a warmth surround his body. He becomes aware of every sound, every touch, every scent around him. He feels as if he is expanding, like he's too big for his body. There's a splash and dolphins enter his awareness. He is experiencing their joy for life. He's experiencing the life of every insect and plant near him. He's seeing without his eyes. He notices the necklaces that Angelica and Stephen wear—the blue stones are glowing. It's all almost too much to bear. Then, it stops...and...he's back in his body. And he feels fantastic! His skin tingles with energy. His sense of well-being is heady. He's holding hands with these two—people? They're smiling at him. He lets go of their hands.

"Okay," says Colin. "Okay. Well, uh. Thank you for that?"

Angelica laughs and leans in to give him a hug.

Colin hugs her back, also laughing. "I'm sure glad you're on our side."

"We are always on the side of light and life and creation," says Angelica.

"Thank you," says Colin. Glowing, he stands and gazes at the two people in front of him. A moment passes, no one moving. "Okay, I have to go now. We'll keep in touch." He gives Angelica another hug, and receives one from Stephen. Climbing on the bike he shoots away, toward his plane.

Angelica turns to look at the ocean. "That was an incredible two days with our new friends. Their dedication to their people gives me hope."

"It makes our mission easier. We have good people with us," says Stephen.

"We still have much to accomplish, but now we have help."

"And now it's time for us to leave," says Stephen. Angelica gets everything left on the beach into the hovercraft. It's still early morning when they take off for the mainland.

WSO HQ, LOS ANGELES

Damien sits at his desk reading the latest dispatch about the two women wanted for disrupting the Denver detention center. Rhotah Mhene already sent several dispatches asking for updates on the search. For some reason the commander is obsessed with these women. Despite having their photos, such as they are, spread throughout the west, they've disappeared.

Damien has a bad feeling about the whole situation. First Doc Crawford reports strangers in the Utah camp. Then things happen in Denver. Nothing has been reported from Los Angeles but Damien suspects that group is involved too. The last report from Juan Carlos detailed multiple instances of a man and woman talking up resistance, revolution. There's evidence that life in the larger survival communities is getting more organized. There's an awful lot of martial arts training going on.

"Time to turn up the heat," Damien says aloud. He calls his aide for dictation. "Urgent dispatch to all STEN outposts. Effective immediately. There are to be weekly surprise raids on all survival communities, never on the same day or at the same time, beginning immediately. Look and listen for any evidence of resistance to the WSO or STEN, particularly individuals who may be talking about or organizing resistance. Report any information immediately to Col. Johnson at Los Angeles HQ. Usable intelligence will be rewarded." He waves a hand at his aide. "Get this out right now, highest priority."

He walks to the window. "That should keep them busy," he says to the view.

SOMEWHERE OVER THE SOUTH PACIFIC

After refueling in Fiji and getting the islanders' agreement to help with the resistance, the Aussies are cruising at a comfortable altitude. They had a bit to drink with the Fijians to celebrate the birth of the resistance on their island. Liam is taking his watch at the controls, but he's dozing. Halfway home to Darwin, he drifts off course.

Alarms sound in the cockpit. Liam snaps awake and Colin appears.

"What happened?"

"Sorry Boss, I drifted off course and STEN radar picked us up," Liam reports as he sends the plane into a deep dive. "I'm going NOE."

Colin sits in the copilot seat as Missy appears in the door with Tommy crowding behind her. "What is NOE again?" she asks.

Colin answers. "Nap of the earth. It's using the contour of the landscape to hide a plane's position. In our case, we're going to hug the surface of the ocean for a while."

"Boss, have any drones been sent out?" asks Liam.

Colin scans the instruments. "No, I don't think so. But we're staying low for a while. You okay to stay in the pilot seat?"

"Yeah. I can finish my watch."

"Good man. I'll relieve you in a couple of hours. Stay sharp." He and Missy and Tommy leave the cockpit.

"Roger." Liam sits back, his eyes scanning ahead.

The radio crackles. "CQ, CQ the mangy bird. Over."

Liam picks up the mike. "Mangy bird here, over."

"When are you getting your raggedy hide here to help with the sheep?"

"Hey, I'm hugging curves here."

"And you stopped to answer the phone?"

"We're both keeping an eye out for wolves. We thought you might have some news."

"No wolves. We'll keep you posted. Go back to the curves! Over and out."

Liam replaces the mike with a chuckle. The lads at home will let him know if STEN starts to get frisky. He goes back to scanning the ocean out the plane's front window.

SOMEWHERE OVER THE NORTH PACIFIC

"We only have two weeks to plan the rescue of our Luminaries," says Angelica. She closes her eyes and leans back.

"Do you have any ideas?" asks Stephen.

Angelica is silent, looking at him. "You've thought of something."

Stephen smiles. "Here's what I'm thinking. You described a delivery system for the drug they're using on the Luminaries. How often do they get a supply of that drug? How is it delivered?"

"Oh, you are brilliant, my love. I noticed in Denver there was a small supply of the drug in the closet where the feeder system originated. Akido, ask GA to search STEN's order and delivery records for the deep sleep drug shipped to Los Angeles, Utah, and Denver. Send emails to Francisco, Garcia, and Jeremiah asking if they have any information about delivery traffic to and from the detention center. We need to know how and when the drugs are delivered."

"On it, Boss," says Akido.

"Thank you. Our task loomed over me for a time. Stephen, you helped make it small so I could think again."

"We do that for each other," says Stephen.

"Yes, we do."

They fly on. Angelica looks out at the sea sparkling in the sun.

Stephen keeps a close eye on his instruments, watching for any sign of the enemy.

After a time, Angelica speaks again. "Akido, we need to send a report to Defense Minister Drail. Here it is: 'Greetings, Minister. Stephen and I are happy to report progress here on Earth. The resistance movement is shaping up, with an organizational structure created and being implemented. Its first operation will be the rescue of Luminaries currently incarcerated in three detention centers in three separate geographic locations. We are formulating a plan for this operation. We'll need to meet *Lightbearer* at a specified location in sixteen Earth days. Exact details to follow. Once the rescue is completed, Stephen and I will start on our final mission order.' Do you have anything to add, Stephen?"

He shakes his head, "No, you've covered it."

"Good. Akido, transmit."

Stephen glances at her. Her bowed head is in her hands. He reaches for her with his mind, touching her anxiety. Fear of failure beats at her while she works to stand strong. Stephen places himself beside her, surrounding her, adding his strength to hers. She takes a deep breath, dropping her hands. She adds her strength to his. A warm glow builds and fills the hovercraft. Stephen pulls back but maintains their connection. They exchange a look.

The hovercraft flies on.

"We swap the drug for a saline solution. But the withdrawal will be vicious. We'll need to add a healing supplement to the saline to help the Luminaries until we can reach them. It'll take at least three days for all that to work." Angelica is thinking aloud. "We need to find out what's happening in the Utah detention center. Akido, message to Garcia: 'Ask Bridgetta if she can get into the Utah detention center to see what's happening there. She needs to find out how many Luminaries are incarcerated there and if the setup is the same as the one we saw in Denver. Please remind her to keep her face hidden as much as possible—STEN is looking for us both after our visit to their detention center in Denver. Thank you, Angelica.' Transmit immediately."

"Messages sent," says Akido.

"Send Francisco a message that we're on our way back and will see him soon."

"Also done," says Akido.

"Thank you," says Angelica. She lapses into silence.

The journey continues. High, fluffy white clouds appear to the north.

After several minutes, Stephen says, "Sure is a good thing we have many people to help us."

Angelica looks over at him. She rolls her eyes. "All right. I'll stop obsessing about this while traveling over the ocean with my love."

Stephen smiles at her.

After two more hours, the horizon darkens with the promise of land. Akido says, "Return message from Francisco. He says, 'Fly to Rincon Point—there will be a signal on the beach for you. Turn 5' 30" N, heading inland for about thirty miles to our camp in Ojai. Look for another signal. We'll meet you there.'"

"Akido. Please acknowledge, 'Understood,' and plot a course," says Stephen.

"Yes, Boss."

Now the sun is moving down behind them. The light is golden. Stephen sends the hovercraft into a dive, coming out close to the waves. They fly in a line just out of sight of the coast, avoiding any radar.

"Rincon Point coming up," Akido reports.

Stephen nudges the hovercraft toward the shore.

"There's a fire on the beach," says Angelica.

"I see it." Stephen is flying low over the short waves. He skims the beach, climbing up the bluff. Still hugging the landscape, he heads northeast. Soon, another fire flickers in the distance. Stephen circles, looking for a good landing spot. He finds one behind a stand of trees. By the time he shuts down the hovercraft and he and Angelica climb out, Francisco and Diego are waiting for them under one of the trees.

"Good trip?" asks Francisco.

"Excellent trip," says Angelica.

"Great. Come eat and meet some people."

Angelica and Stephen spend a relaxing evening with Francisco, Diego and their people in beautiful Ojai.

LATE AFTERNOON, UTAH SURVIVAL COMMUNITY

Bridgetta sits with Garcia in his living room.

"How am I going to get into the detention center?" she asks.

"I have an idea about that. We have new people coming into our community all the time. We've set up a welcoming service to help them find a place to live and get oriented. We find out what skills they have and set them up in that area with a buddy. I get notified if anybody raises a question mark. I just met with a group who came from South Salt Lake. One of the girls used to work for STEN in the detention center as a cleaner. She told me she couldn't be around them anymore. Talk to her. Her name is Betsy. I think she's in the dining room right now."

"I'll find her."

In the dining room, preparation is underway for the evening meal. She finds Betsy and they sit down with a cup of coffee.

"Garcia told me you used to work in the STEN detention center," Bridgetta says.

"Yeah. It was bad. Oceans of pills and—other things," Betsy shudders.

"I've heard," says Bridgetta. "Where did you work?"

"I started in the stadium offices, then they moved me to the building across the street. When I left, I was working in the basement. That was the worst."

"Why?"

Betsy speaks in a whisper. "There were places where doctors worked. They kept the doors closed but a couple of times I saw inside. There were people in there that looked dead. Worse than dead. It was creepy. And the smell." She shudders again. "That's when I decided I had to get out."

"I need to go there," says Bridgetta. Betsy's eyes go wide and she starts to speak.

Bridgetta interrupts. "No, I know I shouldn't, but I need to."

Betsy shakes her head. "Okay. I still have my pass and uniform —you can have them. I just hope you know what you're doing."

"Can I get them now?"

"Sure." She takes Bridgetta to where she lives and hands over her uniform and pass. "Luckily, the pass isn't a picture ID. We were the faceless drones. The first shift starts at six a.m. You should go with this one. Report to the big building, first floor, janitor's room. Volunteer for the basement."

"Thank you, Betsy. I appreciate this. If I can ever help you…" Bridgetta gives her a hug.

"Just be careful, Bridgetta," says Betsy. "I want to take your martial arts class."

"Deal!"

After leaving the dining hall, Bridgetta finds Garcia. "I got a uniform and pass from Betsy. I'm going early tomorrow to look at the detention center. It won't take long to see what I need to see. I'll be back by dinnertime; at the latest."

"Do you want Zack to go with you?"

"No, it'll be better if I go by myself."

Garcia stands in front of her and grasps her arms. "Please. Be very careful. Remember what Angelica said about keeping your face covered," he says.

Bridgetta smiles bravely. "I will. Thank you, Garcia." She gives him a quick hug.

DAY EIGHTEEN

UTAH SURVIVAL COMMUNITY

AT FOUR A.M. Bridgetta gets up, dresses in the uniform. She slides a pair of black, heavy framed glasses she's used as a disguise before, into the uniform pocket. She grabs an apple from the kitchen. Her stomach is in knots but she knows she should eat something. By four thirty she's on the road. Within the community, she uses headlights. Once she reaches the freeway, she turns them off and drives carefully in the moonless dark. The roads are clear and empty. She arrives in the neighborhood of the big building at five fifteen. She parks on a side street and eats her apple. At five forty-five, she drives to the parking lot next to the big building. She stays in her car, watching the front door.

At five fifty, another car pulls in. Two figures emerge and fall in step with three other people walking toward the entrance. She puts on her glasses and pulls a scarf over her hair, arranging it to partially cover her face. She gets out and follows them.

The door is opened by a STEN guard. He checks their passes as they file in. Bridgetta keeps her head down, face averted. "How come there are six of you today?"

The others look at him with dull faces. "Never mind," he says. "Just get to work."

Bridgetta follows the group down the hall to the janitor's room, still keeping her head down. Inside, there are five clipboards on the wall. The other workers shuffle over and each grab a clipboard. They don't look at her. She makes herself look busy organizing the supply shelves. Once they've left, she stuffs a couple of dust rags in her pockets, sets up a mop and bucket and heads for the service elevator. Inside, she rubs her face until the elevator dings and the doors open. Rolling the bucket out the doors, she slips off the scarf and dabs her hair with the soapy water, making it fall over her face and glasses in greasy clumps. She slumps, hanging her head, and pushes the mop and bucket into the hall.

There's no one around. She rolls down the hall, looking for a NO ADMITTANCE door. She finds one that's unlocked. She leaves the mop and bucket outside, in front of the door, and slips in, dust rag in hand.

Another short hallway, desk at the end, and another door beyond that.

This looks like the Denver set up. She moves quickly to the second door and opens it. The smell hits her first. She covers her mouth with the dust rag. Her eyes adjust to the low light in the room. She goes in, peering in the ranks of beds. Almost all are empty. There are only five bodies close to the door. They aren't connected to the IV line. They lie on dirty bedding, slack jawed and drooling. Their eyes are dead, vacant. Bridgetta shivers. She finds the door to the medication room and goes in. There are no cubes of drugs and the delivery system tubes hang slack.

As she exits, she notices something in the back corner of the larger room. Investigating, she finds a table with restraints for feet, hands and head. There's a machine near the head of the table. It's labeled "Electroshock Grade IV." Bridgetta steps back in horror.

She goes back to the five people. She stands between two of the beds, reaching her hands to the people on them, touching them gently. She whispers, "Angelica would know exactly what to do for you, to help. She even has a blue stone that she could use. I don't have one. I just know you don't have to live like this. Leave these broken things! Go to Angelica! She'll help you."

A distant clatter sounds. Someone is coming in. She rushes out the door. She's dusting the desk when two white-coated men enter the space.

"What are you doing here?" the taller one asks sharply.

Bridgetta keeps her eyes down, shaking her head, moving her dust rag over the desk.

"Are you deaf?" demands the second man.

Bridgetta shakes her head again, moving the rag.

"Some sort of retard," says the tall man in disgust. "Get her out of here."

The other man grabs her arm and half drags her to the outer door. He pushes her out, toward the mop and bucket. "And move that right now," he snaps, slamming the door.

Bridgetta shoves the rag in her pocket and grabs the mop handle. She makes it to the elevator, keeping her head down and hair over her glasses and face. On the first floor she puts the mop and bucket away and exits through a back door.

She hurries to her truck, gets in and sits, shaking. It's not until she's safely on the freeway that she can breathe again, gulping in air. She was in the building for twenty minutes.

Back in Margo's kitchen, she hunches over a cup of hot coffee, holding it with both hands. Garcia and Margo sit across from her, waiting for her to speak.

She begins in a low voice. "Angelica and I got into the detention center in the Denver walled fortress. It was terrible. This one was worse." She looks up with stricken eyes. "I don't think we can help the poor souls left there. There are only five of them. They were... empty. Bags of flesh with no spark. I talked to them, but I don't know..." She covers her eyes and tears leak from behind her hands. Margo reaches a hand to her arm.

Garcia stands. "I'll set up the computer so you can send a report to Angelica," he says.

Bridgetta follows him and writes what happened and what she

found. After she's finished, she goes to the nursery school to help with the small children.

MORNING, OJAI SURVIVAL COMMUNITY

"How was the meeting in Hawaii with the Aussies?" asks Francisco.

He, Diego, Stephen and Angelica are sitting on a patio looking over the Ojai valley.

"You both would have loved being there," Angelica says. "Everything about it was remarkable. We hit it off with the Aussies. We talked about how their initial model for survival communities is being adopted and adapted all over the world. We talked about organizing the resistance into effective freedom fighters. And we asked Colin to be the head of the resistance."

"Oh yeah, that's a great idea," says Diego. "Colin's base in Australia is far from any STEN and WSO fortress. The creeps don't seem to have any use for the place."

"Yes," says Stephen. "Colin told us he's training elite fighters, and that he has long range planes that can carry them around. We recruited the Hawaiians on Oahu and they'll recruit the rest of the islanders. They are now freedom fighters. Their islands will be a supply depot, staging area, and training ground."

"Stephen gave Colin plans for a hovercraft—the same one we've been traveling in. Colin has manufacturing capability and he's going to get a fleet made. Hovercrafts will be delivered to resistance groups all over the world," says Angelica.

"There will be many details to work out, including how to handle the sleeper cells," says Stephen. "Francisco, you and Diego and Garcia and Margo and Jeremiah, with Colin and his people, are the vanguard. We have every confidence in you."

Francisco and Diego bump fists, smiling.

"The other thing we talked about was how we can rescue the Luminaries being held in detention centers." Angelica leans forward. "We have the beginnings of a plan but we'll need a lot of help to make it happen."

"We're here for you," says Francisco. Diego nods.

Akido speaks. "Boss, I just got an urgent email from Bridgetta. She got into the detention center in Utah. She says, 'Angelica, it was worse than Denver. There were only five Luminaries in the room. They were not attached to the IV system. They just lay there—empty-eyed, drooling—skeletons with a little flesh attached. It was the most awful thing I've ever seen. And I found an Electroshock Grade IV machine in the corner. I know that machine was used on those poor souls. I talked to them, trying to say what you would say. I told them to leave their broken bodies and find you. That you would help them. I hope that was the right thing to do. Angelica, we have to rescue the others as soon as possible. I'm ready to do whatever is necessary to help. Bridgetta.'"

Angelica gazes at the mountains in the distance. She stands, holding her hand out to Stephen. He takes it. She looks at Francisco and Diego. "We need to step away. Please excuse us."

They nod.

Stephen links minds with her.

Angelica: *We have to release those Luminaries Bridgetta found.*

Stephen: *Yes.*

They walk into a stand of olive trees, clasp their amulets and leave their bodies. They're instantly in the same space as the bodies in the Utah detention center ward. Stephen begins the Fallen Comrade song. Angelica joins him. The music flows around the useless bodies of the five Luminaries, lifting them out and helping them move away. With a thought, they all appear in a mountain clearing. Sun slants through the trees. Squirrels chitter, birds call, insects chirp, leaves rustle, dust motes dance in air that smells of life.

The five Luminaries come to themselves as spirits, not dead anymore. They thank the Soldiers of Light and are gone, into the light.

Another thought and Angelica and Stephen are back to their Earth bodies. They wrap their arms around each other, holding the embrace for a long moment.

"We have to get every one of them out," Angelica whispers. Stephen's arms tighten around her.

The air is still. A distant raptor cry sounds across the valley.

Francisco and Diego look at them curiously when they come back to sit down, but don't say anything.

Angelica says, "I've been giving much thought to how we are going to get the Luminaries out of the medical wards. We touched on it in talks with the Aussies. From the beginning, with our trip to the Los Angeles detention center," she nods to Diego, "I knew we'd have to stage simultaneous raids in as many locations as possible. We've visited three survival communities, all of which have detention centers nearby. I had thought to hit all three. Now it's two. There are no Luminaries left in the Utah detention center."

Stephen says, "We want to sabotage the drug delivery system they use in the detention center wards where the Luminaries are held. The idea is to create a saline solution laced with nutrients, packaged like the deep sleep drug. We'll hijack the delivery vehicles and substitute our 'drug' for theirs."

"The actual rescue will take place during the Founding Day holiday that takes place in two weeks," says Angelica.

"Whew," Diego whistles. Francisco looks thoughtful.

"We'll break into the wards, get the Luminaries out and transport them to a safe place."

"They're going to be in bad shape," says Francisco.

"The saline/nutrient blend will begin their treatment. We also have a way to help them, to give them a physical and spiritual boost."

"How's that?" asks Francisco.

Angelica and Stephen look at each other in unspoken agreement. Angelica reaches under her shirt, pulling out the turquoise amulet. It glows faintly in her open hand.

"Stephen and I both have a crystal. It has special properties that we harness. It helps us direct physical and spiritual energy to assist healing of an ailing body part or the body as a whole. We can use it to forge a link with the person, the spiritual being. We connect our life energy to theirs to speed healing."

"Where does it come from?" asks Diego.

"My parents gave me mine on my seventh birthday," says

Angelica.

"Me too," says Stephen. "Where we come from, there are specialists called Soldiers of Light. The Soldiers are warriors and spiritual guardians with healing ability. We understand both sides of life."

"You two are Soldiers of Light?" asks Diego.

"Yes," says Stephen.

"Well," says Francisco. "That answers some questions." Stephen is holding his amulet in the palm of his hand. Francisco looks back and forth between Angelica and Stephen. Each holds his gaze and their amulets pulse brighter. Standing, they take two steps toward Francisco reaching out their empty hands. He stands, steps forward and grasps their hands. The amulets pulse brighter. Francisco closes his eyes for one, two, three beats. He drops his hands.

"Okay." He plops back down. Diego opens his mouth but Francisco gestures stop. He looks up at Stephen.

"Diego, come over here with me," says Stephen.

"Okay."

They walk to the edge of the patio. Stephen takes Diego's hands, keeping the amulet clasped between their palms. Diego closes his eyes and twitches. The amulet's glow is visible between their fingers.

Francisco watches Diego as he speaks. "What can we do to help?"

"Manpower," says Angelica. "We'll need vehicles and drivers and gas for the vehicles. We'll need uniforms and IV equipment to continue nutrient treatment for the Luminaries once we have them. I'll have to work out way stations on the journey where they can rest."

Diego drops Stephen's hands with a goofy grin on his face.

"That was so cool," he says, sitting down again. "So cool." He looks at Stephen, Angelica, and Francisco. "What're we talking about?"

"Angelica is telling me what she'll need for the Luminary rescue."

"Great. What's my part?

"She'll need vehicles, drivers and fuel for them."

"How far will they be driving?"

Angelica taps on her wristband. "We'll be going approximately six hundred miles," she says.

"Okay, I'll get on that," says Diego. "And I'll look into the supplies. You'll need people to help with the Luminaries too, won't you?"

"Yes, at least one per vehicle," says Angelica.

"And some fighters to travel with us would be good," says Stephen.

"Yeah, I was going to provide that anyway," says Francisco.

"Good." Angelica smiles. "We're set. This will be the first slap on the face of the enemy by the New Civilization Freedom Fighters."

"Good name," says Diego. Francisco nods in agreement.

"Colin's group came up with it," says Angelica. "All right. Stephen and I will be travelling to Utah this morning. We need to see Garcia, Margo and Bridgetta."

"Okay," says Francisco. "We'll get started on what you need."

"Thank you, friend."

WSO HQ, LOS ANGELES

The High Commander's aide taps the door to his boss's office, and enters. He places a dispatch on the desk. Rhotah Mhene is facing away, looking at the wall map. The aide turns to leave.

"Report on the search for the women." Rhotah Mhene barks, making his aide jump.

"There is no new information, sir."

"Why not! It's been days. I want these women found and taken into custody."

"Yes, sir. Every outpost is looking for them. But we only have blurry images of them."

"This delay is unacceptable. The images we have should be enough." Rhotah Mhene's fingers drum the arms of his chair. "Get me Colonel Johnson."

"Yes, sir." The aide scurries out of the office. A minute later the phone buzzes. Rhotah Mhene hits the speaker button.

"Damien, I don't have the women yet. What are you doing about it?"

"Sir. My spies in Los Angeles and Denver report the blonde woman was there but no one has seen her for four days. We haven't found a trace of the other one." There's the sound of paper rustling. "I have a report from my deep cover agent in Utah. It's several days old, but he's confident he's met the women and the man. He's deep undercover so his reports are intermittent."

"Those women, and anyone connected with them, must be found. Do you hear me Colonel!" Rhotah Mhene raises his voice, almost to a yell.

"Yes, sir." Damien pauses. "Sir, may I speak frankly?"

"Speak."

"I think these women represent a major shift in the mindset of people outside the walled cities. I have no concrete evidence, but I think the resistance is gaining some teeth. We could face insurrection, possibly widespread insurrection."

Rhotah Mhene is silent.

"Sir?"

"She is ever a blight on my existence—her and the people who cleave to her. She will not ruin this." Rhotah Mhene seems to be talking to himself.

Damien doesn't speak.

"You find those women and find out what is happening with this resistance. Do your job."

"Yes, s—,"

Rhotah Mhene hangs up. He swivels to look at the map again. "I feel her here. And now this. We are too close to fail!" He stands, pacing, shouting. "It will not happen again!"

He stops his stammering, breathing heavily. "Lieutenant!"

His aide steps in. "Yes sir?"

"Take this dispatch: Implementation of the Electroshock Grade IV protocol to begin immediately in every detention center ward with available machines."

"Um, sir,"

"Speak!"

"Sir, I just received a dispatch that there is a delay in Grade IV machine manufacture. An essential part was made incorrectly. It has to be completely redone."

Rhotah Mhene stares at his aide. "What!? How long?"

"They won't be ready until after Founding Day."

"Are there any operable machines?"

"There's one in Utah."

"Are there any Luminaries in Utah detention?"

"There are five, and they've already been given the treatment. A second dispatch just now reported that they all died."

"Did any of them answer the questions?"

"No, sir. There were no answers."

The High Commander is gritting his teeth and his hands are clenched fists. "These Luminaries are *very dangerous* to our cause. We must continue to locate, capture and incarcerate every one of them. We have to keep them under our boots!"

Rhotah Mhene stares at the lieutenant. After a moment he says, "Send the dispatch. Inform me if anyone reports compliance. I want working machines before Founding Day."

"Yes, sir."

MORNING, SOMEWHERE OVER NEVADA

Stephen and Angelica are in the hovercraft on their way to Utah.

"Here is the plan as I see it," says Angelica. "You and Bridgetta will lead the raid on the Los Angeles detention center, along with Francisco and Diego. I will work with Jeremiah at the Denver detention center. Garcia can come down from Utah with supplies."

"Boss," Akido says. "GA has an idea. She can get the saline/nutrient solution made and teleported to us. In fact, it's almost ready now. She'll teleport it to the same location as the hovercraft was sent." He pauses. "In fact, she's been talking with Colin since the Hawaiian summit. He has identified thirteen other locations worldwide where Luminaries are being held. GA recommends a coordinated attack on Founding Day, targeting all detention centers holding Luminaries. Colin will handle contacting local freedom fighters to brief them on the plan and arrange for them to receive a drug replacement shipment. He'll tell them your plan and encourage them to adapt it to their circumstances."

"Colin is certain he can trust all these people?" says Angelica.

"Yes. He says he has been cultivating them for more than a year."

"This is excellent," says Stephen. "We can concentrate on our plan. Colin will tell the resistance and all the Luminaries in distress will have a chance."

Angelica is jubilant. "We get the drug replaced two or three days before Founding Day. GA can manipulate the computer records to facilitate this. We get STEN uniforms so we can infiltrate during the Founding Day shutdown. Akido, do we know the number of Luminaries detained?"

"GA has found the records that detail how many Luminaries are detained and where. She will provide the numbers to Colin so he can tell the different survival groups how many they'll have to plan for. She will send enough of the saline/nutrients to each location. LA has twenty Luminaries, Denver has eighteen."

"Good. For our rescues, we'll have transport for the Luminaries and personnel to help us get them to the spot where we'll rendezvous with *Lightbearer*. There will be outposts on the way that will help us. We'll recruit Clayton's gang to put us in touch with resistance sympathizers."

"GA has outlined the best route from both Los Angeles and Denver to the first rendezvous point, the meteor crater in Arizona," says Akido. "Her suggestion is that you take the wristband—me—and Stephen uses a hard copy map."

"That will work," says Stephen.

"We can talk with Garcia and Jeremiah. We'll get Clayton on board. We're getting the juggernaut in motion," Angelica says.

"Yes, we are," says Stephen. They share a feeling of euphoria.

UTAH SURVIVAL COMMUNITY

Stephen lands the hovercraft not far from Garcia's house. He and Angelica sit on the front porch, watching Margo and Garcia coming up the sidewalk.

"You're back!" Margo hugs Angelica and Stephen. "I'm so glad to see you. Come in and tell us your news." She hustles everyone into the house toward the kitchen. "I'll make coffee."

Garcia says, "So. Your Akido and Francisco have been keeping us filled in."

"What do you know?" says Angelica.

"You're planning to break out the Luminaries on Founding Day. In fact, all the Luminaries held in detention centers on Earth. Sounds mighty ambitious."

"Stephen and I will be involved with just two rescues. He'll be in Los Angeles and I'll be in Denver. Will you be able to bring supplies to the rendezvous point?"

"Of course, when I know where it is."

"Right. Freedom fighters near any other detention centers will handle the rescue of their Luminaries. Colin assures us that he is in contact with trustworthy people. We'll help with some materiel, that's it. I want Bridgetta to go to LA with Stephen."

"She'll be happy about that. Although she's kinda stuck on that new guy you met, Juan Carlos."

"You've been keeping an eye on him?"

"Yeah. He's all over the camp but he always has a plausible reason. We've made sure he's never alone. I do see what you were talking about, though. There is something…"

"Trust your perceptions," says Stephen. "Make sure he doesn't hear anything about our plan."

"I'll do that," says Garcia.

"Me too," says Margo. "I'll talk to Bridgetta, she'll understand."

"Do you know where Juan Carlos is now?" says Stephen.

"He and Zack are hunting today. They won't be back til night-fall," says Garcia.

"Good," says Stephen.

"Next, we need to talk to Clayton," says Angelica.

"The marauder you ran across in Denver?" asks Margo.

"Yes. We plan to recruit him and his band for the resistance," says Angelica. "And get him to recruit other marauder groups."

"Good luck with that," says Garcia. "He and his gang have a place they like to hole up, over near Dinosaur National Monument. They'll probably be there."

"Thank you," says Angelica. "Do you have any way to contact him, to tell him we're coming to see him?"

"I might have. Don't know if a message will get to him before you do, but I'll try."

"Thank you again," says Angelica. "Now we're going to ask Bridgetta to come with us to find Clayton."

Stephen and Angelica approach the training area, looking for Bridgetta. She's in the middle of a circle of young men and women, sparring with a huge man. She dances away from her opponent's attempts to reach her. She glances up and sees them.

"Hold!" she shouts at her opponent and runs over to them. She hugs them both. "So good to see you!"

"Can you talk for a minute?" says Angelica.

"Of course. Max, take over, will you?" The huge man, Max, waves. Bridgetta loops her arm through Angelica's. "What's up?"

"Angelica wants to find Clayton and recruit him for the resistance," says Stephen.

Bridgetta looks at Angelica. "Really?"

"We have a plan to rescue the Luminaries, and we'll need Clayton's contacts in the wilderness," says Angelica. "You are our secret weapon. That gang respects you."

"You think you can talk him into fighting for our resistance?"

"Yes, I do. Will you come with us? We're leaving soon."

"I did kick the crap out of their top guy. That was a triumph but I am not looking for any kind of rematch. That guy was good and he was much stronger than me. It was pure intention on my part that won the battle that day."

"I know. There will be no rematch. Just talking," says Angelica.

"Okay, I'm in. Meet you at Garcia's in an hour?"

"Perfect. See you then."

Bridgetta heads back toward the training area. Stephen and Angelica go to prepare for the trip.

An hour later they are on Garcia's front porch again. When they see Bridgetta, they meet her on the sidewalk and lead the way to the hovercraft.

"Where are we going?" Bridgetta asks.

"Dinosaur National Monument," says Stephen. "It's east of here, not too far as the crow flies."

"Okay." She looks at both of them. "Can you tell me what the plan is?"

Angelica answers. "Garcia is trying to get a message to Clayton that we're coming to see him. It may not work. We'll have to approach with caution. I'm going to appeal to his better side to help take care of the Luminaries. His daughter is missing and I'm sure he knows others who were taken."

"Angelica can talk water off a whale, as we say back home," says Stephen.

Bridgetta looks at him.

"She can be very persuasive," says Stephen. Bridgetta makes an "Oh" face.

"I'll listen to what he says and use it to make my points, that's all," says Angelica. "I've already started, when we talked in Denver."

"She's started working her magic," says Stephen. He grabs her, giving her a quick kiss. "Let's go."

AFTERNOON

In the hovercraft, flying low over the Wasatch Mountains and valleys, the winter views are spectacular.

"We're getting close to Vernal," Akido says. "That is the town closest to the Dinosaur National Monument. The tracker is active. It is located east and north of Vernal. It looks like they're in what used to be the Jones Hole federal fish hatchery. It is a defensible location."

"Show us a topographical map of the place," says Stephen. A three-D image appears above Angelica's wristband.

Angelica points. "We should set down somewhere around here, out of sight, and walk in."

"Agreed," says Stephen. "Here we go."

"They're going to be one surprised gang when they see us. I can't wait to see the expression on their faces," says Bridgetta.

The freedom fighters land and walk along the road into the hatchery. Stephen uses the infrared function on his binovision, scanning ahead for heat signatures and body images. He sees animal shapes, but no man images. Closer to the hatchery, Stephen scans again. This time he picks up body shapes—sentries posted on the ridges above them.

He stops. "We're here," he says. He slowly stows his binovision in his backpack and lifts his hands beside his head. Angelica and Bridgetta do the same. Two men with shotguns approach, their weapons pointed at them dead center.

Everyone stands still. The men with guns are unmoving. Stephen, Angelica and Bridgetta are also unmoving. The moment stretches.

They hear footsteps and Clayton comes around a bend in the road. He's carrying a shotgun, flanked by two more gun-toting men. He's grinning.

"I just heard you wanted to talk to me. Now you're here. How'd you find me?" He pauses. "Never mind, I don't want to know." He nods in their direction. "Search them." The man on his right comes forward and pats each of them down.

"Clean." The man steps back.

"So," Clayton says, "to what do I owe this dubious pleasure?"

Angelica takes a step forward. "We come in peace—to ask for your help."

"Hmm." Clayton looks them over. "My boys haven't forgotten our first meeting. They made sure everyone here knew about your brashness. Not sure anyone here wants to have anything to do with you. Nice to see you again because you're both easy on the eyes but the boys don't like taking a beating. As I see it, you were lucky in our first encounter." He cradles his shotgun. "Plus, you stole one of my guys." He spits.

"Last time we met, I told you about the resistance movement," Angelica says.

Clayton nods.

"Much has happened since that evening. The resistance has become worldwide. And we are planning to rescue all the incarcerated Luminaries." Angelica lets silence settle around them.

"This rescue could include loved ones your people are missing." The men around Clayton shift.

"What are you talking about?" he says.

Angelica raises her voice. "We are going to break out all the Luminaries in every WSO detention center on Earth. Simultaneously." She locks eyes with every man she can see. "Our best people will no longer suffer at the hands of evil men." She takes a breath. "We came here to ask for your help in this rescue."

Clayton stares at her. He looks at his men and back at her. "You follow me." He goes back down the road. Angelica, Stephen and Bridgetta go after him, with his men trailing behind them.

When they reach buildings, Angelica steps up beside Clayton. "May we talk privately first?"

"Sure." He waves his men off and leads her to a grouping of boulders out of earshot. They sit.

"When we met last, you said you knew places and people all over. Once we take the Luminaries out of the Los Angeles and Denver detention facilities, we'll be transporting them across your country to a location in the southwest. They'll be in bad shape physically, so we'll need way stations where they can rest and be tended to. I'm asking you to be our emissary to your people."

Clayton sizes up Angelica, looking at her closely. There is something about this woman—and her man. They have some sort of power. He can feel the strength of her intention. She'll never stop until she does what she plans to do. Neither of them will. Angelica waits, watching his thoughts run over his face.

She speaks again, softly. "This is a chance to demonstrate why you didn't succumb to suicide. Why you stayed away from the fortress cities. Why you live the way you do. This can give a bigger purpose to your life, and the life of the people you lead. Your Luminaries need your help. Earth's Luminaries need your help."

"What do we get out of it, if we help you?"

Angelica spreads her hands. "What do you want?"

Clayton looks at her again. She's not judging him. She waits for him to speak. He looks at the ground. His voice is low when he answers.

"I want to have my loved ones around me, safe. I want my people to be able to live without fear of STEN reprisals. I want our children to play and learn and be able to choose their paths." His voice becomes stronger as he speaks. "Can you give me all this?"

"That is my goal—for you and for all the people of Earth," she says. She can feel Stephen with her. "Our goal."

Clayton kicks at a rock on the ground. He's not committing. He keeps at the rock, not speaking.

Angelica says, "In addition to the philosophical reasons, there could be a material factor. The resistance movement is growing rapidly and it will need a transport system and mail service. It'll need to be designed and implemented. You and your people could help set it up then perform the service for the United States. You already go between the walled cities bringing news to their inhabitants. You venture out into the faraway places where the settlements are. This service would be natural for your group. You could expand your power base with something you're already doing."

Clayton looks up at the rock cliffs above him. He's silent for a long moment before he speaks. "You're totally different from any woman I know. There's something about you—and your man. I don't know why, but I trust you both."

Now he looks at the ground, running his boot across the hard-packed dirt, thinking hard. Finally, he looks up. "We'll help you with the rescue. What are the details?"

"I'll tell you the plan, but ask you not to reveal it. I think you and your group can help without telling them specifics. I know how you feel about sleeper cell spies, so I'm assuming you don't have any in your group. But we're concerned about the possibility of leaks. As our plan progresses, it will be more and more crucial that STEN be ignorant of it." Angelica fixes her gaze on Clayton. "Their leader will do anything to keep Luminaries under his control."

"They are an evil group," says Clayton. "What do you need from us?"

"Once we have the Luminaries, we'll take them to the meteor crater in Arizona. Stephen will bring the group from Los Angeles east, using highway 40. I'll bring the group from Denver west and south through Utah, near Navajo country. This will happen on Founding Day, so we should be able to stay far away from STEN patrols. We'll need friendly places to stop, to hide, to rest, to provide care for the Luminaries. Can you arrange these spots? We'll need them the evening of Founding Day."

Clayton is nodding. "That's a good plan. You have the details worked out?"

"Yes. They all need to be put in motion, but it's ready," says Angelica.

Clayton nudges the dirt with his foot again. He starts to speak. Angelica waits. He takes a deep breath. "I want to find my daughter. More than anything. Some of my men and women feel the same about their missing family. We realize they may be dead. But they might be alive." He looks Angelica in the eye. "We'll join your fight. We'll make it our fight. We'll find our people." He extends his hand. Angelica takes it. Clasping her hand, Clayton feels a peace steal over him. He doesn't know why, but he's certain, certain that everything will work out. He releases her hand and the moment passes.

They're walking back toward the buildings. Clayton says, "I wasn't the best dad in the world, but it would be good to see her again. If she is still alive, she'd be in her thirties, I reckon." They walk a few more steps. "Angelica, I have to be honest. The WSO has a bounty on me and the gang. They know I've infiltrated their system numerous times. They consider me a danger. I'm a threat because I don't play by their rules."

He's thoughtful again. "This might be for later, but I've heard something from a reliable source inside the Denver fortress about a secret plant in California where they're working on some kind of crop. There's processing involved after the harvest. The person I talked to thinks they're growing poppies to make blue pills here, in the West. He thought it was odd, since blue pills are available by the handful in Denver."

"Hmmm." Angelica is quiet for a moment. "This is good information. I think the WSO may have plans we don't know about yet. You'll keep your ears open?"

"You bet."

Stephen: *They're using Earth as a supply depot to expand their drug and sex trade into this sector of the universe*

Angelica: *I agree. We'll tackle that after we rescue our people.*

Stephen: *Yes, we will.*

They share an image of an army of Soldiers of Light and Luminaries descending on Earth, routing the WSO and capturing the Soulests behind it.

Angelica and Clayton walk up to the group of his men with Bridgetta and Stephen.

"We've been sharing war stories," says Bridgetta. "Some of these guys have had experiences like mine. They've even forgiven me for beating up Harry. Although I guess Harry is still a bit miffed about it." The men chuckle.

"I've been filling them in on the resistance," says Stephen.

One of the men speaks up. "Boss, we want in."

"That's good," says Clayton, "Because I just signed us up."

There's a chorus of "Yeah!" and Bridgetta claps.

"Good," says Stephen. "Now, we have to leave."

"How will we stay in touch?" says Clayton.

"We're using Backdoor Charlie," says Angelica.

"That's legitimate?" says Clayton. "We haven't trusted it. We thought it was too good to be true."

"It's definitely legitimate," says Angelica. "You can trust everything on it."

"Well then, we've got some catching up to do," says Clayton. "Safe journey."

"Thank you."

Angelica, Stephen and Bridgetta leave, walking back toward the hovercraft.

"Let's play," says Stephen. He turns to Bridgetta. "Try this running technique. Lower your center of gravity like this and let your arms swing like this. You can run almost forever. Give it a try."

Bridgetta mimics his motions, taking off toward the hovercraft. Stephen and Angelica are right behind her. They're all laughing when they reach it. Bridgetta is breathing heavily. "That's a great way to run!"

After a short trip back to the Utah camp, Stephen and Angelica drop Bridgetta off and head for Denver.

NIGHT

There is no moon, but stars light up the clear sky. Angelica and Stephen lean back, basking in the night.

"Boss." Akido interrupts. "STEN just made another raid on our three survival camps—Los Angeles, Utah, and Denver. GA warned them all so there were no consequences. But they really want to find you and Bridgetta."

"Is Bridgetta safe?"

"Yes, Boss. She stayed hidden. They still only have blurry pictures of you both."

"Thank you, Akido. Keep us posted."

Angelica and Stephen arrive and park in Jeremiah's backyard.

"You two just missed all the excitement," says Jeremiah. "Those storm troopers have a real bug up their hind ends for you, Angelica."

"I heard."

"You gonna stay a few steps ahead of them, right?"

"Of course." Angelica gives him a fox smile.

"Right. Well, you two probably need food and sleep."

"That would be excellent, thank you. Can we talk in the morning? We have a lot to tell you."

"Sounds great."

Angelica and Stephen have a quick meal then crawl into bed. They are asleep in seconds.

DAY NINETEEN

DENVER, OPERATION BLUE WHALE

IN THE MORNING they're in the kitchen. Jeremiah is flipping pancakes and the smell of bacon and coffee fills the air.

"You two have Backdoor Charlie burning up. You got a plan to rescue Luminaries." Jeremiah hands them each a plate.

"We do," says Angelica.

"What happens next?"

"All the parts need to come together in proper order. We'll be working on that today. Can we use your kitchen table after breakfast?"

"Sure."

"Thank you. Do you understand your part?"

"Yeah. We help break out our people from the Denver detention center. Then we drive down to the meteor crater in Arizona."

"Yes. We've recruited Clayton's Marauders to provide cover for our groups. One will be coming from Los Angeles too."

"What about Utah?"

"No one is left there."

Jeremiah bows his head and there's a moment of silence.

"Okay," he says, "let's finish and clean up so you can get to work."

In a few minutes, Angelica and Stephen are standing in front of the cleared table.

"Akido, please show GA what we're doing here."

"Yes, Boss."

Angelica folds a white cloth napkin into quarters, placing it at the left edge of the table. "This is Los Angeles," she says.

Stephen folds a brown napkin in quarters, placing it to the right and above the LA napkin, saying, "This is Utah."

"Here's Denver," says Angelica, placing another napkin near the center of the table.

"And here's the meteor crater," says Stephen, placing the last napkin south of Utah. He picks up a pepper shaker. "This is you," he says to Angelica, setting it down next to Denver.

Angelica picks up the salt. "This is you," she says, placing it next to Los Angeles.

Jeremiah watches them from the doorway. He leaves, returning with a carousel of poker chips. He sets it to one side on the table. Angelica smiles at him. She grabs a handful of white poker chips. She places a stack of four next to both Denver and Los Angeles.

"These are the nutrient solution," she says. "Akido, how long should the Luminaries be given this solution before we come to get them?"

"GA says they should receive it for at least three days."

"How many days from today to Founding Day?"

"Thirteen days."

"That's December 20th," says Jeremiah. He has a handful of small objects he puts on the table next to the carousel. "Would you like to see a calendar?"

"That would be very helpful, thank you," says Stephen.

Angelica looks at the objects Jeremiah put down—two clothes pins, four polished rocks, several buttons of different sizes, a large spring and two medium-sized metal nuts. She chooses the two clothes pins, putting one on top of the white poker chips by Los Angeles and the same by Denver.

"These are the delivery vans with the nutrient solution." Two buttons are placed with each van.

"Driver and guard—our people," says Stephen.

"Right," says Angelica. Now she reaches for a stack of blue poker chips. "Akido, how many Luminaries are there in Los Angeles and in Denver?"

"GA found records of twenty in Los Angeles and eighteen in Denver," says Akido.

Jeremiah comes back in with the calendar. "Made it myself."

"Thank you, Jeremiah." Angelica puts the calendar in the upper corner of the table. "If we put three Luminaries in each vehicle, that means seven vans needed for Los Angeles and six for Denver." She lines up seven blue chips near Los Angeles and six near Denver. "And they will need to be vans so the Luminaries can lie down. We'll need a driver, a guard and an attendant with each van."

Jeremiah goes to a cupboard and pulls out a bag of pinto beans. He hands it to Stephen. Stephen opens the bag and begins counting out beans for the personnel that will be needed—twenty-one for Los Angeles and eighteen for Denver. He puts the appropriate number of beans next to each blue poker chip.

Angelica picks up the calendar. "We're here, on the 8th. The nutrient solution will need to be in the medical wards, being delivered to the Luminaries, by the 17th."

Jeremiah clears his throat. Angelica focuses on him.

"I don't know if Diego mentioned it, but he and I have been planning for a raid on the detention center for a while now. We both have STEN delivery vans we can use. We have delivery personnel uniforms too."

"Oh, well done, both of you!" Angelica says with delight. "GA is creating orders for the 'new' solution for the psychiatric medical wards, to be special delivered on December 16th, and switched out by eight a.m. December 17th. She'll deliver printed orders with the nutrients. Do you need special badges?"

"No, we're all set with those," says Jeremiah.

Akido speaks. "Jeremiah, your shipment of nutrients will arrive in your backyard early December 16th."

"In my backyard? How…?" Jeremiah looks confused.

"Just stay out of the backyard until it arrives," says Stephen. "Although it might be fun to sit on the back porch to watch for it."

Jeremiah stares at Stephen a minute and shakes his head. "Okay, you get the drug replacement here, we'll get it into the ward."

"You can recruit the drivers, guards and attendants we'll need?" asks Angelica.

"Yeah," says Jeremiah. "Once folks know there's a rescue brewing, I'll have too many volunteers."

"Be very careful who knows about the plan. No part of it can get back to STEN. Be certain anyone you talk to is trustworthy," says Angelica. "Our Luminaries depend on it."

"I know. I'll be careful," says Jeremiah.

Angelica stands, looking down at the table top.

"Akido, is it possible to speak, with visual, using Backdoor Charlie? I need a live conference with Colin, Francisco, Garcia, Bridgetta and Clayton."

Akido is silent for several seconds. "GA will need a camera source at each location that can plug into a computer."

"We can do that here," says Jeremiah. "I'll get it set up. You want it in here?"

"Yes, please," says Angelica. "I want to show everyone the plan." She gestures to the table.

"Great," says Jeremiah.

"Requests have been sent to the rest of the parties," Akido says. "GA added that the locations should be secure, with only the requested people present."

"She thinks of everything," says Stephen.

Angelica touches his hand. "Let's take a walk while we wait for answers." Stephen nods.

"Your neighborhood is secure?" she asks Jeremiah.

"You'll be fine," he says.

They leave by the back door. Outside, they walk around the house to the front yard, turning left at the sidewalk.

"You want to talk with the Defense Minister," says Stephen.

"We need to coordinate. Now is a good time," says Angelica. "Akido, voice contact with Defense Minister Drail please." She points to an empty house with a huge yard. "Let's go behind here to talk." She leads the way.

The next voice she hears is Drail's.

"Angelica, Stephen. Be the light. You've made excellent progress," he says.

"Yes, sir. The people of Earth have proved resourceful. Their plans for resistance were already well underway. We provided some extras that have helped them."

"And now you're ready to rescue our Luminaries."

"Yes, sir. I wanted to coordinate with you. GA has arranged the manufacture and delivery of a nutrient solution to replace the drugs being given to the Luminaries in the psychiatric medical wards. She is working with Earth's resistance leader to make sure all groups close enough to rescue Luminaries have the nutrient solution.

"Stephen and I will be helping in the rescue of our people from two locations near us: Los Angeles and Denver. We've enlisted all the resistance fighters in the area who can help. The resistance leader will be sending an elite guard from another location on the planet to help us secure the Luminaries while we travel. We'll be taking them to the meteor crater in Arizona. Will you let the captain of *Lightbearer* know to meet us there after dark on December 21st? We'll need his full capabilities to help our rescued people."

"The ship and its orbiters are already on their way. Two more Soldiers of Light and another helper are on board, coming to assist you with the Luminaries, and your other mission orders, if you have need."

"Who?"

"Luerin Macobi, and his sons, Soldiers of Light, Gabriel and Virgil."

"We will be very happy to have their help, thank you, sir." Angelica has a big smile on her face. Stephen is grinning too.

Drail continues, "The GA informs me that she will be incapacitating the WSO's computer system starting at western hemisphere sunrise on their Founding Day. Her hack will start small and build to a complete meltdown three hours later. That will keep the enemy occupied. Your people will have an open door for escape."

"Thank you, that's very good news," says Angelica. "That's all we have for now, sir. We will keep you informed. Thank you for your help. Be the light."

"Be the light," says Drail, ending the transmission.

"We should get back," says Stephen, "and see if all our folks have reported in."

"*Folks.* You're going native on me," says Angelica, giving him a quick kiss. "I like it."

They make their way back to Jeremiah's house. In the kitchen, they find Colin already on the computer screen.

"Is everyone here?" asks Angelica. She receives a chorus of voices identifying Francisco, Diego, Garcia, Bridgetta, and Clayton.

"Wonderful," she says. "I want to show you the rescue plan." She trains the camera on the table top.

She explains the plan, pointing to the various items as she speaks. She shows them the white poker chip nutrient solution that will be delivered four days prior to the rescue. Colin confirms he has worked with GA to schedule the supply drop at locations around the world. Diego reports he has his delivery personnel set up.

Angelica now talks about the actual rescue. "The idea is to infiltrate the detention center medical wards while almost all the staff are out celebrating Founding Day. GA has confirmed there is a four- or five-hour window when the medical ward will be locked, with no personnel on duty. They've done this in previous years.

"We'll enter the ward at that time and get all the Luminaries out to waiting transport. They will have been on a nutrient drip for three days by the 20th, so they'll be in better condition. Once they're in the transport vehicles, we'll take them to the meteor crater."

As she describes the journey, Stephen shows the trucks and vans moving along their routes to the crater. Clayton's men, in the form of pinto beans, are shown running interference and steering the blue poker chip vans to rest stops. Everyone ends up together at the crater.

"Once everyone is at the crater, some of our people will be on hand to help out," says Angelica.

"Can't wait to meet them," says Colin. "What do you need from me?"

"Can you get two hundred of your elite commandos here, to the states, in time to rendezvous at the crater?" asks Angelica.

Colin says, "No worries. We fly to the Los Angeles area, drop off a couple of squads to travel with the LA rescue team, refuel, and go on to Flagstaff. How does that sound?"

"It's only about forty-five miles from there to the crater," says Clayton. "I can arrange transport for them."

"That'll work, mate," says Colin.

"Excellent!" says Angelica.

"Okay. Does anyone have any questions?" says Stephen.

Diego speaks. "Do all the other resistance groups have the same plan?"

Colin answers. "They're all receiving the nutrient solution, with instructions on when and how to get it into the wards to replace what's there. They all know that the rescues have to happen on Founding Day. Each location is coming up with their own plan to get it done. And they've set up rendezvous points like you have, Angelica."

"Excellent," says Angelica. "There's one other part of the plan. The WSO and STEN computer systems are going to experience an inexplicable meltdown on Founding Day. This will cripple any response they try to mount."

"Fantastic," says Colin, a sentiment echoed by the others.

"Angelica and I will be available via email if anyone needs anything or wants to talk," says Stephen.

"One last thing," says Angelica. "We call this plan Operation Blue Whale. Thank you all for joining us." She looks into the camera. "When we finish a meeting, we say, 'Be the light.'"

"Be the light," choruses from the computer screen.

Jeremiah shuts down the computer.

"I better get busy putting my crews together," he says. "Stick around as long as you want." He walks out the door, waving.

UTAH SURVIVAL COMMUNITY

BRIDGETTA WALKS toward Margo's house. She has a date for brunch with the older woman. Margo is wise, practical and funny and Bridgetta is happy to spend time with her.

Bridgetta gives a brief knock at the front door, walking in. The house is filled with the smell of coffee and cinnamon rolls. As she enters the kitchen, Margo hands her a cup of coffee. She sips it, enjoying the warmth.

"Let me get the cinnamon rolls out of the oven," says Margo, "then we'll sit and have a chat." She pulls a pan from the oven, slathers on frosting and puts the rolls in the middle of the table. "Help yourself," she says, sitting down.

Bridgetta digs a roll out of the pan, putting it on a plate. "Yum." She licks her fingers.

"Garcia says you're to go with Stephen to help him in Los Angeles," says Margo.

"Yeah." Bridgetta speaks around a mouthful. She swallows, shaking her head. "I'm excited, nervous, ready."

"You may have guessed; I have something specific I need to talk with you about."

Bridgetta nods, taking a sip of coffee.

"You are becoming fond of Juan Carlos." Margo takes a bite of roll.

Bridgetta nods again. "There's something about him. He listens when I talk. He cares about what I think. He makes me feel good, important."

Margo nods. "I'm just going to say this. Please accept it as information, take a look at it…." She pauses.

"What?"

"Garcia and I, Angelica and Stephen, we have some concerns about Juan Carlos."

"Why?"

"He arrived out of nowhere. We don't know where he comes from, where he's been, why he's here."

"He's told me."

"What has he told you?"

"He said he's been wandering the land between here and LA. He spent some time in the Vegas area. He said he wanted to be somewhere colder."

"When I ask him about his people," says Margo, "he speaks a lot of words but says nothing."

"I have noticed he sidesteps specific questions about his family and his life." Bridgetta is thoughtful.

"He also asks a lot of questions about our community and how we do things."

"Yeah. He asks me a lot of questions about the people here—who they are and what they do. He wants to know all about everyone."

"Has he been interested in Angelica and Stephen?"

"Yeeesss. He's wondered some about who they are, where they're from, what they're doing. Yeah, he's pretty interested in them. He's asked about how long they've been around." Bridgetta looks at Margo. "Now that I think about it, he never really asks a direct question. It's more like he wants me to fill in the blanks." She pauses. "Are you thinking he could be a spy?"

Margo is silent.

Bridgetta rubs her face. "Damn! I was really starting to like him. He makes me feel good. I feel like we could work together."

"You can still hang out with him. You'll just have to make sure you say nothing about the plans you're part of."

"Easier said than done. At least I'll be leaving with Stephen in a few days."

"We'll need to find a job for him to do away from the camp when Stephen comes to get you."

"Does Zack know? He and Juan Carlos hit it off too."

"He knows. He's helping keep Juan Carlos away from anything sensitive, and away from anything he could use to communicate outside the camp—like the computer room."

"I'm going to keep talking to him about our philosophy," says Bridgetta. "Maybe we can bring him into the light."

"Maybe," says Margo. She squeezes Bridgetta's hand.

DAY TWENTY

DENVER

STEPHEN AND ANGELICA are sitting in front of Jeremiah's computer. Colin's face is on the screen.

"Things are shaping up on my end, mates," says Colin. "We found an airfield near Bakersfield, California that was used by the U.S. Air Force. We'll land our big plane there and offload the commandos for the Los Angeles team. We've arranged a bus to take them from Bakersfield to LA. If anyone asks, they'll be a bunch of STEN recruits. We'll refuel and fly on to Flagstaff."

"Brilliant," says Stephen. "You've coordinated with Francisco?"

"Yeah. He'll meet the commandos in LA. I'll meet you at the crater."

"You're coming?"

"Wouldn't miss it. Liam's taking command while I'm gone. He's pretty jealous—he wanted to come too." Colin laughs.

"The battles begin," says Angelica.

"The battles begin," echoes Colin.

DAY TWENTY-THREE

DENVER

ANGELICA AND STEPHEN sit in Jeremiah's living room, in front of a warm fire. The temperature outside is in the low twenties.

"Every detention center medical ward needs to be hit at the same time," says Angelica. "If not, STEN will be alerted. They cannot be allowed to figure it out until all the Luminaries are on the road to safety."

"GA has timed it down to the minute," says Akido. "Stephen, she says you'll need to extend your journey from LA to match the time it will take Angelica to travel from Denver. Her trip to the crater will be at least five hours longer than yours."

"No problem. Clayton has my caravan stopping in Needles, California," says Stephen. "We'll be able to stay there safely for as long as needed. According to Clayton, there's a small community there that STEN hasn't paid any attention to."

Angelica says, "I'll be talking to Clayton tomorrow about the stops in my trip." She leans forward, looking into the fire.

Stephen watches her. "What is it, love?"

"Something," she says, staring at the fire. "There's something out there, something waiting for me."

"Bad?"

"No, not bad." She looks at him with full eyes. "I'm hoping it's something we've been searching for."

Stephen moves to her, pulling her into his arms. "Me too."

She wraps her arms around his waist, laying her head against his chest. She listens to his heartbeat and sighs. He lays his head on hers.

The fire snaps and settles.

DAY TWENTY-FOUR

NEAR DINOSAUR NATIONAL MONUMENT

"The convoy needs to stop in Window Rock," says Asta. He's just arrived at the Hatchery.

"How do you know about this?" asks Clayton. He stares at the Navajo man in front of him.

Asta looks at him.

Clayton tries again. "How long did it take you to get here?"

"I've been traveling for two days, mainly at night."

"I see. This stop must be pretty important if you've come to request it in person…"

"Not requesting." Asta stares at Clayton for several beats. He breaks into a grin.

Clayton grins back. "Tough guy. But seriously, what's the deal?"

"We have some people the tribe has adopted. One of them asked for the convoy to stop in Window Rock. I'm here to make sure it happens."

"Okay then, no problem. I'll let the leader, Angelica, know. But seriously, how did you know about the convoy?"

Asta puts on a blank face. "We Indians have our ways."

Clayton gives him a look. The moment holds, then they both laugh and clasp hands.

DAY TWENTY-FIVE

UTAH

Juan Carlos meets Bridgetta walking toward the chapel.

"Hi," he says.

"Hi."

"Where are you going?"

"Church."

"Really?"

"Yeah. Want to come?"

"Sure." Juan Carlos falls into step beside her. He sits next to her during the church service.

After church, they go to the common room for coffee. There are other members of the congregation there, talking quietly in pairs and small groups. Bridgetta gets a cup of tea and sits down in front of the fireplace. The flames warm her. Juan Carlos sits down beside her.

"This is nice," he says.

"Peaceful," she says.

"Umhm." He's quiet, sipping his coffee. He turns to look at her. "Can I ask you a question?"

She nods.

"Do you like me?"

She turns to him.

He continues, "I mean, when I first got here, I had the feeling that we could, maybe, be friends, like *friends*. But you've been distant the last few days. Did I do something?"

She gazes into the fire. He waits.

"It's coming up on an anniversary that always makes me sad. I close up for a while. I'm sorry about that," she says.

"Oh." He touches her arm. "Can I do anything for you?"

"No. I just have to get through it." She pats his hand. "Being here, in Utah, has helped."

"You're not from here?"

"No, Los Angeles originally."

"Wow. Me too." He leans back into the sofa. "You ever been anywhere else? You ever been further east?"

"I went to Denver once."

"By yourself?"

"Oh no, with a couple of friends."

"How was it?"

"Interesting. The country between here and there is spectacular."

"What did you do there?"

"We visited another community like this one. And we met some marauders. Have you been anywhere else besides LA and here?"

"I guess I've been a sort of marauder myself. Mainly roamed the west." He leans forward to put his cup on the coffee table. "Do people leave this camp a lot to roam?"

"Not since I've been here."

"But you did. How come?"

"It was a whim. My friends decided to go and invited me to go with them."

"I'd like to meet these friends. They sound like my kind of people."

"You actually already met them."

"I did? When?"

"Maybe ten days ago. It was brief."

Juan Carlos looks thoughtful. "Wait. That couple that came to see you during a class. You introduced us. What were their names…?"

Bridgetta looks at him, sipping her tea. "Didn't they say?"

"I don't remember." Bridgetta pats his hand. He continues, "Do you know where they are now?"

"They're trekking," she says. "They were vague about where."

"Will they be back?"

"Oh, I'm sure, eventually."

"Okay. Maybe I can meet them again."

"I'm sure you can."

Bridgetta stands. "I have to meet Margo now," she says. "Thanks for going to church with me." She gives him a warm smile and walks away.

Juan Carlos watches her leave, a speculative look on his face. *I have something bothering me too.* And he'll have to figure it out soon.

DAY TWENTY-SIX

DARWIN AUSTRALIA

Colin is in the cockpit of the troop carrier. His copilot Joseph is running the preflight checklist. He has one hundred and twenty commandos in the plane behind him. A surge of pride rushes through him. He sends a brief thank you prayer to any gods listening for the strangers Angelica and Stephen. It's finally happening.

Joseph gives him thumbs up. Colin starts his taxi to take off. The resistance is underway.

GREEK THEATER, LOS ANGELES

Diego and John Boy are in the trees across from the Greek Theater parking lot. It's hazy with a slight breeze.

"Do you know what's supposed to happen?" whispers John Boy.

"Nope."

"We just wait?"

"Yup."

"Okay." John Boy leans against a large pine. He and Diego are dressed in the white coveralls of the WSO Health Group. The white van parked next to the box office building has the WSOHG logo painted on the side.

Diego scans the parking area, eyes moving back and forth. The parking lot is empty. He catches a shimmer at the edge of his vision. There's no sound, but now a pallet sits near the back of the parking lot.

"Wow," breathes John Boy.

"Let's grab it," says Diego. "You bring the van over." He trots toward the pallet. There are cubes packed on it, labels showing that the contents are made in the Philippines. The list of ingredients looks medical. Diego whistles in admiration.

John Boy drives up, pulling beside the pallet. He and Diego load the cubes. Diego climbs in the driver's seat with John Boy beside him. They head for the Los Angeles walled fortress.

As they near the gate, Diego says, "Remember, I'm doing the talking."

John Boy nods.

They stop at the gate's guard station. The guard has a rifle at his shoulder. "What are you doing here today? This isn't the normal delivery day." He peers at Diego, moving to hold the rifle across his chest. "And you ain't the usual driver."

"Hey man. Stop jerking my chain. I got orders, I follow them." Diego hands the guard his documents.

The guard takes the papers and looks them over, grumbling. "Nobody tells us nothing." He hands the papers back. "Fine, go ahead. You know how to get to the back of the detention center?"

"Yeah. The freight loading area, right?"

"Yeah." The guard waves them forward.

They make their way through the walled city to the back of the Staples Center detention center. Diego gets out and knocks on the back door. It's opened by a guard who glares at him.

"Who the hell are you?" he says.

"Special delivery. Can we get some help hauling this stuff in?" Diego asks.

The guard stares at him. "Let me see your paperwork," he says. Diego hands it over. The guard examines it.

"Looks like everything is in order. But this is very unusual," he says, handing the papers back to Diego.

"I don't know, man. I just do what I'm told," says Diego. He stares back at the guard. "Some help?" He waits a minute, shrugs and turns to leave.

The guard watches him. He waves over two others. When they get to the back of the van, John Boy has the doors open and is hauling out cubes.

"What is this?" asks one of the guards.

"No idea," says John Boy. "I just deliver."

Diego speaks to the first guard who is now standing at the edge of the loading dock, watching them. "I'm supposed to take this stuff into the closet and switch it out." The guard doesn't move. The two others stop working and look at him. Finally, he jerks his head toward the door. One of the helpers goes inside and brings out a dolly.

Diego gets all the cubes into the closet under the watchful eyes of the first guard. He hooks up the nutrient cubes to the IV drip system and loads the other drug cubes onto the dolly. He has to walk past the somnolent figures. He confirms there are twenty bodies in the room. He peers at the closest shape. The figure is emaciated and drooling. Diego shudders.

"What you doing man?" A guard is walking toward him.

Diego looks at him. "Just checking out the animals."

"Move it," says the guard. He ushers Diego out of the room.

John Boy is already in the van. Diego climbs into the driver's seat and they drive out of the fortress city, not acknowledging the salute from the guard at the gate as they pass through.

In Denver and thirteen other locations around the world, similar scenes are occurring.

WSO HQ, LOS ANGELES

Damien paces in his office, view from the window ignored. His intermittent raids have turned up nothing. No sign of either of the women. No sign of resistance activity. Juan Carlos is uncharacteristically silent. His last report said he was deep undercover and it could be hard to get reports out. But it's been days. What the hell is going on? Something is happening. He can feel it in his bones, on his skin. The very air is vibrating with tension. He picks up a stapler to throw across the room.

I need to hit something, he thinks, slamming the stapler down. He leaves his office, heading for the training ground.

DAY TWENTY-SEVEN

BAKERSFIELD, CALIFORNIA

A LARGE PLANE lands at the abandoned Bakersfield Airport. A pair of hawks watch from their perch on the control tower. A large group of men disembark. They unload some supplies and gas the plane from a tanker that drives up. About forty men separate from the group, walking to a waiting bus. The tanker leaves. The forty get on the bus. The rest wave and get back on the plane. The bus drives away, heading south. The plane takes off, flying east.

Two hours later, it lands at the Flagstaff Pulliam Airport. The plane is pulled into a hangar before anyone gets out. The hangar doors close behind it. A short time later, men begin to emerge from the parking lot side of the hanger in groups of five and six. They climb into waiting vehicles and drive away.

DAY TWENTY-EIGHT

DENVER

ANGELICA SITS in the bay window in Jeremiah's house watching the snow fall.

Jeremiah comes in, handing her a cup of something warm.

"This will make driving interesting," he says, nodding at the window.

"But not impossible?"

"No, not impossible. Snowy roads mean slower travel. All our drivers have been navigating this type of weather for years. We'll be fine." He sips, watching the snow.

"It is very beautiful," says Angelica.

Jeremiah nods.

The snow drifts in large flakes, settling on the blanket already covering the ground. The silence is absolute.

"Boss?"

"Yes, Akido."

"First, Colin and crew have arrived in Flagstaff. Clayton has arranged places for them to stay for the next two days. They'll be gathering supplies for the crater.

"Next, WSO has issued a memo to all staff advising them to enjoy their holiday and not to get too wasted.

"Last, GA says all deliveries of the nutrients were accomplished with no problem. She has planted a trail to who ordered the change. It ultimately leads back to Rhotah Mhene. It will take some time to unravel. The Luminaries will be safe by the time he discovers it."

"That sounds diabolical," says Jeremiah. "Who is Rhotah Mhene?"

"He's the main bad guy behind STEN and the WSO," says Angelica.

"I've never heard of him," says Jeremiah.

Stephen enters the room. "That's because he stays hidden, working through the people he's corrupted."

"Oh," says Jeremiah. "Like a spider in the center of a web."

"Yes," says Angelica.

"Does that mean he'll get squished in the end?" asks Jeremiah with a sly look.

Angelica glances at Stephen.

"Yes, yes it does," says Stephen.

Jeremiah grins.

Akido speaks again. "This weather will break tonight. Skies will remain clear for the next four days and temperatures will be in the upper thirties."

"I'll leave for Utah before sundown," says Stephen. "I'll pick up Bridgetta and head for Los Angeles. Colin's people have arrived there."

He walks to Angelica, taking her face in his hands. "I'm glad you'll have better weather." He leans in, giving her a soft kiss. "You'll have Akido to help you, too.

Angelica nods. She stands, putting her arms around his neck. They hold each other close.

LATER, Jeremiah, his children, Stephen and Angelica are in the kitchen eating an early dinner.

Angelica says, "Christina. You know we're planning something for Founding Day."

"Yes, but I don't know what exactly."

"We've been keeping it quiet," says Angelica. "In fact, your dad and I could use your help. Are you willing?"

"Yes! Absolutely!"

"What about me?" says Sebastian.

Angelica looks at Jeremiah, eyebrow raised.

"You too, son," he says.

Sebastian pumps his fist.

After their meal, Angelica walks with Stephen to the hovercraft. They embrace for a long moment.

"Ahem," says Akido. "Permission to speak?"

"Of course," says Angelica.

"GA has prepared the virus for the STEN/WSO computer system. It will hit at eight a.m. PT on Founding Day. It'll be reversible, but it will take twenty-four hours to get rid of it. That will give both escape groups time to get well ahead of pursuit."

"Excellent," says Angelica. "Computer malfunction will send any staff left in the walled fortresses and detention centers into panic. We'll be able to get in and out easily."

Stephen grins, rubbing his hands together. "Action!" he says.

Angelica gives him a quick kiss and he's off. She hurries back inside to the warm kitchen. She and Jeremiah's family are up late talking and going over their rescue operation.

UTAH

Stephen maneuvers the hovercraft through the darkness toward Garcia's backyard. He drifts to a landing in the open space. A light comes on in the kitchen. The back door opens and a figure stands in the doorway.

"You ready to go?" asks Stephen.

"I'm ready," says Bridgetta, coming down the steps. "And no one knows I'm leaving except Margo and Garcia."

"Good," says Stephen. "Welcome aboard."

The hovercraft rises into the night. Stephen steers for the mountain shadows. Bridgetta sits quietly next to him.

"Do we know what we're doing when it's time?" she says.

"We'll get together with Francisco, Diego and Colin's people when we get there. Angelica and I want to time entry and rescue to happen simultaneously in both locations."

"That's possible?"

"It is." Stephen smiles at Bridgetta's confusion. "We have a special connection."

Bridgetta nods. *One day I'll have a special connection,* she thinks.

The rest of the trip passes in silence.

DAY TWENTY-NINE

LATE AFTERNOON, WSO HQ, LOS ANGELES

Rʜᴏᴛᴀʜ Mʜᴇɴᴇ ʜᴀs ɢᴏɴᴇ into his pre-Founding Day seclusion. He takes no calls, issues no orders. Normally Damien is happy with the respite. Today, he can't stop pacing. Everyone else at Headquarters is in a holiday mood. They're planning to leave early to get a start on the festivities. Officers have cases of booze to take to their quarters. The best women have been lined up for fun. Usually, he loves Founding Day, but this one isn't right.

His aide enters the office. "Sir, I'm leaving for the day. Do you need anything before I go?"

Damien gives him a vacant look. The aide waits.

"No, no. You can go. Report back on Sunday, 0800."

"Yes sir. Happy Founding Day." The aide salutes.

Damien goes to his bar and pours a drink.

LOS ANGELES WALLED FORTRESS

Diego drives his van to a spot several blocks from the fortress

274

entrance. He knows there are six similar vans being parked in other nearby spots.

He gets out and walks away, melting into the neighborhood north of the freeway. He sees John Boy and moves into step with him. They walk with hands jammed into their pockets, heads down, caps pulled low. They see one STEN patrol, but the men look like they're already drunk. Diego grins at John Boy. They make it to the rendezvous point and climb into the car with two other van drivers.

At the downtown apartment, they meet the rest of the rescue crew. Francisco, Stephen, Bridgetta, and Roscoe, the sergeant in charge of Colin's people.

Diego shakes hands all around and everyone sits.

"The computer virus will be active tomorrow morning at eight a.m.," Stephen begins. "It will take twenty-four hours to get rid of it. Bridgetta and I will begin our infiltration at nine a.m. We'll go in as doctors, get to the medical ward and prepare the Luminaries for travel. The vans should make their way to the loading dock at five-minute intervals. Bridgetta will go with the second-to-last patient. I'll go with the last one."

Francisco speaks. "Each driver will have a walkie-talkie so the convoy can stay in communication. Everyone should get to Victorville separately. We'll meet there, off the first Victorville exit. From there we'll be a true convoy to Needles."

"There's not much cover on that stretch of road so we'll have to be ready for any STEN trouble," says Diego.

"But," says Francisco, "because of the usual Founding Day activity, we should be okay. All of STEN will be celebrating in some fashion."

"And the virus will make communication difficult," says Stephen. "We'll stay in Needles as long as it takes for our Denver group to catch up. We want to arrive at the crater the same time, on Saturday, December 21st."

"You letting Angelica know what we're doing?" asks Diego.

"I am," says Stephen.

"Then we're set," says Francisco. "Diego will give all the drivers their paperwork. Roscoe, your men will get the same stuff. We've got three extra vehicles for you, if you need them. Okay?"

"No worries. We'll stick with our school bus. We'll just have to be careful to drive on the wrong side of the road." He waggles his thumb, grinning.

Francisco stands. "Okay everyone—downtime til 0800 tomorrow."

WSO HQ, LOS ANGELES

Damien is leaving his office for the night. He doesn't feel like partying but he's the only one. Partying staff are laughing and talking as they exit.

"Hey Damien!" Colonel Samson runs to catch up with him.

"Hey, Sam."

"You ready for the weekend?" Sam doesn't stop for an answer. "Man, I can't wait to get out of here. Thank the gods the changeover in the medical ward went with no problem. I could have been stuck here with no Founding Day time off."

Damien grabs his arm. "What changeover?"

"Oh, just a change in the medication for the prisoners we've had forever. The Commander's pet project."

"What kind of change? Who ordered it?" Damien has stopped them in reception, holding Sam's arm.

"What is your problem? Orders came through that the drugs were coming from a new supplier and the change had to be implemented immediately."

"When did you get the orders?"

"Just a few days ago. The new delivery came in Monday."

"Was it for just one medical ward?"

"No, all of them."

"Worldwide?"

"Yeah." Sam is annoyed. "Enough with the questions! I'm out of here." He shakes his arm loose and strides away.

Damien stands still, thinking. He heads back to his office. Once there, he sits at his computer, checking the order. Sam is right. The paperwork for the change is all in order. He traces the order back to —the Commander? Okay. But something doesn't feel right. He checks the Founding Day duty roster for the medical wards. Only one person on duty each shift all weekend.

He leans back. That one person will be drinking and trying to get laid their whole shift, especially down in the medical dungeon. He stands up to pace, talking to himself.

"There's been activity in the resistance lately. Doc witnessed that woman and man stirring things up in Utah. Then two women infiltrate the medical ward in Denver—and disappear. Now there's a new drug for the medical ward, just before Founding Day. What would I do if I was a resistance leader?" He stops at the window, looking out at the lights below.

"I'd use this time when the enemy is not paying close attention. But where would I strike?" He pours himself a stiff drink, gulps it down, pours another. Taking another gulp, he remembers Doc's first report about the meeting in Utah. The woman was ranting about the incarcerated people, calling them L-something. Could they be a target? He shakes his head. Why bother with those walking corpses? He downs the rest of his drink, pours another.

He sits on the couch. What to do? He drinks. "The new recruits get all the extra shifts over Founding Day. I can use them somehow. Maybe order squads to patrol the detention centers' medical wards. Something."

He's hit with a wave of dizziness. Too much alcohol, not enough food. "I'll just lie down for a minute, Then I'll figure it out."

A knock at the door has him weaving to answer it. A young woman stands there, smiling at him. She has long dark hair, wearing a low cut, short dress, and high, high heels.

She speaks in a dark, sexy voice. "Hi, honey. Looks like you got started without me." She sashays past him, plucking the empty glass from his hand. He watches her walk to the bar and pour two drinks. She takes a sip, looking at him from under her lashes.

"Join me baby," she purrs.

"What the hell." He goes to her and she welcomes him with open arms.

DAY THIRTY

LOS ANGELES WALLED FORTRESS

THE RESISTANCE VANS begin entering the fortress at 0800. The first one through reports only two guards, both slow and still drinking. There was evidence of female companionship. By 0900, all the vans are inside the fortress.

Stephen and Bridgetta enter at 0850. As he moves to the gate, one of the guards steps out, holding up his hand. He sways a little.

"What is it?" Stephen snaps.

"There's been a lot of traffic through here for a holiday," says the guard. "Show me your pass."

"I am Dr. Alfonse," states Stephen. "I am called away from my Founding Day celebration with my nurse—," he glances at Bridgetta who waves her fingers at the guard "—to come here and take care of a bunch of drunken idiots." He pulls out the credentials provided by GA. "I hope none of your men die while I'm waiting here for you to sober up enough to see my papers." He gazes at the guard with perfect disdain.

The guard glances at the papers and hands them back. "Move

LUMINATE

along." Stephen takes the papers and rolls up his window before driving forward.

They arrive at the loading dock at 0855.

LOS ANGELES, WSO HQ 0900 PT

Damien wakes with blinding sun in his eyes. He's alone on the couch, half naked, back sticking to the leather. He has a stabbing headache, but he still has some wits.

He sits up, holding his head. "I have to get some recruits to the detention centers, just in case." His voice is rough and he clears his throat. Staggering to the bathroom, he splashes cold water on his face and downs four aspirin. Back at the couch, he pulls on his pants.

His phone rings. He looks at the clock, it's 0845. He debates answering. He has to get people moving. The ringing continues. He sighs, picking it up.

"Good morning, Damien." It's the Commander.

Shit! "Sir."

"Come to my office immediately." The line goes dead. Damien drags on the rest of his clothes. He combs his fingers through his hair as he rushes to the Commander's office.

When he arrives, the door is ajar. He knocks lightly, putting his head around it.

"Come in, my boy." Rhotah Mhene has his feet on the desk. Damien comes to attention, saluting.

"At ease. Take a seat."

Damien sits in the chair facing the desk.

"I see you've started Founding Day celebration," says the Commander. He steeples his fingers. "That's good."

Damien is silent.

"I know you've been working hard for me, for the cause. Give me your year-end report."

Damien is wishing he had a cup—or ten—of coffee.

As if reading his mind, Rhotah Mhene says, "Oh, where are my manners. Would you like some of this coffee?" He waves at a carafe on his desk.

"That would be great, sir," says Damien.

"Help yourself."

"Thank you, sir." Damien stands to pour a cup.

Watching him, Rhotah Mhene takes his feet off the desk. "Instead of a year-end report, tell me what you've been doing recently."

The coffee is lukewarm but strong. Damien takes a gulp. "Sir, I haven't found either of the women, but I think the resistance is planning to hit us today."

Rhotah Mhene leans back, a small smile on his lips. "Did you say the resistance, Colonel? Did I hear that right?"

Damien can't read the Commander's mind, but he forges forward with his theory. "My first hint was a report from my sleeper cell leader in Utah. He reported a meeting where a strange woman was ranting about the people we have in the medical wards. You know, your special project. I think she was one of the women who was later spotted in Denver. Sir, I think the resistance is planning something that will happen today. I intend to send squads of recruits to our detention center here and to Denver..."

A knock on the door interrupts him.

"Come."

A lieutenant enters, saluting. "Sir, we have some sort of computer problem. Tech says it's a virus affecting our computer systems and communication. They're working on it but it's a devil. They said it's lucky its Founding Day weekend or it'd be a real problem."

Rhotah Mhene says, "Fine. Keep me informed." The lieutenant salutes and leaves.

The Commander looks at his fingernails. "Colonel Johnson, your Founding Day is over. Handle this. Redeem yourself." He looks up, his eyes spearing Damien. "Dismissed."

Damien stands, salutes, exits. In the hallway he stops, taking a deep breath. *Handle this? I'm going to assume he means the resistance.* His head is still pounding, but he ignores it. He takes off in a dead run for the new recruits' barracks. It's 0935.

DENVER 1000 MT

The two guards at the Denver walled fortress gate are groggy from last night's festivities. A convoy of six vans approaches. Some have names on the side, the rest are plain. The first van stops at the guard station and the driver's window rolls down.

"Open up," says the driver, an old guy with a scruffy beard.

The guard peers into the van. There's a cute girl in the passenger seat. "What are you doing?" he asks.

"Delivering. What else? I got supplies for Founding Day."

"You behind schedule? Celebration started last night."

The old man rubs his face. "Look, I got this huge order I got to get to the detention center and get unloaded."

"Keep your hair on. You need to save something back and bring it to me on your way out." The guard glares at the old man.

The old man hesitates a moment. "Yeah, yeah, okay. I got some scotch. I can short the big boys a bottle. You'll get it when we come back out."

"Now you're talking." The guard waves him along and watches the other five vans roll past him.

Jeremiah turns to Christina. "That was fun."

"Do we have a bottle of scotch?" she asks.

"Oh, yeah. I keep a case in this van just for bribes."

"Dad! You think of everything." She smiles at him.

Jeremiah pulls his van into the loading area behind the detention center. The second one pulls in behind him. The others line up on the street, motors running.

Angelica jumps out of the second van, hair up in a ball cap pulled low over her face. She keeps her eyes down as she heads for the loading bay door. Jeremiah meets her there.

He raps on the door, once, pause, again. The door cracks open and a red-eyed guard looks out.

"Open up man! We have to get in there to prepare a special Founding Day event," says Jeremiah.

"I haven't heard anything about this," says the guard.

"Not my problem. Call it in if you want."

"Can't. Communication is down—some sort of virus or something."

"Too bad. We got work to do. We're getting on with it." Jeremiah pushes his way through the door, Christina and Angelica right behind him.

The guard's eyes widen when he sees Angelica. "Hey," he says, grabbing her arm. "You look familiar. Have we partied or something?"

Angelica keeps her head down a beat. When she looks up, she has a flirtatious smile on her face. "Oh honey," she says, "if we partied, you'd remember." She leans in, whispering in his ear. "Maybe when I'm done here..." She winks at him, pulls her arm loose and walks away.

Sebastian comes in after her. "Dude, I have this special home brew. Want to give it a try?" He holds up a bottle. "My dad made me come today but I'd rather drink with you." He bends closer to the guard's head. "I have some homegrown herb, too."

"Now we're talking," says the guard. "Come with me to the office." He and Sebastian walk in the opposite direction.

"Let's get busy," says Angelica.

LOS ANGELES 0900 PT

Stephen and Bridgetta pull up to the detention center loading dock. They get out and walk to the door. Stephen pounds on it. They wait. He pounds again. Nothing. He tries the handle—the door opens. Bridgetta raises her eyebrows at him. He shrugs and they walk in. He finds the medical ward door. They look around for personnel. No one.

"Where are they?" asks Bridgetta.

Stephen pauses extending his perceptions outward. "They're

sleeping off their first wave of celebration. We still need to be quick."

He goes into the ward, Bridgetta at his heels. Bridgetta moves forward to the first bed. She leans over, looking at the first Luminary.

"These people look better. The ones Angelica and I saw in Denver looked very bad—gray skin, bad odor. Look, this man has some pink in his skin." She touches his cheek. His head makes a tiny movement into her hand. Stephen watches her.

A tear leaks out of her eye.

"Let's get these people out of here," says Stephen. He walks through the room, looking at each person. "We'll take the better off ones first. Here's what we'll do."

He comes back to Bridgetta. He stoops down next to the man's head. He unhooks the IV, clamping it off. He leans in, speaking softly close to the man's ear. "We've come to take you home," he says. "I'm Stephen, this is Bridgetta. We'll help you walk outside to our van. You'll be safe again. Your strength is coming back. Stand up now."

Stephen takes the man's arm and assists him to rise. He motions to Bridgetta who comes forward, putting her shoulder under the man's arm. His body has little weight. They walk, small steps, to the door.

Stephen speaks into the walkie-talkie. "All drivers, come now. No guards. Helpers, come in for briefing."

He opens his mind to Angelica. She's in the medical ward in Denver. He walks to the next person, performs the same actions, speaks the same words, showing her what he's doing. She acknowledges.

Seven helpers have filed in. Stephen faces them. "Once we're on the road, here's how you can help these people. Keep the nutrient IV's going. There's a supply in each van. If your people become agitated, make physical contact—hold their hand, lay your hand on their head or face—talk to them. Invite them to squeeze your hand if they can hear you. Let them know someone is there who can hear and understand them. Any questions or concerns, call me on the walkie.

"One other thing. If one of your people decides to leave, to die, don't worry. They have that choice. At this point, we can't know what their true physical condition is. If they choose to leave, they can get a new body and come back strong. Do you understand?" He looks at each of the helpers, one at a time.

They all nod, though several look skeptical.

Stephen says, "Please, trust me on this."

They nod again.

"Good. Let's get these people out of here."

The loading goes quickly with Bridgetta and Stephen speaking to each Luminary while unhooking the IV.

Finally, there are two left. They are the worst off. Stephen kneels next to a woman, still pale and immobile. He takes off his amulet and lays it on her chest with his hand covering it. He closes his eyes. Bridgetta watches him. He's doing the same thing Angelica did in Denver for the little boy. A glow starts around his hand, spreading until it engulfs the woman and him. It pulses once, twice, three times. The woman's eyes twitch and open slowly.

"Yes, dear. You can do it. You can walk to safety." Stephen helps her rise, passing her to Bridgetta. Diego comes in and steps to the other side of the woman to help.

When Stephen kneels next to the last man, he gets a wave of intention to stop. He lets it wash over him, recognizing the taint of evil in it. *Not much time.* He kneels next to the man, holding the amulet on his chest. When Diego comes back in, Stephen and the man are standing, with Stephen holding most of his weight.

"We have to go now. The bad guys are almost here," he says.

Diego takes some of the man's weight and they move quickly to the door.

"All the other vans have left," he says. Stephen nods. He locks the outside door on their way through.

At the van door, Bridgetta helps Stephen get the man inside. Diego leaps into the driver's seat, revving the engine. When the man is secured, he takes off. As they pull out, they see running men rush into the loading area and pull at the door.

UTAH 0930 MT

Garcia and Margo are loading the last of the coolers in the back of the old pickup truck. Zack and Juan Carlos are helping. Two other trucks are being loaded by other members of the community.

"You guys got a lot of stuff here," says Juan Carlos. "Where are you taking it all?"

Garcia says, "We make a trip south every six months or so. We contact the people scraping a living along the back roads. In the winter, folks sometimes have some trouble getting by. We want them to come here, to our community, but a lot of them are suspicious. Bringing supplies is a good way to get them to think about it. In any case, it's good to get to know your neighbors and help them if they need it."

"Makes sense," says Juan Carlos. "Who's in charge while you're gone?"

"Me," says Zack, with a grin. "Not that there's much to do. This place pretty much runs itself."

"Yeah," says Juan Carlos. He stands to one side as Garcia and Margo redistribute boxes and duffle bags. He blurts, "Can I come with you?"

Garcia pushes the last bag into place. He turns and gazes at Juan Carlos. Margo and Zack are quiet, watching. "Don't see why not. What do you think, Mother?" he says to Margo.

"The more the merrier." She smiles.

"Okay," says Garcia. "Go get your gear. It'll be cold, keep that in mind. We leave in fifteen minutes."

"Hey, man, I've been wandering my whole life. I know the drill," says Juan Carlos. He takes off toward his quarters.

Garcia, Margo and Zack stand by the truck.

"You think this is a good idea?" asks Zack.

"I'd rather have him where I can see him. I don't want him here stirring up trouble, if that's his plan. This'll give us time to find out who he really is."

Zack nods.

"Send a message to Angelica so she knows he'll be privy to any communication between us."

"Okay."

Juan Carlos trots back, a backpack over his shoulder. There's a bedroll attached on the bottom and a canteen dangles from a strap.

"Here, toss that in the back," says Garcia, holding up the camper shell opening.

Margo gets into the cab, in the middle. Juan Carlos climbs in next to Margo. Garcia speaks to the other two drivers and comes back to climb in the driver's seat. He starts the truck and the journey begins.

DENVER 1055 MT

Angelica has quickly checked all the Luminaries prior to moving them. She goes to Jeremiah, watching from the front of the room with Christina.

"Those three will need extra care," she says, pointing. "They need to be in my van." Jeremiah nods. She motions him and Christina forward to the nearest person. "Here's what we do to get each of them ready." She shows them how to unhook the IV and what to say.

"As soon as there are four ready to be moved, call in the other vans. We'll need to get everyone out fast."

"Right," says Jeremiah. He and Christina began doing what Angelica showed them. She kneels next to the first woman needing more help. She places her amulet on the woman's chest. She closes her eyes and the glow starts, spreading over and into the woman's body.

Freeze!" The young guard stands in the doorway, his gun leveled at Angelica. She gets to her feet. The guard's eyes widen.

"I know you! You're the one they're looking for. You've been here before."

286

"I have," says Angelica, taking a step toward him.

"FREEZE!"

Angelica does, raising her hands from her sides, palms out. "Why aren't you at the Founding Day celebration?" she asks.

The guard stares at her, giving a small shake of his head.

"What's your name?" she asks.

He continues to stare. She stares back. He lowers the gun two inches. "Jason," he says.

Angelica nods. "What now, Jason?"

"What are you doing?" he says.

Angelica doesn't answer right away. Jeremiah and Christina are trying not to breathe.

Angelica looks around at the people on the beds. The ones already unhooked from their IVs are twitching, stirring. Their movement draws Jason's attention for a second.

Angelica takes another step forward. His head snaps back to her. His hesitation is speaking to her. She extends her perception as a soldier of light.

"You don't like the way these people have been treated," she says. "You didn't want this duty today. You've stayed away from this ward as much as you could." She continues to stare at him. "You don't like the alcohol and drugs." Pause. "You don't do casual sex. You want to live a good life and you're not sure you've chosen the right path."

Jason stares at her. His gun drifts down like a feather falling.

"Right now, in this moment, you have a choice."

"What are you doing?" he asks again, gun at his side now.

"We're saving these people."

Jason looks around.

"You can help," Angelica says gently.

Jason says nothing. Angelica waits.

"How?" He holsters his gun.

"Can you keep any other guards from coming?"

"Communications are down right now, but probably not for long. Where are the current guards?"

Jeremiah answers. "They're in the one of the examination

rooms. One is out cold. My son Sebastian is keeping the other one busy."

"I'll take care of him." He turns to leave, stops, speaks to the floor. "You'll take me with you when you leave?"

Angelica answers. "Yes."

Jason leaves.

"Can we trust him?" says Jeremiah.

"We can for now," says Angelica. "We'll keep an eye on him." She goes back to the woman she was helping to find her eyes open.

"There you are," says Angelica, smiling. "I am very happy to meet you. These lovely people will help you out to our transportation."

Sebastian rushes in. "A guard just took out the guard I was with and sent me back here. I thought I was a goner when he appeared in the doorway."

"Yeah son, we know the feeling," says Jeremiah. He picks up his walkie-talkie. "All drivers, bring the vans. All helpers, come inside. Oh, and we have a guard on our side—Jason."

With all the helpers standing in the ward, Angelica gives them the same instructions that Stephen has just given in Los Angeles. Jeremiah and Christina return to unhooking IVs. In a few minutes, there is a small parade of Luminaries being helped out into vans. As each one is filled, it drives away.

Angelica is working with the last two people. She's given both treatment with her amulet. One woman is showing signs of more life but the other is still gray and unmoving.

Angelica speaks to the woman who is improving. "This man will help you to our transportation. We have a long journey, but we'll care for you on the way. Go, sister." Jeremiah lifts her easily into his arms and carries her out the door.

Angelica turns to the last Luminary. She kneels beside her, taking her hand and stroking her head. "Dear one. You don't have to stay. You've seen your people rescued. We'll take care of them. You can rest now, leave this broken body, find a new one, a new game, a fresh start. We will welcome you if you decide to join the fight again. Warrior. Friend. Luminary."

The woman sighs. And is gone.

Angelica watches her spirit ascend, tears coursing down her cheeks. When it's over, she looks for a sheet. She finds a doctor's coat in the nurses' space. She wraps it around the woman's body and carries her out of the medical ward.

Jason is standing at the door, holding it open. "Hurry! HURRY!"

The last van is at the dock, Jeremiah at the wheel. As they exit the hall, Angelica can hear feet pounding inside.

"They're coming!" Jason jumps into the back of the van, reaching for the woman in Angelica's arms. He places her on the floor and closes the door behind Angelica.

Jeremiah drives sedately away from the detention center.

UTAH 1230 MT

The trip south has been uneventful. Margo tries asking Juan Carlos questions about his life, but he answers with non-answers or monosyllables. She gets the idea and stops asking. Instead, she tells stories about life in the community. He asks a lot of questions. She gives him simple answers that reveal no secrets.

Garcia is mostly silent, concentrating on driving. He adds a comment here and there. He holds Margo's hand. He points out landmarks.

They stop at small clusters of buildings. They speak to the people there and pass out blankets and canned goods.

They hit some snow in the mountains west of Bryce Canyon, but nothing they can't handle. After four hours on the road, the convoy pulls into the outskirts of Kanab in southern Utah. It's very quiet.

"This isn't right," says Juan Carlos.

"What?" says Margo.

"I've walked into many towns that feel like this. It usually means the people are either active scavengers with traps set or really hate strangers and won't tolerate them."

"That's a fair assessment," says Garcia. "Let's see what we've got here." He turns left toward the hospital and city park. He and the other drivers pull into the park. Garcia gets out and opens the back of the truck. Putting down the tailgate, he fires up the Coleman stove and starts some water boiling.

Margo gets out the coffee and sandwich makings. The other drivers stand around waiting, mugs in hand.

The first men arrive on horseback, rifles trained on the visitors. More men arrive, some on foot, some in cars, all armed, until there are twenty men surrounding Garcia's group.

"Anyone want some coffee and a peanut butter sandwich?" asks Garcia, his back to the men.

"We'll be wanting what you have in those trucks," says a weathered man on a palomino.

"Not offering that," says Garcia.

"Not asking," says the man. His rifle lowers to point at Garcia. The rifles of all the other men lower to point at the rest of the group.

Juan Carlos shifts his weight. Margo continues to make peanut butter and jam sandwiches.

Garcia leans his hip against the tailgate. "Well, here's the thing. We're down from the survival community in Provo. We have some supplies we've been sharing with people who need them as we travel south. We're happy to share with you. But we're on our way to rendezvous with some refugees who need what we're bringing."

Margo has sandwiches in a basket lined with a cloth. She walks toward one of the men on foot, holding the basket in front of her. She offers it to the man. He has a quizzical look on his face. She lifts the basket a bit and nods. He shrugs and takes a half. She walks to the next man. He takes a sandwich too.

She soon has all the men munching peanut butter and jam sandwiches. Her last stop is the man on the palomino. He looks down at her, scowling. There's one half sandwich left in the basket. She holds it up to him. The horse shifts its feet.

"The jam and the bread are made by the ladies in our community. I had a hand in this batch of jam." Margo pauses. "It's strawberry rhubarb."

"It tastes just like what your missus used to make," says the first sandwich eater.

Palomino Man closes his eyes and lowers his head. He takes the sandwich. "Thank you, ma'am."

Margo nods. She goes to one of the other trucks and pulls out a crate. The driver comes over to carry it for her. They go to Palomino Man and set the crate on the ground next to his horse.

"Here's fifteen bottles of the jam for you," says Margo. "And you are welcome in Provo anytime you run out. If we don't have this, we'll have something else almost as good." She smiles at him.

One of the riflemen hands his gun to the man next to him and comes forward to get the crate. He puts it in one of the cars. Palomino Man sheaths his rifle and gets off his horse. He walks to stand in front of Garcia. He puts out his hand. Garcia straightens and shakes his hand.

"You got a good woman there," says Palomino Man. "She reminds me of my wife."

"Thank you," says Garcia.

Garcia and Palomino Man walk toward the edge of the park, heads together. Garcia gestures. Palomino Man gestures. More talk. Finally, they turn around and head back. Garcia laughs at something Palomino Man says. Margo makes tea for their group.

When they get back to the group, Palomino Man shakes Garcia's hand, nods to Margo and mounts his horse. He waves a hand and the rest of his group disperse.

"There's a gas station on the way out of town where we can fill up," says Garcia. "Let's go."

Gear is stowed and everyone is back in their trucks and on the road in minutes.

Margo leans to give Garcia a kiss on his cheek.

"That was the wildest thing I've ever seen," says Juan Carlos. "What did you guys say to each other?"

"We talked about common goals and the future," says Garcia.

"Works every time," says Margo, smiling.

"Hmm," says Juan Carlos, facing forward.

DENVER 1120 MT

A squad of recruits stares at the empty medical ward inside the detention center. The room is filled with empty beds, IV drips hanging from the ceiling

"What do we do now?" one asks.

"I don't know. Call Colonel Johnson?" says another.

"Yeah, we should do that," says a third. "Are the phones working now?"

The squad goes back to the nurse's station. They hear a moan from the closest examining room and the phone rings. They freeze in confusion. The recruit standing nearest the phone picks it up, putting it to his ear. The one nearest the exam room moves to the door, opening it and looking in.

"REPORT!" comes from the phone.

"Uh, sir, no one's here," says the recruit answering the phone. He mouths, "*It's Colonel Johnson.*" He pauses when the recruit looking in the room waves his arm. "Uh, just a minute."

The other recruit turns his head. "There's two guards in here tied up."

The one holding the phone says, "Two guards are tied up."

"HOW LONG AGO DID THEY LEAVE?!"

The recruit at the door says, "I heard that." He turns and asks the question.

"Like five, maybe ten minutes ago," the door recruit tells the phone recruit.

"I heard that," says Damien to the phone recruit. "Call the front gate and stop any vehicles leaving. NO ONE GETS OUT OF THE DENVER FORTRESS!" The line goes dead.

"Yessir." He looks at the other recruits. "I guess the phones are working." He puts the phone down. "Does anyone know the number to the gate?"

AT THE GATE, Jeremiah has pulled the van a little past the guard shack. He watches the last van disappear around the corner on the street outside the fortress wall. Christina holds two bottles of scotch in her lap. One guard is at her window, the other is talking to Jeremiah.

"So," he says, "you got the goods?"

Jeremiah grins. "My assistant has them for you. Should she give them to your buddy?"

The phone starts ringing in the guard shack. The guard by Jeremiah gives it an exasperated look.

"No, I'll come around and get it." The phone rings again.

The guard next to Christina calls, "You better get that. It's Founding Day. It might be an emergency."

Jeremiah glances in the rearview mirror. Angelica is making a move-along motion with her hand and Jason's eyes are round.

Christina sees this and lifts the bottles to the window. "I told the boss you guys should have two bottles, since it's Founding Day. Now you can each have one." She smiles, handing the bottles to the guard at her window.

He grins, walking toward the back of the van. The first guard reaches the shack. Jeremiah puts the van in gear and pulls through the gate, turning left immediately. In his side mirror, he sees the first guard run into the street, waving his arms. He waves his hand out the window and speeds away.

LOS ANGELES, WSO HQ 1030 PT

Damien slams the receiver down. "They got away," he says between clenched teeth. "They got away here. They got away in Denver. And one of them in Denver was the woman." His face is thunderous.

The recruits with him take a step back.

Damien looks up. "You are all dismissed. Remain ready for further orders today and tomorrow."

The recruits trip over themselves to rush out of the room.

Damien sits at the nurse's station in the now-empty medical

ward. *The Commander is not going to be happy about this. Ha! That's an understatement. He'll ask me what I'm going to do. What am I going to do?*

COLORADO 1215 MT

As the convoy makes its way west, the roads are clear up into the mountains. They hit snowpack before the Eisenhower Tunnel. As the first van exits the tunnel, a snowplow pulls in front of it. The snowplow driver waves a hand out his window. Jeremiah looks a question at Angelica.

"Clayton's man," she says.

Jeremiah nods.

As they approach Glenwood Springs, Angelica goes still. Jason stares at her. One Luminary patient opens her eyes and turns her head toward Angelica.

Only a minute later, Angelica moves. She glances at the patient who smiles at her. Angelica smiles back.

"What was that?" Jason says.

"Communication," says Angelica. She turns to Jeremiah. "Stephen and company are on their way, ending in Needles where they'll stay to wait until we get nearer the crater. We'll stop for a time in Window Rock."

Jason keeps staring at her.

She leans back against the side of the van. Her hand drifts to the amulet around her neck. Her eyes close slowly as she nestles it in her hand. She reaches for Stephen again.

Stephen.

Yes, love.

My amulet. It's pulsing, and not at random. It feels warm. It's like it's been searching for a connection and now it's found one—weak, but there. It's making my heart glad. Are you feeling it too?

I feel it through you. You know what it means.

Do I dare hope?

Hope, dearest.

Angelica sends a wave of love, like a sonar blast, to Stephen. The people in the van start, staring at her. The Luminaries sigh.

CALIFORNIA 1215 PT

The Los Angeles vans meet in Victorville and drive toward Barstow. They've decided to travel from there to Needles in staggered groups.

Diego turns to Stephen. "You know, if it weren't Founding Day, we'd have been caught."

"I know," says Stephen.

"Brilliant plan."

"Thanks."

"Angelica and her group doing okay?"

"Yes."

"Cool."

LOS ANGELES, WSO HQ 1400 PT

Damien is back in his office. With no computer service he's blind. He spreads out a paper map of the west, including California, Nevada, Arizona, New Mexico, and Utah. He's trying to figure out where the prisoners will be taken. There are recruits coming and going with the information he's demanding.

Another man knocks and enters.

"Sir, we're still working on contacting outposts for information on passing medical vans. Nothing so far."

"Someone has seen something somewhere."

"Yes, sir." The recruit runs out.

Damien's phone rings. He jams the speaker button. "Speak."

"Colonel." It's Rhotah Mhene.

"Sir," says Damien. *Working phones are also a curse!*

"Report."

"Yes, sir. The prisoners were taken from the detention center medical wards here in LA and in Denver this morning. They used Founding Day to camouflage their action, putting the prisoners in several vans with medical corps markings. We don't know where they're going yet. I have every recruit from HQ barracks looking for sightings of the medical vans."

"You got authorization to use those men?"

"No, sir. I commandeered them."

"Make sure you get results. I want those vermin back alive—or dead." The line goes silent. Damien can hear breathing.

"Sir?"

"If you fail me, your career will be over and you'll wish you'd never been born." The venom in Rhotah Mhene's voice drips from the receiver.

"Yes, sir." The phone goes dead, then rings again.

"Johnson."

"Sir, I found a bunch of kids who saw two medical vans getting on the I10 heading east."

Damien looks at his map. "Report back to HQ."

He picks up the phone and calls the Palm Springs outpost. When the phone is answered, he barks, "Colonel Johnson. I need to know if any medical corps vans are in your vicinity. They'd be on the freeway, passing through. Put out lookouts and report immediately." He hangs up.

The next call goes to Victorville. Damien delivers the order.

"Sir, we have seen medical vans. There was a group spotted just off I15. They got back on the freeway heading east."

"Send a patrol after them. Report where they're going."

"Yes, sir."

Damien looks at the map again. *Las Vegas? They could be heading to the survival camp in Utah.*

He picks up the phone again to call the new captain in the Utah sleeper cell—Doc Crawford's replacement, since Juan Carlos appears to be offline. The man reports no unusual activity in the camp.

Damien asks, "Are the community leaders there?"

"No sir. They're making a run south. They do it about this time every year. They did take the new guy with them."

"What new guy?"

"He came a couple of weeks ago."

"HIS NAME!"

"Juan Carlos."

Damien hangs up.

COLORADO 1500 MT

Angelica's first rest stop is in Rifle, Colorado. Two of the Luminaries are recovered enough that they take a few hesitant steps. The others are responding well to the nutrient drip.

Now they're entering Grand Junction. The way is clear and they're moving quickly, but there's something on the freeway up ahead. A roadblock. Jeremiah slows the van. As they approach, they see soldiers partying with bottles of alcohol and drunken women.

They pull up and one of the soldiers comes toward the van. His left arm holds a woman, his right hand is waving a gun.

"What are you doing out on the road on Founding Day?" He's shouting slurred words.

The side van door opens and Jason steps out.

"Atten-SHUN," he barks.

The soldier drops his gun and releases the woman. They both end up on the ground. Jason ignores them.

"You are a disgrace! You're disrespecting the uniform and your position," snaps Jason.

"Permission to speak, sir. I was just messing around. It was just a prank," says the soldier.

Jason looks at him with contempt. "You do not mix Founding Day revelry with your duty. Get yourself and your squad out of here."

The soldier gives another salute, but he has a sour look on his face.

Jason returns the salute. "Dismissed!" He makes a sharp about face and strides back to the van.

The soldier picks up his gun and the woman, dragging her back toward the others.

"We've got to move!" he shouts, glancing back at the van.

Jason stands in front of it, feet apart, arms crossed.

The soldier waves his arms at his buddies. "We've got to move NOW!" he shouts, gesturing toward Jason.

The other soldiers finally realize what's going on. They stumble around gathering bottles, articles of clothing and women. These are all stuffed into two vehicles and they drive away.

Jason gets back into the van. Jeremiah follows the soldiers down the freeway until they take the next exit. The vehicles stop on the overpass and a figure watches the convoy drive away.

Inside the van, Angelica turns to Jason. "Thank you."

He acknowledges her with a nod.

LOS ANGELES, WSO HQ 1540 MT

Damien hangs up the phone. The aerial patrols will go out within the hour. He grits his teeth in frustration. Only two! They'll search eastward over the southern desert and the Rocky Mountains in what's left of daylight.

Founding Day *and* the winter solstice. He has to admire the planning of the treasonous bastards.

A knock at the door and his aide enters. "The High Commander has authorized leave cancellation for four patrols. Orders have been sent to the STEN security patrol captains in Denver, Las Vegas, Albuquerque and Grand Junction. They await your call."

"Excellent." Damien picks up the phone. He places the calls, ordering Denver, Grand Junction and Las Vegas patrols to cover the areas south of them. Albuquerque patrol is to go west. All patrols are to ask for sightings of a convoy of vans with medical markings and to follow up on any reports.

"I want hourly reports," he orders.

Now he has to wait. He's standing at the window when his phone rings again.

He picks it up. "Johnson."

"Sir, this is the patrol captain from Grand Junction. We just spoke. One of my soldiers just reported seeing a convoy of medical vans going west on the I70 freeway here. There was a STEN sergeant with them. "

"What time?"

"Around 1500 MT."

"Make sure your patrol catches them. Let me know when you have."

"Yes, sir."

Damien hangs up, going back to the window. The lowering sun shines golden on the downtown Los Angeles buildings. The shortest day of the year is almost over.

SUNSET IN THE WEST

Stephen's convoy has holed up in Needles in the El Garcos hotel. The Luminaries are resting and being tended by the people who rode with them, plus a local doctor. They are responding well to the nutrient IVs. Some are asking for water and food and rising from their beds. Stephen has visited them, giving amulet therapy to each one. Bridgetta is his shadow on these visits. She watches everything he does.

Francisco and Diego are spending time with the people of the community, discussing how to improve their lives—and how they can be part of the resistance. The Australian commandos join in.

Dinner time. The Los Angeles crew are eating together in the hotel dining room. Stephen slips outside into the darkening landscape. The sun has set. He sees lightning flashes in the west and the wind from that direction picks up.

He walks away from the hotel, across the railroad tracks toward the river. He sits in a quiet spot under a scrub oak and opens his mind link with Angelica. He sees she's sitting next to Jeremiah driving south. It's dark, but before the darkness descended, she saw red rocks in beautiful formations.

Angelica: *It reminded me of that one planet where we stopped for R and R.*

Stephen's smile caresses her. *You are safe. Your Luminaries are doing well.* All statements, as he can see the truth of them in her mind.

Angelica: *We lost one. She left from the medical ward. We brought her body with us and laid it under red rock stones near Moab.*

Stephen and Angelica share silence and love for all Luminaries, in any state.

Angelica: *We're heading to Window Rock, Arizona. We'll stay there for the night. Clayton has insisted. We also have a new recruit, a guard from the detention center. His name is Jason.*

Stephen: *Trustworthy?*

Angelica: *He did help us out of a possibly sticky encounter with a patrol in Grand Junction. Although, I think now we have a tail. Not sure if they know we turned south toward Arizona. We got night vision goggles in Moab. We can drive black if need be. If they come up on us, we'll hide in the dark off the road. We'll lose them when we turn off toward Window Rock. Akido is directing us. Your Luminaries are doing well?*

Stephen: *Some are moving and requesting food and drink.*

Angelica emanates a warm glow.

Stephen chuckles. *I love it when you do that.*

Angelica: *Akido says Garcia is in Flagstaff with Colin and Clayton. He brought Juan Carlos. He says the other rescues went according to plan. The gods have blessed these humans this day. Also,* Lightbearer *is behind the moon and has released its Orbiters. They're closing in high over the Pacific.*

Stephen: *I can see evidence of their coming—lightning in the west and weather starting.*

Angelica: *Soon the night UFO show will begin—lights, sights and sounds. The captain of* Lightbearer *will have them scouting the planet, taking readings and mapping.*

They both look out at the night around them.

Stephen: *Tomorrow, stay in our havens for the day?*

Angelica: *You in Needles, me in Window Rock. Meet tomorrow after sunset at the Crater?*

Stephen: *Agreed.*

Angelica: *Akido will dispatch* Lightbearer *with the schedule and will let Colin and Garcia know.* They send each other a wave of love and withdraw.

Stephen sits a bit longer looking up at the stars until his Earth body begins to chill. He goes back to the hotel to brief his people on the plans.

FLAGSTAFF, ARIZONA 1800 PT

The last half hour of driving, Garcia and Margo watch the gibbous moon rise over the desert. Garcia is filled with peace, the peace of rock formations millions of years old, the peace of an empty land filled with wind, sand, sagebrush and the desert creatures who live their lives there. He is overcome by the view. He puts his arm around Margo. She leans into him and he knows she feels it too.

Juan Carlos turns his head away, toward the window.

They arrive in Flagstaff in darkness and meet up with Colin and his Aussie commandos at the motel. In the shuffle of getting room assignments, Garcia speaks to Colin about Juan Carlos. Colin agrees to help make sure he's never alone.

After a meal, sleep.

WINDOW ROCK, ARIZONA 2200 PT

Angelica's convoy pulls into the Window Rock Tribal Park. The moon casts a pale light. Stars fill the sky. Two figures come out of the dark.

"Angelica?" A woman steps forward. "I'm Rosa, this is my husband Raymond. If you follow us, we'll take you to the homes where you'll stay."

A convoy once more, they follow Rosa and Raymond's truck into a residential area. Each van is directed to a house and greeted by the inhabitants. The Luminaries disappear inside with the drivers and caregivers. Angelica watches, making sure all her people are safe.

Raymond speaks to Jeremiah, Sebastian and Jason. "Follow me. I'll show you where you can bunk."

Jeremiah looks at Angelica who nods her head. Christina and Angelica go inside with Rosa. She invites them to sit in the living room.

"Do either of you need anything to eat or drink?" asks Rosa. "Or do you just want to sleep?"

"Thank you, thank you for your kindness," says Angelica. "I think we would like to sleep." Christina nods.

Rosa rises, leading them to beds in a small bedroom. They take off their shoes, lay down and find sleep quickly.

LOS ANGELES, WSO HQ 2300 PT

The aerial patrols have returned with nothing to report. The vehicle patrols are stopping for the night and will resume in the morning.

Damien decides to sleep in his quarters.

DAY THIRTY-ONE

ONE FORTY-SEVEN A.M.

AROUND THE WORLD, there are strange happenings in the sky.

Over the California/Arizona border, there's a hovering object, unusual lights and eerie sounds.

Above western Europe, colored lights streak across the dark sky, followed by a hollow boom that rattles windows and jolts men from their beds.

In Australia, early risers see a shape silhouetted against the moon. It hovers, dips, rises, brightens, then disappears.

By dawn, all evidence of UFOs has disappeared.

NEEDLES, CALIFORNIA

Stephen is up with the sun. After coffee and a muffin with Francisco and Diego, he goes to visit the Luminaries. In the first room, he finds four gathered, with their IVs on rolling stands. They're clustered, two on each side, around a fifth person lying on a bed. They have their hands on her, shoulder/hand, knee/foot. She's shaking.

At his entrance, all four look at him, then turn back to the woman. Stephen comes forward, taking out his amulet. He moves in near her head, placing the amulet under his hand on her forehead.

She stiffens, then a wave of calm runs down her body. The shaking lessens, and she relaxes into the bed. Stephen doesn't move. A soft, golden glow begins around the amulet. It builds, spreading down her body.

Seconds pass. The golden cloud pales, is gone. Stephen picks up his amulet and puts in back around his neck. He touches each of the standing Luminaries, looking into their eyes one by one. He leaves, closing the door quietly.

He finishes visiting the rest of the Luminaries. When he arrives in the dining room, the rest of the crew are having breakfast. He's greeted by various people.

"What are we doing today, Boss?" asks Bridgetta, sitting with Diego.

"We'll let the Luminaries rest up. They all need to stay on the nutrient IV."

The care staff nod.

"We need to take the medical markings off the vans and give them alternate paint jobs. Nothing flashy, just nondescript." He turns to the Aussie commandos. "You guys want to take care of that?"

They respond with enthusiasm.

"Diego and I will help," says Francisco.

"Great. It's a little under four hours to our final destination. Once the jobs are done, take personal time. We'll start getting loaded at 1300 and leave at 1500. See you then."

He walks to the table where the care staff are sitting. "Please let me know if any of the Luminaries are suffering withdrawal. I can help them."

Bridgetta comes up behind him. "He really can," she says, smiling.

"Okay," says one of the staff.

"Good," says Stephen. "I'll be on the walkie if you need me."

WINDOW ROCK, ARIZONA

The morning sun is already warming the day when Angelica starts her visits to the Luminaries. She and Rosa see that every Luminary is doing better. In each house, Angelica tells them the plan for the day and evening.

She meets with Jeremiah, Sebastian and Christina. She asks them to take off the medical insignia on the van and to repaint them with desert colors.

She says, "STEN will be waking up today and we don't want them to be able to spot us from the air. They'll be looking for the medical vans."

"We'll get the drivers to help," says Jeremiah.

Rosa says, "There are several young men who'd be happy to help. Raymond will send them to you."

"Excellent," says Angelica.

She and Rosa go back to her house. In the kitchen Rosa says, "There's someone who wants to meet you."

Angelica waits. A Navajo man enters the kitchen.

"This is Asta," says Rosa.

"I'm very happy to meet you," says Asta. "I've heard a lot about you."

Angelica looks at him in confusion. Her amulet is vibrating against her chest.

A woman enters the kitchen behind Asta. She's older, with gray peppering her black hair and wrinkles on her face. Her step is slow but she glows with life. Without a thought, Angelica stands and moves toward her. They are face to face, eyes searching. Angelica lifts her hand and touches her cheek.

"This is Elizabeth," whispers Asta. "She's been living here with us for many years. She's an artist."

Angelica doesn't speak. She stares. Elizabeth nods as the space widens all around. She reaches for the chain around her neck, pulling on it. A turquoise amulet appears, glowing like a green sun. Angelica gasps and the women fall into each other's arms.

"Mama," breathes Angelica, holding her tight.

"Daughter," says Elizabeth, holding her tight.

The glow from their amulets spreads to encompass both their bodies, then the rest of the kitchen. Rosa fumbles for Asta's hand, tears streaming down her face.

The moment passes. Rosa and Asta sit. Angelica and Elizabeth sit next to each other, hands clasped. The rush of love between them is palpable.

Elizabeth looks at Rosa. "I didn't think I'd ever see my girl again," she says.

"I hoped I would see my mama again," says Angelica. "And now here she is." Angelica is beaming. She turns to her mother. "Can we walk?"

Elizabeth smiles. "Of course."

Outside, they link arms and walk into the desert. The sun is higher in the clear, blue sky. Angelica inhales the smell of sage and clean air. Their universe intertwines.

"Tell me your story," says Angelica.

Elizabeth pauses a moment before beginning. "Years ago, I was given a chance to come to Earth to help the Luminaries here. Your father was gone and you had your calling. It was an exciting opportunity for me, and a chance for adventure. I met many creative people and we made wonderful, artistic designs for this planet. Back on Luminus, I treasured my time on Earth.

"When I learned about David's mission to search for repositories on Earth. I volunteered. Stephen's father needed someone familiar with Earth to handle logistics, and there was a secondary objective in our mission brief. It was to search for hidden art treasures that had been stolen and smuggled to Earth. This project was mine to investigate. He and I were very happy to be working together.

"We got here about eighteen months before the mass suicide, the WSO's rise to power, the birth of their fortress cities and the rest of the chaos. We set up in a commune in the northern California mountains. Using the first thermal scans delivered by the initial Orbital mission, we were able to confirm the presence of the meteor crater in Chile, near a small Incan ruin. We traveled there to find it.

"David's real specialty was encryption and AI. With his amazing skills, he cracked the Soulests' code at that first site in Chile. He discovered the Soulests booby-trapped the entrance with advanced explosives. He figured this was probably the case at any other repositories. We knew this would be important information for the next soldier-of-light mission team. They'd know what to do.

"We covered a lot of territory getting to the site. After David made his discoveries, we were planning our trip back. He'd help me with my part of the mission when we got back to California. We camped outside a village, keeping a low profile. Things were getting unsettled with all the talk about a meteor hitting Earth. I went into the village on a last supply run. Tensions erupted with fighting and it took me a long time to get back to our camp. David had disappeared. I couldn't find a clue as to where he'd gone. The fighting turned into a war. I had to leave." Elizabeth pauses here. She looks into the distance, working to compose herself. "Losing David was hard, very hard. But somehow, I made my way back to Los Angeles.

"I found the Rosario family there. By this time the madness was in full swing. I couldn't go back to the commune, especially without David. The Rosarios were going to Arizona and I decided to go with them. We left in the middle of the night. While we traveled, I used my amulet to send an emergency call to Luminus."

"Wow." Angelica moves to Elizabeth and folds her in a fierce hug. Elizabeth hugs her back. They stand together like that for a long moment.

"I knew Asta's father from my first visit to Earth," Elizabeth says, "and I'd already made contact with Asta when I came into the area. He's an artist too. The tribe was kind enough to let me take refuge with them when STEN started rounding up Luminaries." She pauses again. Angelica puts a hand on her arm. Elizabeth covers it with her hand. She continues, "Asta and I have been working together. He and the Rosarios know everything, my whole story. When Clayton contacted the Reservation, telling us the tale about the two strange people causing trouble for STEN and WSO, I started to hope." Elizabeth lets go first, stepping back to look Angelica up and down. "You got a good body."

Angelica smiles. "I did. So did you!"

Elizabeth laughs.

They link arms again and walk. Angelica feels a completeness walking with her mother.

She says, "I'll never forget the time you found me asleep in the apple orchard. I'd been eating the red, delicious apples and I wanted to take a nap. You found me and picked me up so gently to carried me home. I keep that moment of absolute safety with me always."

Elizabeth takes Angelica's hand. The women walk in silence. Angelica is at peace. She wants to share this with Stephen. She opens her mind and—

Rhotah Mhene is there. His presence is shards of broken glass flowing in a black, viscous mass, stabbing, stabbing, *stabbing*, at her. She drops to her knees, head bowed, fingers reaching for her amulet.

Elizabeth grasps her own amulet and drops to her side. She lays both hands on Angelica's forehead, her amulet between them.

Angelica has both her hands wrapped around her amulet. The force of his attack beats at her, shredding her. She reels. Then she feels her mother's strength flowing into her and she pushes a wall in front of Rhotah Mhene, at first just made of loose dirt. It helps, and the wall becomes higher, made of stone and stronger, and finally thick steel. She's protecting herself and all she knows, but not before he sees the desert around her and knows she has Luminaries near her. Then the light of Elizabeth is with her. She steps inside it, mustering her own light to join her mother's. The explosion they create obliterates her enemy's black mass, and blasts back to harden the steel in her wall. Rhotah Mhene is shut out. In the last second, Angelica feels him reel from the blow. Then she's free.

LOS ANGELES, WSO HQ

Rhotah Mhene is ecstatic! He bested her! Finally, he has overwhelmed his ancient enemy—the one who calls herself Angelica. He knew she was here. Now he's confirmed it and shown her who's in power here! He found her weakness.

He was reading Damien's reports on yesterday's cock-up. This morning, the virus was eradicated and satellite surveillance is back up. He was looking at photos of country around the Mojave Desert. His mind wandered to Angelica and suddenly, he was there, with her. She was vulnerable, soft, full of love so he could attack her. He cut and stabbed, grasping for knowledge about her location and plans. Her mind and body are in the desert of Arizona. He sees a Luminary ship, hovering in the sky above her near where she is now —before she slams him out. He didn't get the whole plan but he is still exhilarated. He won!

He calls his aide and issues a series of orders.

"Cancel all Founding Day leaves for Security forces—ground and air patrols. Every ground patrol to concentrate in desert regions in Nevada, Arizona, New Mexico. Air patrols cover the same areas looking for groupings of vans. They may still be marked as medical vehicles but all groups of vans should be reported.

"Patrol reports to go to Colonel Johnson. He'll coordinate the search. Everyone found is to be returned to LA HQ alive."

Damien enters Rhotah Mhene's office in time to hear the last order. The aide salutes and leaves. Damien stands at attention in front of the Commander.

"Now you have a chance to correct the mistakes you made yesterday," he says. "The woman insurgent is in the southern desert. The air and ground patrols will report to you. Find her. Bring her and everyone with her to me."

"Yes, sir," says Damien. He turns smartly and leaves.

Rhotah Mhene stares at the door closing behind Damien. He begins talking to himself. "I'm not surprised Colonel Johnson is so cavalier about this whole situation. He doesn't know anything about the real conflict." He goes to the bar and pours himself a drink. He gulps some, then heaves the glass against a wall. "If there is going to be trouble for us, you can count on them both being in the middle of it. Every time! All these reports of a woman and a man running the show and stirring up a resistance movement. It can't be anyone else but THEM. Young Damien has no clue what's happening. I have told him repeatedly she's dangerous. He has no idea what she and these Luminaries are capable of. They must be stopped once and for all, and not just here on this backward planet. This has been going on far too long—no more!" He fists his hands at his sides. "Today I proved I can beat her!"

WINDOW ROCK

Angelica is on the ground, her mother leaning over her. She can feel Stephen with her, giving her his strength.

"What happened?" asks Elizabeth, stroking her forehead.

"It was an attack...he got in."

"He?"

"Yes. My heart was so full seeing you again." Angelica grasps her mother's hand and stands. Elizabeth folds Angelica in her arms.

"Can I do anything for you right now?" Elizabeth's face is full of concern.

"I'm okay. A headache—it will pass. He only got a partial location and the fact there's a ship coming."

"A ship is coming?"

Angelica smiles at Elizabeth's surprise. "Yes, Mama. Stephen and I were sent by the Minister of Defense to rescue Luminaries. Luminus got your amulet message." She kisses Elizabeth's cheek. "Now, we have to take care of the ones that are worse off."

"Yes, they'll need a ship's facilities. Do you have to take them far?"

"The rendezvous is near here."

Elizabeth looks at Angelica for a moment. Angelica gazes back.

Elizabeth's eyes get big. "The crater!" she says. "Oh yes! That crater has multiple significances—for me and for Asta's people. They have legends about that place. It's perfect!"

"Significances?" Angelica gives her a curious look.

"Yes. I'll tell you later. The meeting is tonight?"

Angelica mock frowns at her mother, changes to a smile and nods.

"Good. Then we have time. There are some people you should meet."

Filled with joy, Elizabeth links her arm with Angelica's again to lead her back to Rosa's house. Stephen sends Angelica a flood of love and withdraws.

FLAGSTAFF, ARIZONA

Colin and Garcia are up with the sun. One of the commandos has rustled up breakfast and they stand with steaming cups of coffee.

"We'll need to leave soon for the crater," says Colin. "We need to set up camp in the bottom, with shelter and triage."

"Yeah," says Garcia. He's quiet for a moment. "Do you know what's going to happen?"

Colin shakes his head. "We know Angelica and Stephen are not ordinary. I can tell what I think…"

"Please."

"I think they're the scouts for the big rescue party. Tonight, we'll meet the rest of the crew."

"So basically, be prepared for anything." Garcia shakes his head.

"You got it, mate." Colin grins. "Let's get going!" He claps Garcia on the back and they head for the trucks. They're on the road in fifteen minutes.

LOS ANGELES, WSO HQ

Damien issues orders for the search. At least ten Apache helicopter pilots are to be found, brought in and sobered up. He contacts Las Vegas and orders a battalion with artillery and ground troops to be assembled and made ready to roll by 1200. They are to head south into Arizona. He orders any active search parties to head into Arizona. The traitors are there. Find them.

His aide finds him standing over a map of the United States spread out on the conference table.

"Find me someone who knows about this area," Damien says, indicating the southwestern states.

"Sir, I know that area," his aide says.

"Speak."

"Yes, sir. If they're heading toward Arizona, it's probably the central region—around Flagstaff. There are survivalists and other outliers in that area, and the Navajo reservation is not far from Winslow. It's desolate. It's known for unusual meteorite and shooting star activity in the night sky. There have been stories for years from settlers, drifters and helicopter pilots about mysterious objects hovering in the air and darting away. Our pilots have reported aircraft navigation equipment working sporadically there. It would be a good area to disappear into. Also, there's a large crater east of Winslow, about ten miles south of the freeway. They could be heading there."

"Maybe. Why would they take a bunch of half-dead invalids to a crater in the middle of the desert?" Damien looks closely at the map. "Let me know when the troops and helicopters are ready to roll. I'll give the commanders their instructions personally."

"Yes, sir."

Damien paces around the table, looking at the map, thinking. He calls Commander Rhotah Mhene.

"Sir, evidence points to the traitors going to the large crater in Arizona." Damien pauses. Rhotah Mhene is silent. "Sir, does that make any sense to you?"

After a moment, Rhotah Mhene replies, "Find them." A long pause. Damien can hear him breathing. When the Commander speaks again, it sounds like his voice is coming from between clenched teeth. "If they reach the crater, deadly force is authorized. Annihilate them and destroy the crater. Bury them all."

The line goes dead.

When Damien's aide reports the troops are ready, Damien gives them their orders: Everyone converge on the meteor crater in Arizona. Stop and seize any vehicle heading in that direction.

Commander Rhotah Mhene sits at his desk, staring into space. *Damien is capable but I want, no* need, *to be there for the victory over her.* He leans forward and shouts, "Aide!"

His aide rushes in. "Sir?"

"Get a helicopter ready. I'm going to this crater in Arizona. Find out how long it will take to fly there—I want to arrive just after the troops. Report when you have the details."

"Yes, sir."

STEN PATROL

Security unit 16B had been on search duty since the night before. They were ready to stand down when new orders came through. They'd gone northeast through southern Nevada into Utah as far as St. George, then back southwest on I15 into California. Now on highway 164 they're heading east, back into Nevada. Stopping in Searchlight for water and food, they see two boys playing behind one of the empty buildings. When the children see them, they bolt out of sight.

Back on the road, they drive south on 95 toward Needles.

NEEDLES

"We just got word a STEN patrol is on its way down highway 95. It's due here in thirty minutes."

Stephen acknowledges the town leader with a nod. Everyone rushes through the final loading of Luminaries into the vans.

On the road southeast out of town, the vans with Stephen and the Luminaries are in front, with the Aussie's bus bringing up the rear. They get to the bridge over the Colorado River, crossing it quickly. On the opposite side, Stephen heads toward Flagstaff and the crater. The Aussies pull their bus across the road, blocking it. The driver opens the hood. Some of the group stand with him, gazing at the engine. The rest scatter, standing on the bridge and along the banks of the river.

LOS ANGELES, WSO HQ

Damien paces in his office, growling in frustration. It's taking too long to get the pilots and helicopters into the air. They won't be flight ready before 1300 hours.

At least the troop carriers are rolling.

NEEDLES

Unit 16B rolls through Needles. No one in sight, no one to ask about the traitors. They continue to the bridge.

"What is that, Sarge?" asks Private Johns, the driver.

"Looks like some sort of bus blocking the road," Sarge answers.

"What the hell?"

Sarge throws him a look for the language.

"That's more people than we've seen the whole patrol," says Private Jimmy.

"Yeah," says Sarge. "Look sharp, ladies. I'll do the talking."

"Yessir."

The men check their weapons and hold them ready as they approach the bus and the men around it.

WINDOW ROCK

"Mama, it's been incredible to see you and meet the people here. Now it's time to get back on the road. Since Rhotah Mhene knows we're here, I'm feeling some urgency. I want to get our people to the rendezvous point."

"Of course. Asta and I will follow you."

"There'll be danger."

"There's always danger."

Rosa and Raymond meet them at the truck with four large bags. "Food for the journey, and the destination."

"Thank you, Rosa," says Elizabeth. "You're a good friend."

"Take good care, come back to us. And bring your daughter and her man," Rosa says, hugging Elizabeth.

Elizabeth nods, swiping at tears in her eyes. Minutes later the vans are on the road to the crater.

METEOR CRATER, ARIZONA

Colin, Garcia, and their convoy pull up to the old visitor center parking lot at the Meteor Crater National Landmark. The buildings are still there but they're rundown, with broken windows and graffiti on the walls. The overlook platform doesn't look very stable.

"We'll need to drive around the rim to find the best way to get into the crater. We may have to hike in with the equipment. And we'll have to carry the Luminaries down when they get here," says Colin.

"Agreed. I'll go right, you go left."

"Good idea. Send up a flare when you find a spot."

"How about I just contact you on the walkie."

"That works." Colin grins, climbing into his truck.

The commandos and Juan Carlos wait at the visitor's center. Juan Carlos wanders around the building, looking into the crater. He's not sure why everyone is coming here, but he'll find out. *And I'll figure out a way to get the intel to Damien.*

After bumping through the desert, Colin and Garcia meet at the southern side of the crater.

Standing at the rim, Colin says, "Looks like the path near the visitor's center is the best spot."

"Agreed."

"Okay then. Let's get to it."

By the time Angelica and her convoy arrive, there are tents set up in the center of the crater. The western sun is dipping, making long shadows on its floor.

Margo rushes forward to give her a hug as she climbs out of the van.

"You made it! How many have you brought?"

"We were able to save seventeen."

"Can any of them walk?"

"Possibly."

315

"I'll get Garcia to send up some of the Aussies to help them down. There's no road, we have to walk."

"Good. Once everyone is at the bottom of the crater, no one will be able to get to them. Plus, we have reinforcements coming. The bad guys are in for quite a display."

"Oh?"

"Oh yes."

"Good." Margo pulls out her walkie. "Garcia, Angelica is here. Her group needs help to come down. She's got seventeen who will need assistance."

"Roger."

Elizabeth and Asta come to stand next to Angelica.

"Margo, this is my mother Elizabeth and her friend Asta."

"I am so happy to meet you! You're Angelica's mother? How great you found her!" Margo rushes to embrace Elizabeth. She shakes Asta's hand, holding it with both of hers. "So good to meet you. Thank you for joining us!" Releasing Asta, she turns toward the vans. "Now, let's get these people to safety."

Asta and Elizabeth look at each other, turn and follow her.

Akido buzzes on Angelica's wrist. She steps away into the desert to talk to him.

"Boss, STEN has mobilized a lot of manpower coming our direction. That colonel, Damien Johnson, is in charge and he knows we're here at the crater. He reports directly to Rhotah Mhene."

"Understood. What's *Lightbearer's* status?"

"She and her Orbiters will be here at sunset. She is ready to make her entrance just after moonrise, right on time."

"Good. Thank you, Akido. Please let her know we appreciate her assistance."

"Roger."

Angelica smiles at this.

She turns her face west and connects with Stephen. *We're at the crater. How long before you get here?*

Stephen: *We'll be there in an hour.*

Angelica: *Garcia and Colin have a base established at the bottom of the crater. The Aussie commandos are helping my group down to it. Akido reports*

STEN troops converging—they know we're here. Hurry! Lightbearer *is
standing by and her Orbiters will be here at sunset.*
Stephen: *We'll be there soon. We've almost finished the first phase.*
Angelica: *Yes. Soon.*
Stephen: *Soon.*

BOTTOM OF THE METEOR CRATER 1800 MT

Stephen has arrived and the last of the Luminaries in his group
have been brought down to the crater's floor. The tents are set up in
a rough circle with a space in the center. They're warmed with
portable heaters. Stephen and Angelica are working with the worst-
off Luminaries in the largest tent when Colin enters.

"You should see this," he says.

Angelica and Stephen finish and step outside. Six attack helicopters circle the crater's outer rim. They stop, stationary in the air,
facing the camp.

"They've been ordered to destroy everything and everyone,"
says Akido. "They're arming missiles. And the first troops have
arrived. They're deploying around the rim."

The Aussie commandos are forming a human barrier around
the camp. Everyone stands motionless gazing at the enemy. Juan
Carlos is just inside the large tent, watching everything.

With just a whisper of air, two spacecraft drop into formation
over the camp. They're sleek and quick looking. They have a system
of lights along their sides and are eerily silent. The air around them
shimmers as the first missiles launch from the helicopters. The
people standing below see the red glow of their thrusters and the
white trails they leave as the streak toward the center of the crater.
There is a collective intake of breath. The first wave turns downward toward the camp and—explodes harmlessly above the
hovering craft. Angelica and Stephen look at each other and smile.

In a loud voice, Angelica says, "Reinforcements have arrived." A
cheer goes up from the freedom fighters.

Around the rim, ropes are thrown over the edge for troops to
descend. The first men down the ropes hit the edge of the force field

and fall to the bottom, motionless. The nearest commando runs to check the fallen men. He looks up the wall at the faces peering over the edge, back toward the tents and shakes his head. He runs back to where Stephen and Angelica, Colin, Garcia, Francisco and Diego stand.

"The men are alive. I just made it look like they were dead to discourage the rest."

"Good man," says Stephen. "Drag the bodies under a tarp where they can't be seen from above and tie them up. If they start to wake up, we'll gag them."

RIM OF THE METEOR CRATER 1800 MT

While Angelica and Stephen work inside the big tent tending the Luminaries, the troop carriers travel single file down the road to the crater. When they reach the visitor center, they split into two columns to encircle the rim. The STEN officer in charge, Major Rommi, assigns a squad to stay at the top of the path to the crater.

"Check out the bus and vans," he orders.

The squad's sergeant takes two of his men to investigate. They discover Unit 16B tied and gagged in the back of the bus. The 16B men tell a story about being ambushed and captured by a bunch of foreign-sounding men, obviously well trained.

The sergeant listens to their report. His comment, "Whatever." He orders his men, "Get these men armed. They'll join our squad. Check out the vans, then fan out and guard the top of the path. Sparks, let the Major know."

Meanwhile, Major Rommi deploys his troops at strategic points around the rim of the crater. They hear the Apache helicopters arriving from the west. A pack of coyotes howls in the distance, hunting in the high desert chaparral.

The sun has set and darkness in the desert is absolute before the gibbous moon starts climbing in the sky. The major looks down at the tents filled with soft light and moving shadows.

Two silver craft appear over the tents and hover. The Major watches the helicopters arrange themselves to cover the crater center with missile fire. The pilots report ready to launch. The Major takes a deep breath, raises his hand and drops it, giving the kill order. His radio operator relays it to the helicopters.

Multiple missiles launch toward the strange craft and the camp below. They streak through the air—and explode above them. A wave of heat blows back across the rim. Some of the soldiers' clothing catches fire and men nearby slap at them to put out the flames. The helicopters back up to hover outside the crater's edge.

Major Rommi radios Colonel Johnson. "Sir, some sort of force field is protecting the traitors. It's being generated by two flying saucers."

"Repeat."

"Yes, sir. Two craft, not exactly saucers, but not planes either, hovering over the traitors' set up in the bottom of the meteor crater. The missiles from the helicopters detonated above the craft. Blowback set some of my men on fire. No casualties. There are about two hundred military-type personnel surrounding the camp, like a guard."

Already en route, Damien rubs his face. "Secure rappelling ropes and send men down the sides of the crater. They'll take out the guard and kill the traitors. I'll be there in thirty minutes."

"Roger."

Major Rommi issues the orders. He watches his men start down the ropes then fall to the crater floor. He sees a guard approach and shake his head. He leaves, then comes back with others to haul the bodies away.

Major Rommi has a bad feeling about this.

RHOTAH MHENE IS on his way to the crater. No one knows he's coming and he plans to keep it that way. He has to take this opportunity to beat her. He has to get close enough to take her out. He knew this chance would come again; now he has to take it and make it count. Less than half the sun is above the horizon behind his helicopter and shadows are racing across the land below.

As they near the crater in the deepening dusk, he tells the pilot to hug the landscape. Using binoculars, he focuses on the action over the crater. He sees the missiles explode harmlessly. He tells the pilot to set down in the dark area east of the visitor's center. He climbs out and heads toward the rim.

BOTTOM OF THE CRATER 1900 MT

Francisco and Colin stand with Stephen and Angelica. "Looks like we stopped them for now. What happens next?"

"Watch and see," says Stephen.

The orbiters pull back, closer to the crater walls.

"She's coming," whispers Akido.

A breeze starts, whipping up dust devils that dance across the crater floor. An odd singing sound starts, rising and falling, mingling with the helicopters' whoop whoop. The moon and stars wink as clouds roil across the sky and lightning flashes.

This wind rises above the crater and drops toward the crater floor. The singing intensifies until it's just at the edge of audible.

RIM OF THE CRATER 1900 MT

Major Rommi tries to deaden the sound, holding his hands over his ears. The wind whips at him, strong enough to push men off their feet. Lightning flashes split the night, coloring it electric blue and searing vision.

Through slitted eyes, he can just see a shape in the clouds above him. He can make out a wide, delta wing outline set with a contoured design. It's unlike any craft he's ever seen. There's a series of running lights on her front and back sides flickering in rotational patterns.

It's descending—moving straight down in a vertical position. It's huge, hanging over the center of the crater, dwarfing the smaller crafts, the tents below, and the helicopters.

The clouds clear and the spacecraft is fully visible, lit by the moon and its own lights.

Major Rommi and his troops back away from the rim. The helicopters land and their crews step out.

Silence fills the desert all around.

Inside the crater, every able body is standing outside the tents, gazing up.

"See the markings on the side? That's her name: *Lightbearer, The Bringer of Light*," says Angelica. Stephen takes her hand.

"Oh my goodness, she's beautiful," breathes Margo. She's standing with Garcia, Francisco and Diego. Jeremiah, Christina and Sebastian stand near Colin and Juan Carlos. Elizabeth and Asta are near the big tent's entrance.

Akido's voice rings out. "*Lightbearer*. First in the interstellar fleet dedicated to serve the Soldiers of Light in our Confederation of Planets. The people of Luminus and Lumina are dedicated to the birth, nurture and preservation of creators and aesthetics. They are dedicated to communication and understanding among all beings in the universe. Soldiers of Light are dedicated to eradicating any attempts to suppress these things."

A great melodic sound pierces the night air, emanating from *Lightbearer.* The sound is almost too big, composed of deep base and middle tone octaves, played in a rapid succession of waves, slow then fast, each lasting a minute. A counter harmony joins the movement reaching a crescendo of middle and higher melodic, harmonic octaves.

It is a sound in musical language from another world. It repeats and resonates. It bellows out its high and low harmonics and octaves, repeats again, then once more. Everything around feels refreshed in the music's vibrational path, like a spiritual rain has cleansed them. It's joyful, wonderful, uplifting.

The music shifts down until just a heartbeat remains, beating, beating, beating. A radiant light begins to shine from the bottom of the spacecraft. It floods downward upon the center of the crater. The freedom fighters receiving the rays are suffused with well-being and joy.

Angelica starts moving. "Everyone! Get all the Luminaries out of the tents and into this light!"

Cots are pulled from the tents and lined up in the light. It expands to cover all the Luminaries, whether standing, sitting or lying down. Angelica stands at a tent entrance, watching. Then she goes inside, coming out with a box in her hand.

"Stephen," she calls. He goes to her side.

"Look, beamed down by the captain." She opens the box to show Stephen all the amulets. "They'll key to each Luminary when we put them on. He's included some crystal light stones that will be helpful for their recovery."

Stephen and Angelica carry the amulets into the light. They give one to each of the rescued Luminaries. When they're finished, there are extra amulets left in the box. Stephen looks at Angelica. She nods.

He gives the first one to Bridgetta. The next three go to Garcia, Margo and Colin. Francisco, Diego, Jeremiah, Sebastian and Christina are each given one. Elizabeth pulls hers from her pocket and puts it on. Angelica hands her one for Asta. He lowers his head so Elizabeth can put it around his neck. Off to one side, Juan Carlos finds himself feeling left out because he didn't get an amulet. He's not sure where this feeling comes from—it doesn't fit who he is. He decides to ignore it.

All the amulets begin to glow with a soft aqua light that blends with the light coming from the spacecraft. Angelica and Stephen watch the Luminaries, moving to attend the ones who need the most help. Those who are still in bad shape will receive more intense healing inside the spacecraft.

Already a number of the Luminaries have responded well and are coming out of their turbulent mental and physical state. They communicate with the freedom fighters helping them.

Lightbearer's radiant light continues to flitter down like a golden, soothing rain, assisting the healing process.

Above the crater, intermittent gunfire can be heard. The enemy is testing the force field.

The soldiers around the rim have crept forward to look over the edge at the spectacle below. Major Rommi issues orders to his lieutenants to get their men under control. He can hear a helicopter coming in from the west. Colonel Johnson will arrive momentarily. He's glad someone else will be responsible for this cluster fuck.

As the colonel's helicopter lands, the smaller spacecraft slip up over the crater's rim to hover over the troops. Their silent menace gives the major goose bumps.

A lieutenant rushes up. "Sir," he says, out of breath.

"Report."

"My men found a path into the crater, on the south end. We figure they'll have to take down the force field so their people can get out. We can be ready to attack then. I have my platoons getting into position."

"Excellent. The rest of the battalion will move to back up your group. Radio when you're ready," the Major orders.

The lieutenant salutes and makes his way back to his men. The path into the crater is a winding dirt track, narrow and strewn with splintered rocks. The soldiers are three deep on the path, waiting.

They can see what's occurring in the crater, but they're still quite a distance from the flat bottom area where the traitors are assembled. The lieutenant quiets his troops with a series of hand signals, motioning them to be ready for anything.

As Colonel Johnson climbs from the helicopter, Major Rommi comes forward to greet him, saluting smartly.

Damien acknowledges his salute. "Report."

Major Rommi gives a summary of his troops' actions, and the events noted inside the crater.

Colonel Johnson listens without interruption. When the major finishes, he says, "If the helicopter missiles exploded outside the force field, an airstrike with cluster bombs might work."

"Yes sir," says the major, "but it might backfire. The cluster bombs could blast back into our troops."

The colonel is silent.

The major's radio crackles. "Sir, something is happening in the crater. The sound from the spaceship is changing."

Rommi and Johnson walk to the crater rim. Lights on the spaceship are flashing in an intricate pattern. Musical sounds start low, matching the light flashes. The result is hypnotic.

The music swells, stirring. The major and colonel watch as Angelica steps forward.

In the radiant light from the spacecraft and the amulet glow, Luminaries are reviving. The ones lying down are starting to sit up. Others are moving to stand.

The watching STEN troops are overwhelmed with the feeling that something incredible, extraordinary is about to happen.

THE HELICOPTER RIDE got us here faster than I thought. Rhotah Mhene can see the troops on the rim, but their attention is fixed on the spacecraft's spectacle. He is hidden in the darkness.

He fondles the steel-like finish on the custom-made stun gun in his hand. It's fully charged and he has extra charges in his jacket. He begins picking his way down toward the floor of the crater. *Light-bearer* is suspended above the crater, hovering over the spot where the Luminaries and their followers are gathered.

He works his way closer to the tent area and Angelica. There are two sentries standing guard. They both turn away to look at an image from the spaceship. *Now!* Quickly and quietly, he takes them out in the darkness. He snatches a beret off one downed man's head and crams it on his. Now he hones in his attention on Angelica. She's looking in the opposite direction. He reaches for the gun in his belt and fingers the trigger as he creeps closer.

Just inside the tent perimeter, Colin picks up a shadowed figure approaching the spot where Angelica is working. He can't see the sentries assigned to the area. He signals a commando near him and mouths at him, "Get Stephen!" The commando takes off at a dead run. Colin watches the sinister figure as it moves through the shadows. It's wearing a commando beret but moves wrong. *We may have a real situation.*

Rhotah is now within striking distance as he creeps towards *her.* The light coming from the spaceship shines on his quarry. *I can get a good shot at her.* His moment is now. He begins raising his gun. An inner storm rushes through him and the adrenalin pump is intense as he tries to focus on getting the shot. He clenches his teeth. *I have a chance to finish her off right now and end my misery with her.*

THE MUSIC CHANGES, repeating the bellowing refrain from its original blast of bass and mid octaves. It's played in a rapid succession of waves, slow then fast. On the third wave, a counter harmony joins the movement, reaching a crescendo of middle and higher harmonic, melodic octaves.

The sound resonates and repeats once more.

Beautiful music in octaves and harmonics plays in the night air for several more minutes, reverberating and refreshing in the dark, cool air.

Every person in and around the crater is transfixed.

A hologram projection appears just below the spacecraft showing images of the planet Luminus. Then there are images of every star system visited by the Luminaries, where beauty, aesthetics, and music were enriched.

Next are works of amazing art, visual imagery, and heavenly music created on planet Earth and in other galaxies. All are stunningly beautiful. They are aesthetic images of many of the greatest wonders of the world and universe.

ANGELICA SENSES A PRESENCE BEHIND HER. She snaps her attention to the area and knows: it's *Him.* She knows his energy. She focuses on the threat coming out of the dark and readies herself for the attack. Stephen picks up her urgency—he's running flat out toward her.

Rhotah raises his gun to take the shot. He has a second to fire...

Colin is moving behind the tents to flank the figure.

DOWN! Stephen's mental command galvanizes Angelica and she drops to the dirt. The stun gun blast passes over her, flying harmlessly into the desert.

I missed! Rhotah can't believe it. That woman has the devil's own luck! He grinds his teeth in frustration. Looking around, he realizes there are figures moving toward him. It's time to retreat. He melts back into the darkness, holding on to his hatred of her like armor. *She was a goner that last time. And mister stupid here let her be rescued at the last moment by* him. *They're going to see their downfall very soon. Yes they will. Then this will all be over, once and for all.*

He stops near the crater wall and looks back at the activity on the crater's floor and above it. The images and music continue. He looks up at the rim. He can see troops along the edge, just standing and watching. *The Luminaries and resistance will not have* Lightbearer's *resources tomorrow. Angelica and her man are just two people and the resistance is small and disorganized. I have the might of the WSO and STEN. They* will *be defeated.* He permits himself a smile.

He makes his way back to his helicopter. He stands next to it and watches the actions of his troops with binoculars. When he can't stand it a moment longer, he orders his pilot to take him back to LA WSO HQ.

After the aesthetic images there is silence. The radiant light fades. A cool breeze wafts through the crater into the desert above, fresh and clean.

Bridgetta, Elizabeth and Margo hand candles to all the Luminaries, freedom fighters and commandos, lighting each one until the space in front of the tents is filled with soft, flickering light.

Angelica is fully recovered and steps forward onto a small, makeshift stage. She speaks in a voice that carries. "You are holding a candle to light the way for freedom. We are united as ONE in our quest. We are the light!"

Stephen turns to embrace Colin, then Bridgetta. They embrace the people near them until the whole group has hugged someone.

Angelica continues. "You are a special class of beings—the highest caliber in all the universe. You have carried forth the purpose to embrace and create the light of life, to imbue life into the creation of beauty and form.

"From your constant dedication and willingness to do so, you create the extraordinary. You were there, creating in the Mayan, the Egyptian, the Incan, the Ming civilizations. You were there, lighting the way for every renaissance movement.

"Yes, it was you. You are the beacons of light and hope for all Mankind. We salute and honor you for all you have done, brothers and sisters. You are the universe's finest. Every one of you is truly appreciated!"

Angelica goes to the nearest Luminary, sitting on a cot. She takes her hand, looking into her eyes. "What is your name? What is your creation?" she asks quietly.

"I'm Alexa Carter, world architect."

Angelica squeezes her hand, then looks up and announces her name and skill in a strong voice. Stephen stands near another Luminary and does the same. So does Bridgetta. One by one, the names and skills of the rescued Luminaries are called out by Angelica, Stephen, Colin, Francisco, Jeremiah and Bridgetta. The Luminaries who can walk move to the front of the stage. Images of Luminary accomplishments appear in the spacecraft's display.

The commandos begin moving until they form a V—for victory —with the open end encompassing the Luminaries.

The hologram image changes to show what's happening in the crater.

Akido's voice rings out again. "This image is being broadcast worldwide on Earth and to the home worlds Luminus and Lumina."

Angelica steps forward again. She says, "I love you all! You are my truest and dearest friends!" She raises her candle high. Every other hand holding a candle is raised with hers. The spacecraft music dies into a silence that is held for a moment inside the crater.

Angelica begins to speak again. Her space is larger than ever and her voice is magnified, reaching the soldiers outside the crater as well as everyone inside. "I have a proclamation for Mankind, for the Peoples of Earth, and for All Worlds in the Universe.

"Here it is, the Proclamation for All Mankind and Worlds.

Never again will the outright harm and suppression of any individual or being be tolerated on this planet or among any of the peoples in the universe. Mark this statement true now and for all time.

We are Brothers and Sisters, a Brotherhood of Mankind. We have no quarrel with any others of any race, culture, ethnicity, or universe. We possess an affinity for all beings in this world and all worlds.

We respect the right of others to be free and to be self-determined. We are each endowed with our own special abilities, creativities, and individuality. It is our individual right to express these. This names all beings as extraordinary in their endeavors and creative ways.

This innate right to freedom is a universal right. It holds true here on Earth as well as all other places and planets in the universe. This right is held immutable. From this day forward, this right is law on Earth and on all worlds and in all universes.

All individuals of Earth are free men and women, free to create their own destinies and freedoms. They are free to have their own visions of the world, their own determination, and to advance new realities of the future and the worlds of tomorrow. This right to freedom will be upheld and championed.

From this date forward, those who especially seek to suppress creativity in any form are declared to be harmful to society. Those who seek to dominate, hurt or damage others, especially artists, visionaries, and bright thinkers, will be summoned and given swift justice. They will be dealt with quickly and severely.

This is our eternal pledge. Thank you for your dedication to all Mankind and our cause to make this world a better place.

Will you attest that you will honor this pledge, uphold it, and be an example? Come forth and vow with your signature if you are able.

Signed here on this day and witnessed for all to see. A monument will be erected here to mark this historic occasion for all Mankind.

Each person in the crater is given a chance to sign a piece of cloth lettered with the title of the Proclamation. It takes a few minutes, but when it's done the hologram changes. Crowds of people stand, clapping and cheering. They are in many locations. Every heart seeing this spectacle swells with joy.

Akido speaks quietly to Angelica. "Boss, there are STEN troops all around the rim, with a large group ready to rush inside the crater if the force field comes down. The thing is, they don't want to fight. There are many voices wanting to join the freedom fighters. They want to lay down their weapons."

Angelica beckons to Colin. "We have STEN soldiers wanting to switch sides. Can you and your men take charge of them? Jason from Denver can help and we might as well put Juan Carlos to work. The new men should take care of the soldiers who fell off the ropes."

"Good idea. I'll get on it," says Colin.

"Akido, ask *Lightbearer* to take down that section of the force field where the troops are trying to get through. Only fifty should be allowed to come in."

"Yes, Boss."

Colin beckons four of his men to join him, and they find Juan Carlos and Jason. "Come on," says Colin. "We're going to wrangle the new recruits."

They fall into step with him. Juan Carlos says, "New recruits?" Jason is silent.

"Yeah. There are some boys from the other side who've decided they like the look of us better," says Colin.

"Deserters?" says Juan Carlos.

"I suppose. Technically."

"Do we trust them?"

"They'll have to prove themselves before we trust them. But people have a right to change their minds." Colin looks at Jason who dips his head.

"Okay," says Juan Carlos.

"You two collect their guns. My men will keep them together and moving to a holding area."

They approach the invisible barrier holding back the STEN soldiers. Colin's men fan out. Juan Carlos and Jason stand ready. The barrier is suddenly gone and the men in front stumble forward.

"All right, gentlemen," says Colin. "Give your weapons to those men there and come forward." He indicates Jason and Juan Carlos.

The first two soldiers come in, hand in their weapons and move closer to Colin. He shakes their hands and indicates they should walk on. One of the commandos steps forward to direct them.

Now a steady stream of men is coming through the "gate" in the force field. Then there's a disturbance. One of the soldiers is struggling with another, their voices raised. "No, I'm not deserting. I'm not going with you!"

"But you have to. You know that's not the right place for us!"

"It's not the right place for you. It *is* the right place for me!"

Juan Carlos steps up to the two men. "What's going on here?"

"I'm not coming in here. I'm not giving up my weapon. I'm going back to my unit."

Juan Carlos puts a hand on his elbow. "You absolutely have that choice." He helps the man through the throng of soldiers still trying to get through the opening. The man pushes his way back outside the force field. As Juan Carlos lets go of him, he slips a note into the soldier's pocket. Colin is watching him handle the soldier and sees his action. He says nothing as Juan Carlos goes back to collecting guns.

Bridgetta and Stephen walk up to Angelica who is talking with Elizabeth and two of the rescued Luminaries. Bridgetta says, "Can I be in charge of the monument you mentioned?"

"Of course," says Angelica. "Thank you." Bridgetta nods. Angelica smiles, looping her arm through Stephen's.

ON THE RIM, Major Rommi is trying to get his troops under control. He can see men streaming into the crater from the south end. He's shouting orders to shoot them but he's being ignored.

Colonel Johnson stands to one side, watching what's happening inside the crater. Using his binoculars, he sees the hologram of cheering crowds.

"I think High Commander Mhene has not been completely forthcoming," he mutters. "There's more happening here than he's said." He places a call to the Commander's office. There's a delay before he's connected, and sounds of a helicopter come over the line.

He gives the Commander a succinct report about everything that happened after he left the Commander's office that morning. Rhotah Mhene says nothing during the report. There is silence when Damien is finished.

Then Rhotah Mhene says, "Abort the engagement. All troops to return to their bases. Make it known that any deserters will be captured and executed, painfully."

"Yes, sir."

"Colonel, this is no longer a skirmish. It is war. THIS IS WAR. Return to base." Rhotah Mhene disconnects.

BACK IN HIS OFFICE AGAIN, Commander Rhotah Mhene sits straight in his chair. *She* is no longer the only obstacle. The resistance is turning into a force that will need to be squashed into oblivion. He will need all his resources

"Aide!" he shouts.

"Yes sir."

"Let Colonel Johnson know I expect a full written report on my desk by 0800, and that he should report in person at 1200 tomorrow."

"Yes sir."

"I'll be in my quarters. I'm not to be disturbed until 1130."

"Yes sir."

"Dismissed."

DAMIEN STANDS at the crater's edge and watches every person in the bottom disappear. They vanish as if never there. All that's left is tents, flapping in a slight breeze. "Right. A war." *Somehow, I'm going to get the whole story from my High Commander Rhotah Mhene. In the meantime, I'm going to find out everything about the resistance and its leaders.*

INSIDE *LIGHTBEARER*

The freedom fighters huddle for a moment outside the transporter. The captain of *Lightbearer* finds them.

"Captain," says Angelica, "We appreciate you making the journey to help the Luminaries here. And thank you for taking us aboard. *Lightbearer* is a real beauty."

"Of course. The men that joined you from the crater rim are in the cells. I believe they can serve us. The Defense Minister wants to speak to you and Stephen. He's on vid-comm in the conference room. And, my medical staff are evaluating the Luminaries you rescued. So far there are ten who need to stay on *Lightbearer* for treatment and transport home. The rest have recovered well. Several are anxious to speak to you and Stephen. I have a feeling they want to join the fight here. Go and speak to the Minister now. My people will take care of your friends."

"Thank you again, Captain." Angelica takes Stephen's hand and they head for the conference room.

"We'll be here when you get back, mates," Colin calls out. They wave in acknowledgement.

In the conference room a large screen holds the Defense Minister's image. Brief greetings are exchanged then the Minister gets down to it. "You realize the Soulests will redouble their efforts now. Rhotah Mhene especially will not rest until he's found and eradicated you and everyone associated with you."

"Yes, sir," says Angelica. "He'll try."

"Do you know where you'll go?"

"Jeremiah, from Denver, knows of a top secret government facility that still exists. We'll go there for now and make plans to retake Earth and drive the Soulests out. Once that's done, we'll need to nullify them as a power in the universe—finally and completely."

"And the third item in your mission orders?"

"After we help the New Civilization Freedom Fighters get set up all around the world, Stephen and I will undertake that quest."

"Good. As you know, the sacred teachings of our planet and

confederation must be retrieved for the safety of our planet's future."

"Of course, sir. We won't fail."

"Excellent. Another bit of news. The Captain dropped Luerin, Gabriel and Virgil at three of the rendezvous points for the rest of the Luminary rescues across Earth. GA arranged for all those groups to see the video of the spectacle at your crater. *Lightbearer* will go and pick up any Luminaries who need extra care after the captain helps you reach safety. Any of those three can help you with your tasks, if needed. I expect a full report once you've reached a safe place."

"Yes, sir. Thank you, sir."

"Your people are very proud of you." The Minister salutes them. "Be the light!"

Returning the salute, they echo, "Be the light!"

Angelica and Stephen find the freedom fighter leaders in a large recreation area in the spaceship. Colin salutes them, saying, "*Lightbearer*'s surveillance reports that all the troops are withdrawing from the crater's rim. In an hour, they'll be gone."

"Have they left our transport alone?" says Stephen.

"*Lightbearer* protected them. They're just like we left them." Colin grins. "These guys are handy to have around." Stephen grins with him.

Angelica looks around at the faces in the room: Margo, Garcia and Juan Carlos; Jeremiah, Christina, Sebastian; Francisco and Diego; Colin and Roscoe; Bridgetta, Elizabeth and Asta. There are two new faces, two of the rescued Luminaries have joined the group, one of them is Alexa Carter, the architect.

"Thank you all for your work to this point," Angelica says. She sees nods. "We're moving into a new phase. It will start with a trek northeast, into Colorado. Jeremiah knows of a place we can stay in safety to plan our global resistance." She looks at Jeremiah. "Tell them what you told me."

He says, "Akido emailed me when we were preparing for the rescue operation. He said his source found something in the global computer system—a hole, a dead space. It indicates a large system that was shut down. When I read that, I remembered a conversation I had with Big Mike last year. He told me about this military installation his crew found. The place is huge and completely self-contained. Big Mike said he couldn't use it; he just raided it for weapons. He thought maybe my people might need it sometime. That's where we can go."

Angelica says, "We'll leave in darkness and travel along back roads to Colorado. *Lightbearer* will give us cloaking devices to mask our progress. We have to be invisible to our enemies until we reach the mountain. We'll disappear for the time being...but the enemy will be coming hard from now on." She pauses, looking into their faces.

"We'll be ready," says Colin.

ABOUT THE AUTHORS

Robert Frederick

Robert Frederick is the pen name of Bob Cisco. As a young man growing up in Kentucky, Robert was good at any sport that came his way. Not just good, really good. Living across the street from a championship golf course and club, he turned his interest to golf and honed his skills. His dad and brother were also great golfers and they played a lot together.

Robert became a successful golf teacher and performance coach to a number of pro golfers on tour. Between all those lessons and mental game instructs, he ventured into radio broadcasting was a co-host of a national show. He also wrote several popular books on golf, including *The Ultimate Game of Golf.*

But always sitting on the back burner was a keen interest in knights and stories of faraway lands and heroes. When sci-fi movies hit their peak, so did his interest and a new world was awakened: stories about triumph and intrigue and good guys defeating evil.

The day came when just such a story emerged from his imagination, with faraway worlds, soldiers of light, and good guys fighting against insurmountable odds. He told a few individuals about it. They liked it and the story caught fire. *Luminate* was born.

He met Pat Anderson when she edited his golf book project. She was curious to see this sci-fi story he had. He finally shared it with her and she liked it very much. In the process of working on the story together, they became writing partners. Now they write long distance—Pat in Utah and Robert in Florida.

Patricia Anderson

As is so often the case with writers, she's been a bibliophile all her life. Her mother joked that she started reading milk cartons at age three. In the sixth grade, her teacher spent extra time helping kids with learning difficulties, leaving his other students to read what they wanted. Heaven! For her, it's always about the story: How does it start? What will happen? How will it end? How fast can she find out? (She once read *Gone with the Wind* in one sitting to get the answers to these questions.)

Between all that reading, she learned to draw and paint, played piano, sewed her own clothes and cooked for her family. Later, she was a long-distance telephone operator, worked in a typesetting shop, and did quality control at a graphics company. With this book, she's added writer to the list.

She lives with her husband and their toy poodle.

Luminate is the first novel in the Turning Darkness to Light trilogy. Robert and Patricia are hard at work on the second volume. We'd love to hear from you! Please, please let us know what you thought about the book. We promise one of us will answer every message we receive!

Visit the website dedicated to all things *Luminate:* www.luminusuniverse.com